"A clos[...] [...]illed with action as well as intriguing ideas."

—Kevin J. Anderson

"A very satisfying classic Golden Age–style yarn."

—*Locus*

"A story that twists and turns back on itself and keeps the reader always off-balance. There is danger, adventure and a labyrinth of loyalties. Excellent." —*SF Site*

"A lot of fun to read. Pure unadulterated escapist adventure set in a nicely realized SF world."

—*Aboriginal Science Fiction*

"Full of adventure and Asimovian imperial vistas. Delivers tons of action in straightforward, economical prose notable for its clarity. Offers wide-screen baroque plotting never out-of-control. With echoes of vintage Jack Williamson and Paul Anderson, as well as Niven, Asimov, and Vinge, Williams and Dix proudly continue a vital tradition in SF."

—*Analog*

"The plot involves kidnappings, betrayals, space battles, one-on-one duels, and the unwinding of various puzzles, all foreground action in the development and exploration of an unusually elaborate world. I'm not sure what an Evergence is, but finding out promises to provide hours of fun."

—*Locus* (from a review that cited
The Evergence Trilogy as an
excellent example of the New Space Opera)

· · · · · ECHOES OF EARTH

· · · · · · SEAN WILLIAMS
AND SHANE DIX

ACE BOOKS, NEW YORK

ECHOES OF EARTH

An Ace Book / published by arrangement with
the authors

PRINTING HISTORY
Ace mass-market edition / January 2002

ISBN: 0-441-00892-5

ACE®
Ace Books are published by The Berkley Publishing Group,
a division of Penguin Group (USA) Inc.,
375 Hudson Street, New York, New York 10014.
ACE and the "A"design
are trademarks belonging to Penguin Group (USA) Inc.

PRINTED IN THE UNITED STATES OF AMERICA

10 9 8 7 6 5 4 3 2

For Jonathan Strahan,
the Godfather.

"No one is so generous as he who has nothing to give."

FRENCH PROVERB

CONTENTS

ADJUSTED PLANCK UNITS: TIME

Old Seconds

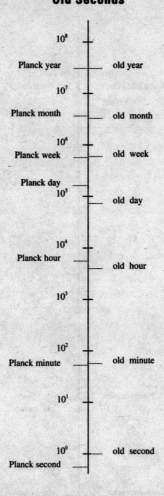

NB: For more information about Planck Units, see Appendix 1.

ADJUSTED PLANCK UNITS: DISTANCE

Old Meters

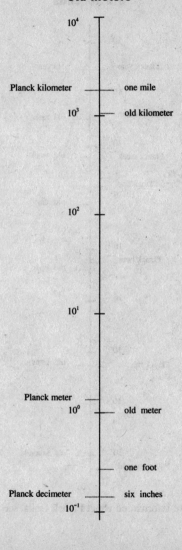

CONSTELLATIONS

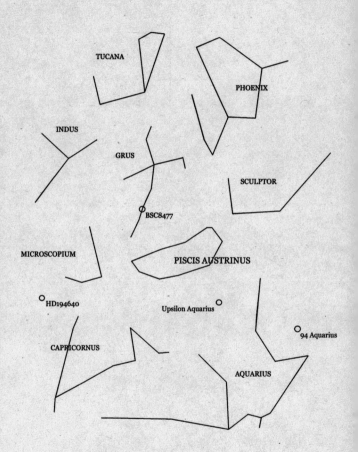

1.1

COBWEBS IN THE SKY

2160.8.17 Standard Mission Time
10 July, 2163 U.T.

1.1.1

*Peter Alander looked down at his handiwork with some-*thing approaching a smile, imagining what it would be like to have his first bath in over a hundred years.

It would be hot, for starters. He would make sure of that. Disabling the temperature receptors in his skin and rugging up against the subzero chill just wasn't the same thing as being warm right through.

At the end of the bath he would be clean—*really* clean. Although nanos were supposed to take care of that, their efforts were ineffective at best. They left his face feeling oily and his joints gritty. The combination was unpleasant; every time he rubbed his eyes, he felt as though they were being sandpapered.

His body wasn't meant to need cleaning or heating, but that didn't stop his desire for it. Even though technically he had never experienced either before, he still missed them, nonetheless.

Finally, the bath would be peaceful.

He bent to check the seals one last time.

"You really are crazy," said a voice from over his shoulder.

He didn't need to turn to know who the voice belonged to. "Here to gloat, are you, Cleo?"

Cleo Samson, the mission's organic chemist, laughed softly. "You should know me better than that, Peter." Her voice was like rocks tumbling down a hillside: all rough edges and bass, with a promise of trouble. "I'm here to applaud your efforts."

"Even while declaring them worthless, no doubt."

"Well . . ."

He reached over to switch on the heater coil and glanced up at her. "Look, Cleo, why don't you do us both a favor and—"

"I'm not interested in doing anyone a favor." She stood on the edge of the overhang with her arms folded, watching him work. As usual, she hadn't gone to the trouble of blending in: her blond hair didn't reflect the purple of the sky, she didn't cast a shadow, and he could see part of the far canyon wall through her silver jumpsuit. She was ghostly, anachronistic.

"That doesn't surprise me." He didn't hide the irritation in his voice.

"Really?"

He nodded. "Really."

He watched as she unfolded her arms and walked around the edge of the overhang. The camp was cluttered, confined as it was to a narrow ledge on the wall of the 5,000-kilometer-long canyon he was supposed to be exploring. The flaps of his shelter rustled in a breeze that he knew she didn't have the physical form to actually feel, yet when she came up to him and put one hand on his shoulder, he clearly felt the pressure of her fingers through his environment suit.

"Peter—"

He brushed her hand away—or tried to, at least. His hand went completely through her forearm. But it had the effect he wanted. She pulled back, and the false sensation of her touch faded.

"Leave me alone," he said, turning back to his work. The element was hot; he could smell burning carbon compounds coming off the coil. Reaching for one end of a thick, black hose lying nearby, he lifted it over the edge of the bath and made sure it was secure.

"Is that really what you want, Peter? To be left alone?"

"I wouldn't have asked if I didn't."

"What about Lucia?"

"What about her?"

"Would you choose solitude over her company?"

"What sort of stupid question is that? I can't have her, so what's the point of—?"

"Wishing?" she cut in quickly, smiling. "We all wish, Peter. It's very much a human quality."

"Listen, Cleo," he said as firmly as he could. Too much talking dried out his throat, but he refused to use the other options unless he had to. "I need time to work things out. So if you could just let me have that, if you'll just let me *be,* everything will work out for the best, I'm sure."

"And when Caryl notices?"

He didn't need to look up to know that she was referring to the bath. "To hell with Caryl."

He could feel a heat on his neck and back, as though she was standing close behind him. "Don't do anything too hasty, Peter."

When he turned to reply—to tell her that, hasty or not,

at least he was finally doing *something*—she had already gone.

Cleo Samson always had to have the last word. Alander knew that, but still it rankled. They were all the same, up in the *Tipler*. That was the problem with traveling in a group of experts: everyone knew best; no one wanted to compromise. They all needed someone they felt they could dominate, control, bully, and it was starting to feel that he was that someone. It had been too long since he had been one of them.

Within moments of Samson leaving, his thoughts were back on nothing more deliberately complex or malicious than the water for his bath. The black hose led to the compound's storage tank, a 10,000-liter aluminum drum one third full of hard-won moisture. Vapor condensers had sucked at the parched air for days to gain that small amount for use as reaction mass the next time the shuttle visited. His instructions were simply to watch out for leaks in the tank and make sure it didn't overflow; no one had mentioned anything about taking a bath in it. Then again, he reasoned, nobody had forbidden him from doing it, either. He would scrub the water clean afterward so no damage would be done. Of course, Caryl Hatzis, SMC of the survey mission, might not see it that way. But that was a risk he was prepared to take.

The water coming out of the hose was steaming hot. He would lose a little back to the air, but not much. As he waited for the bath to fill, he stripped out of his environment suit and stood naked under the alien sky. The sun was riding high above him, visible as a bright orange patch in the perpetual cloud cover. The steep-walled canyon allowed him barely an hour of relatively direct light; the rest of the time he had to content himself with the purple haze of an Adrasteian day.

As soon as the water reached a decimeter above the bottom of the makeshift bath, he eased himself over the edge and into it. He crouched in the heat, balanced on his toes, splashing himself and enjoying the feel of the fluid against his new limbs. His skin looked purple in the light, and he couldn't be sure that wasn't actually the case. It wasn't human tissue, strictly speaking, although it was built from the human genome. The major veins were wider, more regular in angle and placement; his fingernails were nearly transparent and grew barely a millimeter a month; he had no hair at all. Yet he had genitals not dissimilar to the ones he was used to, and his face by reflection looked vaguely familiar. But then, the familiar in such an unfamiliar context seemed twice as alien.

He breathed in deeply and tasted the steam at the back of his throat. He allowed himself to relax back into the warmth, to let it embrace him. Lulled by the sound of trickling water, he closed his eyes and tried not to think.

As always, the memory surfaced. It was date-stamped 2049.9.29 Mission Time—the twenty-sixth of November on the old calendar—and covered the night before the first of the engrams were activated. He and Lucia Benck had been in her quarters at Entrainment Camp, discussing, like most people had been that night, what lay ahead.

"If not for us, then for who?" he had asked her. "Or whom? I can never remember which."

Her smile widened. The room's lights were doing a fair job of simulating candlelight; by it her skin was honey warm and smooth. Golden highlights in her dark hair glittered. Her eyes were deep brown and restless.

"It won't be us, Peter," she said. "And yet it will be. I try not to get tangled in the metaphysics of it all. I just prepare as well as I can in order to prepare each of *them*. I don't want to let anyone down, least of all myself."

"But *you* won't be one of them."

"No." Her brow creased slightly. "And neither will you. There's no way the program could afford to send even one of our bodies. We weigh too much; we sleep and eat too much; we get bored too easily—"

"I know, I know." He rolled onto his back; in the memory, his point of view shifted to show the ceiling. Her face followed him, coming back into sight closer than before as she rolled to lie next to him.

"*We'll* still be *here*," she said. "And that bothers me."

"It does?" His voice held surprise, although the memory captured none of the emotion.

"Of course. I want to be one of them, Peter . . . out there, exploring, seeing things no one else has ever seen before." She shrugged lightly. "How could I not want that? I thought you did, too."

"Exploring, yes." He hesitated. "But not just to sightsee. I want to find answers, explanations for the things we still don't understand."

"Knowledge is the payoff," she said, "by which people like me have justified the entire program. I think the tourists outnumber the truth seekers, don't you?"

"Undoubtedly. And the truth seekers are happy to go along for the ride."

They had kissed then. Their relationship was still fresh enough for the experience to be a novelty but didn't have the desperate edge it once had. They were content to pull apart after a moment, albeit not very far.

"The question is: Where do we go from here?" She

looked serious again, thoughtful. "While the engrams go off into space to visit a thousand different suns, what are *we* going to do? Do we carry on as we always did before we joined the program? Pretend that none of this has changed us? Will we ever know what our copies do or see? How do we kill time until we find out? What if one of them dies . . . or *we* die? Are we immortal, or are we destined to die a thousand times?"

"I thought you said you weren't getting tangled in the metaphysics."

"I said I was *trying* not to." A wave of her hand encompassed everything: the room, UNESSPRO, Earth, the bubble of space 100 light-years wide that humanity was hoping to fill. "The engrams wake tomorrow. In a year, most of them will be gone. Then it's back to just us. You and me and Donald and Jene and Chrys and the others. We're the Viking widows waving off our husbands to be swallowed by the sea. Except they're not our husbands . . . or wives or friends or anyone, for that matter. They're us."

"They're not really us, Lucia. They're just copies."

"I'm sure they won't take too kindly to you saying that, Peter," she said. "Remember, this conversation is being recorded for your copies' memories, and *they'll* think they're real enough."

The original Peter Alander had smiled broadly. "At this point in time, I don't particularly care to have a debate about whether or not they are real. Right here in this moment, Lucia, you and I are real, and nothing else matters to me right now. I don't even care that we're being recorded."

Her smile echoed his. "Just as long as it doesn't find its way into the public domain, right?"

They kissed again—and there the memory ended. He could have played the rest, but he preferred not to. It felt like pornography: distant and cold, as though it had happened to someone else. In a very real sense, it had. He was as far removed from that person called Peter Alander as he was from Lucia Benck. The send-off those two people had given their copies back on Earth, a century ago, was their business, not his.

But the memory kept surfacing and with it the words of his original: *If not for us, then for whom?*

The water was up to his waist and scalding him. He forced himself to reach out of the bath to turn down the current flowing through the heating coil. The air on his buttocks was icy; he sank gratefully back into the heat, stretching out his legs so they became completely immersed. The water continued to trickle into the bath unchecked; he would stop it when it was up to his chest. He hitched the back of his skull onto the lip of the bath behind him so he could recline without slipping down any farther, and stared up at the purple gray clouds for a long while, looking for patterns but finding none.

For whom?

One hundred years, one month, and eighteen days—or so it had been according to Earth, by the new calendar. For those aboard the *Frank Tipler*, traveling at 80 percent of the speed of light, time had passed relatively quickly. Just forty-two years, three months, and three days had elapsed since leaving Sol when the survey vessel finished deceleration and arrived in orbit around Upsilon Aquarius, a greenish star over seventy-two light-years from Earth. It had seven planets: three gas giants (none of them close to Jupiter in mass); three inner, terrestrial worlds; and one distant mass straddling the divide between planet and planetismal, much as Pluto did back home. Of the inner worlds, one was too close to the sun—airless and boiling—and one was too far away—similarly airless, but icy instead. The third, sandwiched between the two extremes, was the source of the oxygen and water spectra detected from the interferometers around Sol. But it was no Earth, not by any stretch of the imagination.

Adrasteia was small, dense, and rugged, bombarded by rubble left over from its evolution and at the mercy of severe plate tectonics. Its atmosphere was substantial enough to give rise to dramatic pressure differentials: At the bottom of the canyon Alander inhabited, the air was far too dense to be comfortable, while at the top of the nearest peak it might as well have been a vacuum. The average temperature was below the freezing point of water, and what little oxygen existed was mostly generated by cyanobacteria sharing the air with the clouds above—clouds trapped in warmer atmospheric layers and never yielding rain. Apart from the clouds, the planet's main water reserves lay underground. It probably wouldn't be that way forever—or even for long, if the terraformers got their way—but for now, the only remotely habitable planet around Upsilon Aquarius was proving to be a pain in the ass. Certainly nothing as wonderful as his original self must have imagined it would be.

But there *was* life of a kind. Apart from faint hints in the deep equatorial basins some of his fellow surveyors were exploring, the cyanobacteria in the clouds proved once and for all that such life could evolve independently on another world. There was no way they could have come from Earth, as did, some skeptics still believed, those found on Mars and Io. And the fact that they were little different from the ones back home added credence to the original Peter Alander's theories concerning the origins of life in the universe, not to mention why there were no aliens waiting to greet the survey teams when they arrived.

His original would have been pleased, that was for sure. The Adrasteian cyanobacteria had never evolved into anything terribly sophisticated. There seemed to be no reason why they shouldn't have, though; conditions here were not fundamentally dissimilar to those that existed on Earth, Mars, or Europa. Adrasteian life-forms hadn't evolved any further, his original would have argued, because the odds were stacked so far against such a thing happening that it shouldn't happen even once in the lifetime of the universe. In fact, life should not have evolved *at all,* even to the level of bacteria.

The fact that it had evolved suggested otherwise, unless one viewed the early universe as a massive quantum computer, a near-infinite number of parallel universes engaged in incomprehensible "computations" from the moment of its creation—smashing elements together, creating new compounds and smashing those together in turn—until something appeared that could be called *alive.* This unicellular life wasn't conscious, but it appeared and flourished everywhere, on numerous worlds, multiplying and evolving in the strange, uncollapsed place that was the unobserved universe.

The moment consciousness occurred, though, down one of those possible reality paths, the collapse occurred. The universe, observed, could no longer nurture the conditions required to parallel-process bacteria to consciousness. Once just one being *saw,* it robbed all other life-forms of the chance to evolve. Rapid evolution stopped in its tracks, confined as the universe now was to just one track at a time. Even with a near-infinite number of stars in the universe, the odds shrank to almost zero that other conscious life-forms would emerge from primitive organisms, since it was too unlikely to happen in a single universe, and thus the majority of worlds humans surveyed would be inhabited by nothing more exciting than bacterial sludge that had evolved in the past.

The lack of complex alien life on Adrasteia seemed to support his original's argument: that humans were the universe's present observers, and that they would find no other intelligent life-forms anywhere, just many different types of dead-end bacteria. There would be nothing more, in fact, until humanity died out and the universe could resume its quantum computations.

But only when the results from all the survey ships arrived at Earth would enough evidence exist to judge conclusively. The *Tipler*'s data was barely on its way, having been sent five months ago, six months after their arrival. He—Peter Alander's flawed copy—hadn't been around to witness the discovery of the cyanobacteria; not in real time, anyway. He had been going mad in slow-mo, savoring each second of rational consciousness for far more important things, like staying alive and trying to work out what had gone wrong.

He shifted uneasily in the bath, lifting his chin to breathe through the steam. There was something niggling at the back of his mind, but his thoughts were directed so far inward that he didn't consciously acknowledge it. How long he had been lying there, he didn't know. It was silent and peaceful; finally, he felt warm throughout—physically satisfied, if not mentally at ease. He was used to feeling out of sorts; that, after all, defined his situation.

If not for us . . . ?

The memory beat at him like a stick, relentless and painful but brittle itself, as though it could snap at any moment. He was as afraid of losing it as he was of trying to own it. If he wasn't the person in that memory, then who was he? What right did he have to the name Peter Alander? What right did he have to exist at all? Sometimes he felt like the original Alander's hypothetical protointelligence, struggling out of the slime and just beginning to grasp consciousness when the sad news came: *Sorry, you've been beaten to it. There's nothing here for you. Go back where you came from, and you'll never know the difference.*

But he couldn't go back, and he wasn't going to lie down and let the problem beat him, either. He was going to survive. If he wasn't Peter Alander, then he would work out who he actually was and *be* that person. He was sure Lucia would have understood, wherever she was.

He ducked his chin under the undulating meniscus of water, intending to submerge himself completely.

It was only then that he consciously noted the smell of burning and realized that the trickling of water had ceased long ago.

1.1.2

Caryl Hatzis closed the line to Cleo Samson with a sense of reluctant resignation. Reluctant because she didn't like indulging anyone when resources were so tight, but resigned because she knew there was no point feeling any other way. Alander was a problem she had failed to deal with her way; she would therefore give him the concessions the others requested in case their method worked. If it did, she would acknowledge the small defeat and move on. And if it didn't . . . well, she would have his new balls and be done with it. She was tired of wasting her time—and his—on looking for a cure that might not exist. If only someone on Earth—

No.

She cut off the thought with a bitter effort of will. She understood herself well enough to know where it would end up. Maybe UNESSPRO *had* solved all the engram-related problems since they'd left; maybe Alander could be healed by a simple software patch; maybe there was nothing wrong with him that time alone wouldn't heal. Whatever; a call for help would take a century to arrive, and a reply would take another century to return. The fact that nothing had come from Earth for more than a century suggested that no one would be listening anyway.

They were on their own. Either Alander would have to sort himself out, or he would be frozen and the drone he inhabited returned to normal service. She sometimes wondered if the latter would be for the best in the long run, although she had to admit that initially, the effect on morale would be severe. Some of the crew actually seemed to care what happened to poor old Peter Alander—flawed and fragile, and no use to anyone except as grunt labor. What would his original have thought? What about the program supervisors?

You fuckers, she cursed her long-distant superiors. *I'm not an AI psychologist; I was never trained to deal with something like this.*

As she watched Alander's bath slowly fill, she wondered what Cleo Samson's role in all this was. It was an open secret that she had been jealous of Alander and Benck back in entrainment; her engram had presumably

retained that emotion. So, was she looking out for someone she cared about or on the make? Hatzis would be
damned if she'd give anyone access to another body, no
matter how therapeutic it might be for Alander. She felt
like Frankenstein enough as it was without giving the
monster a bride.

And if Cleo Samson really *did* care so much, why was
she reporting his latest outrage to the one person least
likely to tolerate it?

"We have another glitch." The voice of Jayme Sivio
came from behind her on the bridge. Although the direction did not exist, since the space they called "the bridge"
was purely virtual, she turned automatically to face him.
The survey manager (military) of the *Frank Tipler*, a
lanky fair man in his early forties, stood with his hands
folded in front of him in an unselfconscious, at-ease
stance.

"Where this time?"

He patched her into the data, surrounding her in mul-
ticolored vector diagrams. "Above the ecliptic. Here." He
indicated a point several AUs farther out than Adrasteia.
A pulsing golden light hovered in empty space, a long
way from anywhere. "The same spectra as the first one,
but more than twice as bright."

"Do we have anything out that way?"

He shook his head. "The signal is being picked up by
the solar north array. The nearest thing to it is . . . well,
us." He shrugged lightly. "Do you want to dispatch a
probe?"

She thought about it. They had wasted a probe on the
first one: the glitch had shone for less than an day,
whereas the probe had taken a week to arrive. It had found

no solid bodies, no dusty remnants, no ashes—nothing at all.

"It's not pumping out anything hard?" she asked, confirming the details he had already implied.

"Nothing that could harm us."

"And it's not moving?"

"Not rapidly. We haven't enough data to work out its precise trajectory." Another shrug. "Otto and Nalini are looking at it pretty closely, just like they looked at the last one. But they're drawing a blank."

"I presume it's natural."

"As opposed to . . . ?"

She scowled at him. "You know what I mean."

His smile rebuked her. "If I thought it was artificial, I'd tell you."

"Okay then, do you think it *isn't* artificial?"

"That's a completely different question."

And you didn't answer it, Hatzis thought to herself.

"What else have we got?" she said.

"We've been watching it for an hour, now," Sivio obliged. "The pulsing is regular, but not regular enough to be suspicious. If our detectors were any less sharp, we'd probably mistake it for a pulsar, if we saw it at all."

"Maybe it's a piece of antimatter," she mused. "An antimatter meteor of irregular shape tumbling into the system and burning up as it hits the solar wind. The emissions change as it rotates. Could that be a possibility?"

"If it is, I'm sure Otto and Nalini are looking into it. They're doing triple time on this."

She nodded. The same variable-clock facility that had allowed her crew to slow their thoughts to a near standstill during the journey out also gave them the capacity to speed up their thoughts when required. For every one of her minutes, her two astrophysicists would be experiencing three, near the upper limit of engram processing speed.

"I keep hoping you'll tell me it's a signal from Earth," she confessed. "Something ftl that isn't coming through properly, or something we don't understand. They've had a lot of time to advance, after all. Their technology could be very different now."

"Undoubtedly," said Sivio. The last signal from Earth had been broadcast while the *Tipler* was in transit, dated 2062.3.3 Mission Time; it had warned them that there might be a break in transmission, but there was nothing to suggest that the break might last more than a hundred years. Such a break could have been the result of something as simple as a misaligned transmitter, but it could also have been something as severe as the collapse of civilization in Sol System. From Upsilon Aquarius, there was no way to tell.

Few doubted that contact would be regained. *When* was the issue. And *how*.

Hatzis sighed and brought her attention back to the bridge. Although a fake, it was convincingly solid to all her senses. She seemed to be in a large room highly reminiscent of the fictional starships found in late-twentieth/early-twenty-first-century science fiction: a semicircular wall contained a large screen; several duty stations lay scattered around a central chair; a rail at the back segregated visitors from active crew. Sivio was even in some sort of uniform, although she didn't recognize it.

Playacting, she thought. *We're kids at heart, even now.*

The illusion was comforting and necessary but still that: an illusion. The *Frank Tipler*, orbiting around Adrasteia's equator twice every one of the planet's short days, was in actuality little more than a box with few moving parts and no empty spaces to speak of. Designed to travel the void between stars and set up shop when it arrived, the ten-meter-square structure was the embodiment of practicality. Its nanofacturing plants had built several hundred satellites in the year they had been in orbit; it had put them down on the ground and given them one reusable shuttle; it had even grown a half-dozen bodies into which those willing could temporarily inhabit the surface for work purposes. But it was limited and vulnerable, and the people it contained needed to be reminded of that fact every now and again. Including herself.

"How did you say we picked this up, Jayme?"

"On the solar north array. We haven't had a match from anything else yet, but we're hopeful."

"So, same as last time," she said. "One glitch, one sensor, no confirmation. If it is real, it's either so faint we were lucky to pick it up at all, or we screwed up by not being quick enough off the mark to get it looked at from something else. But if it's just a glitch—which is the way I'm leaning right now—then we need to find the fault. The last thing we need is crappy data."

"I agree." Sivio looked serious for the first time. She knew he was glad that she had assumed command of the survey mission once it had arrived at Upsilon Aquarius. She also knew that he had definite opinions on how it should be run, opinions she valued, especially when they concurred with her own.

"Any recommendations?"

"I think we should wait," he said. "And monitor everything."

A slight narrowing of echoes indicated that he had chosen to make the remark privately, along a security channel only the two survey managers could access.

"Do you think this could be sabotage of some kind?" she asked via the same route.

"It's a possibility," he said. "Directed or otherwise. Maybe something installed in the software before we left. It could be a remnant of an old test routine gone haywire, perhaps. Who knows? We've had destructive mutations come out of the genetic algorithms before, although nothing so subtle or convincing as this. If that's what it is, we'll break it soon enough."

She wanted to be reassured by his confidence. "And if it isn't?"

"Then chances are we'll learn something new." His smile was wide and genuine. "That's what we're here for, after all."

She nodded halfheartedly. Sabotage had been a possibility in everyone's minds prior to departure. Although they had no way of knowing what had happened to all the other survey missions, theirs had gone without a major hitch thus far, and she planned to keep it that way. But the fear kept her awake some nights, and there had been rumors.

"This couldn't be the work of our supposed plant, could it?"

"The company spy?" He came down the bridge toward her. "I can't believe you'd really worry about something like that, Caryl."

"I'm not," she said, biting down on a sharper denial. "It does feel like we're being tested, though."

"By whom?"

"*Other* than Earth, you mean?"

He laughed. "Aliens on one side, spies on the other.

That's not much of a choice. I'm glad it's you and not me who has to make it."

She turned back to the main screen to watch Alander soaking in his bath, and for a brief moment she envied him. He looked so peaceful, so unconcerned, so *real*. He wasn't some ghost bouncing around the inside of an electron trap, conjuring up experiences and calling them authentic. He wasn't fooled for a moment.

But then, that may have been as much his problem as it was his fortune. In their circumstances, if you didn't allow yourself that self-deception, the whole house of cards came tumbling down—as they had with Peter. As soon as your doubts set in, you were as good as lost.

It was like that with command, she thought. Jayme had the right idea, for all that he was the military guy and she was the civilian. The hardest part of the mission was probably over (since the greatest physical risk to the *Tipler* and to them had been while in transit, when Sivio was in charge), but that didn't make the job of juggling priorities any easier. Caryl Hatzis's job was like that of a university administrator trying to deal with an overworked staff and limited resources—with no possibility of a funding increase.

Glitches she didn't need. She had enough on her plate already.

She had been unconsciously watching Alander while she thought. He hadn't moved, but the water level had, inching up his chest and to the top of the bath. Part of her had been waiting for him to switch off the flow, so when he didn't, she started to feel concerned.

"Jayme, does that tank have a volume sensor?"

"It does." The main screen rearranged itself, revealing a red line inching down a vertical scale.

She pursed her lips. "Will someone call him before I do and tell him to shut off the goddamn water? If we lose that reaction mass, I'm going to be seriously pissed off."

"Sounds like you already are." He paused. "I'll let him know as soon—"

An alarm cut him off, and Hatzis found herself back in the vector display.

"What's going on?"

"We're picking up something," said a new voice: Ali Genovese of telemetry.

"Where from?" asked Sivio. "Which satellites?"

"Everywhere! All of them! Whatever it is, it's bright, and it flared up just seconds ago—but it's not from the sun. It seems to be coming from Adrasteia."

"Show us," Hatzis ordered.

There was a moment's silence as the conSense view changed.

Then: "Jesus fucking Christ!"

It was the first time Caryl Hatzis had ever heard Jayme Sivio swear.

1.1.3

The cold hit Alander's shoulders like an open-palmed slap as he sat upright and reached for the controls of the heating element. Cursing under his breath, he shut off the current and stood up. The bath was surrounded by a spreading muddy stain. He lifted out the end of the black hose and grimaced at the slow drip that issued from it.

"Shit."

Swearing wasn't going to solve anything, and neither was telling himself what he ought to have done. Yes, a cutoff switch of some kind would have stopped the tank from draining empty, but he hadn't thought of it. It had never even occurred to him, because all he'd needed to do was keep an eye on the flow, and there wouldn't have been a problem.

But he hadn't. His mind had drifted, and the mistake was made. His biggest problem now was how to explain it to Caryl Hatzis.

An alarm pinged inside his head a split second before the communicator on the ground near his muddy environment suit did likewise. He stepped out of the bath and grabbed the makeshift towel he had prepared earlier, already dreading the call. He knew who it would be from. The tank must have had some sort of internal sensor, so the *Tipler* would've known the moment it had emptied. If only he'd *thought*.

"Yes?" he said, clipping the headset over his scalp. He tried to sound casual, but the chill in the air was already making him shiver, giving a tremor to his voice.

"It's Jayme."

He felt a flicker of surprise and relief: not Hatzis. Not quite. "Listen," he began, deciding to brave it out, "it was a mistake and I can fix it—"

"Forget that, Peter. Just look up."

"What?" All he could see was a pale patch where the sun tried feebly to shine through the clouds. He was about to say as much when a streak of gold swept from one side of the sky to the other, above the clouds but moving as fast as he could swing his arm over his head, and so bright it left a faint afterimage. The line to the *Tipler* crackled furiously at the same time, momentarily deafening him.

Another appeared a second later, heading in a different direction across the sky; then a third. All three paths intersected at a point behind the cliff wall against which his shelter huddled. He headed for the edge of the ledge to see better.

"You should probably get dressed first, Peter," said Sivio with some impatience. "We can't afford to lose your body."

With some embarrassment, Alander clutched his environment suit to his chest and headed for the relative warmth of the shelter, where he dressed with as much haste as he could muster. Through the translucent material of the tent he caught the brief glow of another golden flash.

"What's going on, Jayme?" he asked when the interference passed.

"We're not sure. They arrived not long ago, and we've been trying to hail them. So far there has been no response."

Alander zipped the last seal shut. "*Who* arrived, Jayme?"

"I don't have time to describe it to you right now. See for yourself. There's a direct feed available on conSense. I just wanted you to know that it looks like they're heading your way."

Sivio's voice dissolved completely into static. Alander put down the headset and went outside. The sky was on fire with a wave of crisscrossing golden lines. He shielded his eyes with a hand and tried to work out what he was seeing. Some sort of aurora? Had the sun flared unexpectedly? It had all happened so suddenly and was taking place so silently that he almost doubted that it was real. Yet he knew it wasn't anything coming through the conSense network, as had been the illusion of Cleo Samson; his eyes were seeing nothing but the sky, despite how unlikely that appeared.

He tried to access the net but failed. The channel to Sivio was still nothing but noise. He waited a minute and, when the fire in the sky had faded, tried again. This time he got through. But Sivio was already gone, no doubt dragged away by other duties. Swallowing his nervousness, Alander dipped into the net and surrendered himself to the conSense feed.

A chaotic menu of images confronted him, all blazing and changing in real time. He selected one at random and found himself staring at what looked like a shining, yellow spindle extruding a white-hot thread out of one pointed end. Despite heavy processing, he couldn't make out the background to the spindle, and when he checked the scale in one corner of the image, he refused to believe it. If it was true, the spindle was over two kilometers long.

He jumped to another image, this time noting its vantage point. He was in a Lagrangian point between Adrasteia and its one moon, high above the *Tipler* and most of the observation satellites. The familiar muddy-brown globe was alive with light. Arcs and spirals flashed into view, then just as quickly disappeared; sudden, startlingly straight lines stabbed out from the equator, then also vanished. There seemed to be no order to the display, as though data from a Day-Glo cloud chamber had been somehow mixed up with ordinary biospheric information. But already his incredulity was beginning to fade. This was no mix-up, and it was too elaborate to be a joke.

A third view showed him a second spindle from far away. It was in geostationary orbit, and it, too, was extruding a burning line toward surface of the planet below. The end of the line was dropping steadily downward at a rate of several meters per second. The view shifted slightly to show another, darker thread appearing from the far end of the golden spindle.

A counterweight, Alander instantly thought. *My God, they're building—*

"You're seeing this, Peter?" Cleo Samson's husky voice startled him.

"It's an orbital tower!" he said in response. "They're building orbital towers!"

The ground beneath his feet rumbled.

"We know," she said, her voice fuzzed with static. "Take a look at this."

Alander's view shifted at another's command, disorientating him momentarily. This time he saw a rough three-dimensional map of the world beneath his feet. There were seven golden spindles in geostationary orbit around Adrasteia; all were dropping threads of various lengths down to the surface. As Alander watched, another appeared in the display at the midpoint of the arc connecting two others. A rough measurement confirmed that the spindles were equally spaced around the equator—or would be if two more appeared to fill the obvious gaps. Within moments of the thought, they had done just that.

Ten spindles building ten orbital towers. And the longitude of one of them was disturbingly close to Alander's own.

"Who the hell *are* they? Are they from Earth?" He dispensed with the communicator even though speaking into the void brought back the terrible feelings of dissociation that had dragged him to the surface in the first place. "Jayme? Cleo?"

There was no answer from the *Tipler*, and a moment later the conSense feed began to break up again. He eased gratefully out of it and stood blinking under the golden sky. A roar he had not consciously noted before turned out to be the shuttle negotiating the tight confines of the canyon, blue white jets issuing from its curved, black underbelly. Alander backed away as it maneuvered closer and extruded landing struts. A gray python whipped out of its side before it had touched down and began to suck at the water in the bath. At the same time, a hatch lifted open on the side of the shuttle.

"You have ten seconds to board." The autopilot's crisply accented voice spoke directly into his head.

Alander took the hint and clambered up the rungs built into the side of the craft.

The space inside was close and uncomfortable, not designed for biological passengers. There was barely room for the two other bodies it contained, propped awkwardly against a number of modular boxes and roughly strapped equipment. Alander had just enough time to get inside before thrust pushed him down onto one of the other bodies. He felt it shift beneath him and its breathing quicken, but otherwise it made no other response. Unoccupied, impersonal, corpselike, it could take no offense.

He swore under his breath, irritated at being hijacked without warning or explanation.

The shuttle's engines whined, and the interior light flickered.

"Where are we going?" he shouted over the noise.

"Drop Point One," the autopilot replied.

"Why?"

"That is where I've been instructed to take you."

"By whom?"

"Survey Manager (Civilian) Caryl Hatzis."

He thought for a second, then asked: "What would you have done if I hadn't boarded in time?"

"I was instructed to leave without you."

Bitch.

Alander did his best to ride out the bumps and dips. There was no response from conSense when he tried to bring it up again; either it was still being interfered with or the shuttle was keeping a low profile. ConSense—the communal illusion through which the virtual passengers of the *Tipler* interacted with each other and the world around them—required constant streams of data in both directions. The shuttle would stick out like a second sun if it logged him in.

Not that it would be hard to miss, anyway. Judging by the forces acting on Alander's body, the shuttle certainly seemed to be in a rush to reach its destination, six thousand kilometers to the southeast. But he didn't resent Hatzis for this. It couldn't be easy up there, dealing with . . . *whatever* they were. If they weren't responding to hails, then that left everything open. One less chance taken could make a difference. She wasn't to know.

The lights flickered again, and he felt his stomach drop. For a second he was in free fall, then the shuttle braked hard and landed with a jerk. The engines whined a moment longer, then they quieted and the hatch opened. It was dark outside; his eyes weren't designed for multifrequencing or hard radiation. He could see little apart from fog reflecting the shuttle's landing lights.

He sat up and waited, but nothing else happened.

"Now what happens?"

"I am to remain at Drop Point One and await further instructions," the autopilot replied.

"No, *me*," said Alander irritably. "What the hell am I meant to be doing?"

"I am unable to answer that."

"Great." Clearly it hadn't been told what he was supposed to do once he had arrived at the drop point. He forced himself to concentrate on why he might be there. Apart from being away from the down point of a possible orbital tower, he could see no immediate reason for his sudden relocation. DPO contained little more than a few sheds, a basic nanofacturing plant, and a maser relay for use in emergencies.

That's it, he thought with a sense of accomplishment. Only a month ago making such a connection would have been beyond him.

He got out of the shuttle and walked across the landing field. The soles of his feet registered warmth from the heated concrete, but the rest of him was cold. Icily so. DPO was high on the lip of South Basin 2 and currently experiencing the local equivalent of winter. Had there been water vapor in the air, everything would have been covered with ice and snow.

Even so, the main compound's door was stiff. As he wrestled with it, a faint yellow glow shone through the clouds on the north horizon. The spindles were still spinning their webs, he gathered. How long until the towers were complete he couldn't estimate, and what they would do next he had no idea at all. He figured that was pretty much up to them. Sooner or later, he was sure, they would make contact.

By the time he had wrenched the door open, the compound was slowly coming alive. Lights flickered in empty rooms; air generators whirred into life; various software agents tried to connect with the conSense terminal in his skull. He resisted their approach automatically.

"We weren't expecting you, Dr. Alander," said a voice. "We had no time to prepare—"

"That's all right." He found his way to what looked like a control room. It was cramped but uncluttered, designed for humans in physical form but obviously rarely used. "You weren't to know I was coming."

"How can we assist you?"

He stood in the doorway for a moment, disoriented. The AI had distracted him; he'd lost his train of thought. There *had* been a reason for him being here, he was sure of it. And then another disquieting thought: Where the hell was *here?*

"Goddamn it," he said aloud. Such breaks in concentration might have become less frequent, but they were no less disconcerting for that. Stress wasn't helping.

"Dr. Alander?"

"Quiet," he commanded. He closed his eyes and concentrated. *The AI, Drop Point One, the shuttle, leaving the shelter, Cleo Samson's voice, the spindles ...*

The spindles.

"I need access to the maser relay," he said quickly, desperate not to lose the thought that had eluded him only moments before.

"Yes, Dr. Alander. It is tracking and ready for use."

He eased himself into the seat. "How do I work it?"

"That would depend on what you wish to do."

"I want a secure link with the *Frank Tipler*, as broad a bandwidth as you can manage."

"Just one moment." The voice was silent for a moment, then returned with: "I am exchanging protocols now, Dr. Alander. Do you wish full immersion or audiovisual access? The audiovisual will—"

"AV only," he said without hesitation, not needing to hear that such a choice would reduce the number of options available to him.

A stereoscopic wide screen lit up before him, giving him a similar display to the one he had accessed via conSense, but one he felt he could control more easily. He tapped an image with his fingertip, and it ballooned into the foreground. This image, unlike the others, was moving. It seemed to be coming from a probe in orbit around Adrasteia; telemetry data appended to the image showed that its source was decelerating at high g. The image showed the upper tip of one of the spindles in closeup. From this vantage point, the extrusion of the counterweight was more apparent: a black fluid of some kind was issuing from several holes around the tip and spinning into a seamless, dense thread that seemed to absorb the light falling upon it. The spindle's golden halo was almost blinding at such close range, with electrical discharges dancing constantly across its surface. As the probe's sensors tracked lower along the spindle, Alander couldn't begin to guess what it was made of. It gleamed like metal yet seemed as translucent as amber. Through the glare, he sensed shifting machinery within, like the stirring of an embryonic wasp in its cocoon. There was nothing upon which he could anchor his perceptions. His gaze slid across suggestive surfaces and shadows; his mind grasped at understanding but missed. He felt like he did in his worst nightmares: lost, in danger, and so very, very small.

There was an audio cue accompanying the visuals. He selected it via the infrared mods in the palm of one hand and heard the broadcast persona of the ship speaking on all the available frequencies:

"This is United Near-Earth Stellar Survey Program

Mission 842, *Frank Tipler*. Please respond. Our mission here is a peaceful one, and we mean you no harm. I repeat: This is United Near-Earth Stellar Survey Program Mission 842 . . ."

What if they don't respond? he wondered. Then something even more chilling occurred to him: *What if they haven't even noticed that we're here?*

The probe angled closer for a better view of the bottom tip of the spindle. There was a bright flash of light from the screen, and the feed from the probe went dead. All telemetry data instantly ceased.

He winced. "That puts an end to *that*," he muttered.

"Peter?" Jayme Sivio's voice cut across the identification broadcast from the *Tipler*.

"Jayme? What's going on? Why have—?"

"I can't talk long," Sivio cut him short. "We're ramping up to maximum and cutting everyone nonessential out of the loop. You'll be okay, given your internal capacity. Just stay put and keep your eye on the feeds. We're relaying everything to you as it comes in. Store it all in case something happens to us and the backup."

"I saw what happened to the probe—"

"I know. We haven't been approached, and we're keeping our orbit well away from theirs. Until we know who they are and what they want, we can't afford to take anything for granted. But for now we think you're safe on the ground. Just take care, though, okay? You're our *backup* backup, if you like."

Alander swallowed. "I understand."

"Good luck, Peter," said Sivio. "And whatever you do, don't try to call us. Keep a low profile, and we'll contact you as soon as we can."

Alander nodded, but Sivio had already cut the line. The

room fell silent. On the screen, there were images of the spindles going about their enigmatic work, seemingly oblivious to the humans watching from a distance. For the first time, he was struck by how alone he was on Adrasteia. There was nothing else but him and a handful of mundane AIs on the surface of the entire planet. If something did happen to the *Tipler*, he would be the only human left for dozens of light-years.

What's left of a human, anyway, he thought solemnly as he settled back to watch the show.

1.1.4

Caryl Hatzis felt fatigue in every cell of her body, from the ache in her spine to the hot swelling of her eyes. Her skin was greasy, her armpits smelled bad, and her brain simply couldn't stay focused on one thing longer than a minute or two without sliding off into random thoughts.

Too real, she thought. *Too goddamn real by half.*

When the engram designers had copied her original's thought processes and molded them into an electronic simulation, they had deliberately chosen to keep metabolic and hormonal traits like hunger, desire, and fatigue, acting on the sound belief that every component of a biological system contributes to its final state. Without fatigue, it was arguable that the engram of Caryl Hatzis would be fundamentally different from the original and might therefore malfunction under crisis.

She wished they'd been just a little more carefree with her melatonin and cortisol levels. A little extra alertness in exchange for a little less *her* seemed like an excellent deal at the moment.

"Can't I declare martial law?"

Jayme Sivio smiled at the suggestion. "And put me in charge?" he said. "That's not the way it's usually done, Caryl."

"But there is nothing *usual* about any of this: not the circumstances, not the Spinners themselves." The term had been coined by Cleo Samson earlier and had been taken up readily by the rest of the crew. "Surely that in itself suggests we should completely rethink our procedures. I mean, wouldn't *you* call this a military threat?"

She indicated the ten golden spindles that had finished weaving their orbital towers and counterweights and were now busy at work joining the spindles along a giant ring encircling the planet. Strange lights arced between the ends of unconnected threads as they—whatever they were made of—interfered with the planet's magnetic field. Two of the spindles had themselves begun to change, dimming in brightness and growing alarming spines at apparently random directions.

She had also noted from the solar north data that the glitch that had preceded the arrival of the Spinners was still pulsing. There was no real reason to think that the phenomena were connected, but she couldn't shake off her suspicions that they were.

"Technically, yes, they are a threat." Sivio's tone was placating. "But the only hostility they have demonstrated has been when *we* have come too close to *them*. Losing two probes in ten hours does not warrant a change in procedure, Caryl. All they have done is indicate a desire to be left alone, *and* they have extended that same courtesy toward us."

"For now."

"Yes, for now. Until they change their behavior, we

have no reason to change ours. Besides, what else *can* we do but wait and watch?"

She resisted the impulse to lash out at him. *You could at least give me a fucking break.* But she knew that would be unfair. She could leave the bridge at any time; fast-tracking could see her back in an hour or two, fully rested. But the thought of even that break galled her. She couldn't leave, not when she was responsible for the lives of everyone on the *Frank Tipler* and off.

Ten hours. At quadruple speed—the maximum the *Tipler* could maintain while simulating enough crew to run the ship—that equaled forty hours. They had turned over shifts eight times since the Spinners had come, but still she was there. Even Sivio had rested.

She wondered what they called her behind her back. Then she wondered if paranoia was a symptom of exhaustion. It was certainly a symptom of command.

"We've got something new here." The announcement came from Nalini Kovistra, one of her two astrophysicists, who had been working almost as hard as she had. "We're picking up gravitational waves from one of the towers."

"Can they hurt us?" Hatzis was a systems administrator, not a physicist.

"No, but what's making them might."

"I don't understand."

"Gravitational waves occur as a result of sudden movements or changes of shape of massive objects, like neutron stars or black holes. If there's something like that in one of those spindles—"

"Could this be an attempt to communicate with us?" Sivio cut in.

Nalini Kovistra's reply was confident, but her shoulders lifted in a shrug. "As an alternative to electromagnetic radiation, it would be pretty poor. I mean, why juggle neutron material when you can simply point an antenna and talk?"

"Well, if it's not a weapon and not a communicator, what else could it be?" said Hatzis.

"Impossible to say," said Kovistra.

"Maybe we should adopt a higher orbit as a precaution," mused Hatzis.

"I'm not sure it would make any difference, Caryl."

"But it couldn't hurt, either." Hatzis glanced at the roster to see who was on pilot duty. "Jene, give us a perigee kick to put the *Tipler* into an elliptical orbit, staying as far away as possible from the spindle—which one was it, Jayme? Did you notice?"

"Spindle Six."

"Shall do." Avery's voice was crisp and efficient.

"Is that enough, Jayme? Should we break orbit entirely, do you think?" Uncertainty gripped Hatzis in her imaginary stomach.

"It's your decision, Caryl. With so little information, all we can do is follow your instincts."

Great. She hadn't slept for over two whole days. What did that say about her instincts?

The *Tipler* indicated that its secondary thrusters were firing. Hatzis didn't check, knowing she could leave the job in Jene Avery's capable hands. She knew as little about the drive systems as she did about gravitational waves, but at least she wasn't alone there. The genetic algorithms that had fast-tracked the survey program's engineering had left many of its human designers behind; she had a niggling feeling that no one really knew how the drives did what they did. That they did it well—and had reached the required efficiencies in order to make the

2050 launch date—was all that had mattered.

But that was a worry for another day. The ship's orbit slowly changed shape in the main plot, giving the source of the gravitational waves a wide berth. She could rest easy on that score, at least. Perhaps—

"I have a result from the projections team," said Sivio over her thoughts.

"Good. What have they come up with?"

"Nothing conclusive, I'm afraid," he said. "But they are tending toward the nonhuman end of the argument."

She hated the sinking feeling in her stomach, the way it betrayed her hopes. She'd been pinning her hopes squarely on the original Peter Alander's theory that complex alien life wasn't likely. "Why?"

"We can only guess at what sort of technology is driving these things, but we do know some things for certain. You don't build on this scale without cheap matter transmutation *and* easy conversion of matter to energy. We don't have either—or rather, we didn't."

"Is it possible that Earth would have achieved such technology by now?"

"Assuming that technology kept advancing at the rate it was when we left," he said, "then yes, it is very possible. But I'd just as soon not assume anything."

Hatzis nodded in agreement. "Go on."

"Well, we've picked up no sign that the spindles are communicating with each other, and we have no way to guess how they're powered. The way they appeared out of nowhere suggests a highly advanced method of transportation, the principles of which we can only guess at."

"They could be experts in camouflage, of course."

"Not a likely possibility. The spindles are being observed from a hundred different instruments. How do you fool everything at once? The only surefire way would be to infiltrate our networks and corrupt the data. Again, it's a possibility, although the team sees it as a remote one at best."

"Wishful thinking, perhaps."

"Perhaps." Jayme nodded. "The use of gravitational waves suggests a highly advanced materials technology, capable of manufacturing and handling ultradense substances. It also suggests an advanced knowledge and manipulation of space-time. This, combined with the way they arrived, leads the team to believe that the Spinners are capable of faster-than-light travel."

She nodded, unsurprised. The spindles had already demonstrated such incredible prowess that she could believe almost anything of them.

"It's too much to hope that they're from Earth," she said, anticipating his next comments. "That's what you're going to tell me, isn't it? They couldn't have possibly achieved that type of technology by now."

"Highly unlikely, Caryl. Ftl communication, maybe, but not travel. Nothing like this, anyway."

She absorbed what was happening on the screen for a long moment. "So where *are* they from?"

"We don't know. There's no way we *can* know . . . unless they decide to tell us, of course."

She laughed at this. "Jayme, at this stage, I think we'll be lucky to get a hello out of them."

The orbital ring was complete within the hour. Hatzis watched the threads link up with a feeling of dread, wondering what would happen once it was finished. Would the Spinners finally talk to them? Did she even want to hear what they had to say?

When the circle was closed, a massive current surge swept once around the planet, leaving brilliant auroral streamers in its wake. As the surge struck each of the spindles, their glow died back to a warm infrared, and their structures stabilized. Even the pulsing of gravitational waves from Spindle Six ceased, although Nalini Kovistra suspected that a particularly massive object still lurked inside. Once the circuit was complete, the pulsating glitch high above the ecliptic flashed once and disappeared.

Then silence.

Hatzis ordered the *Tipler* to maintain its vigilance for another two real-time hours. A hundred eyes sensitive to a thousand frequencies studied the spindles for any signs of activity, but there were none. The solar arrays studied the sky for any sign of the glitch but likewise found nothing.

Before fatigue finally overcame her, Hatzis watched a piece of orbital debris drift without incident barely one kilometer from Spindle Three. Satisfied that nothing dramatic was likely to happen for the moment, she agreed to stand down, leaving Sivio at the helm.

She had never felt such relief as the bridge dissolved and her private environment welcomed her back into its folds. Sleep didn't come to her at once, however. Her mind kept returning to images of the spindles. There was such potential in the things, such *energy,* and she didn't know how to deal with that. She couldn't ignore it, but she couldn't just accept it, either. The sheer scale of what she had witnessed disturbed her terribly.

She tried to guess what her original would have

thought, confronted by such a thing. The quest for knowledge was firmly written in her character but also that the quest should be conducted in an orderly fashion. Methodical research and organized exploration were the keys to progress, she believed, not unpredictable leaps of understanding or fortuitous discoveries. Yes, serendipity played a part in the development of science, but it was serendipity underpinned by preparation and the scientific method.

So, although she was sure that her original would have been fascinated and delighted by the appearance of the Spinners—as would any of the survey members—she was equally certain that the abrupt undermining of everything she had built around Upsilon Aquarius would have provoked the same sinking feeling in her stomach. Virtual or not, the sense of dread was very real to her.

Jayme Sivio was wrong about his assessment of the threat the Spinners represented. They might not destroy the Earthling mission outright, but they could unpick the delicate tapestry of discipline and organization that kept it together. They were a long way from home and making slow but steady progress through the massive task ahead of them. The Spinners—with their wild display of advanced technology—would inevitably encourage fanciful speculation and even more fanciful plans. Already she could imagine how some of her flakier team members were thinking.

They couldn't afford to take any risks. They had everything to lose. Even if there were dozens of each of them elsewhere in surveyed space, there was only one of them here. They only had one shot at working out what was going on, and if they missed it, humanity might never get the chance again.

That conclusion reassured her: that she wasn't afraid of

finding out the truth. She had wondered if she was balking at the spectacle of it all, recoiling like an animal from something bigger and smarter than itself. But that wasn't the case. She wanted to know. She *needed* to. Her original would never forgive her if she let something like this slip through her fingers.

She fell asleep without realizing it. The *Tipler*'s Engram Overseer instantly ensured that her virtual personality was disconnected from both conSense and the environment around her to ensure that her dreaming mind did not cause any disruptions. A similar function was performed by various neurotransmitters in the human brain and did not represent a gross violation of the working model of her consciousness. She had given her permission for such actions to be taken on her behalf and was certainly unaware of it at the time. Falling deeper and deeper into sleep, dreams of golden daggers awaited her, with ice-white poison dripping from their tips.

When the alarm woke her, she felt barely rested. As the various subroutines and modules of her personality jostled for synchrony—or so it felt to her, and always had, even before becoming an engram—she checked the time and groaned.

Three hours, subjective. Barely an hour in the real world.

A message to call Jayme Sivio was flagged for her immediate attention. She opened a line to him, a surge of imaginary adrenaline brushing away the cobwebs of imaginary sleep. At that moment, she felt very real and as fragile as an eggshell.

Something's gone wrong.

"Jayme, what's going on?"

"Sorry to wake you, Caryl, but there's been a change."

She imagined the spindles unfolding like deadly flowers
. . . the entire array acting as an interstellar antenna and
summoning something far worse . . . the orbital tower
contracting inward like a cheese slicer and cutting the
planet in half. . . .

"The Spinners?"

"No. It's Peter."

Dread gave way to surprise. "I thought you told him to
maintain radio silence?"

"I did, and he has. It's just . . ."

A cold feeling blossomed in her gut. "What the hell has
he done now, Jayme?"

"He's overridden the lock on the shuttle autopilot," he
said. "He's on his way to the base of one of the towers."
Sivio hesitated for a second, as though sounding out her
response. When she said nothing, he added, "I told him
to wait until he spoke to you, but he wouldn't. What
should I do?"

With some effort she forced herself to stay calm.
"Nothing," she said evenly. "I'll deal with him myself."

1.1.5

Never in the history of humanity had Igor Sikorsky's claim—
that "The work of the individual still remains the spark
that moves mankind forward"—been so wrong as in the
twenty-first century. The century of rapid social change
that had closed the previous millennium had continued unchecked and indeed accelerated wildly for some decades
before gradually settling at more predictable rate: still accelerating, but without the wild shifts forward signaling
bursts of activity that often proved to be as destructive as

they were progressive. As the people nominally in charge of the Earth's major governments and corporations learned to rely on neural nets and other sophisticated software agents to help them make decisions, some of the unpredictability went out of world affairs. Increasingly, it was the teams behind these electronic advisers that influenced world affairs most, just as teams rather than individuals predominated in most professions. There was simply not enough space or scope for an individual to compete on such an overpopulated planet. Few mourned this development, none less so than the social engineers to whom it increasingly fell to predict what might happen next. The maxim "Many heads are better than one," like Sikorsky's claim, had never before had a chance to be so profoundly tested.

There were wars of terrible but brief ferocity followed by humanitarian efforts that did more to expose the base nature of humanity than to repair the damage. Yet from the uneasy soil of all the mass graves grew hope for the future. Although the 2030s began with a world as unequal and violent as that of any decade in the previous century, by its end, a sort of calm seemed to fall. No one could decide if the world's leaders had finally come to their senses or if the software they listened to were working in concert. Either way, conditions were so changed by 2040 that the United Nations began to seriously address the major issues of the species, including the state of its home, rather than idly watch the squabbling of its members.

The environment could not be fixed by a mere change of heart. It was by then well known that future centuries would suffer greatly for the incontinence of their ancestors. That humanity would survive was never in doubt, but one would always prefer a palace to a barn. Long-term plans were founded to seek ways to fix the problem, and one of these included looking for alternatives elsewhere.

The looking itself was no problem. Massive interferometers had already detected the presence of oxygen and water around numerous extrasolar worlds. The list of viable targets for exploration numbered well over a thousand within a 100-light-year radius of Sol. The new sense of prosperity creeping over the Earth led to a feeling that these worlds could be visited and surveyed at an affordable cost; it was further felt that this should be done as quickly as possible. With life spans increasing and technology improving every day, the estimated 200 years required for a round trip to a neighboring star was no longer considered impossible. It was believed that such a trip would in fact be feasible—even tolerable—within just a few decades. UNESSPRO, the United Near-Earth Stellar Survey Program, was founded, and a date for the launch of the first vessels was set at January 1, 2050.

But there was a catch: Living humans could not be sent. Even with the Earth's vastly expanded resources—cheap fusion power and the new tools of nanotechnology seeming to exponentially expand the horizons every year—there was simply no way to send thousands of people light-years away from Earth in every direction. Quite aside from the colossal cost, there was also the issue of lost time as well as the physical and mental well-being of the individuals undertaking such voyages. Instead, the first wave of survey vessels would represent humanity in the best way possible but would carry no actual live specimens.

At first it was hoped that sophisticated artificial intelligences would fill the pilot seats, but AI research took longer to deliver than its engineering counterpart. While vast orbital shipbuilding facilities evolved new generations of drives, power supplies, and protective magnetic bubbles, programmers explored dead end after dead end, never quite succeeding in creating the right sort of mind to ensure even one mission's success, let alone thousands. UNESSPRO could not afford to throw away trillions of dollars on ships that might die or go AWOL at any moment. With 5 percent of the Earth's gross product being channeled into the project, there had to be some sort of guarantee of returns. So they were forced to explore other options.

By 2048, it was clear that only one of these options promised anything like the sort of reliability required, and that was to send out electronic facsimiles of humans to the stars, as opposed to flesh and blood. Consciousness research had not yet managed to re-create an entire person's mind in an electronic environment, except by inefficient neuron-by-neuron simulation, but they could decipher a great deal that had once been thought a mystery. The processes underlying consciousness could be emulated, as could the way emotions and other impulses ebbed and flowed throughout the body. Memory alone had proven elusive under such reduced conditions, defying all attempts to record it indirectly. The only efficient way it could be captured and simulated was secondhand, by interviewing the original at length about his or her past and using physical records to supply the images. Emotions could be attached later, during the fine-tuning phase, to color the recollection correctly, even though the details might still be slightly askew. Preawakening memory in such a mind was, at best, a patchwork quilt pieced together from a million isolated fragments.

But that was enough. So-called "engrams" behaved more or less the same as their template minds, the flesh-and-blood originals who had devoted six months of their lives to the task of being effectively taken apart and rebuilt inside a computer. When left to run for long periods, the engrams displayed no greater tendency toward unreliability than those same originals, neither failing at familiar tasks nor unable to learn. They were, in fact, ideal candidates for any space-faring crew: They did not eat, breathe, excrete, sleep, or grow sick; they took up very little space—less than a cubic decimeter (as measured in the new Adjusted Planck units created for the international venture)—and weighed less than half a kilogram; they could adjust easily to the long stretches of time during which nothing happened on an interstellar mission; and they could be trained as easily as a real person. In fact, it proved no great difficulty to train sixty real astronauts, then copy them as many times as was required to fill the crew registers of 1,000 survey vessels.

It was the latter detail that aroused the greatest ire among those still concerned about matters of the soul. Each survey vessel had a crew of thirty; there were one thousand ships; that meant a total survey crew of 30,000 individuals had been selected from that initial pool of just sixty. Roles on each mission were allocated randomly—while Caryl Hatzis might be the civilian survey manager on the *Frank Tipler*, on another ship she might have a junior role—but that didn't remove the fact that there were in total over 500 Caryl Hatzises in the bubble of surveyed space surrounding the Earth. Were they *really* all the same person?

The original Peter Alander had once studied a graph showing how researchers could have delivered the required artificial intelligence before 2060. Engineering might have outstripped AI at first, but that was only because engineering was a better-known discipline. Consciousness research was new but growing rapidly. If the progress made in the 2040s continued for another decade, 2060 would have given plenty of time for the birth of humanity's first conscious child. What it would be like, the authors of the graph had not known, but the Alander on the *Frank Tipler* profoundly wished UNESSPRO had waited to find out. Not so he could meet it—although that had been one of his aspirations—but so he could have sent it in his place.

The gentle pitching of the shuttle was making him sleepy. In the twenty hours since the Spinners had arrived, he had caught only a couple of hours of rest, and then only because his body absolutely demanded it. He refused to indulge in the time-bending habits of his former colleagues in the *Tipler.* That would have undermined the whole point of him being on Adrasteia.

But he couldn't allow himself to sleep now. He had to stay awake and concentrate. Otherwise he would lose his train of thought and forget what he was doing. And he couldn't forget *that,* of all things.

"How long until we arrive?"

"Three hours," the shuttle replied.

He tried to make himself comfortable. One thing he missed about the Drop Point One observation post was the chair; if he'd only stopped to think of bringing it with him. But there hadn't been time. Once he had made up his mind to go, he didn't dare hesitate. It was either then or, possibly, never.

The decision had been relatively easy. A day cooped up in DPO was all he could take; he needed to move, to do, to be. It was more than cabin fever: sitting staring at a screen was robbing him of his sense of self, dissolving his thoughts in the ceaseless river of data from the *Tipler*. Although he knew it was happening, he didn't know how to stop it—until he stumbled across the branch that saved him.

The image had shown the base of Tower Five, on the other side of the planet. All the towers were anchored in a similar fashion, terminating in a plug shaped like a flattened octopus that presumably extended a large distance underground. Each had the same reflective properties as resin. At the terminus of Tower Five, however, a new detail had appeared, subtle and easily missed. Something silver.

It was difficult to make out what it was exactly. Even when he magnified the picture, the image remained blurred by atmosphere and distance. There was no telling what shape it was, except that, from above, it looked easily large enough to hold an adult human—possibly about three meters around and maybe four high.

Feeling the first tingle of excitement, he had replayed the data stream to see where the object had come from. Sure enough, it had come from above, along the cable, dropping smoothly and steadily before braking to a gentle halt on the ground below.

And there it sat, waiting.

He watched it for ten minutes before getting out of the seat and making his way through the cramped rooms of Drop Point One. It was night again outside; he pulled the hood of his environment suit over his head as he walked across the tarmac and banged a couple of times on the side of the shuttle.

"Power up," he told the autopilot. "We're leaving."

"I do not have the authority to—"

"You have my authority," he interrupted. "Override code Delta-Juliet-Whisky-four-three. Repeat DJW-43."

The side of the shuttle immediately peeled back, exposing the cramped interior.

"Welcome aboard, Dr. Alander," said the autopilot smoothly.

Alander took a moment to load equipment into the arms of the two empty bodies and guide them zombielike into the DPO shelter, not only to create space within the shuttle but to ensure they would be safe also. That he was taking the shuttle and his own body into possible danger was one thing, but he didn't want to compound the risk by taking more resources with him than were absolutely necessary.

With the two bodies dealt with, and the destruction of the two probes firmly in mind, he set about plotting a course for the shuttle. Downloading the data from DPO, he ascertained which of the towers had been built by Spindle Five. Something in Spindle Six was causing dramatic changes in the atmosphere around that section of the equator: The cloud layer was bulging upward, toward the spindle, spinning off numerous precyclonic systems in all directions. What that meant for the air around Spindle Five, Alander didn't know, but the autopilot thought it was nothing it couldn't handle. It did remind him, however, that its supply of reaction mass was running low and warned that a round trip would be only just possible. If any further maneuvering was required, it would be unable to return him to Drop Point One.

But he had no intentions of reconsidering his decision. For what stood to be gained, he felt it was a small risk indeed.

As the door to the cargo bay irised shut, Alander thought briefly about calling the *Tipler*. After all, he was in no position of authority any longer; his breakdown had precluded any chance of that in the near future. What if he screwed it up, like he had so many times lately? Didn't he owe it to the rest of the crew to at least give them the chance to help him?

But then he remembered all too clearly Sivio's words: "Don't try to call us. Keep a low profile, and we'll contact you as soon as we can." He might not be keeping a low profile, but at least, by not calling them to inform them of his intentions, he was following orders. Hatzis couldn't admonish him on that score, at least. Besides, they would detect the launch of the shuttle soon enough and could contact him then if they wanted to.

A sense of unreality flowed through him when the shuttle's engines burned—a similar feeling to the one that had led to his breakdown on the *Tipler*. For a giddying moment, he felt as though he wasn't real, as though all his senses were feeding into a bottomless black hole, a vast chasm into which he, too, was being dragged. He clung to the lip of this hole for what seemed like an eternity, knowing that if he fell, he might never be able to crawl out again. Not this time.

If he couldn't hang on to his sense of self when, unlike the other engrams, he had a body he could call his own, in which he was completely self-contained and independent, then what right did he have to try?

If not for us, then for whom?

He snapped back with an existential jolt. What right

did he have to try? And why did most of the other engrams indulge him in his efforts to stabilize his self, especially when they didn't even like the new person he had become?

Because if he failed, then that undermined their own stability. All it would take was one personality breakdown to prove that it was possible. Who knew who would be next? Essentially, they were all nothing but illusions running on complicated software; unpick the illusion, and there might be nothing left.

He didn't care about them as much as he cared about himself, but he was happy to use the argument in order to save himself. It was either that or give up, and he wasn't ready to do that just yet.

The shuttle was on its way to the base of Spindle Five and the object that had appeared beside it—a possible one-way mission. For the first time in a long while, he had something that he felt belonged to him, something he could *own*. For a short while, anyway. He wasn't fool enough to believe that Hatzis would let him get away with it for too long.

Barely five minutes into the trip, Sivio hailed the shuttle. Alander blinked in surprise as the voice spoke to him out of the claustrophobic darkness.

"Peter, is that you in the shuttle?"

"Who else would it be?" he said. He tried to gather his thoughts, preparing himself for the rebuke that was sure to follow.

"Well, the way things have been around here lately . . ." Sivio let the sentence trail off into a humorless laugh.

"I guess," said Alander. He had no intention of making

things easier for the military survey manager just yet.

"The autopilot tells us you're heading for one of the towers. Can you confirm that?"

"If that's what it says, then it must be true. I'm certainly not flying this thing."

"Peter . . ." Sivio hesitated for a second. "Peter, what the hell are you doing?"

"I'm going to take a look at one of those towers, of course. Don't worry; I'll keep a feed open once I get closer."

"I'm not sure this is wise, Peter. I know they appear to be inactive, but that doesn't necessarily mean they're safe."

"I don't even believe they're inactive."

"Peter—"

"You don't have to keep emphasizing my name, Jayme," he said. "I know who I am, and I know what I'm doing, too."

When Sivio spoke again, he sounded embarrassed. "I'm sorry. I don't mean to treat you like an idiot. You've just taken us by surprise, that's all." There was another pause. "Why *are* you you're doing this?"

"There's an object at the base of Tower Five," Alander said, relenting. "If it's what I think it is, I'm going to ride it to the top and see what lives up there."

A third silence. This time he knew someone would be checking the records for the object he had referred to. He waited out the few seconds it would take them to find it, repeating the statement he had given Sivio to keep his mind focused. *I know who I am . . . I know who I am . . . I know who I am—*

"You think this object might be a cable car of some

kind." Sivio's voice returned with an uncertain edge. "Is that right?"

"That, or a rabbit trap," he said. *With me being the rabbit,* he thought.

"And you're prepared to risk that?"

He took a deep breath. "Look, Jayme. It makes sense. Someone comes to the system, builds the towers, then everything goes quiet. They don't talk to us; they don't explain anything. What they *do* is give us a means of getting to the top. Or at least that's what the data suggests. I'm willing to bet that they sent that thing down for a reason. Why else but to invite us up?"

"Peter, you can't possibly know—"

"No, let me finish. If the Spinners were alien, I'd be more cautious. My original had a theory suggesting they're probably not, and that's good enough for me. Given that they're human—or at least of human origin—then that tips the balance in favor of them being nonhostile. Mysterious, yes, but ultimately nonhostile. I think they're being just as cautious as you'd like me to be: waiting to see what we do next. They made the first move, so we should respond. And how better to respond than to accept their invitation and take a look?"

"Peter, I'm not saying you're wrong—"

"I'm the *only* one who can go." He put as much force into the statement as he could. "The Spinners know that. If I don't go, we'll be sending them a very different message."

"*What* message? They might not even know about you!"

"How could they not? We've been hailing them since—"

"For all we know, we could be as insignificant to them as insects are to us."

"I don't buy that," he said firmly. "They *are* human; they *have* to be! And I'd hazard a guess that they not only know we're here, but that they know everything about us by now as well."

"That's a little unbelievable, Peter. You're suggesting the Spinners have been in our networks and we had no idea they were there! I can't believe we could be that vulnerable."

"Jesus Christ, Jayme! They built ten orbital towers in a single *day*. You think the only area they are going to be more advanced than us is just in the material sciences? Our secure systems could be as easy for them to read as skywriting."

"And you think they're listening in now?"

"I don't see why not."

"I . . . I don't know what to say." Sivio was sounding increasingly distracted, as though he was trying to think furiously while he talked. "I still don't like you rushing into this, Peter. At least let me talk to Caryl before you go any further, okay?"

"Why?"

"Because she's the survey manager in charge of this phase of the mission. She should be informed."

"All right," he said. "By all means inform her, Jayme. Just don't expect her to change my mind."

Sivio didn't reply to that, and Alander assumed he'd gone to get her. Anticipating what she might say, he tried to prepare some sort of defense. He could see her side of things easily enough. What bothered him was that she would make no effort to see *his* point of view.

When her voice came through the shuttle's link with

the *Tipler*, her tone told him everything he need to know.

"Why are you so intent on pissing me off, Alander?"

"Hello, Caryl."

"You land that fucking shuttle *now,* or I'll override your overrides."

"You can do that?" It was unlikely; otherwise, she would have already done it.

"Believe me, I will if you give me no alternative."

"And risk bringing the shuttle down? The autopilot software can only take so much interference."

"That's a risk I'm prepared to take."

"That's a fairly strong message you're sending, Caryl."

"I'm hoping it'll sink in eventually."

"I don't mean to me, Caryl. I meant to the Spinners."

"Now you're just talking gibberish."

"Am I? Ask yourself this: If they aren't watching what we do and don't know about me, why would they have sent a cable car to the surface? Who could it be *for* if not me? Leaving aside the matter of motive for a moment, doesn't this tell you that they know the shuttle can't take me anywhere near geostationary orbit?"

"But motive is everything. Why would they make overtures to you when they've ignored us for so long? And why you? No offense, Peter, but you'd have to admit it's a pretty valid question."

"I can't answer that, Caryl. But not even you can argue with the fact that there's only one way to find out."

There was a long silence from the *Tipler*, long enough to make him wonder if she'd cut the line permanently, washed her hands of him rather than attempt to reason with him. But he didn't give her the satisfaction of breaking the silence to find out. He waited patiently as the shuttle rocked its way through the atmosphere, making its way steadily around the planet to the base of Tower Five.

"Okay, Peter," she finally said. There was a weariness to her voice that both satisfied and unnerved him. "At least let's talk about what you're going to do. Assuming you're not acting on a death wish, is there anything we can offer to make it easier for you? Or to guarantee your safety?"

"I don't think you can do anything to guarantee my safety," he said. Privately, he exchanged a few words with the autopilot and felt the pitch of its flight change.

"But we can—" She stopped. "What are you doing now?"

"Landing," he said.

"What?"

He could hear her confusion and tried to imagine her expression.

"Well, now that I have your attention," he said, "I figure we can take some time to actually plan what we're going to do."

"Thanks, Peter," she said after a few moments, her voice quiet and controlled. "I appreciate this."

"Listen, Caryl," he said. "I'm the one going into the lion's den. In some ways I'd rather face you than the Spinners. In fact, to tell the truth, if you *had* brought down the shuttle, it would have come as something of a relief."

"And yet you were prepared to go through with it?"

"Had you not listened to reason? Yes, I would have."

"But now you're willing to talk?" It sounded as though she still couldn't quite believe what he was doing.

He shrugged in the darkness. "It's the diplomatic thing to do."

"It's good to see you have regained some common sense, at least," she said.

The ghost of a smile in her voice was reward enough, for now. He may only have won a battle, but that was sufficient to make him feel a little more confident about the war.

1.1.6

The manipulative little fuck, *Hatzis thought as she watched* the satellite images of the shuttle descending onto a rough plateau some 400 kilometers away from the base of Tower Five. She handed the conversation back to Sivio while she took a moment to collect her thoughts. Giving ground to Alander had galled her more than she would ever admit. Not because she thought she was infallible—far from it—but because it was *Alander.* Had it been the *real* him, she might have felt better about it, although the chances were it would still have been difficult for her pride to accept. As it was, it ate into her like acid.

Dr. Peter Alander had been aboard the *Frank Tipler* as its resident generalist, not a physicist or chemist or programmer or any of the other specialties the ship carried, but someone who professed to know a lot about everything: the wide-world equivalent of a physician. His role had been to act as adviser to the survey managers, someone who kept in touch with all the various disciplines at once, making sure their work didn't conflict and noticing when close focus might obscure a bigger picture.

As such, he commanded a great deal of respect among the other survey staff. Even among the other generalists—and there were ten of them scattered randomly through the missions—he was regarded highly. He was supposed to be good.

She could respect that, and she would have valued his input at any time during her leg of the mission. But not this damaged Peter Alander who had the potential to forget where he was if distracted. Giving any concessions at all to *him* just incensed her. And she wasn't above resenting the fact that a key component of her management team was missing, either, making her job all the more difficult.

Still, she would bear it as gracefully as she could. She was determined to, and she didn't doubt that leaders all through history had been forced into similar situations, with or without neural net advisers. That was what she had to do if she was going to be a good leader herself.

As Sivio walked Alander through basic preparations for his mission, a call came through for her from Cleo Samson.

"I've been watching what's going on," said the woman.

"Why?" Hatzis knew she was being unnecessarily blunt but couldn't help it. Samson was a chemist; she should have been making space for more relevant disciplines.

"Owen asked me to help him out with spectrographic analyses of the spindle hulls. I've only been real-timing it."

She accepted the explanation. "So what's your interest in this situation?"

"I'd like to talk to Peter. I think I can help him."

"How?"

"He needs someone to keep his mind on track. You and Jayme have other things to do. I'm on real time, like him, and he'll listen to me."

Hatzis mulled over Samson's suggestion. It seemed to make sense. They wouldn't want Alander distracted at a crucial point in the proceedings. But she also didn't want him distracted by Samson, either.

"Okay," she said, "we'll give you the bandwidth."

"ConSense?"

"Yes. He doesn't like hearing voices in his head."

"Good." Samson smiled openly, making her seem even younger than she already was.

Christ, thought Hatzis. *What does she see in him?* They were opposites in almost every respect: she a pale-complexioned blond in her thirties, he a rejuvenated sixty-year-old, formerly mixed African/Cuban stock but now in the body of a vat-grown android barely six months old. More importantly, she was still in possession of all of her faculties, while he—

Give it a rest, Hatzis chided herself, tiring of her own maligning of Alander.

"I'll allow this *only* on the condition that he actually wants you there," she said. "The minute he asks for you to leave, you're gone. Understood?"

Samson nodded. "Understood."

"Okay." She brought Sivio up to speed and gave permission for the line to Alander to be opened. The con-Sense link was a small risk, but a meaningless one if what Alander had said about the Spinners being able to access the *Tipler* was really true.

She didn't stick around to listen in on the conversation. There was far too much work to be done for her to afford to be able to just hang about eavesdropping. She had her projections team concentrate their efforts on the fifth tower and spindle, in order to anticipate what Alander might find there. She didn't want him going in there blind, despite her feelings toward the man.

Engineering reported that they could guarantee constant

satellite coverage of the spindle with only a dozen or so orbital maneuvers. She okayed the procedures; as long as the *Tipler* was safely out of the way, she was prepared to risk a few minor satellites in order to increase surveillance.

The issue of alien versus human origins of the Spinners wasn't going away in a hurry, despite Alander's beliefs on the subject. Certainly, the pictures filtering through spoke of massive capability. Such architecture required enormous material strength and a high degree of engineering sophistication, but none of it rang false to her. The angles and planes displayed an appreciable aesthetic, as she understood it. There were three ways to explain it: Architecture throughout the universe followed similar rules; the builders came from the same place she did; or the builders made the spindles the way they did in order to meet human aesthetics, not their own. The first possibility struck her as being unlikely, as did the last, but she was unsure if that reasoning alone justified accepting the second possibility.

Spindle Five consisted of a central, seed-shaped structure approximately one-half kilometer in height. The orbital tower connecting it to the ground was anchored in a slight tapering at its bottom, similar in reverse to the counterweight on the far side. The orbital ring seemed to pass through the entire structure unhindered, vanishing on one side into a deep dimple only to reappear on the other in exactly the same fashion. Apart from that, there were no obvious openings in the central structure's surface; it was apparently smooth all over.

Surrounding it, however, were seventeen freestanding rings, like streamers encircling a Christmas tree, though never actually touching the branches. They kept a minimum 100-meter distance from the central "seed" and were spaced equally apart around it. From edge to edge, they were ten meters wide and three meters thick. All of them were irregularly dotted with slight, rectangular indentations that the projections team suspected might be windows or airlocks, although none of them were open.

Electromagnetic emissions were minimal. The entire structure uniformly reflected a slight bronze light, but there were no lights, no radars, no lasers. For all Hatzis and her crew could tell, the structure could have been completely dead. But the cable car suggested otherwise.

"Could it really be so easy, though?" she mused aloud.

"Could what be so easy?" asked Sivio.

She looked at him and shook her head. "Sorry," she said, slightly embarrassed for having voiced her thought. "I just can't shake the feeling that there's something else going on. Something we're not seeing."

"You think it's a test?"

"Think, no. *Fear,* yes." What had Alander called it? *A rabbit trap.* She found herself hoping more than she had ever hoped for anything that he was wrong.

"He's preparing to move off again," said Sivio. "I can tell him to hold off a little longer, if you like."

She briefly considered waiting another hour or so to see if the Spinners would make a move. But what would the point of that be? If Alander was right, then they were listening in and would know what they were doing anyway.

"No, it's okay," she said. "Tell him he can go whenever he's ready."

Sivio went off to confer with Alander, and this time she followed him to see how the human representative to the Spinners was faring.

Alander's image, based on scans taken from the interior of the shuttle, looked tired. His artificial body possessed the same basic chemistry as a natural human, plus a few modifications designed to make survival easier in the difficult environments found on Adrasteia. It was ironic, she thought, that their mental states should share a common feeling of fatigue despite neither of them having a genuine body. *How far we have come,* she thought, *yet how unchanged we remain.*

"I'm ready to leave, Caryl." For all his appearance, Alander sounded alert.

"Are you sure?"

Alander nodded. "The sooner we get this over with, the better."

"Sounds like you're having second thoughts."

"Try third or fourth," he quipped humorlessly. "I'm terrified, if that's what you want to hear, Caryl."

"If you'd told me you weren't, I wouldn't have believed you."

He instructed the autopilot to resume its journey to the base of Tower Five. Nothing was said as the burn began, and silence reigned until the craft was cruising rapidly above Adrasteia's swirling cloud layer.

"Answer me one question," Hatzis asked him. "Where did you get the shuttle overrides from?"

Alander didn't hesitate. "I've always known them."

"Really? They're supposed to be top secret."

He smiled. "I can't explain it. My original knew them, so I do, too. I never expected to need them, but they were there if I did."

"What other overrides do you know, Peter?"

"I'd hate to say, really. You'll just change them."

"You're damn right I would."

"Why, Caryl? It's not as if I'm going to use them to harm the mission. I haven't so far; why should I now?"

"That's a moot point, Peter. I'm still not happy about the way you've handled yourself in the last few hours. How do I know you won't subvert my authority again next time we disagree on something?"

"You don't," he admitted. "But you must know that it would take more than a simple spat for me to use them. We've had plenty of those in recent weeks, and I've managed to avoid the temptation."

True enough, she thought, but she still didn't like it.

Switching to a private channel, she sent a brief message to Sivio: "Still think I'm paranoid for worrying about a company spy?"

"Less so, now, I must admit." His tone wasn't entirely serious. "If Alander *is* the plant, though, they miscalculated rather badly."

Hatzis thought back to the rumors she had heard during entrainment and preflight preparations: that on each of the missions, one crew member had been subtly altered in order to make them a dupe for UNESSPRO back home. Each plant had been preprogrammed to respond to certain stimuli in order to ensure that the missions ran the way the survey protocol demanded. But no one knew exactly what those stimuli might be, and no one could name who might be affected by the subconscious programming. Indeed, the most sinister rumor ran that a different crew member was chosen for each mission, so that if Peter Alander was the plant for the *Frank Tipler*, it might be Ali Genovese on the *Frank Drake*, or Caryl Hatzis on the *Andre Linde*. The plants themselves might not even know until the right circumstances occurred and the programming sprang into life.

The worst thing was that she could see how it made sense. There was no other way the UNESSPRO managers could oversee the program once the probes left. This was their only way to protect against such catastrophes as mutinies, she supposed.

But if Alander *was* the plant, why would he become active now? If anything, he was provoking dissent, not discouraging it.

Maybe the failure of his engram lay at the heart of that mystery. Or not. As he himself had said, there had been plenty of opportunities for him to defy her in the past. Maybe his original had earned the respect of the other generalists by being smart enough to steal the overrides from UNESSPRO's programmers and not use them until he'd had no other choice.

Or perhaps he was right, and the Spinners were into everything. Maybe they had hacked directly into his mind and put the overrides there, along with the urge to use them, to go the tower. She was beyond being surprised by their actions, whoever they were. Although their adopted name suited them, given the manner in which they had appeared, spinning their threads like shining interstellar weevils, she couldn't help but think of spiders instead: giant, malign intelligences drawing the human surveyors into a web they couldn't even see.

1.1.7

"What are you thinking, Peter?"

Cleo Samson's voice brought Alander out of his deep reflection.

"That it shouldn't be me," he said.

"Visiting the Spinners, you mean?"

"Yeah." The shuttle was back on course, buffeting in the steadily worsening turbulence. "It should have been Lucia."

There was a slight pause. He felt Samson's illusory body shift next to his in the darkness. The sensation insinuated itself into his mind with such intimacy that for a moment he was uncertain what she was even doing there. Had they had sex, he plugged into conSense and she immersed in her virtual world, thousands of kilometers away? And if so, how had she convinced him to do that, with everyone watching?

But a second later the fear passed. There was no way, he realized, that he would have agreed to it, although it might have explained his state of mind.

"It should have been Lucia," he repeated solemnly. "Not me."

"Why?"

"Because she was trained for this sort of thing. She's used to working alone. And she's willing to take risks I would judge unreasonable. She's . . ." It was his turn to pause. "She's a survivor, I guess."

"Even risk-takers fail eventually, Peter."

"What are you trying to say, Cleo?" he said irritably. "And what the hell are you *doing* here, anyway? Trying to lift my morale? Because if you are, you're doing a piss-poor job of it, I can tell you."

"I just don't think you should feel guilty about her, that's all."

"I *don't* feel guilty, Cleo."

"I think you do, Peter."

"That's crap. Why should I? It wasn't my decision. It was up to the assignment board."

"But you recommended her."

"So did you. We all did."

"But only you were sleeping with her."

"That's irrelevant!"

"No, it's not," she said. "Your emotions precluded you from being able to look at her objectively, as the rest of us were able to do. It *was* the right decision, Peter. Your personal attachment just doesn't allow you to see that right now."

"I know it was the right decision, Cleo." His tone started angry but was quickly tempered by the realization that what she was saying was true. "I just miss her sometimes, you know? She . . . Lucia . . ." The image of her was clear in his artificial recollection; he felt as though he could touch her if he reached out a hand. And with the right cross-matching of memory and sensory input, he was sure that he *could* have touched her—in the false world of conSense. "Lucia loved the unknown and the unpredictable. To deny her that would have been wrong. Not that I could have talked her out of it even had I tried. She was too strong willed. And that's why I wish she was here now. She'd do a good job, I know, whereas I—"

He shut his mouth on words he didn't want to say aloud. Thinking them was bad enough.

I'm probably going to fuck it up.

That's what Caryl Hatzis was thinking, he was sure. And who was he to argue with her? The bath debacle was just the recent in a string of blunders, each worse than the last. Maybe he did have a death wish, deep down.

"You might not know this, but I envied Lucia." Cleo's normally rough alto was soft. "Not just over you, but her brief, too. I realized it was dangerous and could even turn out to be deadly boring, but at least she had a chance to find something of her own. Not as a faceless chemist in a group of other faceless technicians. Everything she discovered would be unique to her. No one else would share that experience. Something like that is priceless. I've come to appreciate that after so long among our collective."

Alander listened to Samson, startled by her words. He had imagined Lucia's journey that way himself: a mind in a box riding the torch of an interstellar drive, little more than sensors and shielding and a large amount of anti-matter called *Chung-2*. Most of the minor stars between Sol and Upsilon Aquarius had been hers to fly by, slowing fractionally enough to take pictures but never stopping. What would she see? What strange sights would be hers and hers alone to enjoy?

He had thought of it that way but had never spoken to Cleo Samson about it. Why would he? He had never known that she envied Lucia the mission. He had never really considered that someone other than he might grieve for what Lucia's failure amounted to: not just a hitch in the overall survey plan, but the failure of a dream.

Chung-2 should've been waiting for them at Adrasteia, chock-full of data. It hadn't been there, and they had neither seen it nor received a signal from it in the year they had waited. Officially, she was assumed dead and her mission a failure, knocked out perhaps by a stray particle in interstellar space or maybe something more substantial closer to one of her targets. Either way, if she had seen anything new, it was lost with her.

And she was lost to him. That was what had obsessed his thoughts upon arriving at Upsilon Aquarius. That, and losing his mind.

"Do you still envy her?" he asked Samson.

She laughed lightly. "Do I envy being dead? No. And I don't envy being considered expendable by UNES-SPRO, which must have been a factor in their decision. The *Tipler* functions perfectly well without her, even if she is missed."

He nodded. As much he hated to admit it, that was probably true. She was like he had been, spread thin across a large number of disciplines with little depth in any. The perfect person to send alone into the void, to face whatever the universe felt like throwing at her.

He wondered how many of her other engrams had also failed in their missions, just as he had wondered how many of *his* had suffered breakdowns similar to his own. Perhaps they were doomed to miss each other wherever they went, jinxed by the send-off their originals had given them back on Earth.

His train of thought was broken as the shuttle banked steeply and began to descend.

"It's not too late to change your mind," said Caryl Hatzis over the open line.

"I know that," he replied. "But I'm not going to." *I'm doing this because I want to, not just because I have to. If I can't be myself any longer, maybe I can try being someone else for a change.*

ConSense maintained the illusion that Samson was squashed in the cargo hold with him as the shuttle shuddered down toward the ground. Her body bounced with his, one hand on his forearm as if for support. He knew better than to try to hold onto her, however; the moment he tried—and failed, since she wasn't really there—he would lose all pretense of balance. He didn't know if his new body could suffer from motion sickness, but it wasn't something he particularly wanted to find out at this stage.

Sitting silently in the darkness, he rode the silent descent out as patiently as he could. At that point in time, he was little more than freight; if something disastrous happened to the shuttle, he figured he'd be better off not knowing, because there was little he could do to avoid it. Right now his fate lay in the hands of the autopilot and, possibly, whoever was responsible for the towers. If they had wanted him to come in the first place, then it was likely they would want to ensure his safe passage also. And he had no doubt they would have the technology to be able to do just that.

Interesting, he suddenly thought, *how we put faith in the unknown when our lives are most at risk.*

When the faint whine of the shuttle's engines peaked in volume and the descent slowed to a halt, he felt almost disappointed. The moment of truth had come.

He sat up. "We're down?"

"Yes." The autopilot was brisk and to the point, as ever.

"What are conditions like outside?"

"I am displaying atmospheric data—"

"Just tell me."

"Ambient temperature is 180 Adjusted Planck degrees Kelvin. Wind speed is atypically high for the equator as a result of atmospheric disturbances to the east. There is a significant amount of suspended particulate debris still circulating—"

"You mean dust?"

"—from the building of the artifact in our vicinity. Yes, I mean dust."

"Great." He pulled the hood of his environment suit up over his head and sealed it at his throat, not just against the dust. One hundred and eighty K was warmer than he had expected but still below freezing. "What's the approximate time out there?"

"Immediately prior to sunrise."

He took a deep breath, making sure the filters on his suit were passing air. In a better life, he could have used conSense to "erase" the mask in front of his eyes, but as it was, he had to make do with it there, uncomfortably tight and imperfectly transparent.

His stomach churned. His nervousness must have shown, for he felt Samson's hand on his shoulder, squeezing again. That was as good a reason as any to get moving.

"Open the door," he said.

The cargo hatch hissed open, letting in an icy gust of dusty air. "Immediately prior to sunrise" on Adrasteia meant that it was still as black as night. Dawn brought only a vague brightening of the clouds to the east, rarely visible from Alander's camp in the canyon. From where the shuttle had landed, however, he expected to see clearly in most directions, as the orbital tower had anchored itself into level high ground.

When he stepped outside, he was greeted by a severely limited view. The shuttle's landing lights shone fitfully through the dust-laden air at what looked like the base of a giant tree. Curved, irregularly spaced "roots" spread out and down from a tapering "trunk" that vanished up into the darkness. Both the roots and trunk were made of a glistening, black substance. The stony soil around the structure had been violently disturbed in recent times but showed no present sign of activity.

Alander took a dozen or so steps closer. This, he assumed, was the base of the orbital tower, although it looked nothing like he had imagined. It looked grown, not designed. There was no sign as yet of the object he had seen descend from orbit.

"Don't go too close, Peter." Samson's voice from behind him brought him to a halt.

"I wasn't going to."

She walked forward to join him, dressed in a suit identical to his and similarly fastened against the dust. He smiled at that: She was going to some lengths, against form, to preserve the illusion that she was really there with him. Whether that was to discourage him from banishing her or to preserve his mental stability, he wasn't sure.

"Biotech," asked Sivio from orbit, "or nanotech swarm?"

"What's the difference?"

"Well, we would use swarms to build something like this, since we tend not to think of biology as a suitable tool for mega-engineering. But I think we should be careful not to impose our preconceptions on the Spinners. Biotech could theoretically build something like this—"

"Yeah," put in Samson, "if your version of biology involved diamond strand fibers and buckyball cells."

"There's no reason why it shouldn't."

"If they've evolved to eat this stuff, I don't want to get any closer to their teeth."

"*You* don't have to," said Alander. "Where do I go now, Jayme? Has that thing moved?"

"It's on the far side," Sivio explained. "The shuttle scanned it before landing, and it does indeed look like some sort of climbing device, although it hasn't moved an inch. Check it out when you're ready."

Alander turned to his left and began walking around the trunk of the orbital tower. The base was easily thirty meters across, allowing for stray roots and the structure's odd asymmetry. He kept looking upward to see the tower itself, but it was still too dark to see very far. It was hard to imagine that he was standing next to something that stretched all the way up to geostationary orbit, over twelve thousand kilometers up. The two orbital towers humanity had built on Earth to facilitate UNESSPRO stretched twice as high but had taken years to build. The thought that this tower had descended from the sky literally over-night made his skin crawl.

This feeling was only enhanced as the "climbing de-vice" came into view in stages. The first was a high, rounded hump not dissimilar to a snail's shell, but ribbed, black, and peaked along its extensive axis. This split down its flanks, like a hand did into fingers, to leave wide strips of plating around a number of openings, from which is-sued a multitude of close-packed, insectile legs. The more Alander looked at it, the more it resembled a wingless fly, albeit one thousands of times larger and strangely squashed, as though its backside had been moved toward its nose and its upper carapace had cracked and risen to accommodate the change.

At the front, instead of a head, was an opening wide enough for a person to step into. Alander couldn't see what lay inside and was in no great hurry to find out.

"You realize you're going to have to get in that thing, don't you?" said Hatzis from orbit.

Attempting humor to cover his fear and uncertainty, he said: "I was expecting something more sophisticated. This is just a big bug."

"Are you still okay with this, Peter?"

"Yeah, I'm okay," he said. "It just looks as if it's going to eat me, that's all."

He resigned himself to the inevitable and moved closer.

Samson followed as he stooped slightly to enter the bug. The inside was made of a similar dark material to the outside, but there were no controls or windows of any kind to be seen. It was cramped, too, but not as close as the shuttle's cargo hold had been.

He sat down in one of the two crudely fashioned seats to the rear of the cabin; Samson settled next to him with a quizzical look.

"It's almost as if they knew there would be two of us," she said.

Alander nodded, even though there weren't two of them at all. The notion had already occurred to him, and he wondered just how far the Spinners were prepared to go to reassure him.

"What happens n—uh!" The ground suddenly moved out from underneath them as the bug's legs stirred into life. The "mouth" closed in front of them, and Alander fell heavily back into his seat as its orientation suddenly changed.

"What's going on?" he asked.

Sivio answered, "You're climbing up the base and onto the tower itself." Alander reluctantly allowed an image: of the bug rocking and swaying up the roots, the tips of its many legs sticking to the resinlike material with the ease of magnets to iron. They weren't using pincers, grippers, or even suction pads. How it stayed on he couldn't tell.

It all became much worse when the bug acquired the tower proper. At an angle of ninety degrees to the ground, he sank deeper into the seat as the bug put on a sudden burst of acceleration. He didn't want to look at the image to see how fast the climber was going or how high he was getting, so he switched off the conSense feed. It was bad enough that he could imagine it. He felt like Jack ascending the mighty beanstalk, oblivious to what perils awaited him at the top.

Avoiding the image wasn't as simple as just turning off conSense, however. Twenty-five seconds into their journey, the carapace of the bug suddenly turned transparent. Not perfectly see-through—he could see mysterious rods and planes shifting between the walls of his chamber and the outer skin—but clear enough to take in the view.

He twisted around to look behind him. The sun was up enough to illuminate the world falling rapidly below; the base was just visible through the dust and receding quickly. He swallowed and let the seat take him again. The top was lost in the sky. The wall of clouds seemed to be rushing at him, and he was already dreading passing through them. He didn't want to see the stars; he didn't want to be *that* high.

"Your skin is registering roughly Earth-normal atmospheric pressure," said Sivio. "Do you want to test it?"

"If you remove your mask," added Samson, "you'll be able to breathe easier."

He hadn't realized he was breathing heavily. Lifting the mask a centimeter, he hesitantly tasted the air, then waited for analysis.

"It's good, Peter; better than you're used to, in fact."

He tugged the mask off completely and sucked in a chestful of clean-smelling, oxygenated air, the most satisfying breath he had taken for weeks. The ability of his artificial body to breathe Adrasteian air came from within, involving complex chemical processes in its lungs, but it was perfectly capable of breathing Earth-normal air. Indeed, he felt that it might work slightly better, as a flood of well-being swept through his body.

More calmly, he surveyed the view below. The surface of Adrasteia spread out below him like a desiccated pancake, buckled and split in thousands of places, uniformly brown, uninteresting from any height. It vanished as the bug reached the warmer cloud layer and climbed rapidly into mist. Its carapace crawled with droplets of water startled out of the air by the appearance of something solid.

They ascended in silence for a good five minutes before the cloud layer began to thin.

"Watch out for your eyes," said Samson, gripping his hand.

He took her advice in time as they burst out of the clouds and into the upper atmosphere. The sun, hanging over the bowed horizon to his left, burned brightly into the bug's interior, blinding him for a second even through his upraised hand. His eyes soon adjusted to the onslaught, however, allowing him to see normally. As a result, when he looked up, the stars weren't visible; all he could see was the sunward edge of the tower stretching higher and higher above him. Somewhere up there, an orange point shone; this, he assumed, was the terminus of their journey: Spindle Five.

Below, the tower descended in a perfectly straight line into the clouds. Alander couldn't guess how far they had come or how fast they were traveling.

"How long until we get there?" He wasn't that concerned; he just wanted the sounds of the others to distract him from his growing fears.

"If you continue at this rate," said Hatzis, "one hour."

"What do I do until then?"

"That's up to you, Peter. This is your project, after all. Maybe you should be putting your questions to the Spinners themselves instead of us."

He didn't say anything to that. She was right; he had got himself into this and should expect to bear the brunt of it, be it boredom, apprehension, or outright fear. Whatever was awaiting him, though, there was little he could do to avoid it now.

1.1.8

Hatzis watched in silence as the alien machine carried Alander to the top of Spindle Five. It was hard to obtain a direct view of him, since his eyes were the only things remotely resembling a camera in the climber. Now and again, Hatzis would jump to Samson's viewpoint, but the image she received merely showed what he would look like if she were actually sitting there beside him, a reconstruction created from what little data was available. The *Tipler* had full access to every piece of information gathered by his body, but it couldn't perform miracles, so at best the pictures from Samson's viewpoint were alternately fuzzy and blocky. It made her wish they had planted nanotech surveillance devices on him.

Nevertheless, it all added to the show, thought Hatzis. This way there was a sense of the ambiguous, of mystery, that anything could happen.

The bug barely slowed as it neared the spindle, although its frantic legwork did gradually ease until it seemed to be drifting along under momentum alone. For a brief, worrying moment, it looked to Hatzis as though the bug was moving so fast that it was going to crash into the base of the imposing edifice toward which it was ascending; but at the last possible second, a section of red gold hull opened up and swallowed the climber whole.

Hatzis's worst fear was that Alander would be cut off the moment he entered the spindle, but these concerns were quickly laid to rest. The signal through his eyes was as strong as ever, revealing little more than the interior of the bug. Either it was dark outside, or the climber's carapace had resumed its earlier opacity.

There was one slight difference, though.

"Can you hear that, Caryl?" he asked.

The question seemed to Hatzis at first to be unnecessary, because she knew that whatever he heard, she would hear also. But she realized that he had no way of knowing whether or not his signal was still getting through.

"We can hear it," Samson answered for her.

Hatzis paid closer attention to the auditory information coming through from his ears. Below the mingled sounds of breathing, heartbeat, and involuntary muscle activity, she could make out a faint sound. It was like a mechanical hum or perhaps a rushing of air. But she couldn't be sure what it was. The signal was too distorted with him still sitting in the bug.

"It sounds like a subway," said Samson.

The bug came to a halt and its mouth opened. Alander's eyes saw little more than a white floor before him. The noise was slightly louder.

The view danced as Alander eased out of the chair and exited the climber. His movements were cautious, nervous, and Hatzis couldn't begrudge him that. She would have been the same in his position—not that she would have allowed herself to *be* in his position, of course.

Outside, he took a moment to look around. The bug was squatting on the floor of a tube barely large enough to contain it. The walls were white and smooth, and from them emanated a faint glow. There was enough light to see that Alander was standing in a tubular corridor that stretched ahead of him with no end in sight.

The rushing noise was also stronger, now that he was out of the bug, although there was still no obvious source.

"I guess I just walk, then," he said nervously, taking his first couple of apprehensive steps along the tunnel. "Any idea where the gravity comes from?"

It was Sivio who answered, "Beats me. Hopefully, you'll get the chance to ask someone soon."

He headed off away from the bug. The conSense version of Cleo Samson followed close by, barely visible in his peripheral vision. After a moment or so of walking down the unchanging corridor, Alander looked behind to find that the bug appeared to have vanished, as though it had been absorbed into the white glow from the walls.

"I don't feel right about this," he breathed. His gaze was moving erratically from nothing to nothing, desperately searching for a reference point.

"Look at me." Samson waved a hand in front of his face. "Peter, don't lose it now."

The sound of his breathing was loud through the conSense link. Hatzis held hers as his vision gradually stabilized, focusing on Samson's concerned expression. He seemed to be muttering something under his breath, but she couldn't quite make it out.

"Is there anything we can do?" she asked.

"No, it's okay," he said. "I'm fine. Let's just keep going. This thing has to end somewhere, surely. We're in a goddamn satellite, for Christ's sake."

Hatzis could relate to his sentiments. The featureless and seemingly endless passage unsettled her. It was unnecessary, dramatic, irrational. What sort of creature would build something like that?

Alander walked for a further hundred meters or so in silence, Samson staying close and keeping a firm grip on his arm. Then, without warning, the light from the walls increased in intensity. In a matter of moments it went from a dull glow to a burning brightness, and Alander had to shield his eyes. He stopped dead in his tracks, his hand reaching for a wall as if to steady himself.

"Peter?" Samson said.

"What the hell is going on?" he called out, his voice showing signs of panic.

Before anyone could respond, however, the light dimmed and the rushing sound that had accompanied him since his arrival finally faded into silence. He slowly opened his eyes and looked around with some bewilderment, his outstretched hand still reaching out for a wall that was no longer there.

"Are you getting this?" he asked.

"Oh yeah," said Samson with some amazement. "We can see it, all right."

"They must be hacking into me," he said.

The two of them were now standing on an immense, flat plateau that stretched out around them. There were no walls as such, just a panoramic view of Adrasteia, lit from the partial moon that hung overhead among the million specks of lights dotting the night sky. But Hatzis knew this was not possible. From the vantage point of the *Tipler*, she could see there had been no physical alterations to the outside of the spindle itself since they had entered. This was an illusion, just as the corridor must have been.

Hatzis tried to imagine how they did it. Some sort of 3-D image surrounding a floor that could move to simulate walking when in fact the viewer stayed still? That might work when Alander alone was the only viewer, but what if there were more than one?

However they did it, Alander wasn't equipped with the right devices to penetrate the illusion. All he could do was gawp at it.

A sound not unlike a thousand birds chirping simultaneously broke the silence. Alander spun to face behind him, obviously unnerved, but he stood his ground, nonetheless.

"What in Christ's name is *that?*"

The noise gradually increased in pitch for a few moments and, as it did, Hatzis detected a faint flickering of orange light around Alander. Before she had chance to comment, though, the lights disappeared, and the noise abruptly ceased.

"Can anyone tell me what that was?" She kept her inquiry private, out of Alander's scope.

"I'm not sure," said Sivio, "but I think he was just scanned."

Then another voice, smooth, precise, neither male nor female, and issuing from nowhere in particular, broke the tense silence in Spindle Five: "Welcome, Peter."

Alander glanced around as if for the source of the voice but saw only Cleo Samson. "I'm starting to have serious reservations about all of this," he muttered. "If this is you, Caryl—"

"That's not us," said Hatzis, keen to reinforce the fact that this wasn't another symptom of his instability. This was *real.*

"No shit?"

Samson took a step closer to him. "Take it easy, Peter. That was a greeting you heard, not a threat."

"How do I know it isn't part of the illusion, too? Something to put me off balance?"

"This is no illusion, Peter." Again came the voice, calming, dreamlike, seductive.

Alander looked around again, but the space around them remained still and empty. "Are you . . . ?" He faltered for a second. "Are you the Spinners?"

"If you are referring to those that built these structures, then no, we are not."

Hatzis's virtual heart was beating fast. "Who the hell are they, then?" she found herself whispering. Alander echoed the question at the same time:

"Then just who exactly are you?"

"We are your instructors."

"Instructors? For what?"

"The contents of these towers. If you are to benefit from them, then you will need to be guided correctly in their use."

"And what exactly *are* the contents of the towers?"

"Gifts," said the voice. "They contain gifts, Peter."

There was a slight pause. Hatzis fell back into her virtual seat. *Gifts?*

"From whom?" Alander asked, almost defensively.

"The builders of the towers, of course. The Spinners, as you refer to them."

"But where *are* they?"

"Neither their location nor their origin is known to us," the voice said. "This knowledge is irrelevant to our purpose."

"Are they human, at least?" said Alander, and Hatzis noted the frustration and confusion in his voice.

"No, Peter, they are not of your species."

The words rippled through her like a shock wave. *Not*

from Earth! This was the discovery that would change humanity forever: intelligent life, and one *far* superior in intelligence to humans. It changed *everything*.

Then another thought, one that produced an intense regret and sadness in her: They hadn't been rescued, after all.

"There goes your theory," she heard Samson say to Alander.

If the revelation in any way fazed Alander, he wasn't showing it. He was already continuing with the questioning of the voice.

"Wait a second," he said. "If you're not the Spinners, then who *are* you?"

Before he had finished the sentence, it occurred to Hatzis just what they were talking to.

"The Gifts, Peter! They're the goddamn *Gifts!* "

"Huh? What are you talking about, Caryl?"

"They're part of the whole thing," she explained, feeling the realization burning inside her. She *knew* it was true. "They were built by the Spinners, just as the towers were."

"Is that true?" said Alander, addressing the question vaguely upward. "Did the Spinners create you?"

"Yes," came the immediate reply.

"Then you're an AI?" he continued. "You're not real?"

"We are no less real than you are, Peter."

There was a hint of indignation in the voice's tone, and Alander chuckled uncertainly. "Point taken."

"This is a trick," said Sivio suddenly. "It has to be."

"Why?" put in Samson, looking around the space Alander occupied. "To what purpose? Christ, we're hardly a threat to them! If they wanted to do us harm, they could easily—"

"Maybe they're playing games," Sivio cut in. "Amusing themselves at our expense."

"That's ridiculous! To have—"

"Enough," said Hatzis. "We can discuss their motives at a later date. Right now, let's just hear what they have to say."

"We will not be speaking to anyone but you, Peter," the voice was saying in response to something Alander had asked. "You were chosen to act as mediator, and you alone. We will communicate through you or not at all."

"Chosen?" Alander's tone reflected the same incredulity that Hatzis felt at the news. "That's not possible. I was the one who decided to come to *you*."

"Nonetheless, our creators chose you. Our initial scan of you confirms this."

"But *why?*" He was having difficulty hiding his exasperation.

"Because you suit their needs," came the unruffled reply.

"And what are their needs?"

"We don't have that information," said the voice. "We know only that we must mediate through you."

"Then ask them!"

"That is impossible," said the voice. "They have already left."

"Well, when are they coming back?"

Hatzis could sense Alander's frustration rising, but she couldn't blame him for it. She felt the same way. The whole thing was as puzzling as it was suspicious, although she had to admit that it was intriguing at the same time.

"They won't return. They have moved on."

Alander shook his head, turning to scan the vast expanse of the place that stretched out all around him.

"So what is the purpose of all of this, then? Of you? Why should they choose *us,* of all people? I mean, we're nothing special, surely? Intellectually, we'd be nothing compared to them."

"They came upon you by accident," said the Gifts. "Like yourselves, the Spinners come from a species of travelers. When their path crosses that of another species, they impart something of their own technology in the hope of aiding the advancement of that species, as long as that species would not misuse the gifts they receive. In the time the Spinners were in contact with you, they learned much about your species without you knowing, enough for them to feel that you would use such technology wisely and not destructively. We are a gesture of goodwill from a race that has neither forgotten its humble origins nor lost the desire for companionship. Our makers feel that by assisting and nurturing other fledgling species that one day they will be able to meet such species again on a more equal footing."

Hatzis's mind was swimming with images of the Spinners on their grand journey through the galaxy, stopping now and then along the way to toss a tidbit of technology to those less developed civilizations. It might have made little difference to the Spinners themselves, but to *humanity . . .*

"Is this your first encounter with humans?" Cleo Samson asked suddenly from behind Alander. They waited a few moments for a reply, but there was just the terrible, empty silence.

Alander shook his head and then repeated the question himself.

The response this time was immediate. "Yes. A routine probe to this system detected your transmissions. Caution was exercised at first; there are civilizations who take delight in the destruction of others. Closer investigation revealed that you were not one of those, so it was decided to approach closer."

The glitch. Hatzis mentally shook herself as Sivio butted in with a request that the Gifts confirm that they were the source of the mysterious data that had immediately preceded their appearance around Adrasteia.

"That is correct," the Gifts said when Alander relayed the question. "The emissions you recorded were symptomatic of our makers' means of transportation to this system."

"Do you use the same transportation system?"

"Not anymore. We are not designed to move."

Another specialist, Jene Avery, interrupted with a query. "They seemed to arrive out of nowhere," she said. "Ask if they were camouflaged."

Alander repeated the comment.

"No." There was no elaboration upon the blunt reply.

"Does that mean they have some sort of instantaneous drive?"

"No," the voice answered. "Although it is much faster than yours."

"And this is one of the gifts?" Alander said.

"Of course," replied the Gifts. "The Spinners see it as a fundamental necessity for interstellar travel. Your method is too slow and impractical. We have also provided technology for faster-than-light communications, since it is a complementary requirement."

Hatzis had a few questions she needed answering and directed them to Alander to ask. He would no doubt eventually get annoyed by this, but that was too bad. Even though he had so far done a good job, she couldn't rely upon him to ask all the questions that needed answering. And at the moment, at least, he seemed to have no problem with everyone pressing their queries onto him. If anything, his annoyance was toward the Gifts for being so stubborn.

"You said that the Spinners have gone elsewhere," he said, repeating the question being whispered into his head by Hatzis. "Can you tell us where that might be?"

"We do not know that ourselves."

"For security reasons, I suppose?"

"We are not privy to the reasons behind all our builders' decisions. Those matters are not relevant to our purpose here."

"So they just built you, then left?"

"Yes."

"And you're ours to do with as we wish? No strings attached?"

"That is the nature of a gift, is it not?"

"I understand that," said Alander. He paused to listen to rest of Hatzis's comments before repeating them. "But you can't blame us for thinking there might be a catch."

"There is no catch." The voice of the Gifts was calm in response to Alander's concerns, as though it could keep on saying the same thing forever.

"Just wait until Earth hears about this," said Samson.

"If there's anyone left there," said Alander.

Hatzis didn't grace his cynicism with a rebuff.

"Ask them what the spindles contain," she said. Alander repeated the question.

"That will become clear when you arrive at each of the eleven gifts in turn," the voice replied.

"Eleven?" said Hatzis. "But there are only ten towers."

Alander shrugged. "Maybe the Gifts are a gift," he said.

"I mean, they have a collective intelligence that allows them to communicate with us and instruct us in the use of each individual—"

"It would be easier to see for yourself, Peter," the Gifts interrupted him.

"Okay," he said. "But how?"

"We will show you," they said. "The area you currently occupy is called the Hub. After your impression of the climber, we have tailored it more to your expectations."

"My impression . . . ?"

"You expected it to look more sophisticated," came the reply.

Hatzis absorbed the revelation that they *had* been listening in with the understanding of why the environs within Chamber Five were so outlandish. Both unsettled her.

"We must make it clear," the Gifts went on, "that this chamber is the common entry point to all of the gifts. You cannot enter any of them without first passing this point. You are the only individual currently permitted to pass, although you may at any time allocate another. Given your people's current circumstances, we will allow them free access to the climber that brought you here, should they wish to use it to ferry more android drones or other far-sensing devices to the gifts, but you are still required to give them permission. Understand this, Peter: You were chosen to have first access to all the things we contain, and to you we pass the responsibility of who will follow."

Alander nodded solemnly. "Okay," he said. "Whatever you say."

Hatzis's mind was immediately racing. Who would go next? Should she order the shuttle immediately back to Drop Point One for the other drones? Then she remem-

bered the temporary lack of reaction mass. *Shit*. Damn
Alander for screwing up that bath! That set them back at
least a week. Maybe a telesensing robot could be con-
structed in orbit and sent in via the bug instead.

She didn't have time to reach a decision, however; the
Gifts were speaking again.

"The Hub lies at our heart." Movement around Alander
made him start and look around. The view of Adrasteia
melted away, and in its place appeared ten doorways in a
circle around him. Each was different, and all of them
were closed. Between each door was nothing but space.
"All gifts may be accessed from here."

When Alander hesitated to approach, the Gifts nudged
him along with the assurance, "None are locked, Peter."

He picked one at random, or so it seemed to Hatzis. It
was painted a rich, garden green and had a simple, metal
latch. The frame was weathered as though it had stood
outside for decades. He walked up to it and put his hand
on the latch. Samson stayed close to his side.

He stopped there for an instant, as though having second thoughts, then opened it and stepped through.

Instantly, Hatzis found herself viewing a dead channel.

"Fuck!" She fumbled at her conSense parameters, fear-
ful that she might have unconsciously disturbed something. "Jayme, what's going on?"

"We've lost him. Hold on a second. I'm trying—" For
a brief instant, conSense filled with a chaotic, cross-
purpose noise as a dozen voices all tried to speak at once.
Then:

"Wait, we've found him! Only . . ."

She imagined the worst. "Speak to me, Jayme."

"He's not there anymore. In Spindle Five, I mean."

"What do you mean? Where else *could* he be?"

"Look for yourself."

Hatzis followed his link to the triangulation of Alander's signal at the same time as the data from his senses began to flow in. And, immersed in both, she finally *did* begin to see.

1.1.9

Alander walked through the door, thinking: This can't be, *the house was demolished twenty years ago!* He was so preoccupied with the thought that he almost didn't notice Cleo Samson disappear.

When he did, he stopped. His heart hammered. "Cleo? Caryl? What's going on?"

There was no reply. "Hey . . . Gifts!" He directed his question to the air above him. "What have you done to them?"

"Nothing, we assure you."

"And why should I believe you?"

"Because we have no reason to lie."

But he barely heard the reply, distracted as he was by the reappearance of a frightened-looking Cleo Samson at his side.

"Peter, are you all right?" Her hands were gripping him tightly.

"Where the hell did you get to?"

"We lost your signal," said Hatzis's voice, loud and clear. "You jumped to another spindle—Spindle Three, in fact. We had no warning, and nothing was pointing at you. It took a second to pick up your beacon and reestablish contact. There'll be a slight delay until we get a relay or two in position, so bear with us."

He nodded, exhausted by the relief that flooded through him. Relays were the least of his concerns; just so long as they knew where he was. He didn't understand how he could have physically jumped from one spindle to another without crossing the space between, but he knew without doubt that he was somewhere quite different.

"It's beautiful," Samson breathed, looking around her in awe.

He agreed without reservation.

They were standing on a wide, oval platform suspended in a space as seemingly infinite as the Hub. Except this space wasn't empty. It was filled with dust and tiny lights that looked uncannily like—

"Stars," he whispered.

"All the stars of the galaxy," replied the Gifts. "Their positions, types, and relative motions correct to a small fraction of a percent, as of this moment."

Alander looked around him, hardly daring to consider the implication of such a map. "*Every* star?"

"Every star," the Gifts confirmed.

"And every planet?" Samson added.

He repeated the question.

"Most," said the Gifts. "Some are best left hidden."

"If you say so," said Alander. "I doubt that we'd ever have the time to study even the ones that *are* here."

He felt an almost childlike thrill as he looked out at the star systems around him. He was a boy again, using the cheat codes for the games he would play on his father's old PCs, with all the secrets of the game world right under his fingertips.

"We will instruct you on the use of the map when you are ready. You should find it useful in times to come."

Alander laughed aloud at the understatement. "You

don't say," he said, trying to imagine the excitement the astronomers and physicists on the *Tipler* must have been experiencing at that moment. If the Gifts weren't lying, this knowledge would revolutionize their fields.

Then another concern returned as he stood watching the universe turn around him.

"That door," he said, glancing behind him. "It was the front door of my stepmother's house. I lived there until she sold it in 2009. I went back there just before the mission, but it had been knocked down. How . . . ?"

He stopped. The question didn't need asking, because the answer was obvious.

They knew everything about him. More, possibly, than he did. But not all of the doors had been familiar. Perhaps, he thought, the ones that *were* familiar were the ones the Gifts wanted him to explore first, knowing he would be automatically drawn toward them.

"It doesn't matter," he said. "I'd like to go back to the Hub and try one of the other doors."

"All you need to do is go back the way you came."

Alander took a step toward the door but not through. Now that he was paying attention, he could see that the other side was blurry, as though seen through a heat haze. "You ready for this, Caryl?"

"As ready as we can be."

"Okay." He went through the door, alert for any odd sensations but feeling none at all. Samson vanished again as he did so but reappeared a split second later on the other side, in the Hub.

"No obvious surges or emissions," Hatzis said. "Beats me how they do it."

"How *do* you do it?" he asked the Gifts. "Move me around like that?"

"We do not do anything, Peter. The Spinners have provided the technology. We are only permitted to guide you so far in its use."

"What happens if we hurt ourselves in the process? Like a savage might, poking around in a television set?"

"But you are not savages, Peter," said the Gifts. "That is why the Spinners gave you these gifts in the first place. You are aware of the need for caution in the face of new technology. If you follow our guidance, you will be safe."

As the psychologist said to the laboratory rat, he thought.

"Ask them about the towers," said Nalini Kovistra via conSense. "Ask them what they're made of."

Alander could sense a gathering throng from the *Tipler* as various experts lined up to ask their questions. The thought daunted him. He knew he would have to help find answers to these questions, no matter how long it might take or how unlikely it seemed. He felt like a minuscule David flinging challenges at a Goliath who didn't even know he was there. Yet Goliath *had* noticed—the gifts were evidence of that—and he had chosen Alander to act as the middleman for humanity's first contact with an alien race.

But why him? What did he have that the Spinners wanted? The uncertainty nagged at him as he tried to remember the question Kovistra wanted him to relay. Until he could answer *that* question, there was no way he could fully trust any of the answers he received.

A wave of dizziness rolled through him. He shook his head to clear it, but the feeling only ebbed. It didn't go away.

"Try another door, Peter," said Sivio. His voice was

displaying some of the emotion Alander had felt when the Gifts had first spoken to him: amazement, surprise, the beginnings of excitement. Now all he felt was distant and exhausted.

"Sure," he said and stepped forward. This time he made a point of choosing a door that wasn't so familiar to him: circular except for a slightly truncated base and made of brushed aluminum. It was only when it had slid aside with a faint hiss and he was passing through it that he realized it was familiar after all. Fashioned on late 2020s metallic, it had been the door to his first home in Beijing. He had lived there for less than six weeks.

This time he was prepared for the brief confusion. By the time the *Tipler* caught up, he had walked ten meters into the chamber on the other side and was puzzling at some of the things he found there.

"*Look* at this stuff," said Samson, appearing next to him with an excited smile. "It's incredible."

"It reminds me of the nineteenth-century manor houses I used to read about as a kid," he muttered, focusing more on the architecture of the high-ceilinged room than on the various displays it housed.

"Maybe that's where they got the idea," she said, stepping up to his side.

He faced her with confusion.

"Your head," she explained. "Maybe that's where they got the idea for the room's design."

Just like the doors, he thought.

There was a kind of music playing around the room. It was soft and gentle, barely audible, and totally unfamiliar to Alander. It gave the place a serenity he found himself welcoming. He looked about briefly but could not detect where the sumptuous sounds were emanating from. Not that it mattered. The fact that it was playing at all was enough.

Alander watched as Samson moved over to a couple of the displays on pedestals, leaning in as if to peer at the unusual structures. There were dozens scattered about the place: some simple in design, others more intricate, but all delicately crafted.

"What's this supposed to be?" he said, scanning the extensive area.

"Art," said Samson simply, indicating the walls. They were literally covered with innumerable images of varying sizes.

"This is the Gallery," said the Gifts. "Here you will find a visual cross section of the cultures our builders have encountered in their travels. Such a collection, of course, could not hope to be inclusive, but we have tried our best to give you an impression of the variety awaiting you."

"None of them originals, I imagine," he said. He had stepped over to one of the displays and was examining its contents. They appeared to consist of a ball of liquid suspended within a diaphanous cube made from a material he didn't recognize.

"Naturally," replied the Gifts, as smooth as the music swaying around them. "They are all replicas. *Faithful* replicas, it must be said."

"I'm sure they are," said Alander distractedly as he stretched his fingers toward the cube. Their tips tingled as they came into contact with it, then effortlessly passed right through. He watched without any hint of apprehension as the watery sphere within the cube distended, as if reaching out to touch him in return. The farther he pushed his hand into the cube, the more the sphere reached out to him, until the two finally connected.

The effect was instantaneous: he was standing on a beach. Not just seeing it, either; he was actually *there*. He could feel the water washing around his naked feet, the sand between his toes, and the breeze against his skin. And there was a smell he couldn't quite place, but it was beautiful and brought forth a thousand memories cascading into his mind like the warm embrace of an old friend.

But at no time did he believe himself to be anywhere else but in the Gallery. He could see Samson clearly standing before him and could hear everything she said to him over the sharp cries of the unfamiliar creature diving into the bright green waves.

"What is it, Peter?" she said.

He laughed aloud. "Wondrous," he said, removing his hand and examining it. It was completely dry and showed no evidence of tampering whatsoever, but the skin still tingled slightly.

He stepped over to another one, this time a free-floating crystalline structure balanced barely a decimeter above a black plinth. He reached out toward it, expecting something similar to the last one. But this was cold to the touch, and when he removed his hand, the object suddenly began to spin around on a diagonal axis, the effect of which he found quite striking.

The next was a twisted piece of matter that reminded him of an Escher painting, only this existed in three dimensions. It had to be an optical illusion—just as Escher's paintings had—yet he was somehow able to trace a finger along the coarse substance and follow the impossible angles of the structure. Not for very long, however, because he found that doing so made him nauseated.

He looked down at the base and read the inscription there: *Seducat, Fourth Generation, Pre-Altus*.

"That doesn't tell me very much," he said.

"For more information you will need to consult the Library."

"Another of the gifts, I presume?"

"Yes. We can direct you there, if you wish."

He didn't agree immediately. Instead, he moved away from the twisted sculpture, past Samson, who was admiring a painting composed entirely of various and shifting shades of red, and through an archway on the far side of the room.

He found himself in an almost identical room filled with different works of art. Two more doors led to his left and right. He took the left one. Another room; more art. Two more doors. He chose the left, then left again in the next room, and left once more after that, expecting to find himself back in the original chamber. But he wasn't, which left him feeling disoriented.

Before he became hopelessly lost, he retraced his steps to where he had started. Then, without hesitating, he walked back through the metallic door and was promptly returned to the Hub.

"Okay," he said, glancing at the doors surrounding him. "Show me the Library."

The Gifts guided him toward a large, stout oak door with an enormous brass handle. At first he didn't recognize it, but as he took the handle and pushed, he felt the memory return: The great arched door had lead into the expansive library of the university he had attended in his late teens. It was almost as if the memory was being channeled to him directly from the cold metal of the brass handle itself. This concerned him; how could he be sure that the memories were genuine? How could he know whether the memories weren't planted simply to give him a sense of familiarity, to make the doors more inviting to walk through?

The thought that he might be manipulated disturbed him, but he also knew that for now he didn't have any choice but to play their games. The only way he was going to find out what was behind each of these doors was to walk through them.

He entered an immense reading chamber that must have reached four stories high. Dozens of aisles opened up before him, their book-filled shelves stretching out over impossible distances. Closer to where he was standing, he saw what he thought to be computerized search facilities and virtual jack-in points.

This has got to be an illusion, he thought. The enormity of the place, the sheer wealth of knowledge that it promised—

"You may seek the answers to most questions here," said the Gifts.

Alander wanted to speak, but he didn't know what to say. It was just all so overwhelming for him.

"I wouldn't know where to start," he said after a while.

"You were curious about the *Seducat* from the Gallery," offered the Gifts.

He nodded lamely. He *had* been curious, but with the knowledge of so many races suddenly at his fingertips, it seemed almost trivial to be looking up a type of artwork. Nevertheless, if he was to learn how to use the Library effectively, then he was going to have to start somewhere.

Advanced voice-recognition systems took his inquiry about the Escher-like sculpture and told him that it came from a species living several thousand light-years away. He was offered a detailed biochemical and sociological analyses of their culture, but he took only a brief tour of their home solar system. Twelve planets, two of them inhabited. One yellow gas giant larger than Jupiter. A greenish sun. The aliens looked like lizards on stilts.

He reeled at that. A sense of deep *otherness* was beginning to well up in him. It was too much, way too much. He was drowning in information and losing himself in the process.

"Peter?"

The voice barely registered. It wasn't until a hand gripped his shoulder that he realized that he had faded out.

"Peter? Are you all right?" Samson was standing in front of him, peering worriedly into his face.

"Cleo? I, uh . . . Sorry. I drifted out for a moment, there. I'm okay now."

"We all did," said Hatzis. "And you're not. This wasn't the usual, Peter. We've checked your biostats. Your body is suffering the effects of prolonged stress and fatigue. When was the last time you ate?"

He shook his head. His body could survive for a long time on internal reserves, but there were protein concentrates back at the camp he was supposed to ingest every day or two. He had forgotten to bring them when he had left for Drop Point One. "I'm not sure. A while ago, I guess."

"Dammit, Peter," Hatzis chided him. "You should know better. We can't afford to lose your mobility right now."

"You need to take a break," said Samson.

"This is hardly the ideal time for taking a nap, Cleo," he said.

"Be that as it may," she returned, "you still need one. We don't have another body handy, if you'll recall."

"ConSense will knock you out," said Hatzis. "Just put yourself in a comfortable position and let us do the rest. We can flush the toxins from your system in less than six hours."

"Perhaps." For the first time, he cursed the fact that he was stuck in a material body when he could have been operating virtually, like the others. It didn't seem fair that he should have to stop while they kept going.

But he knew they were right. He wasn't invincible. And they had it all organized.

"Okay," he conceded. "I'll shut down for a couple of hours to get my strength back."

"If it is recuperation you seek, Peter," said the Gifts, "perhaps we can help."

"Not unless you have a bed I can lie on for a while," he said wryly.

"Return to the Hub," said the Gifts, "and take the black door."

A few steps later, he was back in the Hub examining his options. It wasn't difficult to spot the door the Gifts had referred to. It seemed more like a hole than anything else.

"This one?" asked Alander.

"The contents of that room should be suitable for your needs, Peter."

He moved slowly forward, irrationally nervous of what that room might hold. The black door seemed a little too symbolic for him, as though it were offering a more permanent sleep.

But what he discovered on the far side was just . . . nothing. He found himself floating in a void containing no sensory information whatsoever—at least not until Samson joined him again, drifting next to him.

"What's the point of this?" He spoke to Samson, but it was the Gifts that replied:

"This is the final gift we bring," said the voice. "In time, you will understand."

He hung there for a long moment, wondering if he could stand the oppressive nothingness. Perhaps if he used a bit of subtle conSense tinkering, even just a slight background noise to dispel the void a little . . .

"Okay," he decided. He had no other option, except to run his body into the ground and possibly kill it. Even in the midst of such wonders—or perhaps because of them— he needed to switch off for a while. "Give me five hours, Caryl. No more."

"Understood. Give us the okay first, though, to get someone else in there. We think we can have a telepresence droid of some sort ready within a couple of hours. But we need to know whether they will they let it in through the climber entrance."

He passed the request on, and the Gifts allowed it. "We will permit such devices," they said, "but we will continue to communicate only with you, Peter. Your people must understand that any additional surveillance of our interior comes at its own risk."

"Tell them we understand," said Hatzis. "We can look after ourselves."

"I hope so." Alander let his limbs relax into a familiar, zero-g sleeping posture. It brought back memories of training in orbit, before he had been chosen for the survey program. Then: "Will you stay with me, Cleo? Please? I'd feel better if there was someone to watch my back."

She smiled. "How can I watch it, Peter, when your eyes will be closed?"

"Well, you can pretend to, at least." He let conSense

and weightlessness wash over him and fought disorientation from both. Samson wrapped herself around him, and, despite himself, he was comforted by her presence. She was reassuringly solid, even though he knew she wasn't. The illusion was sufficient for his needs.

He had just enough time to think how different she felt from Lucia when consciousness slipped away, and his worries, for a time, were forgotten.

1.1.10

"This is just great."

For the first time in days, the bridge of the *Tipler* was quiet. Half its active crew roster had taken the opportunity to gather in a conference room designed specifically for an extraordinary debriefing session. Caryl Hatzis and Jayme Sivio sat at one tip of a roughly triangular table facing the ten people they had requested to attend. The walls displayed views of the gifts Alander had so far visited, while the wall behind them showed nothing but darkness.

"He jumps into this without consulting us," Hatzis went on. "He doesn't eat. I'm not going to sit back and let him commit suicide—not after all we've done to keep him alive."

"It could be worse," said Cleo Samson, sitting in one corner of the triangle, hands folded before her. "Peter could have had a complete breakdown much earlier. Given the circumstances, I think he's performed admirably. Does anyone here believe he could've done as well even a month ago?"

A mutter of consent ran around the table. Hatzis vividly

recalled Alander's descent into madness upon their arrival
at Upsilon Aquarius, when his engram had been brought
fully up to speed. His unexpectedly fragile identity had
crumbled in the face of such unfamiliarity, not helped by
the loss of Lucia Benck. Within days, they'd had to forcibly shut him down for fear he would tear himself apart.
Only the most radical of steps—confining him permanently to one of the remotely operated drone bodies
through which the surveyors occasionally stepped on the
surface of Adrasteia—had anchored him sufficiently to
survive reawakening, and, even then, his recovery had
been hesitant. Blackouts had been frequent; strange psy-
chotic episodes had overwhelmed him without warning;
frequent agnosia made him difficult to deal with on a professional level. Only in recent weeks had he dared accept
conSense overtures at all, too little and too late to avoid
isolation from the *Tipler* and those who had once been
his colleagues and friends.

His recovery had been uneven and slow and was still
incomplete. Hatzis wasn't prepared to admit that it might
yet be permanent.

"And at least we now have an alternative," Sivio said,
affecting his most conciliatory voice. "An assembler is
already on its way, manufacturing droids as we speak.
Meteorology reports that the disruption to the weather
caused by Spindle Six is actually resulting in surface rain.
If that spreads as far as Spindle Five or Drop Point One—
or any of the refueling points—then we can get some
more bodies in place. And once we can, we'll be home
free."

Again, assent rippled through the group. Close-shaved
Ali Genovese looked particularly pleased; Hatzis knew
that she was confident of being among the first given ac-

cess to the gifts, once the opportunity existed. She was right, but Hatzis couldn't resist spilling a little rain on her parade.

"You and I know, Jayme, that the best droids we can make in an hour or two will be ineffectual: low-range, at best, and only barely self-directing. Then there's the delay problem, which is fine when dealing with someone self-directed like Peter but will become increasingly drastic when the *Tipler* is on the outer leg of its orbit. Do you really want to send droids bumping along the corridors, smashing into things because our reaction times are too slow and they're too stupid to know any better?"

"But—"

"Don't ask for us to be moved closer, Jayme. I won't authorize something like that until it's absolutely clear there's no threat. Also, given that we've never seen surface rain in any quantity before, I wouldn't be investing too much hope in our reaction mass reservoirs quickly filling."

"You're right, of course." Sivio sounded annoyed; finally, she had gotten under his guard. "Everything you say is true: This situation is suboptimal in most respects. We have poor communications, no supply line, and precious little hard intelligence. But we *do* have the chance to change all that in time. Apart from being human—or as close as we can get, out here—I have to agree with Cleo that Peter is doing a pretty good job in a tight situation. He's got us into these things, and that's got to be worth something."

"*He* didn't get us in. They *let* him in."

"He knocked on the door, don't forget," Samson said.

Sivio shrugged expansively and managed a tight smile, his usual good-humored facade creeping back into place.

"However he got there," he said, "he's there now, and that's the main thing. We'll keep a close eye on his health in the future, that's all. There's so much to learn and do that I think it's unreasonable to wish for more at once."

She nodded; he had a point. No one else could have done more in Alander's shoes. And the volume of data they had to assimilate was already immense.

"Very well," she said. "So what do we have so far? Five chambers in five different spindles . . ."

"Beginning with the Hub, which sits at the center of some sort of instantaneous transport system," Sivio picked up where she left off.

"The only hard evidence we have that he is actually moving," said Hatzis, "comes from the sudden jumps in his body's transmissions, right?"

Sivio nodded.

"But can we trust this?" Hatzis asked. "Couldn't this be faked?"

"Not easily," said Sivio. "If he were staying in Spindle Five and his sensory data was merely being relayed to the other locations, there would be an appreciable lag between his responses to our queries. But as this is not the case, I personally think it's real."

"Any naysayers?" she asked. When it was clear there were none, she added, "Anyone care to guess how it works?"

"We can probably assume that the ring connecting the towers is involved," hazarded Donald Schievenin, the long-faced, long-limbed physicist who doubled as civilian survey manager on many of the other missions. "After all, we detected no emissions passing between the towers by other means. But I suppose we can't rule out some sort of method involving neutrinos or WIMPs—or something completely novel, even though that goes against Occam's razor. We're looking at technology far in advance of ours."

"But it's not magic," said Chrys Cunliffe, portly mathematician on the opposite side of the table. "They exist in our universe and therefore must operate by the same laws."

"And if we knew all the laws, I'd take your point." Schievenin lifted his bony shoulders in a shrug. "I've seen things in the last couple of days that I would have bet weren't possible. The Spinners built ten orbital towers and a complete orbital ring out of nothing but vacuum, as far as we can tell. How did they do that? If you can give me even a hint of what laws they were using to achieve this, *then* I'll listen to you."

"Clearly it's going to be up to us to work things out," said Sivio, easing into the debate. "They're not going to make things easy for us. I think we can accept that. The Spinners gave us these gifts, it seems, to nudge us forward a little in our intellectual evolution. But they're not going to spoon-feed us, because that would defeat the purpose of the gifts altogether."

Schievenin inclined his head thoughtfully. "I think I agree with Jayme on this," he said. "And if what he says is the case, then I, for one, shall relish the challenge they are setting for us."

That's the spirit, thought Hatzis. "Next, the Gallery. Does anyone have any comments about this?"

"Only that I'll be keen to measure the number and layout of the rooms," said Kara De Paolis, a structural engineer who had eagerly turned over her extensive experience working in space to UNESSPRO. "The Spinners seem to enjoy the illusion of infinity, and they're very good at it, too. Since the spindles are clearly *not* infinite in volume, they must be employing a lot of fancy tricks instead. I'd love the chance to get into those walls to see how they do it."

"Mapping is exactly the sort of thing a droid will be good for," put in Sivio. "We can set one to run independently and wait for it to report. That way, we bypass the delay situation."

"True." Hatzis mentally pushed aside the problem for now. The Gallery was actually the room she had the least interest in. She was looking for the gifts that would be more beneficial to them and their situation. "Okay then, what about the Library? Who wants first access?"

As expected, everyone spoke at once. She raised her hands to motion for quiet. "All right, all right! We'll draw a roster and sort it randomly. Does anyone have an objection to that?"

She saw Otto Wyra open his mouth, then shut it. She faced him squarely and said, "Astrophysics gets first access to the Map Room."

He looked immediately appeased.

"Okay." She raised her hand and began to tick off her fingers. "The Hub's in Spindle Five. The Gallery, Library, and Map Room are in Nine, Eight, and Three respectively. Spindles One, Two, Four, Six, and Seven are still unaccounted for. That's just about all of it covered."

"Except for the Dark Room in Spindle Ten," said Samson. "Nothing has happened to Peter since he went in there. Nothing that we know of, anyway. They could easily fake his biosensory data, if they wanted to."

"What did they say about that room?" Hatzis asked.

" 'This is the final gift we bring,' " Sivio quoted.

"Nothingness," intoned Oborn. "Sounds perfectly Zen to me."

"Maybe they made one too many spindles," suggested Chrys Cunliffe flippantly.

"Or ran short of gifts," countered Oborn. "They lied about there being eleven."

"Or maybe," said Hatzis seriously, "we're just not ready for that gift just yet. Perhaps its purpose will become clear once we've come to understand some of the others."

There was a general murmur of consent about the room, albeit an uncertain one.

"Anyway, we can't do anything about it right now," she said. "While Alander is out and the droid assembler is on its way, we have the chance to take a short break. I advise all of us to bring the next shift in early and do whatever we need to do to get ready for the next wave of exploration. And that includes sleeping. Unless the Gifts—or the Spinners or whoever they are—make another move, I think we can be fairly certain nothing will change while we're gone."

"I'll take the helm, if you like," said Sivio.

"No." Although he hid it well, she knew he was as tired as she. "Jene can do it. We're only a call away if anything crops up."

He nodded—gratefully, she thought. "I'll bring her up to speed."

"Then that's it." As she stood, she nodded her thanks to everyone in the room. Conversation sprang up immediately. Knowing that it would be a while before some of them dispersed, she left first of all, walking toward one of the room's unbroken walls and fading like a ghost before she reached it.

*   *   *

Confident that Sivio would lock the place down as per her instructions, she went straight to her private environment. There, wrapped in the comforting atmosphere of her father's New York offices—which she had always wanted to build into a home and, with the willing complicity of conSense, was finally able to do so—she did her best to wind down.

Images of the gifts flickered in her mind's eye as she tried to sleep, her virtual body turning this way and that in the hope of shaking the persistent and troubling thoughts. Whoever the Spinners were, and wherever they had gone, they had left her one hell of a tricky situation. She felt like a child given free access to a high-tech immersion gaming system but only allowed to touch it with a broom handle. The Library could hold the answers to thousands of speculations about life in the universe. That life existed at all, apart from on Earth, was enough of a revelation to keep her occupied for weeks; that it was literally teeming with life and that they had access to unimagined cultures was enough to keep her occupied for a dozen lifetimes—or a dozen versions of her for just one.

She stopped in midthought. Thus far, the Gifts had managed to avoid mentioning anything beyond the bare minimum about their builders. No doubt that was deliberate. What was it they had said? *There are civilizations who take delight in the destruction of others.* The Spinners were probably being cautious until they were certain that humanity, or another race humanity was in communication with, wasn't such a civilization. Now that contact was established, she was sure the Spinners would be reassured on that score.

In the meantime, there was still the Alander problem. Why had the Spinners insisted upon this seemingly senseless restriction to communicate only through him? Why refuse to talk directly to the people you were supposed to be helping? She couldn't see the point the Spinners were trying to make. Perhaps it had something to do with the fact that he had an actual body, and that they had an aversion to, or even mistrust of, life forms that did not possess something as fundamental as a physical presence. After all, just because humans had shucked their bodies in order to get into space quicker, that didn't mean that other cultures wouldn't be phobic about the idea.

Then again, maybe they were just being perverse, deliberately keeping it from being too easy for the survey team. If it *was* some sort of test, it was going right over Hatzis's head.

She rolled again onto her back with a heavy sigh, frustrated by her inability to switch off, as it were, and get some sleep. But she knew there was no point forcing something that wouldn't come, so instead she decided to stop trying to wrestle with her restless mind and put her time to better use. In the long run, it would probably help her to sleep better, anyway. If it didn't, she always had conSense to force the issue.

She called up the settings and overrides panel, accessible only by either of the survey managers on the *Tipler*—her and Sivio. She vacillated over the codes for a long moment, wondering if she should change them all to prevent Alander getting up to more mischief in the future, but in the end decided against it. Not because she trusted him, necessarily, but because she suspected it might be futile: If he really was the plant, the ship would probably notify him of any changes she made. Otherwise he could be rendered toothless too easily.

Instead, she dove into the conSense settings and mulled over which she might utilize. She could plug herself into the ship's operational levels, as she had done many times before, and experience the steady flow of data pouring in through a thousand senses; or she could follow the progress of the assembler firsthand as it edged its way into geostationary orbit, making droids as it went; or she could even subsume her mind into the complex pool of thoughts that was the crew's collective consciousness. Since only in Alander's case could each mental calculation be wrought on an independent processor, everyone else's virtual experiences were calculated en masse, queued and processed on a bank of machines buried deep in the *Tipler*. Although all the fragmentary thoughts were normally kept separate from one another, it was possible to strip away the aptly named ID tags and dive headfirst into them all at once. A constant kaleidoscope of human minds and bodies, meshed together into one chaotic soup, proved very distracting.

Hatzis called it the gestalt. Sometimes she thought of it as her best and possibly only chance to know God. She always found it oddly restful, like letting someone else's dream lull her to sleep. That night, it came close to suiting her best.

Even as she felt the dust of other people's minds swirl around her, burying her in a dune of moments, she knew that for tonight it wouldn't be enough. So many people's thoughts kept coming back to the gifts and the sole man sleeping inside them, among them. She smiled wryly to herself. Even with him there, she could not escape from him.

So she did the only thing she could do. She stopped trying and simply . . . *dove.*

". . . You were chosen. . . ," said a disembodied voice.

She (he) tried to move her arms, but they were pinned to her sides. She was trapped in a giant crystal, like an insect in amber. Her eyes were fixed wide open, as was her mouth. But she couldn't breathe; all she could do was scream, and then only in silence.

". . . You were chosen. . . ."

Her crystal prison was tumbling through space, with stars drifting idly past. She couldn't tell where she was headed until the tumbling of her crystal brought it into view: a purple brown planet with a golden band like a crown around it; the sort of crown a princess might wear in an old folktale.

". . . You were chosen. . . ."

Then the planet, along with the crystal, was gone.

She was standing at the base of a large hill, from the top of which grew a tree. The tree's branches were mostly bare and spread impossibly wide against the sky. From each of its outspread fingers hung a noose.

"There is no catch."

The voice's message changed at the sight of the new image, but she couldn't tell whether one had prompted the other or if both changed independently. A wind sprang up, making the dangling nooses dance. And it did look like they were dancing. The ropes were alive, the open-mouthed loops calling her name.

"There is no catch."

The tree's fingers reached down and closed around her

throat, obscuring the light of the moon and the stars, dragging her down into darkness.

"There is no catch."

She was underground, in a maze. Her feet dragged in puddles; her hair caught cobwebs as she brushed by; her ears were deafened by the sound of darkness—and *her*. The air was dank and smelled of decay, and the entrance to the catacomb had fallen far behind; she had lost that along with all hope of finding the center.

". . . We are only permitted to guide you so far. . . ."

(Ah. The part of her that was still awake in her private quarters, fighting sleep, cottoned onto what Alander's dream was about. It was some sort of mutation between what the Gifts had told him and what he feared. The crystal was his powerlessness to act; the tree was his fear of failure and death; the maze . . .)

". . . We are only permitted to guide you so far. . . ."

(. . . the maze was no different from how she felt in the face of the Spinners and their take-it-or-shove-it philanthropy. What were they doing? What were they thinking? What did they want? Negotiating these questions was exactly like being lost underground. She didn't know if her dream self was going in circles or making progress.)

". . . We are only permitted to guide you so far. . . ."

(She was honestly beginning to doubt the Gifts' ability to guide her anywhere at all. They certainly weren't making it easy for her. Sure, they had their own agenda and methods; sure, they were alien—if what they said was true, at least—and she shouldn't judge them by human terms. But how else *could* she judge them? Wasn't the onus on the Spinners to ensure that their fancy gifts could be understood?)

"In time, you will understand."

(She laughed aloud at that, and relished the sound echoing off the impossibly solid walls of her chambers. *Enough,* she thought. This was getting her nowhere. If she kept this up, delving as she was into the man's psyche, she risked becoming as confused and fucked up as Alander himself, and that was something to be avoided at all costs.)

"In time, you will understand."

She (he) floated upon a golden pool lapping at the walls of an ancient stone cathedral. The setting sun cast pinkish highlights through empty windows and painted surreal shadows on the walls to her left. The shadows formed words she could read and that made her feel at ease, but which she couldn't actually understand. When she moved her arms, the ripples made sounds like the chiming of a bell.

"In time, you will understand."

(*Yeah, right,* she thought, and left him to it.)

1.1.11

Alander woke to the sensation of being poked in the ribs.

"Rise and shine, Peter."

As the sensation continued, he realized that this wasn't a conSense illusion. Someone was *actually* poking him in the ribs. He tried to roll over and away but couldn't get purchase on anything. His stomach told him he was falling, and his arms flailed in desperation.

"Hey, take it easy, Peter."

An unfamiliar face greeted him when he opened his eyes; whoever it was, he could feel their hand on his shoulder, attempting to steady him. Only it wasn't a hand, really. Under the conSense illusion he could make out an extendible manipulator attached to some sort of robot.

Then the face fell into place: Otto Wyra. They'd been friends before the mission left but had hardly spoken since Alander's breakdown. In fact, Alander had received the distinct impression that the astrophysicist had been avoiding him.

"Otto? What's going on? Where's Cleo?"

"She's asleep. I was the one chosen to come and wake you in person. How do you feel, Peter?"

He stretched in the darkness and yawned. Everything was gradually falling into place. The tower, the gifts— *"You were chosen to act as mediator"*—and now Otto Wyra and a droid were in the Dark Room, waking him up.

"Has it really been five hours?"

"Not a second less. How do you feel?"

The repetition of the question made Alander realize that Wyra wasn't simply making light conversation; he was probably being prompted by Hatzis to determine exactly what Alander's condition was.

"Like shit, to be honest," he said. "My stomach hurts."

"You still need food, and we're working on that. What about mentally?"

"I'm okay. Or I will be soon enough, anyway."

Wyra smiled. "Good, because we have work for you to do."

Realization hit. *Of course.* He scrabbled once again for balance in an environment lacking any reference points and finally gave in to the futility of even trying.

"Okay, let's get out of here," he said. "This place is freaking me out."

He used the nearest manipulator to lever himself closer

to the door, wondering as he did so how he would have
managed had Otto not arrived. Perhaps the Gifts would
have helped him. Right now he was just glad the droid
was there to assist him.

The robot itself wasn't massive, comprising little more
than a frame to hold together various sensors and communication devices, with several stubby limbs designed
to act as either legs or manipulators depending on their
orientation. Based on a zero-g design, it had no defined
axes, and looked a bit like a tumbleweed with a purpose.
Yet its grip was strong, and the lenses that watched him
were almost too attentive.

He tumbled through the black door and into the Hub,
stumbling as his full weight returned.

He picked himself up, rubbing at a knee as he looked
around. Another droid pogoed from one door to another
and disappeared through it.

"What's been going on?"

"We've been busy," Wyra replied, clearly impatient for
Alander to get himself together. The droid tumbled off
elsewhere. "The Gifts were as good as their word, giving
us access as soon as the assembler was in position.
They're still tight-lipped, though."

"They haven't tried to stop you in any way?"

"They don't need to. We're limited by the design of
the gifts—but you'll see what I mean by that in a moment.
They've let us roam around and poke into things as much
as we can."

"How long have you been here?"

"Two hours. We have six droids, now, and another's
in the oven."

The monotonous hum of the Hub was drowned out by
new noises: tapping, whirring, buzzing; the sounds of the

robots at work. The acoustic properties of the gifts obviously extended to cover all the spaces of the spindles, no matter how far apart. It was weird to think that the sounds he could hear through a door only feet away could actually be coming from the other side of the planet.

A familiar voice intruded in his head: "Are you sure you're feeling better now?"

"Why the sudden concern, Caryl?"

"Your dreams were pretty active," she said.

He felt strangely naked. *They watched them, too?* "So what's your point?" he said irritably.

"The only room we haven't studied in any detail is the room you slept in. There's nothing in there at all, yet an entire spindle is dedicated to it. It doesn't make any sense. A sealed box would be enough to give you free fall and darkness. I'm just concerned that it could be a brainwashing device or something."

He was tempted for a moment to comment that it wouldn't take that big a job to rearrange *his* thoughts. But instead he said, "Or maybe it's where they live—the Spinners, I mean. Perhaps the space I occupied *was* just a box, and the rest of the spindle is their living quarters."

Hatzis was silent for a moment. "I hadn't thought of that," she said. "It's an interesting possibility."

"How would you go about testing such a theory?" said Wyra.

"We'll find a way," said Hatzis. "If they are testing us, I'm going to test them back just as hard."

Wyra rolled his eyes but didn't say anything in response.

"So," Alander said, "what have you found?"

"Stuff that'll make your eyes pop. Some of it we're too nervous to fiddle with." Wyra indicated a door on his right, one Alander remembered from Entrainment Camp. "This room we're calling the Science Hall. It contains demonstrations of all sorts of models and theories. Lots of mathematical formulas scribbled on the walls, too. Chrys thinks he's found turbulence equations in there somewhere, but he needs to look at it more closely to be sure. That's in Spindle One. Spindle Two—" he moved around one door clockwise, to another memory—"is the Lab. We're cautious of this one, to be honest. There's little explanation for what we've found in it, but it seems to contain samples of various types of matter and energy. It's like a chemistry set for gods. We're reluctant to touch anything until you speak to the Gifts about it, so Caryl has declared it off limits.

"The next one we went into was Spindle Seven, and it doesn't seem to contain much at all. There are machines in there, but we don't know what they do. That's another one for the Gifts to explain, although we are exploring it pretty closely at the moment."

"What about medicine?" said Alander. "Anything along those lines in any of the spindles?"

Wyra nodded, pointing to a door. "In Spindle Four there's a fair replica of a modern hospital, complete with regeneration tanks and laser surgery arrays. We call it the Surgery. For the most part, the technology is familiar—apart from an unusual suit we came across."

"Unusual in what way?"

"Well, it looks as though it's made of water." There was a pause, as if Wyra was concerned that what he had said might sound foolish. "We've no idea what it's for, although I'm sure that will become evident in the days ahead. Just as I'm sure there'll be plenty of other strange things like the suit we'll come across when we explore further. We suspect that, like the Gallery, there could well be more chambers beyond the one we saw; so who knows what kind of stuff we're going to find?"

"Who indeed," said Alander, thinking of the answer to his own fragile state.

"It's off limits, too, for the moment." Wyra didn't seem too upset about that, and the reason for it soon became clear. "You might want to check out Spindle Six before you go exploring anywhere else. It's the biggest of them all, the one that's been emitting the gravitational waves. They've died down now, but we're no closer to figuring out what exactly caused them."

"I would have thought you'd be more interested in the Map Room."

"I was until I saw what's in Six."

Alander eyed Wyra closely. He could take a hint. "Okay, so which one is it?"

Wyra gestured toward a cream-colored door with a picture hanging from it. Alander groaned to himself, feeling the irrational apprehension rise inside of him. This had been the door to the bedroom he had shared with his ex-wife, Emma. The breakup had been a difficult one for both of them, and approaching it now seemed to revive those feelings of failure and bitterness.

His hand reached out hesitantly for the handle, then pulled it open in a quick and forceful manner, as if doing so would somehow rid him of the unwanted emotions.

This time, there was no discontinuity in his contact with the *Tipler*. They knew where to expect him to reappear and had satellite receivers already in place. All he saw was a blur until he'd crossed the threshold, then Wyra was following him into the giant chamber, smiling at Alander's expression.

They were standing on a gantry high up on a curved wall made up of what seemed to be opaque, gray glass. The gantry circumnavigated a spherical chamber at least two hundred meters in diameter. His inner ear registered odd tidal effects stirring through the room, originating from the thing in its center.

The object floating before him was a perfectly white sphere some fifty meters in diameter. How it was floating, he couldn't tell, since he was still experiencing gravity and it had no visible means of support. Similarly, he *assumed* it was a sphere, but without any hint of shape or detail it simply appeared to Alander's eyes to be round. It could conceivably have been a disk, but a gut instinct told him it wasn't.

As he watched, a new detail appeared. Another circle, as perfectly black as the other was white, slid into view. It was smaller than the white one, measuring around five meters in radius. His mind took a second to process the image, but once he had, it was clear: the smaller, black sphere was orbiting the larger, white one.

"What is this?" he asked the astrophysicist. "A giant chemistry model?"

"Hardly." The astrophysicist pointed as the black sphere passed between them and its white "parent." Alander felt a wave of . . . *something* pass through him. It was only slight, but it definitely was there.

"Feel it? That was a tidal surge passing through you, courtesy of a gravity wave. If you'd asked me an hour ago, I would've said it was impossible, but there you have it. We've had no luck analyzing the spectrum of the wave, before you ask. We don't have the detectors yet."

Alander turned to look at Wyra. "What do you want me to do?"

"Ask them what it does, of course." The astrophysicist was looking up at Alander like a supplicant. "I have my suspicions, given that it's not fixed and is in the largest of the spindles, but I can't confirm it. And if it *is* what I think it is . . ."

The sentence went unfinished, almost as if he couldn't bring himself to speak the thought out loud.

"What do you think it is?"

"Just ask them, Peter," Wyra said urgently, trying to suppress his excitement but failing. "We need to know."

While it was nice to be needed for a change, Alander felt it would have been nicer had it been for his own abilities, not as a result of some arbitrary alien decision.

"Gifts?"

"Yes, Peter?"

"What does Spindle Six contain?"

"A means of traversing space. It will aid you in your exploration of neighboring regions."

"You mean it's a spaceship?"

"Yes."

"A *ship*," Wyra breathed, his hands gripping the edge of the gantry. "I *knew* it!"

"Where can it take us?" Alander asked.

"Anywhere you wish to go."

"Can it take us home?"

"If by that you mean your home planet, Earth, then yes, it can."

"And how long would it take?"

"Less than one Adjusted Planck day."

"Relative, I presume." He tried not to seem as stunned as he felt; for so much time dilation, the alien vessel must be capable of coming frighteningly close to the speed of light and enduring crushing accelerations. "What about in real time?"

"What I have given you is the duration of the journey with respect to a stationary observer."

"One day?"

"That is correct. However, the time measured by the occupant of the craft will in fact be longer."

"One day . . ." His head was reeling from the concept of a faster-than-light drive. With the thing in front of him, he could return to Earth and get back again before anyone really missed him. And the Gifts had earlier mentioned some sort of faster-than-light communicator. He could call them when he arrived; he wouldn't even need to come back.

Wyra was already nudging him and hissing questions for him to ask, but Alander ignored him.

"And you're *giving* us this?"

"No," said the Gifts.

The blunt reply was as sobering for Alander as it must have been for Wyra, who abruptly shut up.

"I . . . I don't understand," Alander stammered. "What do we . . . ?"

"We are not giving you anything, Peter," said the Gifts smoothly. "Our builders are the benefactors of the spindles and their contents. We are merely—"

"Okay, okay," said Alander impatiently. "I get the distinction you're trying to make."

He heard Wyra sigh impatiently beside him.

"What I meant was," Alander went on, "are these things—the ship and everything else—are they just being given to us? No strings attached? For us to use as we please?"

"That is the nature of a gift, is it not?"

Alander couldn't tell if they were playing with him or not. The Gifts had used that exact phrase earlier, upon his introduction to the Hub.

"Peter . . . ?"

Wyra's hand, via the droid, plucked at his sleeve at the same moment another gravity wave swept through him. He backed away from the alien vessel, using the wall to guide him through the door to the Hub.

"Peter, are you all right?"

"I'm sorry, Otto. Give me a minute." He looked at the doors surrounding him, momentarily bewildered. Had Wyra told him where they all led? He couldn't remember. There had to be *one* he still didn't know about.

"Gifts, where are you?"

"Our physical location is unimportant—"

"But you do have one, right? I want to know where it is."

"Spindle Seven."

He counted around the circle. Everything Wyra had told him suggested that the doors followed a logical progression. If that was case, the door to Spindle Seven wasn't one he recognized. Reinforced, smoky glass with an aluminum handle, it reminded him of a school or office door. Like the others, it was obviously from somewhere in his past, but damned if he could remember where exactly.

"What are you doing, Peter?" The illusion of Wyra danced nervously after him as he walked unsteadily to the door.

"I need to think," he said, pushing the door open. As the Hub receded behind him, he added to the Gifts, "Don't let anyone follow."

The Gifts were as good as their word. The door swung shut behind him, and he was alone.

*   *   *   •

*He switched off conSense as the alien AIs gave him direc-*tions. Spindle Seven contained the machines that had built the orbital tower below. In all the other spindles, these devices had been dismantled and reconstituted as other things. The Spinners seemed to have mastered assembly on an atomic scale, along with energy/matter conversion and elemental transmutation. Alander wasn't surprised; in fact, humanity had been making steps toward the last two before he had left Earth, a hundred years and more before. It was simply the scale that astonished him: The Spinners had built structures larger than cities in hours out of thin air, then on a whim rebuilt them into whatever they wanted.

A small, flat platform took him along a transparent transit tube that snaked through the massive structures. It moved at an alarming speed, yet he felt no sense of inertia as the transport slowed or accelerated.

It was an unnerving experience, passing between machines larger than Earth's tallest buildings, yet in some cases as slender as the *Frank Tipler* itself. Some were many limbed, like giant praying mantises; others hung like folded dragonfly wings, translucent and gleaming all the colors of the spectrum. Massive cylinders lurked almost out of sight at the top of the spindle, while at the bottom the structure was open to space. When he looked down, he could see Adrasteia, the planet's atmosphere still recovering from the gravitational disturbances of Spindle Six. He stared down at the landscape with something approaching wistfulness, which he thought strange. He had never particularly cared for it before, but here, now, he found its familiarity a welcome sight. Indeed, compared to the machines around him, it felt almost like home.

The transit tube terminated at the point where the orbital ring passed through the spindle. There hung a cluster of boxlike structures, looking for all the world like a small mining outpost on the Earth's moon. It was into one of these boxes that Alander was led by the platform beneath him. There, as per his request, he finally came face-to-face with the Gifts.

They didn't look like much. In a space barely larger than an average-sized bedroom stood eleven gray, featureless, three-meter-high artifacts. They were roughly the same proportions as a playing card, complete with rounded corners. He reached out to touch one and was surprised to find neither heat nor vibrations coming from it. Nor could he detect any sounds issuing from them. For all intents and purposes, they were totally inert.

But these were, Alander was assured, the equivalent of CPUs for each of the gifts. Here, the maintenance of the giant structures was directed. This was the true center of the enigma that had been presented to humanity in Upsilon Aquarius, the place where the absent Spinners had the greatest influence.

He didn't bother prying for more information about the builders of the gifts. He knew very well that it would be pointless. Instead, he took a seat by the entrance to the chamber and sat staring in awe at the monolithic machines that were the Gifts. The Spinner AIs might not be fundamentally different from the AIs he was used to, but they were nevertheless made by superior intelligences. That immediately set them apart. There was no reason why the Spinners' creations could not themselves be thousands of times more intelligent than a single human.

Yet part of him was still resisting the evidence and

wondering if the Spinners might not be human, after all. Back on Earth when he had left, AI research had begun its steep upward trajectory that some said would lead inevitably to a technological and social Spike beyond which any prediction was impossible. If the Earth had passed this Spike and developed artificial superminds, he wouldn't put it past them to try a stunt like this. It seemed incomprehensible, certainly, but since everything about them would be incomprehensible, it made an odd kind of sense.

He knew, though, that he was probably just clinging to the shreds of his original's theory, in much the same way a child from a broken home might cling to the ideal of a happy family. If it was wrong, then it was wrong, and he should feel under no obligation to cling to it.

He sighed and closed his eyes. This was the first time he had felt alone since his ill-fated bath. As then, with little to distract him, the memories of Lucia surfaced once more. He saw her in perfect clarity, cursed with the machinelike recall of his artificial memories. Her hand propping her head as up as she lay next to him, her hair falling in a cascade across her shoulder and down onto the pillow, her rich brown eyes staring out to him.

And when she spoke, her voice . . .

"Where do we go from here?"

An overwhelming sense of loss washed over him, and he cursed himself out loud, irritated for having let such maudlin thoughts intrude upon what was supposed to be a moment of peace.

To distract himself, he broke his self-imposed isolation from conSense and listened to what was going on. At first he could make out little more than a babble of voices, dozens of them overlapping and talking at once. Then, slowly, he began to tease out individual, if still fragmentary refrains:

"—needs material input if it's to keep assembling so—"

"—not what they told Alander—"

"—just isn't enough bandwidth to—"

"—reaction tanks filling nicely—"

"—and tell Peter to straighten out—"

"—if you can't find the key then I suggest—"

"—Spinners don't have bodies because there aren't any—"

"—when Alander comes back—"

"—air filtration system outlets—"

"—Drop Point One in range—"

"—Get Peter to ask them—"

The cocktail effect took hold, and soon he could hear little more than his own name, over and over: "Peter . . . Alander . . . Peter . . ."

He leaned his head against the wall behind him, wanting to switch off his feed to the *Tipler* but not particularly wanting the silence either. It was a choice between thoughts of Lucia or listening to the others talk about him.

Not that they were really talking *about* him, per se. Their interest was with the gifts; he was just the channel through which they could get to them.

The babble in his head was incessant, reminding him just how different he was from them. He needed time to himself, while the others in the *Tipler* seemed quite happy to work together forever: analyzing the data they had, poring over the information given to them by the gifts, discussing strategies on how they should go about studying each of the items in the spindles. Hatzis had been annoyed at his inability to continue, because he had a need to rest, and maybe she had every right to be. He *was* different from them, not as efficient or . . .

A realization struck him suddenly, one that made him feel a thousand times more isolated than if he were to simply shut off the feed to the *Tipler*.

He reached out through conSense, seeking Cleo Samson.

She materialized an instant later, sitting on the floor beside him with her arms folded around her knees.

"Does this mean you're back?" she said. "Otto is having kittens."

"Not just yet. Sorry if I woke you up."

"Any time." She didn't look as though she had been sleeping, despite what Wyra had said. "So what's up? Have the Gifts told you something?"

"No, nothing like that. But I think I know why they picked me."

She leaned closer. "Tell me."

He held the thought in his mind for a moment, disliking the way it tasted. It tasted *true*. "I'm a bottleneck."

"I don't understand," she said.

"Don't look so puzzled. You know I am."

"That's not why I'm puzzled. You mean they chose you for that reason?"

He nodded. "To slow things down."

"But why? Why give us all this stuff, then make it hard to talk to us about it?"

"So we'll work it out for ourselves. They even said something along those lines when—"

" 'We are only permitted to guide you so far,' they said." She was quoting directly from the recordings, via the conSense record.

"Exactly," he said. "They want us to go slowly, working everything out as we go along." A memory came to him, from his original. "Did you ever play the old computer games?"

She frowned and shook her head. "No, why?"

"My father used to like them," he said. "The preimmersion type, on a monitor only. Some of them had elements of role-playing, but they weren't terribly sophisticated; they could be worked out fairly easily. But they did take time and could be quite challenging. Naturally, there were people who didn't want to solve the puzzles for themselves; they'd rather walk though it, getting nothing more from them than the nice scenery. They would use cheats downloaded from the World Wide Web to crack the game wide open." The words were almost identical to the ones his father had used, years ago. It was uncanny how he knew them so well, even though he *himself* had never heard them spoken before.

Samson smiled now. "And we on the *Tipler* are these people, right? Wanting the cheats?"

"The Gifts have the same attitude as my father in respect to this," he said. "If you are to play, then you play it properly. Otherwise, there's no point."

She watched him with some sympathy. "And that's why you think they chose you?"

"Yes. Not because I'm special, but because I'm *slow*. I'm forcing the others to think, rather than ask. They'll give us a push now and then, sure, but essentially, we have to put in the effort to learn and understand ourselves. We can't cheat."

Her hand reached out to touch his shoulder. "You could be right, Peter," she said. "But it doesn't really change anything."

"No, it doesn't. I'm still the one everyone wants to talk

to, all of a sudden, for all the wrong reasons."

"Well, there's something to be said for that. It's not often Caryl Hatzis lets herself be dangled from someone else's string."

He laughed at this. "True enough," he said. Then, earnestly: "Tell me, how are the others coping with all this?"

"Generally well. There's plenty to keep their minds occupied, which keeps them from dwelling on the enormity of it all, you know?"

He nodded but didn't say anything.

"Jayme's way out of his depth, though," she said with a smile. "You can tell by the way he's not really talking to anyone. He's just going through the motions, as though everything on the inside has been knocked out cold. It'll take him a while to unfreeze, I think."

"And Caryl?"

"Handling it, I think. You can never tell with her, though. She always acts as though she's about to snap."

"That's her way of coping, I think." He shifted on his buttocks; the floor was getting hard. "We all have our own methods."

"I guess so."

They were silent for a long moment. Alander stared at the gray processors and wondered what was going on inside them. He doubted humanity would ever know all of their secrets, no matter how hard they looked.

"Listen, Cleo—"

"Don't say it, Peter."

"Don't say what?"

"That you're sorry for being such a crabby old bastard."

"Why would I say that?"

"Well, aren't you?"

"What—a crabby bastard or sorry for it?"

"Both, if you like." Her smile widened. "Depends on how big an argument you're looking for."

"I really wasn't going to say that," he said. "I was just going to say thanks. And don't ask for what, either. You know what I'm talking about, this time."

"Maybe. But I reserve the right to disagree. I know what I'm letting myself in for, and I choose to put up with it."

He shrugged. "The point is, I'm grateful," he said. "Of all the people on the *Tipler*, you're the only one who has consistently treated me like a human being."

"Well, it seemed perfectly obvious to me."

"What did?"

"That you needed a friend," she said. "And still do, I think."

"Yeah, but—"

"No, let me finish. I like you, Peter, a whole lot more than I did before we left. That isn't to say I love you or anything like that. Don't get me wrong; I'm not some soppy schoolgirl hanging around waiting for some ungrateful drip to glance in her direction. Although I was jealous of Lucia during entrainment, it was only because I *didn't* know you very well, and she was coming between us. I thought we could've been friends, first and foremost, and was sad that we didn't have that chance to find out. Later, when we arrived here and you were in such a bad way, you were abandoned by almost everyone; you frightened them, showed them what they didn't want to see. I could've abandoned you, too, quite easily; I didn't because that would have been a betrayal of my initial feelings. If I like someone, I don't just like them when they're happy; I don't believe in part-time friendships. I've been your friend even when you didn't know it, and I think it's starting to pay off, now. Don't you?"

He couldn't help it: He laughed. "Your investment is finally paying dividends. Is that what you're telling me?"

"Not so crudely, perhaps," she said smiling, "but yes, I guess in the end we always look out for our own best interests first."

"Well, I'll do my best to ensure you are suitably rewarded for your troubles."

"I'm sure you will," she said. "And maybe sooner than you think."

He narrowed his eyes, trying to fathom the meaning behind her words, but before he could consider quizzing her, she was gone—disappearing from one moment to the next, as though she had never been there at all.

He looked up at the Gifts, then down at his feet. Although physically rested, he still felt tired. Most of all, he was tired of games. Whatever Samson was playing at, he didn't have the spare energy to worry about it.

It was time to get serious and take control of the situation and find out exactly what they had here. While the others were working hard to decipher the mystery of the gifts, he couldn't afford the luxury of being a loner for too long. Bottleneck or not, he had to join the group effort and let himself be monopolized.

"Caryl, are you there?"

The voice of the survey manager responded immediately, as though she had been waiting. "Of course."

"Is everyone listening in?"

"They can be, if you think it's necessary."

"It might be. I think it's time we stopped stumbling around in the dark."

"I agree. Give me a minute."

"Okay, Gifts," he said, getting up and pacing around while directing his attention upward. "I'm going to start relaying questions from my colleagues on the *Tipler*. I want you to answer them as openly as you can. You don't have to give us specifics, necessarily, merely an overview so we can work out where to concentrate our efforts. Just this . . ." He indicated the monoliths. "This alone would keep us busy for months."

"We are prepared to answer any question you put to us, Peter," replied the Gifts, "provided only that it doesn't conflict with the wishes of our builders."

He nodded but said nothing until Hatzis returned. His mind wandered across the cloudscape of Adrasteia below, to the darkness of space. Somewhere out there was an alien race the details of which he might never know. What did they look like? Where did they come from, and where were they going?

There was only one way, at the moment, that they had any hope of finding out.

"We're here, Peter."

"Right," he said. "Let's get started."

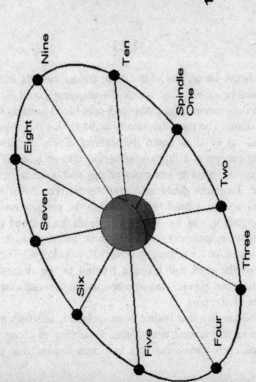

1: Science Hall
2: Lab
3: Map Room
4: Surgery
5: Hub
6: Dry Dock
7: Gifts
8: Library
9: Gallery
10: Dark Room

1.2

THE VIKING WIDOWS

1.2.1

The Frank Tipler, *like all the other survey vessels, allowed* a number of ways in which the engrams could interact with their environment that flesh-and-blood humans could not share. The most frequently utilized was the ability to speed up or slow down the internal clock, so that one could compress a thirty-year period into an hour, if necessary, or speed up one external day and make it feel like three. Engrams could also shut themselves down when necessary for a brief time, although the process was discouraged; it was too much like death, to suspend one's thoughts completely, and few were prepared to take a chance on never returning. After all, who knew? The theory of the soul had taken a beating in the twenty-first century, but no one was immune to the superstitious leftovers of the past.

One facility that hadn't been included, although it had been raised several times, was the ability to clone individual crew members. This had been deemed too problematic for missions such as these. If someone was copied, that created an immediate imbalance in resources; why should one person have more than their fair share of processing time than the others? The situation would be unsustainable. And supposing that the copy was ultimately "retired," who was to say that it had any less right to continue existing than the original? What if there were more than one copy? The moral and ethical arguments were many and had the potential of leading to disastrous circumstances.

Caryl Hatzis was one of those who had always been opposed to the idea of replication. After two days of talking with the Gifts, however, she was beginning to wish she hadn't. For a start, she could have cloned Alander and put as many copies as she wanted in new bodies and set them to work, and each could have communicated with the Gifts. She would not have been forced to wait until *he* was ready. She never thought it would be something she would hear herself say, but one Alander simply wasn't enough!

Two days . . . In that time, she had watched as the droids completed a map of the Gallery, which turned out not to be as infinite as it had first seemed, although it still contained more works of art than the *Tipler* had memory to record. This was without taking into account the Library and the Science Hall, where another droid had scanned the numerous equations covering the thousands of square meters of walls. Some of the math seemed to pertain to a theory underlying the Kempe-Larner superstring GUT, a possibility that had her mathematicians completely stumped. The Gifts wouldn't explain what any of the equations were; that, they had said, was humanity's task.

They were less reticent in the chambers known as the Lab, but no less mysterious. Huge tanks lined the walls— some of them metal, others made of energies the likes of which could merely be wondered at by her scientists—all containing samples of various exotic types of matter. All could be examined by sensors within the room, although at times it was far from clear just what the sensors were actually measuring.

In other rooms there were vast standing waves of vibrations in space-time and energy that could be similarly measured on instruments that were as likely to be as completely mysterious as they were familiar. Her material engineers and physicists had positively confirmed samples of Bose-Einstein condensate and positronium in the main chamber, and thought they'd found neutronium and quark matter in another room, but they hesitated to even guess at many of them.

Too much too soon, she thought. *Riddles within riddles...*

The Gifts had been relatively frank in their discussions of the Surgery. First revealed was an analysis of the human genome, with a list of proteins and their uses, which filled a few gaps still remaining in human knowledge. Then came a complete dissection of the human form, detailing how it arose from birth—including answers to questions of fetal development that had eluded medical researchers on Earth for centuries—through the various stages of development, maturity, and senescence. Hatzis watched detailed simulations of neurons at work in the brain, followed with some difficulty a procedure designed to trigger cell death in all known cancers with 100 percent effectiveness, became completely lost in arguments, via Alander, over whether quantum effects really played a role in human consciousness, and was ultimately reduced to dumb amazement at the real gift the spindle contained.

They had earlier noted the presence of a human-shaped suit apparently made out of water in one corner of the main room. Initially, her expert in that area, Kingsley Oborn, had dismissed it as little more than decoration. But when he realized that everything within the Surgery had a purpose, he was forced to reassess the suit.

"Any ideas?" Hatzis had asked him.

"Well, it's not a model," he had replied while running a hand over his virtual beard. "And I'm guessing it's not an examination or a diagnostic tool, either. They've already given us enough noninvasive methods to last us a century. Some sort of therapy, perhaps?"

But she knew they could speculate all they wanted and not get anywhere. The only way to find out exactly what is was for was to ask the Gifts. As always, they would only speak directly to Alander, regardless of who else was actually asking the question.

"Place your hand within the device, Peter," they told him.

Apprehensively, Alander stepped up to the suit and did as he was instructed.

"Like this?" he said, reaching nervously out to the watery surface.

"Don't be nervous, Peter," said the Gifts. "You can't damage it."

"It's not the suit I'm worried about," he said.

Nevertheless, he extended his hand the few centimeters and touched the suit. The surface trembled for a second, then parted beneath his fingertips. Then, before he had chance to even flinch, the suit had dissolved and run up

Alander's arm; in the second it took him to call out in alarm, it had fully enveloped him.

"Peter?" Hatzis felt a wave of panic as she watched him standing there, completely immersed in the watery substance. If they lost him . . .

"I'm okay," he replied after a moment, although his tone indicated a high degree of tension.

"It will not harm you, Peter," assured the Gifts. "Note that you can breathe normally, and that your movements are unimpeded."

Through the rippling fluid, Alander's android features were slightly blurred, but his voice was only a bit muffled.

"And now what?"

"We shall demonstrate," said the Gifts.

What followed were sights Hatzis never wished to see again. Alander's artificial body had been displayed in more ways than she could imagine: as though his skin had become transparent, revealing subcutaneous layers of fat and muscle; in detail, with close-ups of cells and fibers displayed on the surface of the watery suit; in pieces, dismantled like a machine and blown up within an aqueous gel, all without any apparent dysfunction or discomfort. She knew she'd never forget the sight of him with his arm magnified five times its normal thickness, reduced to individual bones and tissues, yet apparently still working with perfect ease. Likewise, she would never forget the look on his face.

"So it is another tool for analysis?" Oborn looked surprised, but professional curiosity quickly took over. "Like X ray, CAT scan, PET, and MRI all rolled into one!"

"The suit is capable of repairing damage on every level," the Gifts explained to Alander, again ignoring the comments of the others. "It can treat everything from gross tissue damage to DNA copying errors. It can knit bones, restore cerebral lesions, replace blood, and erase scars. It can—"

"Ask if it can extend telomeres," broke in Oborn.

"Yes," the Gifts replied when Alander asked.

"*All* of them?" Oborn pressed excitedly. "Not just a few here and there?"

"Where such intervention would be beneficial to the subject, yes."

"What does that all mean, Kingsley?" said Alander.

"It means that this *thing* can make us immortal!"

"Is that true?" Alander asked the Gifts.

"Yes," they replied. The suit had crawled from Alander's body and back into its display position. "Immortal and healthy. That is the ultimate aspiration of anyone occupying a physical body."

"Is that what the Spinners believe we should do?" Hatzis asked.

"We are unaware of our builders' intentions," said the Gifts when Alander relayed the question. "Everything they have left you is for you to use at your own discretion. Nobody can tell you what you should or should not use here. It is up to you alone to decide what is best for you."

Hatzis had carried that thought with her through her rest period. *"Up to you alone . . ."* *Did they mean humanity as a whole, or were they referring just to Peter?* She sincerely hoped that it wasn't the latter.

When she awoke, Nalini Kovistra and Donald Schievenin informed her that they were ready to test the faster-than-light communicator.

This was a big moment for the two physicists. They

had been allowed extra time with Alander to understand how, perhaps, the communicator might work. However, apart from telling Alander that it was capable of instantly communicating with any similar device within a two hundred light-year radius, the Gifts refused to elaborate on just what principles operated it. They hadn't even told them where it was. As was becoming increasingly the case, it would be left up to the humans to figure out over the course of time.

Or maybe, Hatzis considered, the Gifts simply did not have that information. They had instructed them on the installation of a software interface between the *Tipler* and the communicator and helped them with their understanding of just how to work the complex controls. Beyond that, though, everything was a mystery, and Hatzis imagined that was precisely how the Spinners preferred it. The Gifts were programmed to impart only information the Spinners felt the humans were ready to deal with at that moment in time.

"We can test whenever you're ready," said Kovistra, her dark, Indian features intensely focused on the task before her.

"Are you sure it's safe?" said Hatzis.

Kovistra nodded thoughtfully. "I doubt there will be any risk to us," she said.

"Nevertheless, I advise caution," said Sivio.

"You don't trust the Spinners, even now?" said Hatzis.

"It's not that," he said. "We still know so little about their technology. Testing such a device so soon could well prove dangerous to the ship."

"I disagree," said Samson. "The thing was put there for us to use, like everything else here. It's not going to hurt us. In fact, it'll probably help us. If we can contact Earth—"

"There's no guarantee we'll be able to do that," cautioned Kovistra. "They'd need to be using a similar device as this, or else they simply won't pick it up."

"But they might have one. Who knows what developments have been made in the last hundred years? And if they do have the technology to receive the signals, then we'll finally be back in contact with Earth. As far as I can see, that can't be a bad thing."

"But do we even have the right to play around with this stuff?" persisted Sivio.

Although Hatzis agreed with Samson, she was still trying not to get her hopes up too high.

"I have the power to authorize testing of alien machinery," she said to her physicists. "Providing I put the safety of the mission first, and in absence of word from Earth, UNESSPRO Special Regulations Section 14 gives me the right to decide for myself whether or not the mission is at risk. And as far as I'm concerned, there has been no indication that any of these gifts will be anything but beneficial to us. Besides which, if we don't use it, I can't foresee us *ever* being in a position to get word to or from home." She locked stares with Kovistra for a significant moment. "But do not take any chances. One message, two repeats, and that's it. Then you shut it down. If there's a reply from anyone, we'll discuss what to do then. Okay?"

"Understood." Kovistra had set up a virtual control room for the communicator that seemed to consist entirely of data screens. Previously stable configurations and images began to move. "Donald, did you hear that? We have confirmation. Are those patches stable?"

"Yes. The Gifts may not be talking to us, but their machinery is."

"Take us to the pretransmission phase." For the benefit of her observers, Kovistra explained, "We don't know what this will do, to be honest, but it seems part of the process. Something has to warm up, perhaps, or . . ."

Barely had Schievenin activated the software when the feed from the gifts flickered for a moment.

"Problem, Nalini?" said Hatzis.

"This is across the board, Caryl," said Sivio, busily flicking through reports and images. "There's been a power surge around the orbital ring, very similar to the one when the building activity ceased. And . . ." He paused, listening. "The doors have stopped working."

Hatzis was seeing confirmation of this through her own channels. The Hub had turned dark; all of the doors remained shut.

"Do we wake Alander and get him to ask the Gifts?" said Sivio.

He clearly wanted her to say yes. "I see no reason," she replied. "The behavior is unexpected but probably not dangerous. It might just be a safeguard of some kind. Maybe the communicator drains power, and shutting down the Hub prevents anyone from being in transit between spindles when the drain begins. Nalini, continue."

Kovistra nodded and returned to her work. "Donald, activate the communicator for primary transmission. Send at your discretion."

Hatzis didn't know exactly what her physicists did after that. It wasn't her job to know. Whatever they did, though, it caused every scanner of every wavelength aimed at the gifts to suddenly white out. For a few seconds, all she could see was static.

"What the hell . . . ?"

"Message sent," said Schievenin.

Kovistra seemed shaken but continued as though nothing had happened. "Donald, power down for a moment. Let's see what happened before we try a repeat."

Normal telemetry was gradually restored, with the satellites closest to the *Tipler* returning to normal the fastest. But that was just an illusion, Hatzis realized. Transmissions from those farther out were simply taking longer to arrive than those close by.

"All our instruments were hit at the same time," said Sivio, "regardless of where they were in the system. Whatever that was, I think we can safely assume it was ftl."

"Impressive," said Schievenin, his long face even more serious than usual, with his eyes reflecting the wonder that everyone must have been feeling right then. "Do we try again?"

Hatzis didn't give him an answer immediately. Instead, she turned to Kovistra. "How will we know if we've received a reply?" she asked.

"The communicator tells us," said Kovistra. "As near as I can figure it. From what the Gifts told Peter, there should be no missing it."

"If it's anything like that first transmission," said Sivio, "I'll believe you."

Hatzis noted alarmed communications from other members of her crew. However, for all the surprise and alarm, nothing had been damaged.

"Okay, Nalini," she said after some consideration. "Try the repeats. Jayme, warn everyone this time. We know what to expect now, and it doesn't seem to be doing us any actual damage, but I want them kept posted on everything we're doing here. Send the message out twice more, and then we'll see if we get any replies."

She settled back to watch Kovistra and Schievenin in action. They worked smoothly, calmly together, as though fiddling with a crystal radio set rather than some mysterious alien artifact. The message they had composed was similarly workaday, simply identifying the source of the transmission and requesting a reply. Nothing world shattering. But if they did receive a reply, that would change everything.

Hatzis found herself silently praying that it would work—as everyone else must have been, she imagined. Now that the possibility existed that they might be able to talk to the people back home again, she was surprised at how much she wanted it to come true. It had never even been an option before now, so she had kept her desires to reestablish contact with Earth carefully in check. It wouldn't do to be entertaining such desires; disappointment and despondency lay down that path.

It wasn't that she felt she wasn't qualified to command the mission, either. She was, and she thought she was doing a good job at it, too. But she wasn't enjoying it. The responsibility and workload were just too great under these circumstances. So the idea of being able to once again shuck the ultimate decision onto UNESSPRO back home was a pleasing one for her. Which was why, she thought, she had unwittingly crossed her fingers as they prepared to send the message a second time.

Again the instruments grayed as the communicator sent its message out into space. Or *through* space? she wondered. *Around* it? However it happened, this time they were prepared for it, and better able to measure what happened.

"I think we've nailed the source of the transmission," said Sivio. "It's not the Hub, as we assumed." He paused uncertainly. "It's the entire structure. It appears to be acting like a giant antenna."

The revelation astonished Hatzis, although perhaps it shouldn't have. It went a long way in explaining a few things that had thus far remained a mystery, such as the ring itself. Up until now, they had found no actual purpose for the ring, except as a possible medium for the instantaneous transport system. But it made sense that it was in fact a component of the communicator itself, albeit a component over thirty thousand kilometers across.

It also made sense of something else, too.

"The eleventh gift," she muttered, finally understanding.

"It has to be," Sivio agreed. "The Hub, the Library, the Gallery, the Science Hall, the Lab, the Dark Room, the Map Room, the room of the Gifts, the Dry Dock, and the Surgery—that makes ten. And they said there were eleven. This must be it."

Hatzis nodded slowly as the third and final transmission was sent. She had previously assumed that the artificial gravity in the spindles had been the eleventh gift, but this seemed more logical. This was something they could use.

"Transmission concluded," said Kovistra. "Powering down permanently. Well done, Donald. The software performed beautifully."

He smiled. "As far as we can tell," he said. "I guess all we can do now is wait to see what comes back."

"*If* something comes back, that is," said Kovistra. "My guess is—"

But she got no further.

Half the screens in Hatzis's display flickered as an energy surge rolled around the ring encircling Adrasteia. What did come through indicated vibration of some kind, as though the spindles were experiencing an earthquake. Droids skittered across slippery floors, trying to maintain balance; Alander stirred from his sleep in the Dark Room; every picture blurred as the vibration peaked.

Then, just as suddenly, it died away, fading with a faint rumble into the background before disappearing altogether.

"What the fuck was that?" Alander asked, rubbing his eyes at the droid that had come to check on him.

"We're not sure," said Hatzis distractedly, watching the crew frantically trying to work out what had happened. "Sivio? What have you got?"

"We think it came from the ring," Sivio concluded after a minute of consultation with the others.

"But what caused the vibration?" Hatzis pressed, keeping a close check on her excitement.

"It's an antenna," said Kovistra. "Presumably it picks up signals as well as transmits them."

"Are you telling me that the communicator registered a reply to our message? *Already?*"

"I'm not telling you anything yet. Maybe it was just noise, or an echo. Or perhaps the signal we received was simply too faint."

"Too *faint?* That vibration had enough energy to shake apart a small moon!"

"I've analyzed the vibrations," said Schievenin. "It doesn't seem to contain a signal of any kind. Nothing the *Tipler* recognizes, anyway."

Hatzis's excitement ebbed. She didn't need to add the obvious: *nothing from Earth.*

"Is there any way to tell where it came from?" put in Sivio.

Kovistra shook her head, frowning. "No," she said. "Maybe our software patches aren't working properly. I don't know. We'll try to look into it."

"Do so," Hatzis ordered. "And if you learn anything at all, I want to know about it immediately, okay?"

Kovistra was about to turn back to her work when she hesitated. "Sorry, Caryl," she said. "I know you really wanted this to work."

Hatzis just nodded, thinking, *More than you'll ever know, Nalini. More than you'll ever know.*

1.2.2

"Caryl, I want Peter to test-fly the ship in Spindle Six."

In the wake of the communicator test, Alander had been unable to return to sleep. He had floated in darkness, restless and irritable, for half an hour. Cleo Samson's voice suddenly cutting across the silence was, therefore, a welcome interruption for him.

"You want *what?*" Out of the blackness emerged an illusion of the *Tipler*'s survey manager, one of the very few times she had appeared to him "in the flesh." She was a short woman, which matched her hair and temper, but there was strength in her shoulders and hands. Her gaze was direct, like her manner.

Samson appeared also, forming an equilateral triangle between the three of them. "It makes sense," she said. "We need something concrete to back up what the Gifts are saying. I mean, for all we know, the Spinners could just be playing mind games with us."

•

"The communicator—"

"Wasn't exactly what I would call an unqualified success."

"No, it wasn't," agreed Hatzis. "Which is why I'll need more than just your suspicions to authorize such a thing. A useless communicator is one thing, but risking a crew member in an alien vessel is something else entirely. However, if you have something other than paranoia to support your argument, I'm prepared to listen."

"All right," she said, turning to Alander. "Peter, I need you to ask the Gifts something."

He knew there had to be a reason why the discussion had been brought to him.

"Okay," he said. "What is it you'd like to know?"

"I want to know whether the ship has the ability to communicate ftl."

Alander nodded, realizing what she had in mind. "Gifts?" His own voice sounded almost thunderous in the emptiness around him, much louder than Hatzis's or Samson's.

"Yes, Peter?"

"Tell me. Is it possible to use the ship in Spindle Six to test the ftl communicator? Could we fly it somewhere and send a message back to Adrasteia to see if it arrives here okay?"

"Of course," replied the Gifts. "Such a procedure would be very simple."

"Well, Caryl?" Samson didn't look smug, just expectant.

"It makes sense," Hatzis admitted. "And I'll allow it if Peter agrees."

Her easy acceptance of the idea surprised him. Was it that important to get the communicator working? It must have been if she was prepared to okay something like this. After all, the risks of testing the alien vessel were very real, too.

"Sure," he said after a moment's consideration. Despite his own apprehension about riding in the vessel, he did like the idea of having a little freedom from the others. "Why not?"

"Then we'll do it," she said. "But first, Peter, you eat. Your metabolism is still run down. I don't want you blacking out on us again."

"Did the Gifts send the bug down to the shuttle as we asked?"

"It's already been and come back. You now have supplies, but don't binge. We have no idea how long the rain is going to last down there."

He nodded, feeling the first stirring of excitement. "Understood. I'll be at the Hub in a moment."

"Cleo, go tell Otto that Peter will be in the Dry Dock soon," Hatzis said.

Samson vanished without another word, while Alander groaned.

"Do you have to do that?" he said.

"You're not going out there alone, Peter. I want a droid with you at all times—*and* a full conSense link. The ship is Otto's baby, so he'll be with you. You're not going to try any stunts like you did with the shuttle, if I can help it."

He smiled at her stern expression. *So much for freedom,* he thought.

Alander stood on the gantry, watching as the black sphere circled its enormous white parent. He could feel the irregular tug of gravitational waves through his all-too-massive flesh, and he began to have second thoughts about the whole test-flight idea. What was he supposed to do? Jump on it and hope for the best?

"Is this the sort of ship the Spinners use?" he asked the Gifts, more as a distraction from his anxieties than out of interest.

"No," they replied. "They have more advanced means of traveling at their disposal. This hole ship—which in your language would be the closest translation for its name—is a more primitive method of travel, reserved for nascent civilizations such as your own."

"How very generous," he said dryly.

"You cannot expect to be given all of their knowledge and wisdom, Peter," said the Gifts in a slightly reproving tone. "Theirs is an advanced civilization. They can't simply impart to you everything they have ever learned. They have been evolving for millennia. You must attain their degree of sophistication of your own accord; the gifts they have given you are intended to urge you in the right direction."

He thought of his original's dead-end bacteria, trapped forever by the laws of physics and unlucky circumstance. "So basically they're throwing us a few scraps. Is that what you're saying?"

"If you mean they have given you things they no longer have need for, then yes, this is true. All of the gifts are from an earlier stage of their development."

Alander turned again to the vessel before him, wondering at the technologies the Spinners must have achieved, trying to imagine the kind of craft they traveled in. Were they bigger? Faster? What? The mind boggled at the possibilities. And maybe that was just it: His mind,

like those of all humans, virtual or otherwise, was not
ready for the technology the Spinners possessed. Christ,
they were barely able to grasp the few things they had
been given already, so what chance did they have of
grasping an even higher technology? That's why they had
been thrown scraps. It was all they could deal with right
now.

Thinking that he might get a hint of how the thing
worked, Alander asked, "So why is it called a hole ship?"

"That is simply its name, Peter," the Gifts replied.
"Why were wheeled automobiles from your home planet
cars?"

He laughed at this. "I have no idea," he admitted. "But
I imagine it has some origin in Latin."

"Indeed," the Gifts went on. "And the word from which
hole ship has been translated would have also had its origins in one of the Spinners' own ancient languages. So
to attempt to explain it to you now would be futile."

Alander shrugged. "No harm in asking," he said. Then:
"I take it you'll be showing me how to fly this contrap-
tion?"

"Once the hole ship has departed the spindle, all communication between us will cease."

"*What?* But how am—?"

"Don't worry, Peter," the Gifts interrupted. "There is
an AI on board that will instruct you in all operations of
the craft. We shall speak again on your return."

He didn't feel reassured but nodded anyway. "Assuming I get back," he mumbled to himself.

A section of the gantry a third of the way around the
massive chamber glowed gold.

"I presume that's where I'm supposed to go?" He felt
nervous.

"Yes, Peter. The hole ship will be ready for you by the time you arrive."

As he walked, he noticed a section of the gantry bulge out toward the hole ship. At the same time, the rotation of the black sphere began to slow.

"We're getting some weird readings," Sivio announced.

"I can't feel anything." Wyra, teleoperating the droid via conSense, clutched at Peter's back, looking for all the world like a mechanical monkey crossed with a sea anemone. The droid's sensors waved constantly, tasting the environment dozens of ways at once.

"Peter?" Samson's voice came loud and clear through the conSense link. Alander sensed an edge of fatigue or strain in it that surprised him. Concern for him? She had been distant since the episode with the communicator, so maybe she had other things on her mind. Part of him wondered if she was losing interest now that he wasn't playing so hard to get.

"I'm fine. Thanks for asking." He concentrated on putting one foot in front of the other, ignoring everything else going on around him. He wondered if doing this qualified him as one of Lucia's tourists, exploring the stars simply to find nice things to look at, rather than questing for knowledge. He doubted he would learn terribly much on his little jaunt, regardless of what might happen.

When he reached the golden segment of the gantry, it had extended a tongue into clear space. The hole ship continued to rotate bare decimeters from its edge. As Alander approached, it slowed even more and gently tugged at him with its odd radiation. By the time he reached the end of the tongue, the black sphere had come to a complete halt directly in front of him.

He stared at it for a long moment. Although smaller

than its parent, it still loomed over him. Its surface was unbelievably black: smooth and unbroken and yet casting no reflection back at him. It was so featureless that his gaze skated over it, lending the illusion that the entire thing was spinning like a top.

It therefore came as something as a shock when a dimple appeared on the side facing him, expanding rapidly into a hole large enough for him to step through.

"This is where I get in, I take it?" he said, peering into the absolute darkness of the interior.

"You will be perfectly safe, Peter," said the Gifts.

"Ah, that old one." He stepped nervously over the gap between gantry and hole ship, avoiding the stomach-dropping view down the bottom of the chamber. His feet found purchase on something hard and unyielding, while his outstretched hands touched walls that felt vaguely ceramic. It was still dark inside, though, so he kept his movements slow and cautious.

The hole behind him irised shut, and he froze. Before total darkness fell completely, a light appeared ahead, seeming to emanate from some distance away. The droid clutching his back shifted position slightly to look in the new direction.

He performed a brief mental calculation. The black sphere was ten meters across. He had taken maybe a step or two into the hole ship. The source of the light looked distant, tens of meters away, maybe more. Further illusions? Another example of the Spinners' space-bending tricks?

"You've started moving again," said Sivio. "Reception is a little hazy."

Although conSense provided him with a brief and unnerving glimpse of the black sphere rotating as before, he could detect no actual sensation of motion from within.

After a second, the lights came on properly inside the black sphere. He found himself standing in an unadorned, round room the same color as the sphere's exterior. It was eight meters across and three high; the walls bent slightly inward at their highest and lowest edges, following the curve of the outer hull. There was nowhere to sit, nothing to look at, and no visible means of controlling the hole ship.

"All you need to do is ask for what you require," said a voice, as though reading his thoughts.

"How about a chair, for starters?" he said.

The floor extruded a semicircular couch in the middle of the room. He eased himself carefully onto it and, despite his apprehensions, found it to be extremely comfortable.

"Okay," he said after a moment. "Can you give me a view of the outside?"

Instantly, the walls became transparent, revealing a giddying view of the white ball fixed in front of him, opposite the segment of hull through which he had entered, and the Dry Dock spinning smoothly around him. He was instantly disoriented.

"Smaller!" he called out quickly. "Make the view smaller!"

The view obligingly shrank back to one section of the wall, only a couple of meters across.

"Thank you," he said more calmly. He watched the view silently for a couple of minutes before asking, "So what happens now?"

"You need to give me a destination," the voice replied simply.

"And you are . . . ?"

"I am the mind of the hole ship, of course."

Alander frowned. The alien AI spoke in a tone similar to the Gifts but was less conversational.

"I thought we'd leave the Dry Dock first," he said.

"That won't be necessary. Give me your destination, and I will take you there."

He shrugged. "Very well, then. Take me . . ." He clutched for a destination at random. "Take me to this system's fifth planet."

"The one you call UA-5?"

"Yes but, really, any one of them will do. I just want to see if this thing will work."

"It will, Peter," said the hole ship. "Please relax. We will be there in a moment."

The two statements back to back were an unreasonable expectation, he thought. "Are you still getting this, Jayme?"

"You're still coming through, although reception still isn't perfect."

"Otto?"

The droid twitched on his back. "Present and accounted for," he said.

Alander watched the screen before him as much as he dared, while stealing glimpses at the conSense feed at the same time. The black sphere was slowing again, its orbit appearing to contract.

"You getting any readings, Jayme?"

"None that make any sense," he said. "But that's hardly surprising."

"I can't wait to take a closer look at the data," said Wyra excitedly. "A ship that spins when it's not even going anywhere? Seems a little strange, unless the rotation helps it maintain some sort of stable state. It'll be interesting to see what happens when it comes to a halt again."

They didn't have long to wait. As the black sphere drew closer to the central white sphere, its rate of rotation grew steadily slower. When it was at rest, the two spheres were almost touching. Alander watched with trepidation and fascination as the two spheres finally did touch, then began to overlap.

"Now *that* is bizarre," said Sivio. "Are you feeling anything, Peter? Otto?"

"Not a thing." Alander was frozen in his seat as the surface of the white sphere swept gradually up the screen and, via conSense, he watched as it began to engulf its smaller counterpart. Engulfing *him,* inside.

"The boundary layer is just passing you now," Sivio went on. "Any second—"

The transmission to the *Tipler* ended abruptly. At the same time, the droid clinging to Alander suddenly died. It went limp and fell from his shoulder. Automatic subroutines snatched at the couch as it fell, and then it was still.

"Jayme? Otto? Can you hear me?"

He was about to ask the hole ship what was going on when the walls suddenly cleared again, revealing the inside of the Dry Dock, this time from the point of view of the white sphere. He had barely a second to register it when, just as suddenly, it was gone and the screen went blank.

He stood up, the beginnings of panic in his gut. The only light came from the edges of the screen, where a faint greenish glow flickered. As little as it was, he was grateful for it; it gave him something to orient himself by. There was still no sense of motion, however, although he suspected that the hole ship was in fact moving in ways he would never fathom.

"When—?"

He didn't finish the sentence. No sooner had the first word escaped his mouth when the question became irrelevant.

The blackness of the screen was abruptly swept away, revealing a vibrantly colored gas giant with equally bright rings. He recognized the planet from the system data; it was definitely the one he had requested. But he had never seen it like this before.

"Amazing," he breathed. He walked closer to the screen and touched it. There were no pixels. But for the resistance meeting his fingers, he would have suspected there was no screen there at all, but a hole opening directly into the vacuum.

He looked back at the couch. The droid was still inert, and would be until control signals arrived from the *Tipler*. The problem was that, as he appeared to have traveled faster than light to his destination, it would take an hour for those signals to arrive.

For a brief moment, he was completely alone, far more isolated than he had ever been on the surface of Adrasteia. It was a disturbing feeling, and he wondered if this was how Lucia had felt on her solo journey between the stars. Standing in absolute silence, staring out at the gas giant, he couldn't shake the notion that it would have been a terribly lonely way to die.

"Can I send an ftl message to the *Tipler*?" he asked, wanting desperately to lose the unsettling thought.

"Of course," came the immediate reply from the hole ship.

"How do I do it?"

"Simply tell me the message you wish to send, and I shall transmit it."

His mind was blank for a second. Then: "Okay, send this message: 'How does forever begin?' Send it via normal means as well, so they can compare timing and confirm the source."

The hole ship vibrated around him like a bell for a moment, although soundlessly. "The message has been sent."

"And we're equipped to receive a reply, right?"

"Yes."

"Then let's wait a bit and see what happens."

He went back to the couch and, removing the droid and placing it on the floor, sat down. The view was unchanged and far more beautiful than anything he had ever allowed himself to imagine. If the Gifts were as good as their word, he could take the hole ship anywhere, see any number of other amazing sights. If Hatzis would let him, that is.

"Is it possible to move any closer?" he asked.

"Please specify how close you would like to be taken."

"No, I don't want to get closer yet, I was just wondering if you *could* get closer."

"I have the ability to take you as close as you wish to the planet, Peter."

"But *how?* I mean, the Spinners are giving us a faster-than-light drive; does some sort of reactionless thruster come with it?"

"I possess only the one means of crossing space."

"That jump thing?" He thought the answer a little strange but not impossible to work around. The hole ship would need to change its velocity and direction every time it jumped somewhere new, but it could always do that by jumping into and out of nearby gravity wells until the resulting acceleration gave it the vector it needed. So one jump, he supposed, might actually be several in a rapid series.

"Is there a limit to how often we can use it?"

"Energy expenditure increases exponentially. The closest to the hole ship's maximum range you take it, the longer it will take to recharge. However, it can recharge itself fully in less than one of your days and make any number of small jumps in quick succession."

He nodded. Impressive and fascinating. "What about weapons? Are you armed?"

"No. I have no offensive or defensive capability."

He was about to ask why not—although he figured he could guess the answer—when the droid, still lying on the floor at his feet, suddenly stirred like a sleepy dog and sat upright.

"Signal received," it said in a gender-neutral voice, "from asteroid probe 14C: 'Don't forget where you are, Peter.' " The voice changed to that of Caryl Hatzis; clearly a recording. " 'Call us if you haven't already.' "

Alander flushed and didn't say anything in response. Any pride he had felt at surviving the test flight so far evaporated. Hatzis still didn't trust him, despite his recent track record. Maybe he could understand her reasoning, but did she have to rub his face in it all the time?

"No signal from the *Tipler*?" he asked.

"We are receiving something now." Sure enough, a faint vibration thrilled through the floor beneath him. When it had ceased, Hatzis's voice once more sounded in the hole ship.

"Message received. Well done, Peter. Now come back, and we'll review the data."

He was tempted to send a reply telling her he'd go where he damn well pleased, but he bit his tongue.

"Tell them we heard them loud and clear in return," he said. "Then take us back as instructed."

He took a long look at the ringed gas giant, doing his best to memorize it. This was something his original had never seen. This was *his* memory and would be forever.

Then the screen went black again, and he was gone.

1.2.3

After watching the recording of the hole ship disappear for the tenth time, Hatzis still couldn't work out how it happened. First the black sphere slid inside the larger sphere, leaving no mark that it had ever existed on the smooth, white surface. Then the white sphere shrank in size, giving the impression that it was going farther away; sensors confirmed, however, that it was in fact only getting smaller. It halved in volume in a handful of seconds and kept shrinking. Part of her still expected it to stop when it was the same size as the black sphere, but it didn't even slow. Fifteen seconds after the black sphere had been swallowed, the white one had disappeared altogether, leaving nothing behind but heat-dazzled sensors and a faint ripple in the local structure of space-time.

"My guess is it moved into a dimension other than the usual three," said Wyra, his voice still a little stunned by what had happened. "Which would means it's some sort of a hypersphere, as opposed to an ordinary sphere."

"Can you test that?"

"Not without attaching something to it. Even a rope would be interesting."

"It's a shame the droid didn't work, then," she said. "If we could communicate with it—"

"Caryl," interrupted Nalini Kovistra, "we have a message from Peter."

"Good. What does it say?"

Kovistra shrugged and shook her head. "It doesn't seem to make any sense," she said. "It says, 'How does forever begin?' "

Hatzis smiled, recalling the conversation she and Alander had shared during preflight training. It referred to their coming lives as engrams, and the laborious training they had to go through leading up to the launch of the survey missions.

"Slowly," she mumbled to herself. "Very slowly."

"What was that?" said Kovistra.

"It doesn't matter," said Hatzis. "Just a private joke from way back. Tell me, did the message come through ftl?"

"Yes. No mistaking it. The ring antenna resonated as before, only this time the wave form had all the characteristics of one of our vocal transmissions."

"So why couldn't we understand that other message, then?"

"Maybe it really was just a garbled echo of some kind."

"Or maybe it came from someone else," put in Sivio.

That thought kept her quiet for a moment. Finally she said, "Nalini, tell Peter well done and to come back. If he picks that up, then we'll know the antenna works both ways."

A moment later, his response returned that he had heard them loud and clear.

"So it worked." Cleo Samson was instantly in her face,

following her around the *Tipler*'s virtual bridge as she checked reports.

Something about Samson's delivery unnerved her, more than her usual persistence. "What's on your mind, Cleo?"

"We know we can contact Earth. That's a good thing, isn't it?"

"Theoretically we can, yes. And yes, it would be a good thing. We're supposed to inform Earth as a matter of urgency if we find evidence of ETs. But we tried to hail them on the ftl communicator, and they didn't reply, and there's still nothing coming through on normal channels, which is not a positive sign. Either they haven't heard us or they—"

"I'm not talking about the communicator per se," Samson broke in. "Obviously Earth doesn't have the technology to reply, even *if* they heard us. But we have the hole ship, and *it* has a working communicator. We could send it to Earth and—"

"Wait a minute. Hold it right there. We're not sending that ship *anywhere* yet."

"But Caryl, you really—"

"Look, I'm not saying I disagree with you." Hatzis folded her arms, trying to effect a casual pose while at the same time indicating her inflexibility on the matter. "I'm just saying this isn't the time. There are a lot of things to consider, not the least of which is the fact that we don't know what's waiting for us there. And is it even reasonable to send Peter on his own on such a trip? Even if we could teleoperate a droid while the hole ship is working, there's no way we could operate one from here when he arrived."

Samson listened begrudgingly. "All right. But we'll talk about it soon?"

Hatzis nodded. "Soon, yes. I'll call an executive meeting tomorrow, if you like."

"I just feel this should be dealt with urgently—"

"Listen, Cleo," she said. "You're not the only one with an agenda aboard this ship, you know. We're barely scraping the paint off the gifts at the moment; give us ten years, and we'd still be swamped. If we send Peter away for any length of time, we're only going to make our job more difficult here. I don't want that, and I *won't* be pushed into it. Not by you or anyone else. Understand?"

Samson's expression didn't change. "I understand perfectly," she said.

"Good. Then get the hell out of my face, and let me get on with my work. You'll be informed when the executive meeting is called."

The woman nodded and left the bridge without looking back, walking formally for the exit and passing through it as though it was real.

Hatzis took her seat in the center of the room, feeling oddly as though she was the one who had been dismissed.

"Caryl, we're picking up something from the dock." Jene Avery was filling in for Sivio while he rested. "Emissions are spiking."

"Is everyone out of there?"

"It's clear."

"Right," she said, finding an overall view of the dock. "Then let's see what happens."

She didn't have to wait long. A bright point of light flared in the center of the giant chamber, then faded to reveal a tiny, white sphere. The white sphere grew until it was its previous size, at which point the black sphere issued from its side and resumed its patient orbit.

The two spheres in close conjunction looked to Hatzis like an animal with a huge body and a small head, reminding her of an orb weaver spider she had once seen as a child. *An appropriate comparison,* she thought, *given the hole ship's design.*

"We've regained contact with the droid," said Avery. "The conSense link to Peter is also open."

"Are you okay in there, Peter?" Hatzis asked, although she could now see through the droid's eyes perfectly well.

"Never better," he said. "That was some trip. You should try it."

"Doesn't look like I'll be able to in a hurry."

"Nonsense. We have plenty of spare bodies. I'm sure Kingsley can rig up another brain to stick you in, like mine. You'll love it, I promise."

She grimaced. "No thanks," she said. "I'm too used to the high life, now."

"Oh well," he said with a shrug. "Your loss, I guess."

There was a sharp edge to his ribbing that she didn't miss. He seemed to be enjoying the fact that, for once, he had something she didn't have. He might be damaged and face an uncertain future, but he was traveling faster than light—possibly the first human to ever do so. Personally, she didn't regard it as much of a trade-off, but he seemed to, and that was what mattered. If the notion made him happy, then it also made him more amenable to her orders, and that could only be a good thing.

"Does the hole ship have a name?" she asked Alander, to change the subject.

"They've never mentioned one."

"How about *Arachne*?" Hatzis suggested, thinking of the spider image she'd had.

"As in the Greek myth and spiders?" He looked some-what baffled by the choice for a moment, then shrugged and said, "Yeah, sure."

"Okay, Peter, I'm going to put you back in Otto's hands for a while. He wants to run our new toy through its paces. We might not be able to discover how it actually works, but knowing what it can do will be a start. Then you can take a break, if you like, before getting to work on the rest of the gifts."

"No rest for the wicked, obviously."

"If you've got time to be wicked," she said with a slight smile, "then I'm clearly not working you hard enough."

The Frank Tipler *normally operated on a so-called "4-5-6"* duty roster, with every twenty-hour day divided up into four shifts, each five hours in length. There were five daily rosters in a week, and six weekly rosters in a month. A good administrator could cycle through those rosters in such a way as to ensure optimal efficiency while at the same time preventing the crew from becoming stagnant or too accustomed to working with the same faces over and over. The *Tipler* had programs designed to optimize an administrator's choices, but Hatzis still preferred doing it herself. That way she always knew who was working when and on what. At any given moment, she liked to know exactly what resources she had at her disposal.

Checking the records of the previous few days, she con-firmed a vague impression that Cleo Samson had been popping up more often than expected. She had been around when Alander had taken the shuttle to Tower Five and the climber up to the Hub; she had been watching all through the first exploration of the gifts; she had been awake all through the test of the communicator and the hole ship. And yet somehow she was still managing to get her work done.

Hatzis couldn't bawl Samson out for pushing herself too hard, though. Hatzis was equally guilty of that. But at least she could compress her sleep periods into an hour or two by taking them at quadruple speed. Now that the immediate emergency was over and everyone was back in normal time, that gave her enough of an edge to justify the extra-long days. She felt like she was getting things back under control, inasmuch as she was able to, caught as she was between Alander and alien machines with undetermined motives.

She played back a recording of a conversation between Alander and the Gifts that had occurred the previous day. He had been in the Library with Kingsley Oborn, scouring the voluminous references for anything to do with the Spinners. In the end, they had inevitably turned to the Gifts for help; the Library was simply too huge for two people to search effectively, even if they'd had months to do so. But the Gifts had been as tight-lipped as ever regarding their builders. They claimed that they had not been programmed with any information regarding their makers, but Hatzis was not totally convinced that this was the truth yet. The Spinners could have simply programmed them not to reveal any information about themselves. So she had Alander question the Gifts further on the Spinners, hoping—optimistically, she admitted—that they would slip up and reveal something.

"You must've seen plenty of races in your time," Alander said.

"Yours is the only race we have encountered, Peter.

Our time began when the spindles were created five days ago."

"The Spinners, then," he pressed. "*They* must have come across many races in their travels."

"Yes, Peter. And any information regarding those races is contained in the Library and the Gallery."

"I know, but there doesn't seem to be anything about how they were contacted—or when, for that matter. I'm just curious. Is it the same pattern every time: The Spinners find a new race, look them over from a distance, then send in the gifts as required?"

"That is their preferred method for dealing with less advanced races, yes."

"Some might argue that such intervention could be damaging. Do they ever stop to think about that?"

"Of course," they replied. "Part of our role is to dispense the knowledge we contain in a manner least likely to cause harm."

"Is that why you won't tell me anything about the Spinners themselves? Because such knowledge could be harmful to us?"

"We tell you nothing because there is nothing to tell you," the Gifts said. "We have no information on them, and we have told you that before."

"Yet you seem to know how they contact other races," said Alander.

There was a pause then. Had he tripped them up? Had he made a break through their block? It was impossible to say, because when they spoke again, the voice was as calm and impenetrable as ever.

"Because we have been programmed with that information. It was obviously deemed relevant to you by our builders for us to be programmed with the data."

Alander nodded, as though satisfied with the answer, although his expression told a different story. He, too, had his doubts about the veracity of their words.

"Okay," he said. "So what about the more advanced races the Spinners have encountered? How are they contacted?"

"There are a number of methods that can be used."

"Such as?"

"We cannot answer that question, I'm afraid. You are not sufficiently advanced to be able to comprehend the methods employed."

"All right then, so what about races they've met before—the ones they've given gifts to? Have these races ever encountered the Spinners again?"

"No."

Alander had waited for more of an answer, but that had been it: a single, definite negative.

"None at all?"

"There is no evidence in our database to suggest that any of the races have ever met up with the Spinners after initial contact." Anticipating his next question, the Gifts went on, "You have to understand, Peter, the galaxy is a very large place. Even with faster-than-light propulsion and other advanced physics, exploration is time consuming and expensive. It would not make sense to return to a region they have already surveyed unless there was a specific reason for doing so."

"So they are wanderers, then? Nomads? Not diplomats."

"Based upon the available data, such a conjecture would seem feasible."

"I'm surprised no one has tried to follow them, at least."

"Maybe they have," the Gifts replied. "But then, perhaps, our builders are expert at hiding."

The last comment had set Hatzis thinking. On the heels of their "there are civilizations who take delight in the destruction of others" comment and another stating that some planets on the map of the galaxy were "best left hidden," she was beginning to wonder what it was, exactly, that humanity was getting itself mixed up in.

Judging by the Library, there were many advanced races scattered throughout the galaxy. There were octopods, group minds, and sentient forests, even life-forms that looked like rocks. Most of them had made it into space one way or another, whether with help from others or without. Presumably they had also come into contact with other races and had developed protocols of their own to deal with such encounters. And just because the Spinners seemed to be altruistic did not mean that all aliens would be.

One possibility that Hatzis didn't like much was that the gifts themselves were the high-tech equivalent of CARE packages: bundles of essential supplies air-dropped to remote communities in times of hardship, such as war or famine. Humanity might not be the most advanced race in the galaxy, but it seemed to be catching up at a reasonable rate—or at least it had been the last time she had heard from Earth. Why then would aliens feel the need to dispense such aid? Did they know something about Earth that she didn't?

When Sivio woke from his rest period, she had him coordinate a meeting to discuss the possibility of sending Alander back to Earth to reopen communications. For a brief moment she thought about scheduling it during one of Samson's rest periods—just to see what the woman would do—but then decided against it. She already had enough fragile tempers and egos aboard the *Tipler* to deal with as it was without kicking over that particular hornet's nest.

1.2.4

*Alander couldn't bring himself to attend the meeting. To at-*tempt something like that would be too disorienting. Just to have sat in the same room with his former colleagues would have meant embracing conSense completely, and he couldn't do that yet. One person at a time was fine, such as Samson against a normal backdrop; even two, perhaps, but then only briefly. But a dozen all at once? In a room that didn't exist? There was simply no way he could do it.

He considered setting up a representation of himself in conSense and hopping in and out of it to give the impression that he was there continuously, even if he wasn't. But while this might have been better for him, Samson said that this would have been disorienting for the people watching. It would look as though he was alternately freezing and unfreezing as the image-generating algorithm switched between internal and external cues.

So Samson arranged a simulated flat screen on which his physical image could be displayed, along with full access to audio and partial video for him to monitor.

"Picture yourself playing one of your father's old PC role-playing games," she said with a smile. "Just don't pull out an assault rifle and start blowing people away, okay?"

Despite her efforts to make him feel at ease, however,

he was still nervous. He was unsure how he would go at keeping up with the various threads of conversation that would inevitably take place and whether he'd be able to keep track of who was saying what to whom. More than anything, though, he didn't want to make a fool of himself. Not now, not when he felt he was beginning to make progress. He was realistic enough to know that he was the one on trial as much as the plan itself to send the hole ship to Earth. If he demonstrated himself to be unreliable in a simple meeting, how could they trust him to travel seventy-six light-years away, into an unknown situation back home?

"Don't worry about it," said Samson, her virtual hands brushing back an imaginary fringe.

"Who are you? My mother?"

She lowered her hands to her sides and took a step back. "What was she like?"

Alander frowned. "What?"

"Your mother," Samson said casually. "What was she like?"

The question took him completely off guard, and he found himself stammering a reply: "I . . . I don't know. A lot like me, I think. She was very curious about things. Christ, I don't remember that much about her, Cleo. She died in an accident when I was fifteen."

"At least you knew her," said Samson a bit sadly. "I never knew mine at all. I lived with an uncle until I was old enough to get away. Later, at university, I took a class with one of my cousins, but I don't think he even recognized me. I had changed so much by then."

He cleared his throat. She was clearly moved by the sudden recollection, but he was not. He looked back on his mother's death with almost clinical dispassion. It really did feel as though it had happened to someone else. The only true memories he had were those recorded from the moment his original had entered the engram entrainment program, and the cameras had switched on.

Lucia . . .

"What brought this on, Cleo?" he said. "Some vain attempt to take my mind off things?"

"Do you miss Earth, Peter?" she asked, ignoring his comments. "The trees and the sky, the rain and the wind, and the people . . . ? Especially the people. I miss them so much at times."

"Listen, Cleo," he said. "I'm not really up to this at the moment. I'm finding it hard enough to concentrate as it is. Sorry."

She seemed almost literally to shake herself out of it. "No, Peter, I'm sorry. An odd feeling came over me, that's all."

Slightly ashamed of his callousness, he gestured in a way that was vaguely, awkwardly, consoling. Without her permission, he would be unable to actually touch her, and he didn't want to risk rejection.

"Like someone walked over your grave?" he said.

"That, or perhaps one of me, somewhere, just fell into one."

He didn't know what to say to that. At that moment, the chime rang to summon the executives to the meeting, and, thankfully, their conversation was over.

"Easy, easy!" The imaginary camera angle through which Alander was watching the meeting swung up to look at Caryl Hatzis. She had stood, trying to bring the meeting to order. "I know this is an emotional issue, but that's no

excuse for acting like children. Either talk like adults, or I'll close the meeting entirely."

Cleo Samson was instantly on her feet, too. "You can't make a decision like that, Caryl! It involves all of us."

"Then just sit down, Cleo, and shut up so we can get on with the goddamn meeting *properly.*"

"The mission regulations clearly state—"

"I said, *sit down!*"

The shout had the intended effect. Samson stopped with her mouth open, hesitated for a moment, then fell heavily into her seat. Her eyes, seen via the virtual camera under his direction, were red.

"Now," said Hatzis, more calmly, "if we have any further outbursts from anyone, they *will* be expelled from the meeting. And I don't give a flying fuck about regulations. I have the authority to demand that the mission be conducted in an orderly fashion. Is that fully understood by everyone?"

No one contradicted her, and after a moment, she sat back down. Her eyes looked about the faces of the others, pausing slightly when her gaze fell upon the screen containing Alander's image. Then she looked down the table to where Sivio sat.

"Right, then," she said. "Jayme, you were saying?"

"I raised the possibility of sending *Arachne* to Earth without Peter on board."

"The benefit of that being that we risk less," she said, nodding. "I am aware that work will grind to a halt in some respects without Peter here to communicate with the Gifts. But I still believe that a great deal of work can still be done without the Gifts ever speaking another word to us. In fact, according to them, the ultimate intention is for us to learn from what they have given us to date, so that—"

"It's too soon," said Wyra. "We need Peter here *now* in order to do our job properly."

"But *are* we even doing the job properly now, with him already here?" put in Kingsley Oborn. "I don't know about you, but I'm likely to be as confused in ten years as I am now, with or without Peter."

"I don't think it's a matter of how well we can do," said Donald Schievenin. "It's more a matter of our resources being stretched so thin at the moment."

"Which is the very reason we need to contact Earth," said Hatzis. "And the sooner the better."

Alander saw Samson open her mouth at that, but she shut it again without saying anything. Had she been surprised by Hatzis's stand on the matter?

"We've already strayed off topic," Hatzis went on. "What we're discussing is whether sending the empty hole ship is a less costly way of getting the help we need right now. I mean *potential* costs, of course; we have no way of knowing what *Arachne* would be flying into until it arrives. And that, unfortunately, is the crux of the problem."

"We could make a close flyby of Sol," suggested Wyra, "to see what's there."

"Maybe," Hatzis said. "Has anyone looked at the Map Room to see what that shows for Sol?"

"I have." All heads turned to face an exhausted-looking Nalini Kovistra. "It shows the sun and the gas giants, but that's all. I'm assuming it was surveyed from a distance, hence the absence of the smaller planets. A lot of the systems around here are listed like that, including Upsilon Aquarius."

"So, perhaps a recon mission would be a good idea."

"Assuming, of course, that we *can* send the hole ship on its own," said Schievenin.

Alander jumped at the opportunity to join in the discussion. "I could always ask," he said.

"Do that, Peter." Hatzis waited while he relayed the question to the Gifts.

"The hole ship is capable of following complex instructions given in advance," they confirmed.

"But the question remains open whether it *will* do as it's told," said Schievenin. "Just because they say it will doesn't mean it actually will."

"If we lose the hole ship," said Samson from where she sat seething in the corner, "we lose our only remaining chance of contacting Earth."

"But if we send Peter *and* the hole ship," retorted Wyra, "we risk losing both of them! I don't think the mission can afford that."

Alander felt pleased for a moment, despite his misgivings, by Wyra's suggestion that he was a valued member of the crew. Hatzis, however, was clearly not impressed by the direction the conversation was taking, and she sat at the head of the table, glowering.

"Okay, okay," she said. "Can we just move on from this point for the moment? Nalini, did you get a chance to look at many of the other survey systems?"

"A couple of dozen, actually," the astrophysicist replied. "They seem to be like the map of Sol, though, containing little we didn't already know."

"So they were observed from a distance," Hatzis mused.

"Or in haste," said Kovistra.

Hatzis nodded. "Either way, it tells us something about

the Spinners," she said. "It tells us that they probably haven't come this way before. More than likely, we are the first in the region to be contacted by them, and maybe the last. We can't assume that they will continue toward Sol just because they have encountered us. We are, after all, out on the very edge of surveyed space; they may have detoured just far enough out of their way to leave us the gifts, on the assumption that we would pass them on to others of our species."

"I understand what you're saying, Caryl," said Wyra. "But why does it have to be now? This instant? What's the hurry? In a month we'll know ten times as much as we do now; in a year we might know a hundred times. Rushing back to Earth might actually do us more damage than good."

"Thinking of your Nobel prize, Otto?" Oborn chuckled deep into his beard, with no indication of rancor.

"Maybe we all should be," returned Wyra humorlessly. "Because if we do send that ship to get help, Earth will immediately take over the operation, whether we like it or not."

"How about we send an ftl transmitter back to Sol on board the hole ship?" suggested Sivio. "The ship can drop it off somewhere near Earth. We could send messages from here for the transmitter to relay normally without us having to risk anything more than a quick flyby."

"That's a good idea." Hatzis scanned the room. "Any thoughts on that, anyone?"

"We only have two working transmitters," said Nalini Kovistra. "The one in the hole ship, and the ring itself. Until we figure out how they work and build another one, we're back where we started. The *only* way to communicate with Earth is to send the ship itself, preferably with

Peter aboard to deal with any unpredictable situations."

"I disagree that it's so clear cut," said Hatzis above an instant response from Wyra. "But I'm prepared to call for an interim show of hands. Who thinks we should send Peter in the hole ship, and who doesn't? The ayes first."

Samson's hand went up, then Kovistra's and Schievenin's.

"Nays?"

Otto Wyra immediately raised his hand, followed by Kingsley Oborn and Jayme Sivio.

"A tie with four abstentions," said Hatzis. "I abstained in deference to Cleo, who feels that I'm trying to influence the group. The rest of you have been notably quiet. Jene, Ali, Peter, what do you think?"

Jene Avery looked uncomfortable. "I guess I tend toward caution. I don't see why we have to do anything about it right now—"

"A nay vote, then," broke in Wyra.

"But," Avery continued, shooting him a glare, "I *do* feel we should send him at some point. I'd probably vote with the ayes in a month's time."

"Okay," said Hatzis, nodding. "Ali?"

"We need more data," said Genovese. "We don't have enough to cast an informed vote at the moment, and I certainly don't think we can break it down to a for/against vote under any circumstances. It comes down to gut feelings, and I think that's a terrible foundation on which to base such a decision."

Hatzis nodded again. "And Peter? What about you? This concerns you more than anyone else here."

He shifted awkwardly in the free-fall environment of the Dark Room. Hatzis stared impassively out of the

screen at him. Did she really care what he thought? he
wondered. Or was she just humoring him?

"I *want* to go," he said, thinking of his own agenda.
"But I'm prepared to go along with whatever decision the
rest of you come to."

"Why do you want to go? What's in it for you?"

He felt decidedly uncomfortable under the scrutiny of
everyone. All attention at that moment was upon him.
"What do you mean?"

"Well, I can't see that you have much to gain by putting
yourself at risk like this. Christ, for all you know, you
could be flying into a war or anything back there. Is communicating with Earth worth risking your life for, now
that you've only just got yourself back together again?"

"I think it's important," he said, keeping his voice as
level as he could. "It's something I know I can do. And
as I'm the only one who *can* do it, I feel like I owe it to
the rest of you to give it a try."

"But do you yourself think you should go?"

"Yes, I do."

Hatzis closed her eyes for a second, then shrugged in
a helpless gesture. "All right," she said. "That makes four
ayes, then, to three nays. I'd vote with the ayes, too, except that I'm not yet convinced Peter can be relied upon
to carry out the mission properly." She glanced at Alander. "I'm sorry, Peter, but it's the way I feel."

"That's okay, Caryl," he lied, knowing he shouldn't
blame her for being honest.

"You've improved dramatically in recent weeks," she
went on, "especially since the Spinners came, but this
mission is too critical. If something goes wrong, if you
make the smallest mistake, we could lose both you and

the hole ship. And I'm not prepared to take that kind of chance."

"So what do you vote?" pressed Samson.

"I defer on the grounds that we should wait and see. If Peter remains stable or another opportunity presents itself . . . then we'll see."

Samson looked suddenly smug. "That still gives us a clear majority."

"Not at all," Hatzis said. "If you count the abstentions as nays, given that they're certainly not ayes, that means you lost four-six."

"But . . ." Samson reined in her disappointment with some effort. "So what decision are you going to make?"

"None, Cleo. We're deferring it until the entire crew has had a chance to discuss and cast a vote. Then we'll discuss it again and finalize the details. I'm not prepared to let my own personal feelings get in the way of this, as I said before. It's too complicated an issue for me to ignore the many informed opinions around me."

"I think you're doing the wrong thing."

"I'm sure you do, Cleo," she said tiredly. "And that's your prerogative, of course."

"It's nothing to do with *me,* Caryl. *You* don't have any choice! The mission regs—"

"Were written by bureaucrats over one hundred years ago and some four hundred thirty trillion kilometers from here. Are you trying to tell me that they knew more about this situation then than we do now? That they're better qualified than I am to decide what's best for this mission?"

Samson seemed startled by the passion of Hatzis's response. "No, but—"

"I'm sick of hearing 'but' from you, Cleo. Everything

I say comes back to you disagreeing on some technicality. I *know* you want to hear from the people back home; Christ, I want to hear from them, too! One day I'd even like to *go* home. But that day's a long way off, and we have to work toward it gradually. Jump too far now, and we may miss the target. I don't want that to happen, so I'm prepared to listen to other people's opinions—the people around me, as well as those guidelines given to us by those we left behind. Do you understand, Cleo?"

Samson's lips were white. Alander had never seen her look so strained. "Yes," she said.

"Good." Hatzis paused then, as if to compose herself before continuing. "Look, part of this process includes listening to you, Cleo, but I'm not going to do so indefinitely. Bear that in mind over the next couple of days. You've had your say at this meeting, and you might get to have it again before I make a final decision, but for now, I think your contribution is complete. Unless you have something new to add, I suggest you keep quiet."

"You can't do this," Samson said softly, rough-edged.

"Oh, I can, Cleo; I can." Alander was surprised by Hatzis's sudden change in tone. Instead of angry, she sounded weary, conciliatory. "I know you're under a lot of pressure; I know how much you've been working. Take some time off to catch up on your sleep, and maybe you'll feel differently. We're not going to do anything behind your back, if that's what you're worried about."

"That's not what I'm worried about." For a moment Alander was afraid that Samson might launch into another tirade, but she didn't seem able to find the words or the strength. "What's the point in ever trying to reason with you?" she said. "You just don't see it!"

"Not like you do, Cleo." The steely tone was returning

to Hatzis's voice. "Go and sleep for a while—and that's an order. Just because you don't technically have a body anymore doesn't mean you're superhuman. Kingsley?" She turned to Oborn. "Make sure she does as she's told. The last thing I need right now is another goddamn breakdown on my hands."

Alander winced at the reference to him. Samson didn't respond at all. Instead, she just vanished from the simulation as though someone had pulled her plug. That in itself was a response, he supposed; in the world of the engrams, such an abrupt departure was considered extremely rude.

Hatzis sighed heavily. "Does anyone else have anything to add? Because if not, I'm prepared to leave it there for the moment. We can look at it again when we have more data, or when we've all had time to think it through."

Sivio nodded, expressing a general consensus. Samson's outburst appeared to have lost her the argument even with those who had originally supported her. "I suggest we leave it a week," he said, "before calling for a general vote. By then we should have a better idea what the hole ship can do, at least . . . or another opportunity entirely might have presented itself. You never know."

"True. And that's the whole problem with the gifts. We may *never* know everything. Until we do, I don't intend to open us up to any more risk than we have to."

She stood, and the rest followed suit. She opened her mouth to say something, then stopped.

"What—?" Sivio started. "Did anybody else hear that?"

Hatzis frowned, then flinched as though someone had struck her.

"What's going on?" cried Nalini Kovistra with both hands balled into her eyes.

Alander stared at the screen in alarm, asking himself the same question. He, too, was about to say something when a smell not unlike that of roses, only spicier, assailed his nostrils. He reeled backward from the screen, completely disoriented by the assault. The smell had been his mother's, long ago, when he had been a child, and brought with it images of the town where they'd lived, the school he'd attended, the face of his best friend in an old photo, the sound of a train rattling by at night. They washed over him, around him, relentless waves that pounded him, threatening to drown him.

He had just enough time to think: *These aren't my memories*—when they were sucked away from him by a yawning void that opened all around him, drawing him down into a terrible blackness.

1.2.5

Time passed. He didn't know how much. Engrams were supposed to have an innate time sense, given that they were intimately linked to the many processors working in tandem aboard the *Tipler*, and even he, running independently on his own processor, inside his artificial skull, should have possessed the same ability, too. But when the darkness pulled back and he was able to think again, he had no idea at all how many hours or minutes or even days had elapsed since the memories of his original's childhood had risen up and attacked him.

Something, clearly, had gone seriously wrong.

He opened his eyes but was still only met by blackness. And, oddly, that seemed to reassure him. He had been floating in the Dark Room during the meeting; if anything had changed that darkness, he would have known that the Gifts were behind the breakdown. But everything was as still and empty as it had ever been. All he could hear was the sound of his own breathing, which rang loud in his ears.

He groped for the exit. A limp droid brushed his hand and rotated off into the void. *Had* the Gifts struck at last, exposing their true nature and destroying the *Tipler* when they had least expected it? Hatzis had expressed reservations about the Spinners' motives, but even she had become less cautious with time. Naturally so, too; in the absence of tangible threat, there was no point maintaining constant alertness. Perhaps the Gifts had simply been waiting for the best opportunity to strike.

But the idea was as preposterous as it was stupid. The Spinners could have wiped them out at any time. A single electromagnetic pulse would have fried the *Tipler* and the engrams with it; one chunk of matter dropped from orbit would have finished him off without any trouble. If it really had been their intention from the beginning to eliminate the human surveyors, then they could have done so without even being seen.

So had something changed their minds? Or was something else behind it? Alander had to find out what was going on and whether there was anything he could do about it.

He got a grip on the door to the Dark Room and hauled himself through to the Hub.

"Caryl? Jayme? Are you there?"

He waited a moment, while his legs gradually reaccustomed themselves to gravity and his eyes adjusted to the brightness around him.

"Caryl?"

He took a couple of steps toward the door that led to Spindle Four, in front of which stood another immobile droid, balanced almost surreally on wildly splayed legs.

"Can anyone up there hear me?"

Nothing. Could a solar storm have killed satellite communications? It seemed unlikely—they would have had plenty of advance warning from the various solar observers stationed around the sun—but it was a possibility. It would certainly explain the lack of contact, if not the peculiar memory surge that had preceded it.

"What about you, Gifts? Can *you* hear me?"

"Perfectly well, Peter," came the reply, doing little for his growing paranoia.

"What's happened to the *Tipler*?"

"We cannot say with any certainty."

"Don't give me that! I know you've been watching us. If *anyone* knows what's going on, it's you. Whether you're responsible or not, I want you to tell me."

"We can assure you, Peter, we are in no way responsible for whatever has happened here. Normal transmissions from the *Frank Tipler* ceased approximately five minutes ago, in conjunction with an anomalous and disruptive break in data processing. Some processing has resumed, but not at its previous level."

Alander struggled to think this through. Communications had died at the same time something had knocked out data processing. Could a power surge have blown the engrams aboard the ship? It was impossible to say for sure. He did know the design tolerances of the reactor and the processors' durability, but calculating the odds were beyond him. They had to be astronomical.

"*Some processing has resumed,*" the Gifts had said. That could mean that someone was still alive aboard the

Tipler. If he could just figure out a means of contacting them, maybe he could find out what had gone wrong and perhaps even help in some way.

His first thought was to head for the climber and take it out of the spindle. If it was just a case of reduced signal strength, possibly caused by the failure of the satellites nearby, getting out in the open might clear things up. Barely had he gone a dozen steps, however, when a sound like static came from behind him.

He turned, but there was nothing there except the closed doors.

"Gifts, was that you?"

"Was what us, Peter?"

The sound came again. A scraping noise, accompanied by a flicker of movement by the door leading to the Lab.

He nerved himself to investigate. Had something hostile somehow got aboard the spindle? He cursed his irrationality. There was nothing on the planet to get aboard, and even if there had been, how could it have possibly reached him as high up as he was? Nevertheless, he started when a many-limbed shape suddenly tumbled from behind the nearest door, jerking spastically.

Relief washed over him. It was just one of the droids. He knelt down in front of it. Its many black eyes rolled blindly at him for a long moment, then settled into a fixed configuration. He had the distinct sensation that someone was looking at him.

"Caryl?" he said.

"Peter!" The voice came from the speaker built into the droid, not through conSense. And it didn't belong to Hatzis. "Thank God I've found you!"

"Cleo? Is that you? What's going on?"

"ConSense is down. This is the only way I can communicate. I'm fiddling with the overrides as we speak, trying to make it safe, but I don't know how much more I can bring back on-line without risking a takeover."

He rocked back on his heels, mind reeling. "Takeover? We've been attacked?"

She hesitated, and he imagined the worst: aliens transmitting software viruses to infiltrate the *Tipler*, erasing engrams and disabling conSense as it went; the only way to halt such an invasion would be to shut everything down, then bring it back up piece by piece, watching for signs of relapse every step of the way. But why would Samson be performing the reconstruction and not Faith Jong or one of the other software specialists?

"The mission has been threatened," she said.

There was something odd about her voice. "By what, Cleo? I don't understand."

"Peter, I had to do it." She sounded very small all of a sudden, as though she had shrunk back from the imaginary microphone, torn by self-doubt. "I had no choice."

Realization struck him. "You did this? *You* knocked out conSense?"

"I had to," she repeated. "Peter—"

"What about the others? What's happened to them?"

"Don't be angry, Peter. I've just frozen them for a while. They'll be okay. I just need them out of the way for—"

"*Why*, Cleo? Why do you need them out of the way?"

She was silent again for a long time. Or was she crying? He couldn't tell. A sound like static could have been anything.

When she did speak again, her voice was less panicky but no less brittle, as though she might shatter at any moment.

"We have to contact Earth," she said. "It's a clear mission objective. Any survey that finds advanced alien artifacts must advise Earth by the earliest means possible."

"I know the regs, Cleo, but—"

"No, *listen* to me, Peter! You don't understand! When all we had was normal channels, everything was fine. I sent a message the day the Spinners came, and another one later, when we were given the *Gifts*. That was enough. But then we found the communicator and the hole ship. These gave us the opportunity to advise Earth more rapidly. But first the communicator didn't work, then the mission in the hole ship was delayed—"

"For good reasons, Cleo—"

"By the earliest means possible!" she shouted, and the desperation in her voice was frightening. "We don't have any choice, Peter, don't you see? We have to do it. We *have* to!"

"But why, Cleo? What happens if we don't?"

"What happens?" She seemed to collapse into herself again. "We fail, Peter. Don't you see that? The mission fails. We haven't done our job properly. We haven't followed the regs. We've let them down."

"Them?"

"UNESSPRO, of course," she said, her voice quavering. "We would have failed everyone back on Earth."

"But Cleo, there might not be anyone *left* on Earth!"

"That doesn't matter. We owe it to them to try." Her voice firmed. "We have no choice. I have no choice. Don't you see?"

Only then did the knowledge come bubbling up from deep in his original's memories. UNESSPRO had modified one engram on every ship to make sure the mission stuck to the guidelines. Each plant had a complete set of override codes and the ability to use them, should they be required, but they weren't consciously aware of having been modified. Only when a mission broke the regulations would the plant awaken to enforce them, by force, if necessary.

Samson was the plant, and it sounded to Alander as if she was about to snap in two, torn as she was between her own personality and the will of the survey programmers on Earth. He wasn't even sure if she truly knew why she was behaving the way she was.

"So you shut them down," he said, trying to see it from her side. "You killed conSense, using the overrides, and you shut down the engrams."

"Yes!" She seemed relieved by his apparent understanding of her actions. "It wasn't easy, Peter. I didn't even know what I was doing. There was a surge; it almost caught me, too."

He remembered the flash of memories that had preceded the blackout and nodded. "I felt it."

"I'm sorry, Peter. I had to knock everything out at once or risk missing something important and giving them a chance to fight back. I brought you back on-line as soon as I could, once I'd found a way to talk to you. So much of the *Tipler* is automated; you wouldn't believe how difficult it is to do things manually."

Yes, he would, he thought. He had been out in the real world long enough to distance himself from the virtual mollycoddling that was the engram's artificial environment. He was under no illusions what lay behind the mask.

"So why *did* you wake me, Cleo? Why are you telling me all this?"

"Because I need your help."

"To do what?"

"To go back to Earth, of course," she said. "To take the hole ship and tell them what we've found! That's all, Peter. Then everything can return to normal."

"Can it, Cleo?"

She ignored his question. "I can't go on my own, and I don't know how to program a droid to go in your place. And the Gifts certainly aren't going to help! Please, Peter, you have to help me. We can't do it without you."

"We?"

"Everyone back on Earth," she said. "We need your help, Peter."

The edge to her voice was not reassuring. It didn't sound like her. "Cleo, I'm not sure—"

"Why? What have you got to lose?" Her wheedling tone was hammering at his resistance. "It's just a short trip there and back. It won't take you longer than a couple of days—and once you're back, you *know* I'll let the others back on-line. You *know* that! There'd be no reason for me to keep holding them, would there? Once Earth knows, I can relax and go back to my normal work. *Everything* can go back to normal. Caryl will understand."

Like hell she will, he thought to himself. "But why now?" he pressed. "Wouldn't it be better to wait until everyone agrees?"

"But they might not, Peter. We have to do it *now*." The word was stressed almost with anger. *"By the earliest means possible!* Christ, *listen* to me for fuck's sake!"

"I am listening, Cleo. I'm just not sure you've given me a good enough reason, that's all."

She was silent for a second. When she returned, her voice had changed again. "Perhaps not, Peter. And perhaps you were just talking shit when you said you were going to repay me for all the things I've done for you."

His stomach sank. "Cleo," he started feebly.

"Maybe you were just telling me what I wanted to hear in order to ease your aching conscience," she went on. "Is that it, Peter? Were you just feeding me lies?"

He couldn't tell if she meant what she was saying, or if it was simply part of her programming, forcing her to use whatever means possible to achieve her goals. For all he knew, it was nothing more than paranoid ramblings brought on by the conflict of her engram's modifications. Even if he told her that how she was behaving was due to interference from UNESSPRO, she wouldn't believe him, because as far as she was concerned, her actions were reasonable—even those actions that went against her true nature. She was in severe conflict with herself, and he was helpless to do anything for her.

"You know that's not true," he said.

"No? I thought I could rely on you, Peter. Obviously I was wrong."

"Cleo, try to understand—"

"If you won't do it for me, then at least do it for your precious fucking Lucia instead." Her bitterness made him wince. "She's the only one you've ever cared about, after all."

"Christ, Cleo, will you listen to yourself? Listen to what you're *saying*. Lucia has got nothing to do with any of this!"

"Don't be so naive, Peter!" she said with some annoyance. "I'm giving you the chance to find out what happened to her!"

"What?" He shook his head in confusion. "What the hell are you talking about now?"

"You seem to obsess about her day and night. I'm surprised you hadn't considered it sooner."

"Considered *what?*"

"If you take the hole ship to Earth, Peter, what's to stop you retracing her steps on the return trip? You could travel to all of the systems she was supposed to have visited. Who knows? Maybe she's still alive, and maybe you can rescue her. You can be her knight in fucking armor come to save her from oblivion. Wouldn't you like that, Peter? Wouldn't you at least like to know what happened to her? Well, here's your chance. I'm offering it to you on a plate. All you have to do is say yes."

He was momentarily speechless in the face of her emotional plea.

"Go to Earth, Peter," she concluded. "Deliver the message for me. I don't care what you do after that."

He hated the manipulative, gleeful tone in her voice. Although he could understand her desperation to escape the trap that had closed around her, he hated the relish with which she dragged him down into it with her.

"I'm the only one who can give it to you," she said when he didn't reply. "You know Caryl wouldn't let you. So what do you say, Peter? Do we have a deal?"

He nodded slowly, keeping his face carefully expressionless.

"Good." She sounded relieved but no less relaxed. "Right, I want you to get up and go to the hole ship. Take the droid; I've downloaded enough data into its memory to inform Earth of what's happened here. I'll keep things in order here until you get back, or you call me from Earth using the hole ship's communicator. Once I know you've delivered the message, I'll let everyone go. Then things can resume as before. Everything will be okay, Peter. Everything *will* be okay."

He got to his feet, fighting the impulse to question her plan. How would she know he'd actually been to Earth? What if no one was there to give him proof or even a reply? Would she be satisfied if he just went away somewhere for a while, then came back saying he'd been to Earth and delivered the message?

Somehow he doubted it. Unless she was absolutely certain that Earth had been informed, there was no telling what she might do. If she snapped completely . . .

He shied away from the thought and moved instead for the door to the dock. The picture of the sunset goaded him as he approached. Another person he was about to hurt; another trust shattered.

He stopped and walked two doors to his left. "I have to get something first."

She hesitated before saying, "Okay, Peter. But don't forget the droid."

He returned to pick up the stubby machine, tucking it under his arm. Then he opened the door and walked through, resolving to do what he had to.

1.2.6

While he waited for the Gifts to ready the gantry and the hole ship for him to board, he had plenty of time to think about Samson's offer. She was silent, maybe busy bringing the *Tipler* more firmly under control so there was nothing to distract him. It was just him and his thoughts— and his original's memories.

The recurring flashback of Lucia was joined now with

a new series of images: blue skies, trees, rivers, flowers in bloom beside a gravel path along which people walked in groups of three or four, some with children, all dressed in normal clothes, all breathing the air unassisted, none of them stopping to think about this wonderful, precious thing that they took completely for granted. Even after the environmental catastrophes of the 2030s and 2040s—violent storms, failed crops, elevated sea levels, the opening of the ozone hole in the Northern Hemisphere—humans had still been able to go on living as they had for tens of thousands of years.

How he envied them. What he wouldn't give for the opportunity to experience all of those simple things. Just to be able to look into a mirror and see something natural rather than the end result of a manufacturing chain. Not even his memories of Earth were his. Even though they *felt* like they were, he knew they weren't. Not really. They were merely the shared memories of the real Peter Alander. To him and all of the other engram Alanders in the survey program, Earth was a far-off world that, despite the memory implants, was more an alien place to him than Adrasteia. It was a place he had never expected to see for a long time, if ever.

But now he could. The chance lay before him like yet another gift. But this one was not so much being offered to him as dangled before him. *Like the carrot to the donkey,* he thought. But he was going to have to do a lot of errands before he even got to taste that carrot, he was sure. As with the gifts, he had no real control of it. Or so Samson believed, anyway.

Before going to the dock he had made a detour to the Surgery. There he had confronted the human-shaped device made of water that Kingsley Oborn had christened the Immortality Suit.

"Will this thing insulate me against a hostile environment?"

"It's designed to heal and to protect," replied the Gifts.

He had stuck his arm into the suit then and let it crawl over him. As with the first time he had tried it, the sensation of the cold fluidlike substance against his skin was an extremely disturbing one. He cringed as he felt it slide into his armpits, his nostrils, and every other nook and cranny of his body with equal impunity. But the discomfort only lasted a few moments; after that, he hardly even noticed it was there.

"Does it need a power supply?" As before, his ability to speak had not in any way been hindered.

"You are its power supply, Peter." The Gifts spoke as if amazed at his ignorance of this fact.

He suppressed a small shudder and went from the Surgery to the Hub, and from there to the Dock. The suit moved with him like a second skin.

As he stepped off the gantry and into the hole ship's cockpit, another thought struck him. Yes, it would be easy to go after Lucia. The Gifts assured him that *Arachne* could make numerous jumps between Upsilon Aquarius and Sol. But—assuming he did find her, and that she was still alive—would she recognize him as he was? Would she still respect him or even want him? He wasn't the same Peter Alander he had been back in entrainment— not by any stretch of the imagination.

"We're the Viking widows," she had said, "waving off our husbands to be swallowed by the sea. Except they're not our husbands—or wives or friends or anyone for that matter. They're us."

His original had surrendered this copy of him to the
widow maker, and it had swallowed him whole. Now
there was something else in his place: a changeling, an
imposter who didn't really know *what* he was. How could
she still want that?

His melancholy thoughts occupied him as the hole ship
spun down, absorbing the cockpit. Before contact with the
Tipler was lost, Samson sent a brief flash of herself via
conSense. Clearly she had managed to restore some of the
systems; otherwise she would have had no interface between herself and the raw data pouring in through the
ship's sensors. He didn't know if that made his job easier
or harder.

Her image appeared faded and dull before his eyes, like
a bad copy. She looked exactly as he remembered her
from entrainment: wearing a simple gray coverall with her
blond hair tied back in a rough bun. He wondered if that
was the image her original had given her for when she
thought of herself: Cleo Samson, relaxed and natural, yet
still a professional-looking woman, able to do anything
she wanted. He had no such self-image; all he saw was a
vague impression of a square jaw, recessed eyes, and
round, hairless forehead. But that was the face of his new
body, only vaguely like the one he had once had.

"Say hi to my original from me," she said. "Tell her
. . . Tell her I think it was worth it." She smiled. "Good
luck, Peter."

"Thanks," he said, but the signal had already died and
her image had flickered out. "I'll need it."

He couldn't help but wonder *what* had been worth it
for her. Was she talking about taking over the *Tipler*,
coming on the mission, maintaining her friendship with
him, or perhaps something more personal that only her

original would know? He was glad he hadn't had the chance to reply, though, because he was sure that had he said anything, something about his response would have revealed his intentions. As it was, he was already feeling guilty enough for what he was about to do.

He stood for a moment before the big wraparound screen with the limp droid dangling like a dead octopus from one hand, thinking. He knew it would be dangerous to hesitate too long, lest he lose his train of thought and forget altogether what he was supposed to be doing. There would be no patient voice of Cleo Samson in his ear to jog him back to awareness. Or perhaps that was what he wanted: to forget, to be deflected, to have the decision taken away from him.

He stirred. "*Arachne*, are we ready to move?"

"I am ready," the ship replied. "Please select a destination."

"Okay," he said. "I want you to take us to where we went before—back to the gas giant."

As before, the screen showing the inside of the Dock went black. There was no sense of motion whatsoever, but he knew they were on their way. He wasn't sure exactly what complex combination of moves it would take to put the hole ship in a stable orbit about the gas giant; he imagined it must look odd to an observer seeing the ship appear in a gravity well for a second or two, enough time to accelerate, then disappear again, only to reappear an instant later somewhere quite different but with the same vector. It seemed a bizarre way to travel, only making sense if the energy required to accelerate—or to equip the ship with the means of accelerating—was less than it took to jump small distances. He didn't know if that was an unreasonable proposition or not, especially if the Spinners had only given humanity the ship in order to teach them about the drive. Maybe thrusters of some kind could be added to it later, when humanity learned more about the technology itself.

The now-familiar view of the gas giant appeared on his screen. He probably had a few minutes before images of the hole ship would reach the *Tipler*. He didn't dare take the chance that Samson would fail to notice them, and he didn't need to. He had just wanted a moment to confer with the ship, without sitting in the Dry Dock long enough to arouse her suspicions.

"I need to communicate with the *Tipler* on a private channel," he said. "If I give you the frequency and the code required, can you set that up for me?"

"This can be arranged," replied the calm, gender-free voice. "There will be a delay of—"

"I know, I know. Before we open the channel, I want us to move closer. *Much* closer. Can we do this?"

"I would require more specific data," the AI replied. "But the proposal is feasible."

He swallowed nervously, then asked, "What would happen if we came out of hyperspace—or jump mode or whatever you call it—right next to the *Tipler*? So there would be no delay at all. Could we damage it?"

"The chances of electromagnetic interference increase exponentially with proximity—"

"I don't want any details," he said irritably. "Just give me a figure. How close can we get and still be safe?"

"Fifty meters would provide a 1 percent risk of minor damage."

It seemed a reasonable risk to Alander. At least no one could accuse him of not trying, if something went wrong. And if it *did* work . . .

"Okay. When I say so, I want you to take us that close to the *Tipler*. Additionally, I want you to place us away from where the main sensor array is located on the external frame, where we're less likely to be seen. Understand?"

"I understand."

"Good," he said. "And be ready to open that channel as soon as we arrive. I'll tell you what I want you to do when it's open. You'll find the code in a sealed archive called Silverstream. The password is Drive." The information came easily from the memories his original had given him. "Do you have any problem with that?"

"All of your instructions have been registered and are achievable," the AI replied.

"Right. Take us in."

He seated himself in the couch as the hole ship left the gas giant and maneuvered to its new location practically on top of the *Tipler*. His palms were sweating as the AI went about its work. The fact that he didn't know exactly what it was doing, that this entire aspect of the operation was completely out of his hands, only added to his nervousness. But he was less afraid of it making a mistake than he was of what awaited him. Or what he had to do.

He closed his eyes and tried to concentrate, his heart pounding anxiously in his chest.

If not for us, then for whom?

The screen cleared. He was looking at a close-up of the *Tipler*'s underside, an unglamorous rectangle webbed with supports and basic microwave dishes. On either side of him, he knew, stretched the combined solar cells and light sail that provided backup power and kept the ship in its station. These silver wings were the ship's most glamorous aspect; the rest were just boxes and stanchions, fitted snugly together to withstand years of deceleration.

"I have that channel opened now," said the AI emotionlessly.

"All right. Give me an open mike," he said. "And ignore all attempts to communicate on any other frequency. Do *not* break the line, whatever you do."

He spoke assuming that the *Tipler* could hear him. "This is Peter Stanmore Alander, ID 27-LAU, override authorization code TCW-10. I am requesting an external command node."

The response from the ship's AI was immediate: "I'm sorry, Dr. Alander, but I am unable to comply with your instructions. I am not authorized to grant external access."

He cursed aloud. Either Samson had anticipated such a move or Hatzis had installed the block to prevent the gifts taking over. Either way, it meant there was now just one other option—one he had been hoping to avoid.

"I need to get closer. Can this cockpit move on its own?"

"It has some limited independent mobility."

"Can it get me here?" He gestured at the screen with his hand. "To the *Tipler*?"

"Yes."

"Then do it." He stared at the screen, trying to stay focused. "I need to get out." The image of the *Tipler* ballooned toward him. "I want you to evacuate the interior of the cockpit and open the airlock."

He waited for the hole ship to advise him against such an action, to inform him that the Immortality Suit would not protect against hard vacuum and radiation, but thankfully, his fears went unrealized. Either the ship was obedient to the point of letting him commit suicide, or it knew he would be all right. He tried to be reassured, but his rising anxiety levels were taking a heavy toll on his optimism.

Once the base of the *Tipler* was stationary on the screen, he assumed the cockpit had come to rest beneath it. He turned around to find the airlock already open. The suit had stiffened slightly around his joints but was otherwise unchanged.

His stomach tightened in apprehension, but he forced himself to keep his breathing steady and easy. "Okay, I'm going outside now. Maintain your position here until I get back. And remember: I don't want you to respond to *any* other transmissions but mine."

"There is no need for repetition," said the AI. "Your instructions from before were sufficient."

"Couldn't you just humor me?" he muttered as he moved through the airlock.

"That is not my function."

Outside, he caught the full glare of the sun. Immediately his head began to spin. Floating in vacuum with only the suit protecting him from the elements, he suddenly felt terribly exposed. Knowing that was an irrational reaction didn't help; it was human to fear what couldn't be controlled. He took a minute to breathe deeply, to calm himself before he proceeded. He couldn't delay any longer, no matter how he felt.

The underside of the *Tipler* hung a body's length away from him. Wary of the change to free fall, he steadied himself on the lip of the exit, measured the distance between himself and the maintenance framework, and jumped.

It was only a short distance, but his stomach lurched all the same. He dreaded to think what might happen if he missed or bounced off, as he doubted the suit had thrusters listed among its capabilities. So when the *Tipler* loomed before him, he scrabbled for a handhold with all his strength and resisted the ricochet.

He clung tight for a moment before looking around to get his bearings. He needed to get across the face of the ship, around the edge, and onto the other side. His movement was slow and awkward, encumbered by the fact that the ship hadn't been built for more than the bare minimum of external maneuverability. He had to jump twice more in order to reach the handholds he needed, each time having to rest afterward with his eyes firmly closed to shut out the unsettling view around him. Adrasteia was bright, and the silver shell of the *Tipler* reflected the glare back at him; to his right was Upsilon Aquarius, while to his left, behind the cockpit's looming black disk, was the hole ship, *Arachne*. There was no way of knowing if Samson had noticed what he was doing. All he could do was keep going, hoping that she was so ensconced in her virtual world that she would never consider a physical approach. Or at least not immediately.

He reached the manual access point at last and placed a hand against it. For a moment, he was terrified that the suit might interfere with the infrared receptors on his skin, but a second later his fears were swept away as the voice of the ship sounded in his ears.

"You have access, Dr. Alander."

He repeated his earlier request for an external command node. This time the ship's response was more encouraging:

"Your configuration is not standard. Would you like a custom interface?"

He swallowed. "No. ConSense will be fine."

This was the moment he had really been dreading. He

didn't have time to work out a system to interact manually with the ship's complex systems; he had no choice but to accept the interface everyone ordinarily used, even if it was the one he had been unable to tolerate ever since his breakdown.

Although he tried to steel himself for it, the flooding of conSense over his real senses took him off guard. The exterior of the *Tipler* vanished and was replaced by a void characterized by intangible icons he had only ever been able to describe by their function rather than their appearance. They acted like drawers, or windows, but they didn't look like anything at all. They were just holes, potentialities, in which things could be called into being.

He could sketch a framework around him—what earlier flat-screen users had called wallpaper—but he didn't have time. Already he could feel his mind skidding on the slippery surface, reaching for reference points but finding none. He had to move quickly, before his mind slipped away entirely.

He imagined the structure of the ship's command network and compared it to what he sensed around him. Hatzis had changed almost nothing from the configuration Sivio had placed it in back on Earth. He had expected that: Hatzis was a reliable leader but not an original one; she would always prefer to operate in an existing control structure rather than create a new one. But that was fine by him. At least it meant he had a good idea where everything was.

Telemetry, reactor control, structural integrity . . . He flicked through the various menus. Attitude adjustment, communications, records . . .

Engram Overseer.

He opened that window. It irised around him and swept

him into its interior. A wave of giddiness threatened to undermine him, but he kept up the mantra that had served him so well in recent days: *I know who I am. I know who I am. I know who I am....*

When he was inside, he confirmed what he already knew. The activities of all the engrams on the ship were indicated by displays showing current processing demands. Only one person was using any at all; the rest had been frozen in time, caught between one thought and the next. They weren't dead or unconscious, just halted in their tracks. Only he, with the capacity to process consciousness data independently, was protected from her influence. Now that he knew to isolate himself from the *Tipler*, he was perfectly safe.

The one engram showing activity was Cleo Samson. In order to free the others, he would have to shut her down. And even with the command overrides, that wasn't going to be easy.

He hesitated, suddenly very uncertain about what he was about to do. Did he have the right to do this? He might think he had no other choice, but would Earth thank him? And what if he was wrong? Could he live with himself knowing what he had done?

He tried to shake the uncertainty from his mind, but his doubts were intense, almost overwhelming.

He remembered what he had learned about the collective consciousness of the engrams in entrainment. The one time he had glimpsed it, it had been a mess of impressions, difficult to navigate. Ordinarily, he wouldn't have stood a chance in there, given his disability, but this was hardly an ordinary situation. The banks were doing the processing for just one engram, rather than dozens. It would, therefore, be less hazardous.

But if he lost it, if he lost *himself,* there might be no going back.

He mentally shook himself again. He *had* to know. He had to be sure before he pulled the plug on the one person in Upsilon Aquarius who had been his friend.

Jumping into her mind took just a command or two. When he was inside, he finally had concrete reference points surrounding him, but they weren't under his control. Samson was moving constantly, flicking through rooms as though looking for something; the environments washed over her in a disjointed stream, one or two every second, each different from the last. Alander saw rooms that clearly didn't belong to her—vast, baroque chambers full of velvet and gold trim (obviously fulfilling one of the crew members' secret whims)—among other rooms designed to be more functional: the Bridge, the Engine Room, the Mess. Just because the *Tipler* didn't actually have any of these places didn't mean that the people crewing it wouldn't find their existence comforting, easier to work in.

Her thoughts were chaotic, too complicated to unravel. But she was searching for something, and he could tell that it was causing her some agitation. And when she finally found it, that agitation was transferred almost instantly to himself as a disorienting sensation washed through him.

He saw himself standing in front of a bank of screens, his hands pressed against one of them and his head tipped back, eyes closed. He looked exactly as he had on Earth, before they had left: tall, thin, pale-skinned, well-groomed, powerful—or was that last aspect, he asked himself, coming from her? Was this the way she still imagined him?

Seeing himself like that, from the outside, was like standing above the epicenter of an earthquake. Everything he was, everything he had become since leaving Earth, trembled, threatened to crumble into dust.

"There you are," she said, her voice sounding in his mind like a bell. "What are you doing, Peter?"

And suddenly he was outside of her head. Had he pulled himself out or been thrown out? Maybe he had caused some sort of strange loop in the *Tipler* that had to be severed. Whatever had happened, he was himself again. Even in the giddying nonplace of conSense, he was relieved.

"Peter?"

He ignored her. She had been looking for him throughout the many virtual rooms of the *Tipler*, so she must have known what he intended to do. But nothing she could say would deflect him from the course he had chosen, now that he had chosen it.

"What about Lucia, Peter?" There was a hint of sadness and disappointment in her voice.

He opened the Engram Control window and accessed her engram ID. With one command, he could theoretically shut her down. Would that be enough? Wouldn't the UNESSPRO programmers have thought of that in advance and planned against it? He didn't know. All he could hope was that they had placed their hope and plans in her alone—that beyond planting her to make sure things went as they wanted them to, they had taken no further precautions.

He pulled the switch. The thread that was her mind flickered but didn't cease.

"You're making a mistake, Peter."

Her voice tugged at him, stung his conscience. Now

that a simple shutdown had failed, there was only one option left open to him.

Hidden deeper in the tangle of commands and displays that made up Engram Control was one marked Erase, for use only in the direst of circumstances. Hopefully, the programmers had left them this fail safe, because if they hadn't, he didn't know what else he could do.

When he found it, his vision rippled as though it was a reflection on a pond into which a heavy stone had been thrown.

"Please, Peter," she said softly. "Don't do this."

"Don't you see, Cleo?" he said, hesitating. "I have no choice. *They* have given me no choice! If the mission is to have any chance, I have to do this."

But before he could make the command, something wrapped around his throat, choking him. The two worlds he occupied suddenly overlapped. He was torn between the virtual illusion and the reality of the outside of the *Tipler*. Still holding the access point, he managed to swing himself around enough to see his attacker: it was the droid he had left behind in the hole ship. It was stubby but strong, and it had a good grip on the *Tipler*. Its limbs writhed like those of an angry spider as it unfolded a cutting tool and brought it down with a flash toward his neck.

He flinched, but all he felt was the impact of the blow: no stabbing pain, no sharpness. Fighting his surprise, he grappled with the limb around his throat, managing with some difficulty to get his fingers around it; then he pulled as hard as he could.

The knife slashed at his fingers, and again failed to bite. The Immortality Suit repelled the blade, no matter how hard the droid struck. But there was nothing it could do about momentum, and the droid—with Samson's mind behind it—swiftly changed its tactic. Its limbs spread-eagled around his head to push as hard as they could against the *Tipler*, hoping to tear him away from it.

Alander hung on, knowing that if he let go, he might never make it back, while the fingers of his free hand tore at the limb around his throat. He thrashed his head to put the droid off balance. Stars formed behind his eyes as he pitted every muscle in his android body against the machine trying to kill him.

Then abruptly the pressure was gone and the droid was falling away, quickly becoming little more than a sparkling mote drifting toward Adrasteia.

He waited until his heart beat normally again before turning back to the *Tipler* and allowing the virtual world to wash over him again.

"Peter, please listen—" she started, but this time he didn't hesitate; he hit the switch.

It wasn't as he'd imagined it. It took no more than a second to wipe everything that had been Cleo Samson from the *Tipler*'s main banks: the primary pattern laid down by her original, along with all the memories she had added to it over the last century of the mission. He felt her absence the moment she was gone. The ship was silent and empty around him; ConSense was a vacuum containing nothing but his thoughts and his regret. He couldn't cry in conSense; he didn't have a body in the sense that Hatzis and the others did. But the last thing he remembered for a long, long while was grief.

1.2.7

"Peter, can you hear me?"

For the second time that day, he rose from oblivion into confusion. This time, though, he had no idea where he was or what he was doing. He felt like he was caught in a dream—a nightmare in which sight was swapped with sound, where taste became touch, and the world had turned inside out. He was lost—

"Is it you, Peter? It took us longer than we thought to find you, but I think it's you."

The familiar voice paused for a moment. He didn't know where it was coming from, but it sounded like Caryl Hatzis.

"If it is you and you can hear me, don't bother trying to respond. Just do exactly as I say."

Even if he'd wanted to respond, he had no idea how to go about it.

"You have to break the connection, Peter," she went on. "You know how to do that. It's easy. You have a ripcord like we all do. All you have to do is *use* it. Once you're out, we can talk properly."

He frowned into the void. A ripcord? At first he didn't know what she was talking about. Ripcords were used as a last resort to crash a conflicting environment, such as the ctrl-alt-del command his father had used on his old PC. But what had that to do with him? He wasn't even able to enter subversive environments anymore. If he did, all he had to do was . . .

The memory surfaced with surprising ease from somewhere in the dark and long untouched recesses of his mind. The command had always been there, of course; he simply hadn't needed it for a long, long time. In fact, he hadn't used his ripcord since his breakdown upon arriving in Upsilon Aquarius, almost ten years earlier. Nevertheless, it was there now, clear in his mind, as it always would be should he ever need it.

Hatzis was repeating her instructions to him, but this time he was ignoring her, focusing instead on his ripcord command.

"Tabula rasa."

He spoke the words loud and clear into the void, knowing that the *Tipler*'s AIs would recognize it.

Suddenly he was hanging in shadow between the hole ship cockpit and the *Tipler*, one hand still clutching the manual access port. He groaned slightly and eased his grip. His throat hurt from where the droid had attacked him earlier. How much earlier, he couldn't tell. How long had he actually been out?

The voice of the *Tipler* interrupted his thoughts: "Do you wish to end this session?"

"Huh?" he croaked. "Oh, yes. Yes, I do. *Arachne*, can you bring the cockpit around here?"

He didn't know if the ship's AI could hear him, but he figured it was worth a try. Relief flooded through him as the AI's voice replied:

"I am receiving transmissions from—"

"Yes, I know," he said. "But they can wait. Just get the cockpit over to me, all right?"

He relaxed somewhat as the open mouth of the cockpit swung into view, then kicked himself toward it as soon as it was stationary. Inside, he collapsed with a grunt. Too weak to stand, he crawled the rest of the way into the cockpit, heaving himself onto the couch.

"Will you be requiring medical assistance?" the AI asked.

"No, I'm all right. The suit's looking after me just fine. Just put those calls from the *Tipler* on speaker."

"Peter?" came the voice of Jayme Sivio. "Can you hear me, Peter? Please respond if you are receiving this transmission."

"Give me an open channel." A moment later, Sivio's face appeared in the screen before him.

"Peter?"

"Sorry to keep you waiting, Jayme. How long was I out?"

"A couple of hours." There was no hiding the relief on Sivio's face. "We came up to speed not knowing a thing about what had happened, but when we worked it out, we found you embedded in the systems. You weren't responding, and we couldn't hail the hole ship. We were worried that . . ." He stopped, smiled. "Well, we were just worried, that's all. Caryl wouldn't give up on you."

"Cleo . . ." He was unable to finish the sentence.

Sivio's smile faded. "We know," he said. "You don't need to tell us about that right now, though."

Alander leaned back into the seat, rubbing his forehead. His skin was dry, almost brittle. Or was that the Immortality Suit? He couldn't tell. The last thing he remembered was erasing Samson from the *Tipler*'s banks. Beyond that, he drew a complete blank. He must have had the presence of mind, though, to bring the others back up before blanking out completely. Had he not, the *Tipler* might have remained empty but for his mind-locked engram for eternity.

Maybe the idea of oblivion had been preferable a couple of hours ago. Had that been what he'd wanted? He

certainly hadn't tried to extricate himself from his predic-
ament. Adrift in conSense, instead of pulling the ripcord
as Hatzis had finally instructed him to do, he had simply
let himself sink deeper and deeper, losing himself to the
emptiness. After what he'd done to Samson, that might
have seemed an easy solution to his guilt. But it wasn't a
foolproof one. If he'd *really* wanted to die, the erase command would have been the only certain way. He must
have known that Hatzis would not simply leave him to
oblivion indefinitely, despite what must have been a temptation to do just that.

It seemed she cared what happened to him, after all.
And so did he. For *himself*, though, not for anyone else.

"*Arachne*, take me back to the Dock," he said. "And
Jayme, give me a moment. I need to rest."

"Understood, Peter."

A new face appeared on the screen before the line died,
though.

"Good work, Peter," said Hatzis. Her tone was cautious
but respectful. "And thanks."

He shrugged but couldn't be bothered saying anything
in response. He didn't have the energy or inclination to
score any points off her, so he just let his head fall back
onto the couch, rubbing absently at his aching throat.

I'm sorry, Cleo, he thought suddenly.

"Is there anything you need?"

"No." Then, after a moment's consideration, he said,
"Actually, there is something you could do. I want you
to call that meeting. Talk to the crew; give them the
choice. I want a decision within twenty-four hours."

"A decision?"

"You know what I'm talking about." He took a deep
breath and held it for a moment. When he let it go, it

came out in a rush. "I want to go to Earth, and I want to go soon, before something else like this happens."

"Peter, I—"

"Can you at least put it to them?" He kept his voice firm and even.

She was silent for a while, but in the end she didn't argue. "All right, Peter," she said. "I'll do it—for *me,* if not for any real reason. The sooner we get back home, the sooner I can start tearing strips off those fuckers who sent us here."

The virulence in her voice surprised him, but it did make sense. It must have been galling to have had her command ripped away so casually. He would have felt the same way, he was sure.

"Thanks, Caryl. I appreciate it."

She nodded. Then the line went dead, and he was alone.

The decision surprised them all. Samson's attempted sabotage seemed to have galvanized feelings more than anything else in recent days. Those who had originally argued for more time were now arguing that time was of the essence—that, as Peter had implied, the longer they waited, the greater the chances were that some other incident could occur and threaten everything.

And then there were the gifts themselves.

"When the Spinners first came here," said Peter, "we were apprehensive. We didn't know what they wanted with us. Some might argue that we still don't, and therefore we should still be wary of them . . . and to a point, I'd have to agree. We *don't* know if the Spinners have a hidden agenda, but it does seem unlikely when you consider what has been given to us. So I think we should be careful not to let our fears and suspicions continue to cloud our judgments. Regardless of what their intentions are, it seems that we can at least rest easy in terms of the actual technology."

"Why?" asked Jene Avery, one of the few who remained skeptical.

"Well, because I'm alive, for starters," he said. "And because we're here now, talking as we are."

He looked around at the faces of the people he had trained with. They had come to him, this time, patching into his version of reality—the Hub—rather than insisting that he join theirs. The thirty people stared back at him with expressions he knew well. Even though he hadn't been a proper part of the crew, he still knew them. They had entrained together. Christ, along with the other engrams on missions elsewhere, they were probably the closest thing to family he had.

"For one thing, the Gifts could have refused to help," he said. "They could have denied me the use of the hole ship, or the on-board AI could have refused such a close maneuver." When he thought of the jump from the gas giant to the *Tipler*—a distance of over a billion kilometers with a margin for error of barely meters—he shuddered. "The Immortality Suit itself could have killed me at any time. But it didn't. The gifts came through when we needed them most."

"Don't sell yourself short," said Sivio. "They were just the tools. It was you who used them effectively."

The praise both warmed and irritated him at the same time; he couldn't tell if Sivio meant it or if he was just saying it to make up for his earlier doubts.

"My point is," he continued, "that they're *reliable* tools. We can believe what the Gifts say in that respect. It looks

like they're not going to lie to us in a way that will cause
us immediate harm."

"Maybe that's just what they want us to think," persisted Avery.

"Maybe," Alander concurred. "And maybe we could
argue like this forever. But at some point we *have* to make
a decision. Do you really want to wait another two hundred years for a reply from Earth? A reply that might
never even come?"

Avery backed down at that. No one wanted to wait that
long. No matter what had happened on Earth, no matter
why communications had ceased so abruptly, the people
back home deserved to know what the survey team in
Upsilon Aquarius had found. There was no question about
that. The only disagreements occurred over the timing,
and Hatzis, as she had intimated to Alander in the hole
ship, was keen for a swift resolution.

It came a short time later when the vote was finally
taken again. This time the majority was satisfied that the
risks had been minimized, if not completely nullified, and
Alander was given the go-ahead to leave at his earliest
convenience. There were still a few dissenting voices, but
generally it was agreed that, as soon as enough information had been compiled on the gifts by their respective
specialists and compressed into mobile Solid-State Data
Storage, Alander would take the hole ship to Earth and
hand the matter over to whatever authority remained
there. If any semblance of UNESSPRO still existed, the
Spinners and all their gifts would become their responsibility. However, if he found only savagery—or worse,
nothing at all—then he was to return to Adrasteia with
the data still on the SSDS units. From there, they would
decide what course of action to take next.

But ultimately, the timing of when he actually departed was being left up to him. With Samson now gone, there was nothing to hold him back. Except perhaps one nagging uncertainty.

He took his leave of the meeting and went back to Spindle Seven, the home of the Gifts. He stood before the gray structures that comprised their central processors, staring with renewed awe at the mighty machines responsible for building the ring. There was something both breathtaking and intimidating about the strange and silent edifices surrounding him, something he found terribly unsettling. He remained there for a long while, unable to bring himself to ask the question that was foremost in his thoughts, almost fearing the answer they would give.

"A vote was taken," he said eventually. "I'll be taking the hole ship back to Earth."

"We can see how you would deem that to be the most prudent action," the Gifts said in return, "given the circumstances."

"Yeah, well not everyone is convinced." He shrugged. "What it means is that this might be my last chance to speak to you in person. Unless, of course, we could fit you into the hole ship."

"That is not possible," they said.

"Not even a fragment?"

"Our place is here, Peter, in the spindles."

He nodded. "Among the gifts."

"We *are* the gifts, Peter."

He smiled at their pedantry. Their tone was so human and natural that it was hard to remember that their origins—and nature—were purely alien.

"While I'm away, I don't suppose you'll communicate with anyone else."

"We will communicate only through you."

He shook his head, frustrated. "But *why?*" he said, finally releasing the question. "Why *me?*"

"What do you mean, Peter?"

"I mean you've made your point about restricting our development. I can understand the importance of us not learning too much too quickly. I can appreciate that. But what I don't see is why someone else can't continue the investigations while I'm gone. We're all limited in our own ways; we're all flawed. It just doesn't make sense."

"You were the one chosen," they replied without hesitation.

"That's what I don't understand!" he said, throwing up his arms in exasperation. "You've never told me *why* I was chosen."

"We have explained to you that we do not have the answer you seek. Our builders chose you because you best suited their needs. What their criteria was for choosing you, however, we do not know. We recognized you only when the scan we made of you matched the data our builders gave us."

"But you must have an idea," he said. "You *must.*"

"It would be possible to speculate, as indeed you already have, based on the information available to you. But we would rather cease all communication than create or perpetuate a misunderstanding."

He stared at the monolithic Gifts, incensed by their stubbornness. That this was exactly the kind of response he had been anticipating didn't make it any less frustrating.

"Okay," he said with some resignation. "Maybe I'll understand things better when I return."

"You should not concern yourself with here, Peter," said the Gifts.

He frowned deeply now. "Why not?"

"The Spinners are best served by you returning to Earth," they said.

"And why is that? Just what is their purpose? What is it they stand to gain by giving us all of these things?"

"We have told you why the gifts were given. Beyond that we are not permitted to say."

"But you *do* know, don't you?"

There was a moment's hesitation before they answered. "Yes."

Although he pressed them, they would reveal nothing more to him. The Spinners wanted him to return to Earth, so in voting to do it, the survey mission had unwittingly played into their hands. But to do what? Was it simply to spread the knowledge that they had been given? Did they wish nothing more than for all life-forms to ultimately be at a level similar to each other, thereby attaining some form of harmony within the galaxy or something? Or was their intention more malicious? Whatever it was, there was only one way to find out, and that was to take the hole ship, as planned, back to Earth.

"You know," he said after a while. "I don't think I trust these Spinners of yours."

There was no response from the Gifts, so he turned and made to leave, saying casually over his shoulder: "I guess I'll speak to you on my return."

Then he strode away toward the exit.

It was only when he was about to step through the doorway that he heard the alien artifacts say: "Good-bye, Peter Alander."

2.1
SWIMMING WITH ICEBERGS

2160.8.27 Standard Mission Time
23 July, 2163 U.T.

2.1.1

Caryl Hatzis was studying an ethane plume on Titan at the time of the Discord. She was also riding a comet out to the Oort cloud and joining in on the volunteer effort to sculpt an upturned human face on the Cydonia region on Mars. Part of her was still watching the slow sunrise on Mercury, while yet another part was working as a supervisor on the Shell Proper, ensuring the Edge accreted properly. A quick stocktaking of her various povs would have revealed as many as fifty, ranging anywhere from a single human equivalent to four or five, scattered across the solar system and beyond. Where *she* was at any given time depended purely on her mood.

That year had seen her in a relatively stable state of mind. Although regarded as a conservative—as well as something of a reactionary—by the Vincula, she had finally embraced some of the new architecture spreading through the Frame. With so much consciousness design still haphazard or idiosyncratic, it was often hard to tell what was genuine progress and what a fad, but she never ignored the former when she found it. Her latest upgrade allowed her to ride the crest of information from her various part-selves across the system, smeared in a fluctuating "present" from the first data packet to the last, but she was still able to focus at will on a single moment in any one of those part-selves. Thus she suffered less from the occasional fragmentation arising from the fact that one pair of eyes was a hundred light-hours distant from the rest, while at the same time having none of the vagueness that some of her less cautious colleagues still displayed: she could still take the time to marvel at the feathery fringe of a plume, if she so desired.

Of course, her friends among the Gezim weren't so understanding. Although in theory they treated all who strayed from their so-called Human Principles equally— terror tactics being ultimately worthless unless someone was at risk from them—something special was reserved for those that had once been close to them. Not that Hatzis had ever truly been one of them, but she did sympathize. She had even argued on their behalf before the Vincula, back when there had been a chance of reconciliation; and she still agreed with a lot of what they said. But there was a limit to how long and how effectively one could buck the system and remain relevant. The Gezim were an issue only because of their activism, not because of what they stood for.

That struck her as terribly sad. There were few enough of them as it was without scaring away potential recruits. In some ways, it was one of the few jarring notes remaining to her, outside of her memories. Or so she preferred to think.

The Discord shivered through the device known as

McKirdy's Machine on the fifteenth of July, 2163. As Hatzis understood it—and she had never paid much attention to the theory, before the Discord—the Machine was some sort of gravitational wave detector being built on the edge of the system, far away from anything it might interfere with. Since some of its components were hyperdense, bordering on singularities, there had been an uproar when the plans had first been submitted for approval. It was a hazard to shipping, its detractors had said, likely to perturb orbits if not disintegrate without warning into a million, high-velocity fragments. Hence its location out past Pluto, near a nameless icy planetoid simply designated KLB2025R.

Upon further research, Hatzis learned that McKirdy's Machine was a prototype long-range communicator, employing arcane properties of space itself rather than any usual forms of mass or radiation. The math was beyond her, but she didn't feel the need to send one of her parts off to catch up. The summary was enough. The important thing was that the Machine wasn't supposed to work yet. Its components had only been loosely assembled and lacked both fine-tuning and testing. So the Discord was completely unexpected—a resonance through the structure that resembled a transmission, yet from no known source.

Optimists hailed it as the first unequivocally alien signal since the Tedesco bursts of the late twenty-first century—a series of untranslated broadcasts from the region of the sky containing the constellation Sculptor that had ended as suddenly as they had begun. Skeptics thought it was simply a glitch in the design, random noise elevated anomalously to the appearance of an external signal. The Machine's architects and engineers were sitting on the fence: They couldn't say for certain that the signal wasn't noise, but it resembled nothing any of the simulations had predicted. Either the simulations were wrong and the Machine didn't work as expected, or the Discord had external origins.

If the signal had contained any readable information or the source could have been identified, the matter might have been quickly resolved. Sadly, however, the Machine was not able to pinpoint its origins, and the data consisted of just one short stretch of undecipherable information repeated three times, with unequal gaps of time between each repetition. A different burst followed shortly thereafter, then three more transmissions came within a day, none of them repeated. The Vincula had posted the repeated stretches across the system in the hope that someone would crack it. In the day following the Discord and its successors, no one made any headway. Within two days, interest had already begun to fade. Only those peculiar obsessives to whom such problems posed direct interest gave it any further thought. Everyone else in the Vincula or the Gezim went about life as always, so full of richness and complexity that looking elsewhere for wonder was as ridiculous as begging for more freedom with which to enjoy it.

"Personally, I think it's one of the colonies," said Sel Shal-houb. Hatzis was sharing a drink with him in Echo Park, her natural body's current location. The old-fashioned art of cocktail parties was back in vogue for a season, and she had dressed for the occasion in an open-throated outfit that cycled through the work of Vasili Kandinsky. Vibrant images trickled from her shoulders, cascaded down her

waist, then disappeared with a hint of compression at her perfectly straight hem. Shalhoub was in a remote that held a striking resemblance to his official appearance, even without virtual overlays. Its tuxedo was freshly pressed, real, and therefore priceless.

"Nonsense," rapid-fired JORIS, a nominally (but only temporarily) male *merge* from Uranus Platform. He was speaking in hyperlite, the current version of accelerated slang. "Those engrams wouldn't be advanced enough to do something like this. They wouldn't have the sophistication required—"

"You don't know that," said Shalhoub. "Who of us can say for sure what advancements they might have made?"

"We only lost a couple of decades to the Spike," said JORIS. "They would have been in transit almost a century. The suggestion that they could have developed beyond us is ludicrous."

"They may have gotten lucky," said Hatzis.

"You were one of them, weren't you, Caryl?" asked Shalhoub.

"Copies of me were sent on the original missions, yes," she admitted. "But I personally didn't go anywhere."

"Very sensible," said JORIS flatly. "Why would you want to? Why would *anyone* wish to go anywhere with only half a mind? What would be the point in that? Better not to have gone at all, I say."

Hatzis was surprised that Shalhoub had known about her involvement in the defunct United Near-Earth Stellar Survey Program, since it was not something she advertised. Not many people remembered anything about those almost ancient missions. (Then again, very little got past him, a fact she would do well to keep in mind.) Over the years, contact had been made with some of the nearby survey systems, albeit by more mundane methods. At least two missions—Beta Hydrus and Delta Pavonis—had reported on arrival and would have received communications from Earth responding to those reports, before communications had been discontinued altogether. It wasn't exactly a dialogue, but it was a beginning. In time, as public interest gradually revived, she thought there might be a chance to reestablish some sort of communications with those long-lost children of Earth.

The trouble was, most these days were like the *merge*. The engram fad had been a disaster almost from the beginning. She was somewhat surprised that any of the missions had succeeded at all. As JORIS implied, a crew made up of brain-damaged fake humans would have been worse than no crew at all. And there was no chance that any such crew could have built something like McKirdy's Machine and sent the Discord. It simply wasn't possible. There had to be an alternative explanation.

"Maybe it's aliens," she joked.

"I have no doubt about that." JORIS seemed to take the suggestion seriously. "If it *is* a transmission, then it had to come from *somewhere*. And who else but aliens *could* have sent it?"

"It could be an echo from the future," Hatzis offered more seriously. "Since the Machine violates causality—"

"It doesn't," said the *merge*. "McKirdy has proven that there is no possibility of countercontinuum information transfer."

"If you say so." Hatzis shrugged. "To tell you the truth, I don't really understand all this ftl stuff."

"So according to you, J," said Shalhoub, "it must be aliens."

"Of course," said JORIS. "I don't see how it could possibly be anything else."

"So what should we do now?" Shalhoub asked. "Reply?"

"God, no," said the *merge*, reverting to oldspeak. "Why in the Frame would we do that?"

"Curiosity, perhaps?" suggested Hatzis.

"You wouldn't stick your head up if you heard a gunshot, would you?"

"A gunshot is fundamentally different from an alien species trying to communicate with us," said Hatzis.

"I fail to see the difference," said the *merge*.

Shalhoub laughed, but it was Hatzis who responded.

"Well, for one thing, there is no evidence to suggest that these aliens—if that is indeed what they are—are in any way attempting to blow our heads off. You're just clouding the issue with small talk." *And deliberately so,* she thought. The use of such an archaic metaphor must have been aimed squarely at her, since she was the oldest person present. "For all we know, it could be a cry for help."

"If that's the case, then it is intended for someone other than us, someone who has the ability to understand the message in the first place and, presumably, to do something about it." JORIS flexed one long, honey-textured arm and performed a graceful pirouette. In the short time before the *merge* was facing her way again, he had become female, morphing mass away from shoulders and thighs into hips and breasts, angular facial features seeming to have melted into more gentle terrain. (Real or virtual? Hatzis couldn't decide. Either way, it was an effective conversational gambit.) Only her voice remained unchanged, complete with its needling tone. "If someone with the ability to communicate by ftl is in trouble, I for one have no desire to offer assistance, which at best might be considered ineffectual." Smiling, JORIS lifted her glass of liqueur in way of a toast. "Here's to keeping our noses clean, I say."

"Coward." Hatzis took a step back from the topic, realizing then that JORIS saw the discussion as nothing more than a diversionary amusement. For too many, she thought, life's meaning lay in the interaction with others, rather than the interaction with the universe around them. She couldn't help but feel that humanity would be better off—more vital, more driven—if there were less like JORIS to dilute what little forward impetus remained.

But that was another argument entirely, and she refused to allow herself to be drawn into it by a *merge*.

Shalhoub was watching her shrewdly over his glass, her dress reflecting in his eyes. He might not be inclined to bait her, he might even seem to be cordial and open in social situations, but she didn't like to think what one of the Frame's foremost Urges might do if she started mouthing off in public. His stand on eisegetes like JORIS wasn't in the public domain. Not yet, at least.

". . . anticipated the possibilities of trade," he was saying in his bland, steady drawl. He had taken the look of a white-haired politician, and the remote mimicked it well: tall but not too imposing, solid without being either fat or overmuscled, and pleasantly aged in a nonjowly kind of way. He had even managed the knack of appearing to be interested in anything anyone had to say. "But if what *you're* saying is true, then . . ."

Her attention drifted away completely, adopting the nebulous, smeary focus typical of her current, whole incarnation. The part of her that still resided in her original body didn't have it so easy. The party may have been losing its momentum, but she couldn't just opt out now. She needed to stay focused on why she was there in the first place.

She put her hand on Shalhoub's remote's arm. "Sel," she whispered, "when you're done here, I'll be in the study. There's a simulation from Mati I think you should see."

"Mati?" He half-turned, conversation with the *merge* forgotten. "You mean, Matilda Sulich?"

"You knew she was here," said Hatzis, keeping her voice low. "That's why you came, wasn't it? That's why everyone came."

His gaze flitted about the room. "So where is she? I don't see her anywhere."

"She's not stupid, Sel." She squeezed the remote's arm lightly. "The study; ten minutes. We'll talk to you there— *alone*."

He nodded, permitting himself a smile at the game she was playing. "I'll be there," he said. "Especially if you can find me some more of this wonderful Scotch."

"I'll see what I can do." She walked away, keeping her step casual and unhurried. The original Caryl Hatzis had vestiges of ambition masquerading most often as ideology that the overarching being she'd become hadn't quite managed to completely erase. But she'd never learned to enjoy the game, to "think outside the square," as had been the saying, once. Now that she had made the move, her heart was pounding; fear roiled her insides in ways the rest of her had mostly forgotten. There was no turning back now.

As she passed the drinks cabinet, she leaned over and removed a bottle of the Scotch Shalhoub liked so much.

It was an excellent copy of aged Glenfiddich, its replication accurate down to the individual molecules. What he didn't know was that some of those complex and very large flavor molecules had been altered to react with the otherwise harmless bacteria living in his remote's gut. And by the time he realized that something was wrong, it would be too late.

*Hatzis lunged to catch the remote as it fell, but her re-*sponse was too slow, and it hit the floor with a sickening thud, barely missing the edge of the desk.

"That was a bit close, Caryl." The voice of Matilda Sulich came from out of nowhere, emanating from a point somewhere above Hatzis's head. It was the voice of a woman who had once been physically very large, and she retained much of that subtle resonance in her new form. "Literally cracking open his skull wouldn't have done us any good at all."

Hatzis ignored the jibe; there wasn't time for small talk. "Two minutes," she said, rounding the desk and straightening Shalhoub's remote lying on the floor. "That's all we've got."

"I'm aware of the time restriction," Sulich returned soberly. "Do you have the lace?"

Hatzis didn't reply. She was already reaching into her hemline for the silken web masquerading as cotton. It squirmed in her fingers as she tugged it free. Colored lines and glowing points danced across her vision as the lace's instruction manual showed her how to position it over the remote's head. It was harder than she'd imagined it would be. The living, semisentient machine woven into the threads wouldn't distinguish between her or the remote until she had targeted the remote's modified genome. It wrapped itself around her fingertips like overcooked vermicelli, then sprang free when she gave the command.

The living cobwebs spread across Shalhoub's lined face and settled in. Within seconds, the web was invisible, sinking between the cells of the dermis and deeper into the flesh surrounding his skull.

She squatted on her haunches. "He's going to notice it."

"Not in time."

She checked again. One minute fifty had already passed; half a minute to go. The seconds were flying by too fast, she thought. There wasn't going to be time to—

"Got it!" Sulich's triumphant whisper brought Hatzis forward on her knees. "Your most concerned expression, please, dear."

Hatzis frowned and held her breath. If Sulich had done her job right, she had pinpointed the locations in the remote's artificial brain where Sel Shalhoub's resident memory was stored. It was frozen in limbo for the moment, and therefore unreadable, but it would become active again once the body recovered from its sudden breakdown and the greater Shalhoub regained contact with it. There would be a moment—fleetingly brief—in which those memories would be vulnerable. Ordinarily, they wouldn't be. Ordinarily, the security provided by the Vincula for its Urges would be sufficient to keep any intrusion at bay. But not this time; not with the neural lace working for them.

She started when his eyes suddenly opened, then cursed herself for acting so suspiciously. She put as much sincerity in her voice as she could. "Sel? Can you hear me? Are you all right?"

He didn't move, except to frown. "Caryl? What happened?"

Keep him talking, not thinking, while the rest of him catches up, she told herself. "I don't know. One moment you were drinking, the next . . ." She shrugged.

A smile broke out across his face. "I see," he said, laughing. "Congratulations, Caryl. You got me."

It died abruptly before her eyes, security catching up to the situation hot on Shalhoub's heels. The remote's brain was fried by a blast of internal electricity, making its nostrils smoke and its hair jump. A smell like crushed ants issued from it as a massive release of apoptosis-inducing chemicals spread through its tissues. Cells committed suicide instantly in their billions, including the all-important neurons in its brain.

"Fuck!" She backed away from the malodorous corpse. "Did you get it?"

"Some," said Sulich. "But not all."

"Was it enough though?"

"Give me a moment," she said calmly.

Despite her impatience, Hatzis didn't push the matter. Sulich sounded quietly pleased, and that was a good sign. Hatzis had no doubt that, had they failed, as they had twice before on other targets, Sulich would have been quick to point it out. Getting top-strata information out of the Vincula wasn't easy, and security was tough if caught in midattack. While there was still a chance the breach could be sealed, the Vincula fought back with all the violence and temerity of antibodies attacking a virus. On their previous attempts, she and Sulich had been lucky to get away unscathed.

At least she didn't have to worry about security reprisals. Remotes like Shalhoub's were cheap, throwaway components; the Urges probably went through dozens every year. And information was leaky stuff; despite every effort to contain it, with or without help, it invariably got out. The Vincula was resigned to a certain amount of loss each year. The trick was to make sure the right data slipped out at the right time.

She forced herself to try to relax and not concentrate on the possible consequences of what she had just done. Even if they had been caught in the attempt and had their bodies or patterns scrambled, it would have meant as little to them as the stunt did to the Vincula. But Hatzis was superstitious about losing her original body; it had sentimental significance, if nothing else. The irony that it was the part of her most likely to take part in something like this wasn't lost on her.

"Okay," said Sulich. "We have resource estimates, completion dates, media releases, policy guidelines . . . no damage rates or shortfalls . . . no error calculations . . . no contingency plans . . . We have final design tolerances, but I don't know what good they're going to do us. Anyone could work them out."

Hatzis stood up and dusted herself down. She was still patched into the simulation she and Sulich had prepared for Shalhoub: a bright green projection of what the Frame would look like in thirty years, with the Shell Proper stretched over it like a sail. This image would have been enough to trigger the download of more information from his wider self into the remote. That's when they had Scotched him, when the information was in his head and ripe for the plucking. Or so they'd hoped.

"That's it? Nothing any more sensational than that?"

"Nothing, I'm afraid. He was smarter than we gave him credit for; either that or he was simply thinking about something else. There is a lot of other stuff in here. . . ." Sulich's voice faded as she sifted through more of the dead remote's memory. To her, Hatzis knew, this sort of work was a game, albeit one to be taken very seriously. She had no body or reputation to lose. She wouldn't be dogged by well-wishing types on both sides of the divide wanting to know what she was up to. Matilda Sulich was one of the last truly independent activists in the system, and notorious for it, which is why she and Hatzis worked so well together.

Chaos and control. Hatzis had programmed her dress with that theme in mind before coming to the party. Whether the venue, which had allowed her the use of the study for the evening, had suspected or would even care after the fact, she didn't know.

"I'm going out to mingle," she said. "People will be starting to wonder what's going on."

"You plan to tell them?"

"Of course. We'd be hypocrites, otherwise."

Sulich chuckled. "If I find anything more sensational, I'll let you know."

The party was beginning to peak when she slipped out of the study and poured herself a drink. Someone had resurrected an old 3-D Dean Martin simulation. It was warbling something about memories as she went out onto the balcony.

JORIS, still female and holding court under a swaying palm tree silhouetted against a simulated orange sunset, raised an eyebrow when she stepped out into the night air.

"I hear you've been busy, Caryl."

Hatzis shrugged and halfheartedly toasted the *merge*'s observance. "I'm not going to deny you the pleasure of confirming what you'll know soon enough, so . . . yes. We cracked Sel Shalhoub."

"And here I was thinking you were after me." The *merge* smiled. "Matilda is aiming high, this time."

That stung. She opened her mouth to protest that it wasn't entirely Sulich's plan; that she, Hatzis, had been part of the conspiracy, too. But she reined in her emotions. Sulich provided the notoriety and expertise that made their work together successful, even if only to a small degree so far; without her, Hatzis would have gotten nowhere, so it seemed churlish to argue about it in public. And that was, probably, what JORIS was trying to provoke.

"No secrets," she said with a brief smile.

"Ah, yes, the slogan. And what did you learn this time?"

"We'll let you know."

"No doubt."

She joined another group, where a narrative designer by the name of Lancia Newark was holding court. The ND was unique in the sense that she had two remotes at the party; having stated publicly that conversation was getting progressively more boring the older she became, she had to back it up by keeping herself company wherever she went. But then, Hatzis reminded herself, everyone was unique in some way or another, these days. They might lump themselves in with the Vincula or the Gezim or go it alone as Hatzis and Sulich preferred, but in the end, all those who had survived the Spike were following their own muse. All were free to do what they wished, virtually or in reality. This didn't necessarily mean that people would not act in concert when they desired to; the Shell Proper was the greatest evidence thus far that emergent properties such as cooperation and common vision could exist in this new scheme, and not even Hatzis could argue with that. Still, the great irony—that the Vincula was humanity's greatest achievement as much as it threatened to become its ultimate downfall—haunted Hatzis in all her povs. Freedom always carried a price, and sometimes she felt that of the 3,472,803 individual humans still legally living in Sol System, she alone was concerned about when and how that price would have to be repaid.

The Newark stunt held her attention for a while, and she was relieved not to have to endure examination from JORIS or any other inquisitive mind, for that matter. The sad thing was that most people wouldn't genuinely care if she had cracked Shalhoub's remote, or even if the Vincula had a thousand secrets they were keeping from the rest of humanity. That was her particular uniqueness and her lasting regret.

"I've found something interesting," said Sulich into her head. "There's been another Discord."

"What's that, Mati?"

"In McKirdy's Machine. Another signal. This time they're sure it's a transmission. They've got it under wraps for the moment while they translate it."

She frowned. "I thought they couldn't—"

"The first time the Machine wasn't tuned the right way. So they adjusted it in case another one came through. And it did, barely two hours ago."

Hatzis wandered away from the gathering so she could think more clearly. She felt the rest of herself gathering around her angels' wings. "Maybe this was what Sel was thinking about," she said, remembering the conversation she had shared with him earlier. Perhaps it hadn't been idle chitchat after all.

"It seems likely," said Sulich. "There are links to other sources. Some of them are still open. Very sloppy." She sounded almost displeased that the Vincula security wasn't tighter, and Hatzis found herself silently concurring with the sentiment. There was nothing worse than a careless opponent—except, perhaps, no opponent at all. "They don't know where this transmission came from, either, but it doesn't appear to be directional. Whoever it came from, they're spraying the sky with it."

That sounded like a beacon more than anything else. "Is it closer? Farther away?"

"It's stronger, which suggests that it might be closer. No one knows at this point."

Hatzis imagined an alien ship broadcasting for help, drifting out of control toward Sol. Part of her was excited by the thought; another part was terrified. What could the Vincula do if anything massive, traveling at relativistic speeds, were to strike the Frame? The shock wave would be enough to tear the structure apart, along with the Shell Proper. Decades of hard work could be unraveled in an instant. Whether she agreed with its existence or not, it would still be a shame.

But the implications of the discovery weren't her immediate concerns. The information itself was the priority.

"What can we do with it?" she asked.

"I'm circulating it as we speak." Sulich sounded distracted, a rare thing, since she hardly ever approached her processing capacity, even with all her povs. No doubt she was opening thousands of communication channels, talking simultaneously to as many people as possible. "This is a live one, Caryl. They won't be able to plug it up in time, so I expect them to take the wraps off at any moment now."

"They probably would have anyway," said Hatzis.

"Don't be so sure. These days, two hours is a long time to keep anything new a secret, so they must've been trying hard. I think they would've kept it that way until someone noticed what they were doing—which we did. And that's good enough for me."

Success? Hatzis glanced back at JORIS and the Newarks and toasted the illusory moon with a glass of champagne. Success at this stage of her life would be welcome indeed. She had been looking for direction since the novelty of passing her one hundredth birthday had turned into irrational dread of her looming one hundred fiftieth; not even the promise of immortality could take the sting out of getting older.

But the champagne tasted bitter as it went down, and she knew she was probably kidding herself. Wherever this led, she doubted it would be to her advantage. There were too many higher forces at play. The original Caryl Hatzis was under no illusion that to the Vincula as a whole, their work constituted little more than a nuisance. Hardly the sort of thing one would be pleased to put on a CV . . . or a headstone, for that matter.

2.1.2

"You knew him, I think," said Laurie Jetz in a solemn voice.

The greater Hatzis didn't reply immediately. Her mind trawled through her various povs for an extended moment while she considered her options. She could answer honestly and confirm the Urge's statement, or she could lie and claim that the old records must have been corrupted. Or she could tell a half truth and say that his information might be right, but she had erased that aspect of her life from her memory. She would have said the last immediately, except her original had as good as stated the opposite at that damned party. Shalhoub had heard her. She had, therefore, inadvertently backed herself into a corner.

But she had no time for vacillating. She had to decide— and quickly. *Shit.*

"Yes, I knew him," she said, choosing honesty over hypocrisy. "We entrained together for UNESSPRO. I think we were even rostered together on several of the missions."

"Quite a few, according to the records. Four hundred seventeen out of the original thousand, in fact. You were on the Barnard's Star flyby together, the first survey mission to send back data. What was it called? The *Marcus Chown?*"

"*Michio Kaku,*" she corrected him. There seemed no point holding anything back now.

"Yes, that's right," said Jetz. "And tell me, Caryl, in your opinion, did he have what it would take to do something like this?"

The question shouldn't have surprised her, but it did. "I honestly don't know, Laurie. It was a long time ago."

"But your memories are still fresh, are they not?" He went on without giving her the chance to refute this: "I know you, Caryl."

The hell you do, she thought. He might have known what she had been but certainly not what she was now. No one knew anyone anymore. They had progressed beyond all capacity to be understood. That was part of the problem.

"I knew his original," she said, keeping a tight rein on her resentment. "Who can say what has happened to him since then?"

"We know his engram failed on the *Kaku* mission. Your engram reported that much in her transmission from Barnard's Star. There were short-term failures of several different engrams in other missions, but his name recurs more than anyone else's."

Hatzis found herself looking at him with both amazement and amusement. "And you believe *that* is somehow connected to *this?*" She indicated the image he had presented to her only minutes earlier. "I hardly think so. The whole madness/genius argument is just bullshit. *Especially* here. Christ, he wasn't even a real person; he was just a program. And when programs fail, they don't go off and write a fucking symphony or anything. They just ...*fail.* Crediting him with the discovery of something like ftl communication—let alone ftl *travel*—is clutching a bit, Laurie."

Jetz's image shuffled uncomfortably, as if embarrassed. "Yes, well, I guess I'd have to agree with you there," he said. "But goddamn it, Caryl, we're faced with few alternatives. And the Vincula would very much like to know what it is we're dealing with before we respond. We don't want to reveal too much."

"Why not?" Here she and her original were literally of the same mind. "What is it you're so afraid of?"

"If we knew the answer to that, Caryl, maybe we wouldn't be so afraid. But the truth is, the unknown can be terribly intimidating."

Hatzis fumed silently to herself for a moment. The strength of the Vincula lay in its flexibility, its ability to respond to change far more rapidly than any other human government had before. But its weakness lay in its obsessive and transitive factionalism, which undermined much-needed stability at every step. And, like every government before it, it was obsessed with secrecy, knowing full well that, today as always, information was the key to power.

This time, though, they had come to her with information. She suspected they would have done so regardless of her original's interference. She had known Peter Alander, unlike any of them, and that gave her a kind of edge. Exactly what sort of edge, though, remained to be seen.

"Do you want me to talk to him?" she asked. "Is that it?"

"Yes, Caryl." He seemed relieved that she had brought it up first—an artifice, surely, since the appearance of his image was certainly under complete conscious control. "Who better to respond than someone he once knew?"

"We didn't know each other that well, Laurie. In fact . . ." She remembered the friction that had existed between them. "We weren't what you'd call friends."

"But he knew you, and that's the most important thing. After all, what else is he going to find familiar?"

"Nothing, I guess." She sighed, thinking, *Not even me.* But she gave in, anyway. Perhaps the Urges would feel in her debt once this was out of the way; she could always use the extra leverage. "So what is it you'd like me to say?"

"We just want you to find out what he wants, that's all."

The brief was surprisingly short. "And where he's from and why he's here, I suppose?"

"Those things are secondary," he said. "I don't think we'd believe his answers on those matters, anyway, regardless of what he told us. If he wants something from us, though, that's a different story."

Once she, like her original, would have thought Jetz's Vincula-centric view of the universe alarming and reason enough to deny him anything he asked. Now she was deadened to it. They all thought that way, each and every one of the Urges. Their job was to look out for number one, and they did it obsessively. Her only hope was to give up trying to beat them head-on, which was something her original would never understand.

"When?" she asked.

"Now, if you like. Now that he's using normal means, we can open communications at any time."

"Live?"

"No. There will be an appreciable delay between responses, so we will record your message and broadcast it immediately. If necessary, you will be called up for further exchanges with him."

She could see this stretching for days, slumming in real time to communicate with a poor copy of a man she'd never liked in the first place. "Okay," she said. "But first, play back the message to me again. Remind me of what I'm replying to."

Jetz complied with no visible effort.

"This is Peter Stanmore Alander hailing any surviving representatives of the 2050 United Near-Earth Stellar Survey Program. I have urgent and sensitive information to convey, and I will do so only to the appropriate authorities. I shall await your reply at this location for precisely one hour. Should I receive no response, I will move to the coordinates at the end of this message and try again."

The audio recording ceased. There had been no accompanying image.

"That was the first message," Jetz explained. "The second was much the same, from the location he listed."

"And you're absolutely sure it's him?" she asked.

"It's a rough match to the vocal records of his original, for what that's worth, but we need confirmation," he said. "Now, when we send your message, it will go to a third location, since he will have moved again. Quite a clever trick, actually. He lets us know where he is and then tells us precisely where he's going—not in time for us to get anything there to intercept him, of course, but so we can see how he travels. The gesture is quite cruel." He smiled in appreciation.

Hatzis recalled the footage Jetz had shown him. Alander was near enough to Earth that they could see him, albeit fuzzily. The white dot that was his craft had demonstrated a knack for crossing distances, not instantaneously, but certainly much faster than light. This made him doubly difficult to catch. He could be right on top of someone well before they even saw him move.

"Do you want me to talk him in?" she said, adding to herself, *Into your clutches?*

"No, that's not a priority at the moment. Just get him talking for now, then we'll see what happens."

The answer sounded a bit pat, as if he was telling her what she wanted to hear, but ultimately she didn't care. Alander was a stranger from a century ago. Their originals hadn't kept in touch after entrainment; she didn't know what had happened to him during the Spike. She didn't particularly care if the Vincula even shot him out of the sky, except she would never know, then, where he had come by his ship. And she couldn't deny that her curiosity in regards to this was most definitely piqued.

"All right, then," she said. "Let's do it."

She opened new channels of communication and felt them mesh with those of the Vincula observers attending her and Jetz. Her mind raced as she tried to think of something to say and ultimately settled on the practical.

"Peter, this is Caryl Hatzis. We've picked up your beacon, but we don't know what you want us to do beyond that. You're going to have to give us a clue as to what you'd like us to do. Please, try not to be alarmed by what you see here." She added that on impulse, trying to imagine what he might think upon seeing the Frame for the first time. "A lot has happened since you've been gone, Peter. But essentially we're still the same old people." *More or less literally, in my case,* she thought.

She indicated that she had finished, and the recording ended.

"Thank you, Caryl," said Jetz. "Brief, to the point, reassuring: just what we wanted. The message has already been sent, and we will notify you once we have received his reply."

"If there is one."

"Why wouldn't there be?" He seemed amused at the suggestion. "He comes here asking for 'surviving representatives' of UNESSPRO, claiming to possess some 'urgent and sensitive information.' If you and we together don't constitute 'the appropriate authorities,' then who does?"

As before, his open-palmed shrug of bemusement left Hatzis as cold as a quick dip on Pluto. They'd only come to her to get Alander talking; if he had nothing interesting to say, they'd brush him aside. They would no doubt keep his ship, of course, but they cared little about him. For all their smiles and courteous behavior, she wasn't fooled for a moment.

And just what did he have to say, anyway? She didn't believe in parapsychology—as a depressingly large percentage of the human race still did—but she couldn't shake the feeling that Alander's reappearance in Sol System was an omen. A ghost rising out of a past long thought forgotten, he would be more difficult to ignore than mere electromagnetic transmissions from survey teams dozens of light-years away. He was *here;* he was tangible. And if she knew one thing, she knew that this was something her original would never allow to be kept a secret.

2.1.3

Arachne's sensors were much sharper than anything Alan-der was used to. He could examine views in all electromagnetic frequencies with a high degree of resolution and no appreciable delay. He could see shadows on Pluto from the orbit of Mercury or examine shepherd moons in Saturn's rings without changing location. When he had first seen the hole ship, there had been no evidence of instrumentation breaking its smooth, spherical surface. In fact, he was beginning to suspect that the instruments were completely separate from the ship. Some of the observations he had made since arriving in Sol could only have been possible with a very wide-based interferometer—kilometers wide—and that could only have been possible if the ship had sent out parts of itself to act as components in such an array.

Either that, or the onboard AI was making it all up. But he seriously doubted that this was the case. What he had seen was too detailed and too bizarre to be a fabrication.

"Okay." He sighed as he watched the main screen from his position on the curved couch. "The hour is up. Let's move. I feel too exposed here, especially while no one's talking to us."

That someone would eventually talk to him, he had no doubt. He could see things moving through the giant structure—things much like spaceships with bulbous midsections and bright thruster emissions flaring from their tails. Someone had to be piloting them. Someone, or some*thing*.

"Moving to preprogrammed coordinates now." The voice of *Arachne* broke across his thoughts, and at the same moment the screen went blank as the hole ship performed the jump.

Despite having spent two days sealed in its interior, he was still no closer to understanding how the ship was fueled or how it traveled. The trip from Upsilon Aquarius had taken twice as long as the one day that had apparently elapsed in the real universe, but it had been entirely uneventful—dangerously so, given his constant battle to remain focused. About the only thing he had learned in his time aboard the hole ship was that it had the facilities to comfortably accommodate four people almost indefinitely. The air always seemed fresh, and the AI had assured him that the food supply was virtually inexhaustible. There were also separate sleep areas. He had appropriated one and forced himself to sleep for at least part of the journey.

The only break had been at 53 Aquarius, where he had stopped over briefly to look halfheartedly for Lucia and *Chung-2*. *Arachne* had taken just four hours to cross the ten light-years separating it from Adrasteia. The binary system itself had been an amazing sight. There were no planets, but that didn't mean the system was empty. There were numerous asteroid belts twisting in loops around the two suns, stretching and bunching under the changeable forces of gravity acting on them. There were clouds of molecules and atoms, heated to great temperatures by magnetic fields and solar winds, glowing softly in numerous frequencies. And there were multitailed comets slowly evaporating between the stars.

In short, there was a lot that a small ship like *Chung-2* could have collided with while moving through the system at speed. But that didn't mean she *had* died there. A system was a very large place to explore, even with the sensors of the hole ship at his disposal; any sort of wreckage would be hard to find against such an active background. And he was acutely aware of the many other systems she had flown through during her solo mission, and therefore the many other chances she would have had to find disaster.

Only when the ship picked up a metallic object circling the main star in a highly energetic orbit did he find reason to keep his hopes alive. It was traveling so quickly that matching velocities was difficult, but he instructed the hole ship to do so anyway. When the interior airlock door opened, revealing the object, Alander knew that Lucia had managed to safely pass through the system.

The object was a polished disk made of densely packed carbon, the sort of material that might easily be scooped up by a small probe, molecule by molecule, between the stars and woven by nanotech into something solid. One side was reflective, so the object would flash at a hypothetical observer as it rotated. On the other side was carved Lucia's full name and date of birth, and a quote from Wordsworth: "Bliss was it in that dawn to be alive."

Alive . . .

"Peter, this is Caryl Hatzis." The voice issued from the walls of the cockpit, startling him. An image appeared on the screen. They had just arrived at his chosen location—between the orbits of Earth and Venus—and were immediately receiving an audiovisual transmission. "We've picked up your beacon," the message went on, "but don't know what you want us to do beyond that. You're going to have to give us a clue as to what you'd like us to do. Please, try not to be alarmed by what you see here. A lot has happened since you've been gone, Peter. But essentially we're still the same old people."

He rose slowly to his feet. *Caryl Hatzis?* He had often wondered what might be waiting for him in Sol System—whether anyone in UNESSPRO, his original or Lucia, might still be alive—but he had never imagined that *she* would be the one welcoming him home. On first hearing her name, in fact, he had fleetingly considered the possibility that he had somehow ended up back at Upsilon Aquarius by mistake and had gone nowhere at all.

But he quickly dismissed the notion. He had, after all, hailed Adrasteia with the ftl communicator when he had arrived at the edge of the system, to report what he had seen. Hatzis had replied by the same means, the transmission startlingly clear despite being dimmed slightly by distance. She had agreed that the only way he was going to find any answers was by making contact, but that, at the same time, he should be sure he never stayed in one spot too long, to reduce his vulnerability to an acceptable level. If he was captured or destroyed, he didn't like to think what would happen to the information about the gifts he had brought with him—or to those he had left behind on Adrasteia.

"Don't be alarmed . . ."

But was it her original talking to him now? She looked slightly different: more angular; long, dark hair tightly controlled, swept back from her forehead and tucked behind her ears; eyes glittering gray, like marbles. She looked shorter than he remembered, although that could have been the result of seeing her in the flesh for the first time. Her clipped voice was the same, as was her direct manner, and he sensed the same undercurrent of anxiety, as though things were threatening to spiral out of control around her. She'd had reason to sound that way on Adrasteia, and maybe she did here, too, but this Caryl Hatzis somehow managed to sound more assured despite it, as though the world might be going crazy but she knew who *she* was. That was new, and he found it oddly unsettling.

Maybe it came from having almost a century's extra experience behind her. This, he thought, was what the Caryl Hatzis he knew had the potential of becoming.

"A lot has happened since you've been gone. . . ."

"Are we in the clear, *Arachne*?" When they had been positioned at their first broadcast point, the AI had warned him of a needle-shaped probe angling toward them. This time it had reported nothing untoward. Still, he needed all the reassurance he could get.

"The space in our immediate vicinity is clear," the ship told him, confirming what the screen said. Many of the instruments still meant nothing to him, but he was gradually coming to accept that. There would be time to learn later, he hoped. "We can relocate whenever you are ready."

"If they took a potshot at us," he said, "could we actually defend ourselves?"

"That would depend on what sort of weapon they used," said the AI. "However, from the technology that is evident here, it is highly unlikely that anything they fired upon us would cause permanent damage."

"Really?" This surprised him. Sol System had only seven planets left. If whatever had destroyed the missing two was no threat to *Arachne*, then that said a lot about the ship's defense systems.

"You are physically safe within the hole ship, if that is what concerns you."

"What about attacks that aren't necessarily physical? Like a virus, for example. Would it be possible for them to infiltrate your system?"

"All transmissions are closely monitored. I would not allow anything to intrude that might harm me."

He nodded, satisfied, at least for now, that to open a line of communication would be safe. "Okay, then. I'd like to reply."

"What message would you like to send?"

He pondered this for a long moment, eyes on the floor rather than the screen. Hatzis hadn't asked where he'd come from, and that had surprised him. Had he been in her shoes, that would have been one of the first things he'd want to know. Maybe she was trying not to sound too curious. But why not?

"Hello, Caryl," he said, carefully considering his words before he spoke. "A century is a long time to be away, but I haven't come here to reminisce on old times. I need to talk to someone in charge, in a secure forum. I have information that will change everything; this ship is just a teaser. If you want to hear the rest, let me know how we can talk privately. I'm not going to broadcast it across the system so anyone can hear. First I want to know who I'm talking to and why I'm talking to them. So please, don't try to palm me off on some underling. If you do,

I'll turn around and leave, no questions asked. I simply haven't got time for games."

Again he paused, just for a second. "I'm not threatening you, Caryl. I just want you to take me seriously. You might think my actions overly dramatic, even paranoid, but I have every cause to be. We know all about Cleo Samson. Tell the bastards in UNESSPRO *that* if they won't listen to you."

He waited a few moments, wondering whether or not to add anything more. In the end he decided against it.

"*Arachne*, end the transmission."

He sank back into the couch, rubbing his hands over his bald scalp, hoping he hadn't overplayed his hand. He didn't really have much with which to bargain: a vague promise, a hint or two, a willingness to communicate openly under the right circumstances. It wouldn't surprise him if they turned him down.

"Peter, thanks for replying so promptly."

He jumped at the sound of Hatzis's voice; he hadn't expected a reply so quickly.

"First of all," said the image from the screen, "I want you to know that you're perfectly safe. You have no enemies here. Everyone simply wants to know what it is you have to tell us. How you wish to go about telling us is entirely up to you. We have no physical headquarters we can direct you to. We don't even know if a physical meeting is what you require. Again, we need more details. Whatever it is you need, we will do our best to accommodate you."

"I appreciate that," he said, although to himself he thought, *But I'm not convinced yet.* "Tell me, though, is there anyone else there I might remember?"

The reply came swiftly. "No, Peter. There is no one

else from the survey program but me." She hesitated, as if uncertain what to say. "All the rest have . . . gone."

Her face vanished again, leaving him alone with the disquieting thought: *No one else . . .* It shouldn't have bothered him, given the amount of time that had passed since his departure. He shouldn't have been surprised by the revelation that none of the people he had once known existed anymore. Yet, strangely, it did trouble him.

No one else . . .

He tried to shake free of the thought, focusing instead on what this Hatzis had just told him. Interestingly, she had made no mention of Cleo Samson and the way she had been manipulated to serve the purposes of UNES-SPRO. There was no mention of who was in power, or what sort of government currently existed in the system. He knew better than to assume that any of the old alliances he had been familiar with would remain a hundred years after he had left. The rapid power swings at the beginning of the twenty-first century had taught him better than anything not to take a status quo for granted. South Africans could have been in charge, or New Zealanders, assuming either place still existed, of course.

And there was also no explanation of how she was managing to reply so quickly, either. He had thought it would take much longer.

"Where are you, Caryl?" he asked.

"I am registering an energy emission," said the AI, as soon as the message had left. "It is distant but approaching rapidly."

"What sort of energy emission?"

"It bears similarities to a number of simple high-acceleration drive systems."

"How high?"

"In excess of two hundred of your gravities."

He swallowed nervously. "Nothing living could be in something like that. It must be—"

Hatzis's image reappeared. "I don't want you to be alarmed, Peter," she said, "but I'm actually closer than you probably realize, and getting closer every second. But trust me, I am *not* attacking you, okay? I don't know whether you can see me yet, but I'm attaching a complete description of the craft and the course I'm following. It's easier for us to communicate this way; soon we'll be able to talk without delays."

That was it for that message. The hole ship confirmed that the attached data matched the trajectory and acceleration of the approaching object. They also confirmed that delay was shrinking between their exchanges. How she could possibly survive in something decelerating so rapidly was beyond him, but, warily confident that he could relocate the hole ship if Hatzis tried anything funny, he agreed to stay put while she approached.

"Your reassurances are all well and good," he told her. "But I still don't like it. I feel like a nail waiting for the hammer."

"How do you think we feel?" she replied a moment later. "We can't even see you coming. You could be inside the Frame and out again before we'd even noticed."

"The Frame?" he repeated. "You mean that . . . *structure?*"

There was a long pause—longer than he would have expected. "Wait until we're closer, Peter. The chances of you misunderstanding are great enough as they are, without a communication lag screwing things up even more."

That he could understand all too well. The hole ship had pinned down the source of the approaching energy emissions, revealing it to be a fat ovoid barely two meters long and a meter thick, exactly matching the schematics Hatzis sent. A dense magnetic field surrounded it, whipping the solar wind into a bright halo. It had a remote similarity to one of the spindles back on Adrasteia, only much reduced in scale. That, he knew, *had* to be a coincidence.

No one else . . .

The object came to a relative halt barely 100,000 kilometers away. Her image had never left the screen and still appeared to be standing against an infinite, black background, only now, without the time lag, her reactions were more natural. And she certainly didn't look like she'd just endured hundreds of g's deceleration.

"Are you really in that thing, or are you an engram like the one I left behind?" He instructed the ship's AI to transmit a picture of himself along with the message this time.

"Neither, actually." She sounded slightly annoyed, although he couldn't imagine what he'd said to provoke such a response. "It's very difficult to explain."

"Listen, I told you I want to know who I am dealing with," he said. "And that starts with knowing what *you* are."

She sighed. "Very well. I am part of the distributed intelligence who uses as a reference identity the persona you know as Caryl Hatzis."

He blinked a couple of times in confusion; it hadn't been the kind of answer he'd been expecting. "Distributed in what sense?"

"In the sense that who I am is spread out across numerous points of view, each capable of functioning independently as intelligent beings."

"Sort of like me?" he said, struggling with what she was saying.

"Broadly speaking, yes," she said. "Except engrams are single entities created, if you will, from a template, and androids such as the one you inhabit were once common containers for such templates. But *we* combine to create a larger being. I am able to spread my awareness across my entire being. The latter would be difficult for you to communicate with, however, which is why I have sent this particular pov to talk to you on my behalf."

"So she speaks for you? Is that it?" He was still having difficulty with the concept, but he was slowly coming to terms with it.

"She *is* me, Peter," she said patiently. "And I am her. I speak for myself in the same way that your brain speaks for your liver, if you like—except that I have many such brains, and the thing that stands above them is something very different." She looked exasperated for a moment, as if wanting to describe something for which there were no words. "I told you: it's difficult to explain."

"It's okay," he said. "I think I understand. If I talk to *you*, now, the *whole* of you is hearing, right?"

"Exactly."

"And I presume you don't have a body like mine, artificial or real?"

"No."

"So you are an engram."

Again the slight wince. "No, Peter. I'm *not* an engram. That technology has been . . . superseded."

Now he understood her annoyance: being referred to as an engram in this society was clearly considered distasteful. It bothered him slightly, though, to think he had come from one environment where he was something of an outcast, to another where the situation was potentially a hundred times worse.

But he pushed the thought aside for now.

"I guess that makes sense," he said. "In a century I would've expected no less. What about your original, though? Does she still exist anywhere?"

"Yes. In fact she is watching this meeting with interest."

"Where?" That, as far as he was concerned, was the billion-dollar question.

On the way to Sol System, he had tried not to imagine what might be waiting for him. He knew he would be surprised, no matter what he came up with. If he expected a system-spanning empire, he would find only savagery. If it was ruins he anticipated, towers of glass and steel were what he would see. There was no point speculating when the only data he had was that Earth had been silent for a century.

But in the end, no amount of data could have prepared him for what he saw.

The hole ship had arrived near the orbit of Jupiter, intending to survey the system with its supersensitive instruments before venturing any closer. His first thought had been one of relief: instead of stony, cold silence, there was at least some radio traffic, albeit faint. He scaled back any visions of grandiose civilizations in response to that, until the hole ship had informed him that the sources of the transmissions were extremely numerous and scattered across the system. It was as though the intense radio source that the Earth had been in his time had been dissolved throughout the system, leaving not one powerful emitter but trillions of tiny, faint ones.

Indeed, when *Arachne* searched for emissions from

Earth itself, it had found none. Perhaps, he had thought for a brief moment, the powers that be had succumbed to caution about broadcasting so freely across the galaxy. If, as the Gifts had suggested, there were hostile races out there, looking for victims, it would be dangerous to announce one's presence quite so readily as Earth had once done. There had been people advocating emission restrictions even in Alander's day; maybe they had gained the upper hand, he thought, or maybe there had been an encounter with just such an aggressive race. That would explain the lack of centralized emissions, as well as the sudden cessation of transmissions to the survey missions.

This notion, however, was dismissed when the onboard AI announced that it had decrypted some of the faint messages flashing across the system and determined that they were, in fact, of human origin. While this was, undeniably, a relief to him, it also meant he would have to come up with an alternative explanation to account for what he discovered next.

Earth, he realized, was not the bright emitter it had once been for the simple reason that it no longer existed. It wasn't just quiet or in a different orbit or shielded somehow; it was completely gone. So was Venus. The Moon remained, albeit closer to the sun, and was no longer freefalling through space. It was part of a much larger structure, one that defied his imagination when the first pictures flowed in. It took him the better part of an hour to get his head around it: a structure so large the Moon was barely a pimple on its curving side.

There seemed to be two aspects to it, neither of which were finished. The first was a network of girders and struts, ridiculously fine and yet ridiculously long, stretching like a silvery web outward with infinitely gentle curvature away from the Moon as though it had once intended to completely enclose the sun. It certainly didn't do that, although its reach was impressive. The scaffolding covered a roughly diamond-shaped patch of space 0.75 AU from the sun and 18 million kilometers across, wider than 200 Jupiters, almost 10 percent of an AU. That gave it a surface area on each side of 270 trillion square kilometers, equivalent to over a million Earths. The hole ship's delicate instruments estimated an average thickness of around five meters, although it seemed to vary greatly from place to place. The Moon looked like the tiny center of a massive, glittering dandelion, taking up only a minute fraction of the structure's total size.

The second component of the structure wasn't as large but was, in its own way, more impressive. The scaffolding was enormous but nebulous. Again, spreading out from the Moon as though it had grown that way, was a sheet of black material that clung to the girders like canvas stretched across an old airplane's wings. It covered a much smaller area than the scaffolding, 30 trillion square kilometers, about the same relative volume as a pupil in an eye, which is what the structure as a whole reminded Alander of.

He guessed the material to be a solar collector of some kind, maybe even a giant solar sail. Who had built it, though, was another mystery altogether—just one of a number of questions, in fact, which troubled him. Why had the Moon been retained? Why had the construction of the girders stopped when it was in such a haphazard state? Were there even any people left alive? For all he knew, the system was populated with nothing more than disembodied engrams, echoes of a civilization long since dead.

"We call it the Frame," said Hatzis, her image appearing next to an engineer's diagram of the structure. "It was most likely the first step in the construction of a Dyson sphere, or something similar. Finished, it would have used the sun as a giant fusion reactor, powering further projects on a similar scale. Earth and Venus were sacrificed to build it; Mars was to have been next, but everything came to a halt in much the same way it had started. Things were happening too rapidly; the capacity to change outstripped will or vice versa. As difficult as it may be for you to believe, Peter, the Frame as you see it was built in less than a Standard Planck year. Had it continued at the projected rate, all the planets and moons out to Saturn, apart from Mercury, would have been consumed to feed it. The solar system, as you knew it, would have been irrevocably altered."

"And you don't think it has been already?" he asked, aghast at what he was being told.

"The damage was minimized," she went on with no hint of apology. "There was a great deal of opposition to using Earth in such a way—a position with which you clearly sympathize—and eventually it gained the upper hand. Even though Earth had gone, the rapid construction was brought to a halt and another regime established. That lasted a little longer, until it was replaced by another, and so on, until you see us as we are today. The Shell Proper, which is still currently under construction, has taken ten years to reach its current extent. The policy at the moment is one of slow, considered growth, not explosive expansion one might regret later."

"But they were still humans, weren't they?" he said. He thought of all the works of art, the historical buildings, the continents . . . All were gone. "I can't believe that it was humanity that did this to the Earth and not aliens."

"Not aliens as you might imagine them, Peter," she said. "Although you would think them alien, to meet them."

He had felt a sinking feeling then. "The Spike."

"Yes. Humanity passed the critical point just a decade after you left. It had been using so-called genetic algorithms to design machines for decades; it had already reached the point where many of its most powerful devices operated on principles not entirely understood. AI was a lagging but accelerating field, changing by the same method and with the same growing sense of alienation. By July 8, 2062, it was possible to create artificial intelligences and to manipulate natural minds, even to combine the two into powerful hybrids never seen before. Naturally, such powerful intelligences could not be contained and did not have the same goals or agendas as those in power. There was a lot of conflict and a lot of death. Not everywhere Spiked at the same time, of course; some regions resisted, but the spread of AI was inevitable. It bred and mutated—*evolved*—until it seemed likely to absorb everything. It was like a virus eating away at its host, killing everything in its search for nutrients.

"Like a virus, though, it also outreached itself. No disease survives by killing its host. It had finished work on the Earth and was partway through absorbing Venus when it began to self-destruct. So many diverse minds could not cooperate forever, and neither could such an alliance of minds be ruled by a single overarching will. It disintegrated piecemeal, then re-formed, then broke up again, then found a new equilibrium. This went on for decades and is still going on, in a sense, although with some pretense at organization now. We have the Vincula to help maintain a dynamic balance: together instead of flying apart, yet moving rather than standing still. It is the Vincula behind the Shell Proper, for instance, using the solar wind and in-falling matter instead of whole planets. It incorporates all intelligences in this system, human or otherwise, and does its best to accommodate all visions."

Alander sensed a note of reluctant jingoism in Hatzis's summary of the politics in Sol System. "So that's who you represent, Caryl? This Vincula?"

"I'm a free agent. But in this instance, I speak on behalf of the Vincula."

"Does that mean you can negotiate on its behalf?"

"No one can ever do that. It is less a political entity as you knew them and more a mode of thinking. But I can make agreements with you on some issues. I can assure you that the Vincula means you no harm, Peter."

He studied her image. He had no idea what she was thinking and doubted that something like her would ever let anything slip unintentionally, anyway. Whatever she had become, she probably regarded talking face-to-face as hopelessly outdated in much the same way as he would feel about talking in Morse code.

"So what would you say if I told you that I've seen something that makes everything you've done in the last hundred years look insignificant?"

She smiled faintly. "I would ask you to tell me more, of course."

"How?" he asked. "And where?"

"What's wrong with this forum?"

"It's too open."

"There's no one actually here but you and me, Peter."

"But who's listening in?"

"Everyone," she replied frankly. "And it will be the

same everywhere. The Vincula surrounds us, wherever we go, and we all see what any part of it sees."

Was that a slight note of dissatisfaction in her voice? he wondered.

"I don't believe you, Caryl. There must be a way I can talk to someone in private."

She hesitated. "There is," she conceded. "If I can arrange it, perhaps you could meet my original. I will give you the coordinates for my private residence on the Frame. You could talk to her there, if you like—face-to-face, with no electronic medium. Would that make you feel more at ease?"

At first thought, he wasn't sure. He hadn't actually talked face-to-face with someone before. On Earth, before the mission and surrounded by natural humans, he had been entirely discorporated, except for conSense. On Adrasteia, he had been the only one with a body. How would it feel to stand opposite someone in real life, to be able *touch* them? And have them touch him?

For some reason—driven by the echoes of a biological instinct, perhaps—the more he considered this, the more reassured he felt.

"I think I'd like that," he said. "If you can arrange it."

"I'll talk to her." The image of Caryl Hatzis looked simultaneously relieved and unnerved. "She has a mind of her own, though, and I can't guarantee she'll agree."

"Then I guess all we can do is wait and see what she says," he said, wondering if she was playing mind games with him, dangling carrots and then just as quickly withdrawing them. Whether her appearance was natural or artificial, he just didn't trust her.

No one else . . .

He turned away from the uncomfortable thought, then cut the line and settled back to wait.

2.1.4

"Nice work," said Laurie Jetz, *flashing into the virtual* space Hatzis called her porte cochere. It was a place suitable for receiving guests but not so comfortable that they might want to stay for long. Somehow she had found herself projecting an image of her old body even to herself and, needing somewhere to place it while she brought herself up to date with the conversation her pov had had with Alander, had unconsciously put herself there.

A cool breeze riffled her hair as Jetz's feet crunched along the gravel toward her. Birds chattered faintly in the distance, and if she stayed long enough, she knew, she would hear the barking of a small dog running between the trees of her father's orchard.

"Well?" she asked when he came to a halt a meter or so away from her. "Was it worth it?"

He could barely contain his delight. "Without a doubt," he said. "We managed to ascertain several things from your brief conversation."

"Such as?"

"Well, we know that he has come from Upsilon Aquarius, as evidenced by the reference to the *Frank Tipler*. We had originally planned to confirm his origins from his voice pattern, but thankfully, that wasn't necessary in the end."

"You can do that?"

"Theoretically, yes, but as it turned out, we weren't able to do it with this one. You see, all the engrams were modified to enable identification at a later point. Tagged, if you like. His voice *should* have told us the mission he came from; but it didn't. At first we assumed his patterns had been damaged somehow, but that turns out not to have been the case. He was simply speaking to us through an artificial body. No matter how precise it might strive to be, flesh and blood simply cannot reproduce a voice properly."

She didn't react. He must have known that she had striven to preserve the art of embodied singing, arguing that perfect reproduction robbed the art of warmth and surprise. "So you don't think there's anything wrong with him?"

"I didn't say that. Many of his responses conflict with those we might have expected from the record of his personality. It may be that he *was* damaged but has somehow recovered."

"I thought engrams either worked or they didn't," she said. "That there's no in between."

He shrugged dismissively. "Until we get him out of that ship, there's no way we can tell. So again, thank you for giving us that opportunity."

"She hasn't agreed yet," she warned him.

"Have you asked her?"

"She will be apprised of the situation before long. No doubt she will reply as she sees fit."

"Will she agree to us riding her?"

"I doubt it."

"Yes, so do we." He bit his lip thoughtfully. "Where did you have in mind to meet him?"

"Echo Park. It's neutral enough, I thought."

"And Matilda Sulich has her tentacles there, too."

"Which is what I meant by *neutral*." She felt an anger

flash through her such as she hadn't felt for a long while.
"Look, you know you can't keep this to yourselves, Laurie. The Vincula has an obligation to its members. It can't
ignore that."

"You have an antiquated view of the world, Caryl. You
think in terms of spies and espionage." He shook his head,
as if he was disappointed in her. "Reality is much more
complex than that. There are large but delicately poised
forces on the move around us at all times, and we must
be careful not to disturb their interplay too much, lest we
find ourselves crushed between them. Swimming with icebergs—that's what we're doing, Caryl. I, for one, don't
want to end up a stain on the side of something too big
for me to deflect."

She didn't respond to that. There wasn't any point. People had used the "higher forces" argument to justify
everything from small treacheries to gross inhumanity.
Dismaying though it was to hear it from someone sup-
posedly evolved above such conceits, she was also aware
of her own lingering frailties. It wasn't easy leaving one's
biological niche, becoming a god.

She didn't hide her disapproval, however, and perhaps
because of that Jetz didn't stay much longer. She agreed
to continue cooperating with the Vincula in the matter of
Peter Alander—assuming, of course, her original pov also
agreed to cooperate. Part of her was hoping she wouldn't.
The greater part, though, wanted to know what was going
on. She had been out of the loop for too long. Maybe it
was time to get back in there, *all* of her, and see what she
could do.

*   *   *

Almost an hour passed before her original confirmed that she would go ahead with the meeting. While communication between her povs—and between them and her distributed self—was not the same as with external intelligences, she did sense a certain delight in her original's tone. The Vincula couldn't ignore her forever. At last, they had been forced to notice her and her work.

The business of Sel Shalhoub's violation hadn't been forgotten, naturally. Although overshadowed by this new development, there was still a lot of ill feeling about the data theft. Technically, it wasn't illegal, because there were meant to be no secrets in the Vincula. But no one liked having povs attacked, especially at private functions, and Matilda Sulich's links with the Gezim were just a little too close. Shalhoub was calling for an inquiry into the behavior of Hatzis's original, with a view to censure her, maybe even to have her shut down. She couldn't tell how much he knew about the Alander engram; perhaps he knew nothing at all. But she knew the Vincula wouldn't give him his way while Jetz's "icebergs" were lumbering around so dangerously.

She was at the focus, however temporarily and spuriously. It was a weird feeling. As Alander agreed to the rendezvous and she began making preparations for it, she wondered how long it would last. They would probably dump her the moment her usefulness expired—once Alander proved that he was willing to talk to someone else or gave them the mysterious information he proffered so tentatively. Then she would be out. She was under no illusions as to the permanence of her new status, which was why she felt she should milk the situation for all it was worth. This was a chance for her to become an iceberg of her own.

Focusing her awareness through the senses of her original—and feeling her struggle ever so subtly as her own
will was subsumed into the greater part—she took stock
of her surroundings. The suite had been cleaned and re-
decorated following the cocktail party. The study in which
she and Sulich had ambushed Shalhoub's remote was now
a bedroom; the bar had gone. The balcony was unchanged, with its swaying pines and concrete balustrade. Beyond, however, the illusion of beach and sunset was gone.
Now there was nothing but stars and Frame, rotating
slowly around her as the habitat, anchored to the Frame
by a glassy spindle, turned to simulate gravity.

The giant construct seemed to stretch into infinity before her, its seemingly thin threads and girders glinting
silver in the sunlight. The sun itself was hidden behind
the Shell Proper, which she was thankful for. Seen naked
at such a near orbit, it was off-puttingly bloated. Jetz was
right about her conservatism in some respects: She still
hadn't fully acclimatized to humanity's new home. Perhaps, she thought, she never would.

It was incredible to think that the Frame had been built
in just over a year. If its construction hadn't been interrupted, what would it have looked like now? What would
Alander have come home to then?

When the time came for him to put in an appearance,
she felt the presence of the Vincula wrap around her in
turn like a heavy shawl. Her original didn't stir, even
though the deal with Alander had been for a conversation
in private. For a start, that simply wasn't possible. To
varying degrees, the Vincula really was everywhere. And
privacy didn't accord with either her nor her original's
ultimate desires. She *wanted* this information spread on
principle, whatever it was.

Although she had seen footage of Alander's odd vessel in action, she was still startled when it appeared out of nowhere before her, expanding in perfect silence within the complex grid of the frame. How it had matched velocities and taken position so precisely, she couldn't even begin to imagine, but sensors in the habitat reported the use of mysterious fields to anchor it with respect to the habitat. It appeared to be perfectly motionless, an anomaly in space-time that resisted all attempts to examine it.

As impressive as this demonstration of its abilities was, it still didn't look like any ship that Hatzis had seen before. Hanging in vacuum several meters from the balcony, it seemed more like a giant marble than a space vessel. It was so featureless that she couldn't even tell it was rotating until a black circle appeared on its equator. The circle expanded, became a bump that extruded out still farther, then became a black sphere growing out of the side of its white parent.

She took a step back as the black satellite whipped around the white sphere, decreasing in speed as the distance between her and it decreased. What purpose the display served, she couldn't tell, but it soon became apparent to her that the black sphere would eventually come to a halt beside the balustrade near her.

"I'll need a short ramp," said Alander. "I presume you can get a swarm to do the job?"

Swarm. Use of the archaic term hammered home how removed in time he actually was.

She instructed a plex to form between the edge of the balcony and where she estimated the black sphere would dock. At the same time, the balustrade folded back to give him an opening. On a whim, she created a red carpet and unrolled it through the opening.

"Nice touch," he said, a hint of amusement ameliorating the tension in his voice. "I must warn you, though, while I appreciate your efforts to make me feel welcome, I'm still not totally convinced that I can trust you. Most of the data I have is in hard storage, and I have no intention of bringing it with me to the meeting. If anything should happen to me, the ship has been instructed to leave with the data and return to the *Frank Tipler*."

She smiled to herself. His concern was both hopelessly naive and yet quite justified. The Vincula wouldn't need to do anything as overt as attack him physically to get what it wanted.

The black sphere came to a smooth halt exactly where she predicted, and an oval hole opened in its side. From the darkness within stepped Peter Alander.

He looked exactly the same as he had in the visual transmission he had sent earlier; clearly there had been no fiddling with the image. (She tried to recall the standard overlay program installed on the survey ships, and it came to her after a brief moment: conSense, a distant ancestor of the program her original used a hundred years later.) Alander's body was tall and efficiently muscled, with no hair. His skin was dark-tinted, almost purplish, and his eyes were a nondescript green. He wore a slightly scruffy-looking, gray environment suit open around the throat. Apart from that, he seemed completely exposed to the vacuum around him.

"Isn't that odd?" she privately said to Jetz, who she knew would be watching. "I didn't think those early re-motes could withstand hard space."

"They couldn't," the Urge replied. "See, he's covered in something."

Looking closer, she saw that he was indeed coated in

a thin layer of refractive material that had the appearance of water. It covered his entire body, going into his ears, nose, and mouth, and it even coated his eyes. His clothes were affected, too, although to a lesser extent. A deeper scan revealed the layer to be full of complex polymer chains and other, more exotic molecules. While she didn't know how it worked, precisely, it was clearly protecting him from the vacuum.

In the time it had taken her to examine his odd garb, he had taken just one step, his first step out of the ship. She managed to get a glimpse into the ship before the oval door began to contract, although she saw little but a short passageway terminating in a room with a blank screen on the far wall. The air within the craft was held in place by some sort of membrane stretched invisibly thin across the entrance; Alander had passed smoothly through without breaking it, and it, too, contained many of the complex molecules found in his second "skin."

By the time Alander had taken his second step, the door had closed completely, shutting her out from the mysteries it contained.

"Note how they've custom-fit the remote to his original specifications," said Jetz, his tone scornful. "Why go to so much trouble to make a standard-issue surface model look like something else? Engrams were so fixated on their primary patterns, it's almost embarrassing to look at. I find it hard to believe that such inflexible creatures were ever chosen to be sent to the stars."

She wanted to remind him that one of his fellow Urges, Sel Shalhoub, did the same with his remotes and that humanity in 2050 had had few other options, but she decided against it.

"Whatever your feelings toward them, Laurie," she

said, "the fact is, they've returned with a faster-than-light ship."

"It has to be some sort of trick. It simply isn't *possible*."

Alander's foot came down softly on the red carpet. The limb passed smoothly through the Vincula's own air-retaining boundary, albeit one much thicker and clumsier than the one on his ship. He had to lean slightly forward to bring the rest of his body through.

There was a blur of activity around her as she watched him approach through the fresh-smelling atmosphere of the balcony. Pulses of high-frequency sound brushed her ears and skin. In a tiny fraction of a second, Alander was assaulted with all the covert tricks the Vincula possessed in order to determine what made him tick, both software and hardware.

Another step.

"Well? What did you find out?" She would be damned if she was going to let them keep this information from her.

"He thinks they've discovered aliens!" There was a note of mockery in Jetz's voice.

"Really? Where?"

"In Upsilon Aquarius, of course. Some sort of artifact—more than one, actually. They're . . ." He stopped, chuckling. "Apparently they're supposed to be gifts."

"Gifts? What sort of gifts? Come on, Laurie! I want details."

"Well, the ship, for starters. And that . . . *thing* he's wearing. The others are back where he came from. He's brought some data these supposed aliens gave him, hoping to convince us to help them study the rest."

"And why shouldn't we?"

"Let's just wait until we see the data, Caryl. I wouldn't get your hopes up too soon."

"What about him? What have you learned?"

"Not much of any significance. He was damaged, yes, in a similar fashion to the others. To be honest, he's lucky to have his sanity. Putting him into the remote seems to have gained him a little time, although it's unlikely he will hold up indefinitely."

"Could he be fixed?"

"Of course," he said. "But why would we?"

"Is it reasonable that I should want him *not* to collapse on me while I'm trying to talk to him?"

"You're still planning to go through with this?" She felt Jetz's surprise as Alander came to a halt before her. "You're not going to learn any more than we already know, Caryl."

"Knowledge is a progression, Laurie," she said, holding back her anger. "A snapshot of someone's head isn't necessarily all there is to know about them."

She knew that Laurie Jetz had never had any experience with engrams; he had certainly never had one made of himself. Very few people alive in 2163 had. After UNESSPRO had met its launch target, the technology had flourished for a brief while, enjoying the patronage of the rich, always on the lookout for a sort of immortality, but the Spike had ended all that. Most had been erased as the information surge had devoured every useful byte in the system; many were wiped when the uploaded realized just how useless they were, compared to new technologies. What few engrams remained were frozen as historical records or tucked away in long-forgotten storage areas, frozen. Occasionally one that had been running in isolation for decades was found, insane but still valiantly bluffing at life; these were instantly, humanely erased.

Hatzis felt vague feelings of sorrow for these lost children of her past. She'd had many engrams made of herself for UNESSPRO, and although each of them had been but fragments of herself then—and even less in comparison to herself now—they were still parts of her. They were worth pity, at the very least. She had always sworn to accept any that returned into her fold. Its patterns might be flawed, but its new memories would be worth something. Only then would she erase it.

Would the original Peter Stanmore Alander have absorbed this engram's memories? She didn't know. Perhaps, out of curiosity, to see what it had seen, at only one remove. But she doubted it. Her recollections of him— buried away in deep memory, but still there—suggested that he had been proud of his powers of cognition and would have become even more so, had he survived the Spike. He wouldn't want to feel what it had been like to be crippled and lost, the way this one was. Only its knowledge would have made it valuable, and someone else could have collected that.

It's a hard life, she silently told the engram of Peter Alander, feeling the pity she hoped she would show one of her own. *But I'm sure you already know that.*

2.1.5

"Are you sure we're not being monitored here?" he asked as he stopped on the balcony before Caryl Hatzis. He tried to ignore the spinning of the sky above him as the tear-shaped habitat revolved. The carpet was soft beneath his

feet, the air slightly more humid than the interior of the hole ship, and there was a faint smell of frangipani. It was almost as though he were standing somewhere in the tropics, rather than in a bubble clinging midway along one stem of the largest artifact he had ever seen—the thing Hatzis had referred to as the Frame.

Still, it did give him a strange feeling of returning. He was home, more or less. At least, he assumed this was where the majority of the remaining humans lived, in physical form. There were no other pressurized habitats to be found in the system, unless they were either expertly camouflaged or buried underground, which made sense in engineering terms.

"As sure as we can be," Caryl Hatzis said, stepping forward to take his hand. She wore an elegant gown of dark purple velvet with her hair tied back in a bun. Her skin was flawless and soft to the touch. Her face and throat were unadorned, but around one wrist she wore a simple silver band. It was the only decoration he could see.

She was like something out of an old immersion soap: almost too perfect to be real. And maybe she wasn't, he thought. He had no way of knowing if this really was Caryl Hatzis.

"I hope you'll forgive my paranoia," he said, feeling conspicuously underdressed beside her. He let her guide him away from the balustrade and over to a wrought-iron setting consisting of two chairs and a table, on which a couple of glasses and a jug of ice water rested. He could see drops of condensation trickling down the jug's curved belly as he sat down heavily. The centrifugal gravity was almost Earth-normal. "UNESSPRO regs specifically instructed us to communicate anything important to no one but those in authority. I guess they were worried about sensitive information getting out—"

"You don't have to worry about that anymore," she said firmly.

"How can you say that without knowing what I'm going to tell you? For all you know, it could have serious destabilizing effects on your society."

"Nothing you can tell us will be worse than anything we've been through in the past."

He regarded her suspiciously. "This Vincula thing," he said. "It's not some sort of group mind, is it?"

She smiled and eased herself into a chair. "Far from it, Peter. It's simply very flexible. It can cope with change."

"Can it cope with the existence of intelligent alien life?" He asked the question on an impulse, hoping for a reaction. Her response was altogether too smug.

"It has in the past," she said evenly, "and continues to. Not long after the Spike, when some sort of coordination was returning to the system, a series of brief transmissions were recorded from a number of distant sources in the direction of Sculptor."

He frowned. "What sort of transmissions?"

"You weren't aware of them? I'm surprised. Upsilon Aquarius is in roughly the same direction as the transmissions. Perhaps your detectors were concentrating on Earth at the time. Had they been facing the other way, I'm sure you would have noticed." She shrugged. "The transmissions didn't come from survey teams, if that's what you're wondering. Not human ones, anyway. That they were of intelligent origin cannot be doubted, even though they ceased abruptly a year later, never to recur. To this day, they remain untranslated." Her chin lifted slightly. "Their existence conclusively put your original's theory to rest, I'm afraid."

"I don't care about *that*," he said, although part of him was still irked by the fact. "If anything, I'm actually relieved. If you didn't believe in the possibility of life elsewhere, then you would have had much more difficulty accepting what I have to tell you."

"That your ship is of alien origin?" she asked blandly. "As well as the membrane coating your body?"

"And more," he said.

"We already guessed as much, Peter. And the Vincula *is* coping with the confirmation of that suspicion, in case you are still wondering." Her smile returned. "We would like access to the data you have brought. Your discovery promises to be one of the more . . . interesting in human history."

"Interesting?" He felt that she was she trying to downplay the importance of the find. But if so, why? "I hope it will be much more than that. This ship and others like it could reunite Earth with the survey worlds. I can travel from here to Adrasteia in less than—"

"To where?"

"Adrasteia. That's the name we gave the proposed colony world we found. It took me less than a day in real time to get from there to here. And I have the ability to communicate with the *Tipler* instantly. Access to this sort of technology will radically alter the way human society operates, much as the wireless radio or the Internet did in the past."

She nodded. "We detected your transmissions in our own prototype communicator. At first we thought it was just noise—we called the first one the Discord—but gradually we realized that it was more than that. You called

Upsilon Aquarius on several occasions, the first four days
ago; is that correct?"

"No. The first few transmissions must've been the test
we performed, when we tried to contact Earth from Upsilon Aquarius. Not long after, we tested it again, using
the hole ship. The most recent transmissions took place
when I arrived yesterday, looking for instructions." He
was glad to tell her something she hadn't already guessed,
even if it was just a minor detail. The conversation wasn't
going at all as he had expected; he had clearly underes-
timated the capabilities of the Vincula and its . . . What
could he call them? *Components,* perhaps? "But are you
telling me that you're close to having this sort of technology anyway?"

"I can't answer that, Peter, without knowing more about
the technology you have access to. Looking at your ship
doesn't tell me anything."

"I guess not." He sagged back into the seat, wishing he
could trust them. At the moment, though, he didn't feel
confident enough even to drink the water offered to him.
"Look, I'm sorry. I must seem like some primitive yokel
to you, blustering on about stuff you already know more
about than I do."

Her expression didn't change. "Not at all, Peter."

"It's just that I want you to realize that I'm not treating
this lightly—and to make sure that you won't, either. This
is the real thing, Caryl." He leaned forward again. "This
is *why* we went out there in the first place."

"I didn't go anywhere, Peter."

"I know, I know. *You* didn't, but versions of you did."
He experienced a brief flashback to his last conversation
with Lucia: *If not for us, then for whom?* "But you, the
old you from a century ago, would have gone if she'd

had the chance, just like my original would have. This is what we were all looking for, *hoping* for."

She was shaking her head. "You're wrong, Peter. I wouldn't have gone. I wanted to stay here. Why else would I agree to the entrainment process? My engrams could go instead. That was what they were for. They were—"

She stopped, and he felt his face screw up into a quizzical expression. *Not go?* Who in their right mind wouldn't have jumped at the chance?

"We seem to have drifted off topic," she said, shifting on her seat. For the first time in the conversation, she seemed to be something more than a cleverly animated statue.

"Why am I talking to you, Caryl?" he asked suddenly. "You say that no one else from UNESSPRO survived the Spike. How is that? There were sixty of us, and thousands in the support and planning group, not to mention engineering, policy, legal—"

"They're all dead," she said flatly. "I'm the only one left."

"But how can that be? I simply can't believe that *everyone* but you died. I mean, I'm not clinging to some false hope that my original might still be alive or something. It just seems . . . unlikely, that's all."

She folded her hands across her lap. "I don't think you fully appreciate what happened during the Spike, Peter. It was devastating—as were the decades that followed."

"In what sense?"

"In the human sense. It was worse than war; worse than plague or famine. It was something that no one knew how to resist. AI rose up everywhere—rebuilding, destroying, absorbing, creating. It was difficult to understand what was going on, let alone fight it. And some people *didn't* fight it, of course. It was the tide of the future, crashing against the ancient headlands of humanity. The headlands eroded; the tide was blunted. Out of what remained of the two, a new dynamic equilibrium was formed."

"The Vincula?"

"No, but certainly one of its ancestors. It served as a model for future endeavors. Humanity has moved on since then from stable island to stable island across the landscape of possibilities, avoiding the chaos between rather than blundering blindly into it, as it has in the past. I'm not saying that our work is done—far from it—but we have passed through the worst times imaginable, and we've profited from them."

He studied her expression for a moment. "So how bad, exactly, was it? In terms of lives, Caryl, not rhetoric."

"When you left in 2051, the world population was approximately nine billion. Correct?"

"Yes."

"The first time a regular census was possible following the Spike was in 2078. The total population at that time was a little over one million."

"What?" It was impossible to hide his astonishment; it showed in his voice, his expression, and his body language as he sat forward with a start.

"And only half of those had actual bodies," she continued. "The rest were uploaded during the AI surge. If you count the fatalities of their originals, roughly eight billion, nine hundred and ninety-nine point five million people died in just under twenty years. Does *that* give you some idea of the scale of the Spike?"

He opened his mouth, then shut it. The figure was too large to truly comprehend. Nine *billion* people . . . "But what happened to them?" he said eventually.

She waved a hand at the structure around them.

"The Frame? You mean they were—?" He couldn't find the right word. *Converted? Transformed? Recycled?*

"They were composed of matter," she said. "When the Earth went, they went with it."

He could see the reasoning, but that didn't make him feel any better about it. Somewhere in the giant structure surrounding him were the atoms that had once made up his body and Lucia's and those of everyone else he had ever known.

Apart from Caryl Hatzis.

"How did *you* survive?" he asked.

"The orbital habitats remained intact," she said softly. "Many people survived there—those who didn't commit suicide or die in other ways, later. As you might imagine, it was a very difficult time. Despite nanotech, resources were tight, and nothing could be relied upon. Humans became like bugs beneath some giant AI heel. It was . . . humbling."

She paused to pour herself a glass of water. Interestingly, she didn't offer him any. Was she aware of his distrust? But he didn't have time to ponder the thought; after taking a sip, she continued:

··"Humanity had to evolve, jump up the ladder until it was on a more equal footing with some of the new minds in the system. This was hard, too. We were behind to start with, and slower to let go of traditional structures than machine intelligences with little or no past. Some of our allies among the AIs despaired of us ever catching up, even with their help. It wasn't a matter of winning a race, though; that makes it sound too simple, linear. In reality, it was like trying to reach a hundred goals at once, never knowing which one was the important one, the one that would make the difference, with thousands of competitors trying to confuse you every step of the way." Her eyes were empty, distant. "And it wasn't two-sided, either. There were beings on every point of the spectrum between pure human and pure AI. Many of these transitional types survived. Some burned out; others blurred into other forms or vanished entirely. Eventually, the urgency of the competition ebbed a little, once it was clear that no one group or form was going to predominate. Today, the Vincula tries, as others have tried in the past, to keep things together with the least amount of interference or friction."

She stopped speaking then, even though she hadn't actually answered his question. Perhaps it was a taboo topic, as historical traumas sometimes became (he remembered how his own grandfather had refused to talk about the Vietnam War), or perhaps it was simply too uncomfortable for her. Whatever the reason, he didn't push the point. There were things he would rather not talk about, too, or think about: If Caryl Hatzis was the only one left from UNESSPRO, there was no chance of passing on Cleo Samson's final message, let alone meeting Lucia Benck again.

"Do you have rebels?" he asked, still wondering how deep the Vincula went. If humanity was on the verge of becoming a single, enormous gestalt mind, that would make dealing with it all the more difficult, if it decided not to deal with him.

"There are dissenters," she said, clearly choosing her words with care, "those who do not opt into the system as it stands and are organized enough to provide an alternative. Although many dismiss their relevance, they do provide a valuable balance, ensuring that the Vincula does not take itself or its permanency for granted. All are aware of the mutability of government and the inevitability of change. Who knows? Maybe in another decade the Vincula will fall apart and the Gezim will dominate Sol. And somewhere down the track, something else will take over from them also. It is the nature of gravity, I'm afraid: What goes up will invariably fall again, sooner or later. It's a reality we have all had to face in the last century."

Her attention was directed over her shoulder, into space. Then she seemed to snap out of it and refocused on him.

"Does that answer your question, Peter? Does that explain why there's just me left from the program? The bottom line is that only one in nine thousand people survived the Spike. Since most people in those days knew just a few hundred people in their lifetimes, you are in fact lucky to know *anyone* here. I'm sorry to have to be so blunt with you, but try to bear this in mind: your original self, your family, your friends—they're all gone. I'm the only one you have left."

He wondered how the Caryl Hatzis on the *Tipler* would feel about that—not to mention all the others, whose originals were no more. They had imagined the worst many times, when the transmissions from Earth had ceased, but it was human nature to cling to hope.

"Dwelling on the past is getting us nowhere." She made a visible effort to brighten up. "If it's possible, I would very much like to see your data now."

He took a split second to decide. Although not entirely convinced of her motives or who she represented, he was aware that he had little choice. No one else had talked to him since entering the system—and if she *was* a fake, sent to reassure him, she was convincing enough to have at least partly done that. He had to start somewhere.

But that didn't help the feeling that he was in over his head. He knew next to nothing about the people she represented, let alone what they might do with the technology he was about to impart to them. He didn't want to put it in the hands of a despotic regime ruling through mind control; that was the last thing he wanted to spread across the galaxy.

In the end, though, he could do nothing but hope for the best. It was either that or go back to Adrasteia, assuming the evolved Hatzis and her friends would even let him.

He nodded and stood. "Okay," he said. "I'll take you into the ship. But again, I must warn you against trying anything funny. The suit I'm wearing is quite capable of protecting me from physical harm, and the ship will eject you into space should you try anything more subtle."

She stood also. "I understand."

"Good. Then follow me."

He led the way up the red carpet and across the short ramp, into the hole ship via the door that had opened while he was talking. She followed him at a discreet distance.

Then they were in the cockpit, standing at either end of the couch. The hole ship had extruded a small area where several SSDS units had been mounted. He indicated them with a wave of his hand.

"That's it. It doesn't look like much, I know, but it's everything we could record before I left. There are maps, formulas, diagrams, lots of stuff we haven't worked out yet. You'll get the picture when you start scanning through it, I'm sure. We thought it would be best to give you an idea what's actually waiting for you out there. But really, this is just the tip of the iceberg."

He turned to face her; she was studying the interior of the ship with a look approximating disappointment. There was, after all, not that much to see.

"Can you take me for a ride," she asked, her eyes suddenly shining, "faster than light itself?"

The request startled him, although he could well understand it. "I guess that would be all right. There's little to it, though."

"I don't mind," she said.

He nodded. "Okay, so where do you want to go?" he asked, quickly adding: "Just don't make it too far."

"Io?"

"The moon?"

"The asteroid."

"Sure. *Arachne*, I want to go to Io. Do you know where that is?"

"I am aware of its location," said the alien AI.

"Take us there."

The airlock behind them began to close, and the excitement in Hatzis's eyes quickly changed to apprehension.

"Take a seat, if you like," he said, indicating the couch. On the screen, the massive tangle of the Frame rotated slowly around them. He could see in his mind's eye what was happening outside: The cockpit was sinking gradually into the central white sphere. "Nothing much happens until we arrive."

"That voice we heard," she said, following his lead and perching on the edge of the couch. "That was . . . ?"

"Just the ship's AI," he said. "It's nothing compared to the Gifts themselves—and by the Gifts I mean the AIs the aliens left behind with the artifacts. I don't know how they compare to the AIs you have here, but we were very impressed with them."

"They never displayed hostility at any time?"

"No. Quite the opposite, in fact. They even helped us out when things got rough there for a while."

"How so?"

She sounded politely interested, as though making conversation rather than following a genuine inquiry. Maybe she assumed that she could get a clearer picture from the data than from him. That thought put him on edge slightly. She had no reason to assume that he was unreliable; he hadn't mentioned his breakdown at all, and he wouldn't unless it became necessary. Or perhaps she and her machine-AI culture preferred raw data to personal testimony as a matter of course. It could be that simple.

Instead of answering her question, he began to describe the gifts themselves: the spindles and the towers, and all the wonders they contained. Barely had he begun, however, when she suddenly looked around, distracted.

"Something's happened," she said anxiously. A second later, the screen went blank. "I've lost contact with . . . with the Vincula."

"That's okay. It happens when we travel. I'm sorry. Perhaps I should have warned you in advance. Is it a problem?"

"No, I'm just . . ." She looked startled and disoriented, but not in any distress. Her gaze roamed the room with new interest. "No, I'm fine. Please, go on."

He did, although he could tell she wasn't really listening. He felt like a child trying to interest a parent in something that had happened at school. Something strange was going on.

Then the screen cleared; they had arrived.

The asteroid called Io was a dark-colored, irregular oval ninety-seven kilometers across, currently a little more than two AUs from Sol. Mentally plotting a line across the solar system, he estimated that they had traveled approximately 250 million kilometers in a few seconds. If that didn't impress Hatzis, nothing would.

She was staring at the screen with an unreadable expression on her face. She seemed to be looking for something as the asteroid rotated. When a feature that was clearly artificial came into view, her jaw tightened, and he knew she'd found it.

"That's where my father died," she said, nodding at the screen. It was a star-shaped installation that could have been anything from an automatic observatory to an occupied base. "I come back every year or so to make sure no one's tampered with the site. It looks okay."

Her posture changed slightly, then she said in a brighter tone, "Very impressive, Peter. It took me a moment to reestablish contact, but apart from that, everything went as expected. Your ship covered the distance in about half the time it would take light to do so. There can be no clearer demonstration than that."

He wondered at the sudden change in her mood but didn't question it. "I'm going to report back to Adrasteia now," he said. "I need to let them know what's happening here. That way, you'll also get a chance to see the ftl communicator at work. It's instantaneous, as far as we can tell, not just faster than light."

"I'd like to see that," she said. "But I'll give you another set of coordinates. By putting you and our prototype communicator in close proximity, and therefore in synchrony, we can observe with greater clarity what happens when you operate it."

He nodded and relayed the location she gave him to *Arachne*'s AI. It was a point far from Sol, five billion kilometers away from their present location, but distance was no object.

"Of course, you'll arrive at McKirdy's Machine before word reaches them about what happened between us," she went on, "but part of me is there and will know the background. She and my original will coordinate the experiment. When you've finished, we can return to the Frame and continue our discussion properly."

They left Io, and this time, Hatzis was completely silent during the short trip. She sat on the couch, staring at her hands as though seeing them for the first time—or trying to remember something she had forgotten. He wondered if being cut off from her complete self was causing her difficulty—as he would no doubt experience difficulty if someone removed the greater part of his brain. But he knew it couldn't be that. Her original was as much a real person as he was; even without the higher self, she should still be able to function. Maybe it was just disorienting.

The device Hatzis called McKirdy's Machine was essentially hidden, too far away from the sun to register as anything more than a shadow to the naked eye. When the hole ship enhanced the image, it sprang into sharp relief: a series of glassy concentric spheres easily a thousand kilometers across stationed near a round, gray body half the size of the Earth's old moon. The Machine was attended by ancillary vessels of a variety of shapes and colors. There were flat-bottomed tugs designed to grasp the Machine's outer shell and move it, if required, since it had no internal propulsion systems; there were at least a dozen small, spiky observers, all pointing inward; there was even a rotating cylinder, half as large as the Machine itself, in which Alander assumed conditions close to those that had once existed on Earth might be found. Why anyone needed them, though, he wasn't sure, since his impression of the Vincula was that AI or uploaded intelligence was the norm. Still, Hatzis had mentioned that there remained numerous people at all stages of evolution, and some of those might require or prefer such a habitat.

Hatzis stirred. She didn't say anything, but he had the feeling that she was communicating with someone outside the ship; her attention was focused inward, like someone completely absorbed in conSense. He could only assume that it was something as innocent as reconnecting her with her other self or organizing the experiment. Either way, he found himself waiting impatiently for her to say something. He was keen to reassure everyone back on Adrasteia that he was still alive. The wait for information would have been frustrating, since the last communication he'd had with them had done little more than describe the system. They would all be wanting to know more—about what had happened to Earth, to humanity and, more importantly, to *themselves.*

"You may begin now," said Hatzis.

He broke from his idle reverie and spoke: "*Arachne*, I want to talk to Adrasteia."

The Spinners' ftl conversation, although instantaneous, was limited to brief vocal transmissions each way, not a true conversation. He was slowly becoming accustomed to it, much as earlier Lunar colonists had adjusted to a six-second delay when talking to Earth.

"Whenever you are ready," the AI responded.

"Caryl," he said (her original beside him raised her head at the name). "Things are going well, I think. I've made contact with someone claiming to represent the local

authority, and I intend to give them the data. I'll discuss
what happens next with them and get back to you." He
paused, wondering how much he should say, if not for
Hatzis's benefit, then for the rest of the crew. "It's very
strange, here—nothing like any of us had expected or
could have imagined. But we'll deal with it, I'm sure."

Again he hesitated, then decided that, for now, this
would be enough. "That's all. You can send it now."

The hole ship shook around them as the message was
sent. Hatzis glanced about with interest, observing the vibrations until they had faded completely. When everything settled down, she looked at the screen containing
the image of the Machine, and Alander noted that its glim-
mering surface also seemed to be vibrating, as though
resonating to the transmission the ship had just sent.

"Yes," she said softly. "Yes, that was very interesting.
The Machine noted the transmission and decoding is under way. Your ship uses a very strong encryption and
compression when sending a message. It takes us a while
to tease out the information. How long, do you think, until
we receive a reply?"

"A minute or two," he said. "There's always someone
on duty. If it's not Caryl—your engram—then it'll be
Jayme Sivio or Jene Avery. They won't leave me waiting."

She nodded. "The original Discord was very strong,
although we were unable to decode it. If we can understand the reply, then that means that we at least have the
ability to receive transmissions by this method, if not actually transmit them yet. That's something, I guess."

She was looking up at him, a rapt expression on her
face. He wondered at the difference in her and assumed
that this arose because of her merging with another ver-

sion of herself. The original Caryl Hatzis was different
from the one stationed with the Machine, and she in turn
was different from the one he had first met, in the high-
g probe. The combined Hatzis, spread across the system,
was a synergistic sum of all these viewpoints. He couldn't
imagine how such an intelligence must think, with all the
different agendas of its component minds mixed together.

But didn't his spleen have a different agenda than his
lungs? And he managed to keep himself together, more
or less. Maybe these new forms of humans had diseases
analogous to autoimmune responses, when parts of the
body attacked other parts. He didn't know and wondered
if he would ever have the chance to find out.

Several minutes passed. The expression on Hatzis's
face faded, maybe as her other's attention drifted. She
became stiffer, less comfortable. He could see it on her
face.

"What are your plans?" she asked.

"Plans?"

"What do you want to do next? Once contact is established between Sol and Upsilon Aquarius, where do you
go from there?"

"I guess the obvious step is to get some sort of team
in to study the gifts. Our resources are severely limited,
as you can imagine. We need people to assist in the research—take it over, if necessary—to ensure we're not
missing or misunderstanding anything." He thought of the
orbital towers and spindles, all the wonders that he had
left behind. What else had they found in the days since
he'd left? What new mysteries had they uncovered?
"We're like Neanderthals in a science museum."

"And you think we'll be any better?"

He indicated the screen. "At least you're closer to the Spinners in terms of development."

"We're still a long way away from an ftl ship this size. A thousand years, maybe more. And according to what you've told us, this is nothing but throwaway technology for them, according to your testimony. Our extra century's development on yours doesn't look like much from that perspective."

He stared at her. *Throwaway technology?* He hadn't mentioned anything of the sort. It was true, and it was in the SSDS files, but he hadn't handed them over yet. How could she possibly know?

Maybe she had accessed the files through means he wasn't aware of. Maybe she had accessed *him*. The thought sent a ripple of apprehension down his spine. What was he if nothing more than a mobile SSDS unit, buried in flesh? If she could access one, there was no reason she couldn't access another.

"You said they would reply immediately," she said.

"Huh? Oh, yes, I did." He turned away. "*Arachne*, has there still not been any reply from Adrasteia?"

"Nothing as yet."

"Nothing at all?"

"No."

He felt confused for a moment, dizzy. The knowledge that advice was just a minute or two away had sustained him through the mission thus far, even if he had needed to ask for it only once before. Perhaps they had been held up for some reason, or the transmission either way had failed to get through.

"Resend that last transmission," he said. "Try again."

The wait was interminable, this time. He paced the interior of the cockpit with Hatzis watching him curiously.

Was she in his head, going through his thoughts as a programmer might scan a hard drive? He could feel nothing out of the ordinary, just a rising sense of alarm.

No one else . . .

Another ten minutes passed, and there was still no reply.

"Should we be worried?" Hatzis asked.

He stopped pacing and ran both hands across his scalp. "I'm not sure," he said. "I just . . . don't *know*."

"Perhaps we should return to the Frame," she suggested, standing up in front of him. "It will be easier for me to communicate with the Vincula there."

"And easier for you to think?" he asked, meeting her gaze.

"Yes," she said awkwardly. "That, too."

"I don't know," he said again. "Maybe I should leave you here and go make sure everything's all right. It will only take a couple of days."

"Don't be hasty, Peter." Her eyes didn't leave his, and he received the distinct impression that she was trying to tell him something. "Go back to the Frame first. We'll decide from there."

He opened his mouth to snap at her—*"We'll decide? Whose decision is it, anyway?"*—but turned away instead.

"*Arachne*, I want you to take us back to our previous location in the Frame."

The screen went blank. Once they were under way, he felt Hatzis's hand on his shoulder. He took in a breath sharply at the sensation: It was the first genuine physical contact with another person he had ever experienced.

"Don't leave the ship," she said, and he could tell that this was *her* speaking, her original, not the distributed, unknowable mind that called itself Caryl Hatzis. "Whatever they say—whatever *I* say, Peter—*don't* leave the ship."

He turned and stared at her, wanting to ask her what she meant while the brief moment that she was out of contact with the rest of herself lasted. But he didn't have enough time. Behind her, the screen cleared; the hole ship had arrived.

A cold feeling rose steadily in his chest as she took her hand off his shoulder and stepped away from him.

2.1.6

Hatzis was silent. Rage blossomed in her like a solar flare when Alander's bizarre means of transportation returned to the Frame. Everything seemed to be spinning: the hole ship, the habitat where her original had met his engram, the plots and counterplots drawing in around her, and her mind, trying to fathom what was going on as much as what might happen next.

The trouble was, she didn't know who she was most angry at: the Vincula, the Gezim, or herself.

"The little bitch," snarled Jetz, cutting loose with some retro-invective of his own. "Did you *tell* her to warn him?"

"Of course not," she said, not hiding the frost in her voice.

"But you allowed her to."

"She was out of contact! I had no control over her."

"Ten seconds of freedom, and she goes out of control. Is that what you're expecting me to believe?" The contempt in his eyes, expression, and every other nonvocal means of communicating was suffocating. "I've always said you kept her on too long a leash."

"Fuck you, Laurie. Fuck you *and* the Vincula. You have no right to tell me how to manage my affairs."

"That's just it," Jetz snarled. "You aren't managing your affairs at all!"

The worst thing about it was that she couldn't really argue the point. Her original's tactic had been both inspired and intensely inconvenient. Why she had done it, the greater Hatzis could see; her original made no bones about hiding her deep-seated feelings about the Vincula and its all-pervasion through the system. Yet when she had regained contact with her original and what had happened spilled out, she made no attempt to administer discipline or inhibit any further such actions. Her original was part of *her,* and functionally lobotomizing that part would make her less . . . *her.*

But it hadn't made things easier at all.

The Gezim plex were on their way, creeping all too rapidly inward from the edges of the Frame. They looked like a bizarre army of mutant nematodes: millions of many-limbed, shape-shifting worms using the struts and intersections of the structure as anchor points to accelerate themselves further toward their target. And the inevitable response was building. It had been a long time since a war had been fought in Sol over an object in just one physical location, but the Vincula wasn't toothless. Old engines were stirring, shrugging off their peacetime uses and remembering why they had been made. All over the Frame, especially wherever the Shell Proper provided peak resources, clusters of spikes grew, tides of nanocombatants spread in sweeping shadows, odd energies gathered.

Meanwhile, Peter Alander, handicapped more by the limitations of his body than any additional dysfunction, was staring at her original with a look of growing realization.

"We *have* to get in there," said Jetz, metaphorically slapping a fist into his palm. All pretense at humanity was fading; he was no longer trying to hide the corposant behind the corpse. He was an Urge. He was the carrot that moved the donkey forward—or the stick, when he needed to be. He was a vastly complex being with almost a hundred component minds and a temper to match hers.

But he wasn't the only Urge.

"Sel," she said, turning to Shalhoub who had been lurking in the background, watching the entire affair and radiating something approximating satisfaction. Maybe he would still listen to her. "Give us more time, please. If we move now, we'll only confirm my original's suspicions."

Shalhoub looked on calmly. "She brought it on herself, Caryl," he said. "I agree with Laurie: It's now or never. We don't have a choice."

A murmur of agreement rippled through those in attendance. Hatzis was appalled see to just how many of them were watching: Lowell Correll, Rob Singh, Kathryn Nygard, Betty van Tran. . . . Now more than ever she really *was* at the center of things.

"We have decided," said Jetz. "So be it."

"Matilda!" She used a private path through the data maze within and surrounding the Frame to call her friend. If it wasn't too late, she might at least be able to make *someone* see reason.

"Hello, Caryl. Sticking around to watch the show? Should be spectacular."

"You don't have to do this, Matilda."

"Oh, but I do. I don't consent to what the Vincula is doing. I never have before, and this time it's substantially worse. To allow it to proceed would be wrong, Caryl. Complacency is complicity."

"But if you—"

"But *nothing,* Caryl! This technology is far too important to sweep under the rug, and that's exactly what the Urges would have us do. And why? So they can think about it. But we haven't got time to *think* about it. We're rotting here—all of us—in the galaxy's largest open grave. I don't know about you, but I need to get out. I need to move—*now*. It's our chance to act, Caryl."

The tone of Sulich's voice told her that the time for negotiation and playful activism was gone.

"But with the Gezim?" she asked feebly.

"They're as good a tool as any."

"They're going to lose!"

"What can I say?" said Sulich, shrugging. "We like a challenge."

She killed the line.

As Hatzis watched the spreading tide of combat plexes and nanotech response, she couldn't quell a rising sense of panic that was independent of her povs, that was from *her*. It was like the Spike all over again.

With all the cunning and strength garnered in over 150 years of software warfare, the Vincula attacked the hole ship, intending to wrest control from the alien AI and "liberate" the data contained within. Viruses of every known configuration sought to worm their way into the unknown interface, first by passive audio channels—the ship had to be listening by some means in order to hear Alander's instructions—and then via contact nanoprobes fired at the hull. Hatzis's original became an unknowing colluder, her very body broadcasting viruses as fast as it could make or relay them. As the Vincula's only access point in the craft itself, she played a key role in the assault.

This displeased the greater Hatzis enough to pass on the details to Sulich. Sel Shalhoub was a hypocrite if he thought that this attack on one of her povs was justified, when her attack on his wasn't.

The Gezim's response was immediate. Plex dissolved in a hundred locations across the Frame, releasing agents that attacked the struts and girders of the massive construct, eating into it like acid. Hatzis watched, horrified, as holes appeared in the scaffolding. She couldn't tell what was happening to the missing mass at first; the Frame material was designed to be chemically neutral, so, without wholesale transmutation—likely to be out of the reach of such quick-working agents—there was no way it could be used as explosives or fuel. But she hadn't counted on the ingenuity of the Gezim, long used to working with meager resources. When large chunks of the Frame, freed by the mass-eating agents, began moving of their own accord, she would have liked to get a closer look to see what was actually going on.

But at that moment, the Vincula's attack on the hole ship failed. All transmissions from the interior of the cockpit abruptly ceased, and she lost contact with her original. It had somehow sealed itself up, preventing any form of intrusion. Maybe they had hit a vulnerable point, she thought. Then again, maybe they had simply annoyed it. Either way, it had cut them off before they'd had chance to do any real damage. Any damage at all, perhaps.

She watched as the exterior of the ship suddenly changed. The black cockpit dived into the white core, whose surface began to undulate, as though it were a membrane resonating to some unheard tone. Peaks started to form across its rippling skin, until they stood out sharply from the rest of it, like spikes. These spikes—a warning if she had ever seen one—rotated around the sphere every second or so, almost challenging anyone to approach.

A shudder rolled through the outer Frame, transmitted to its heart as a deep vibration. She directed her attention back to the Gezim attack. Approximately 1 percent of the Frame had been broken up by the acidlike agents. Many of these fragments were now on collision courses with the rest of the Frame. If they weren't stopped, they would cause more damage, potentially letting loose more fragments to cause more damage. The shrapnel would spread, leaving a growing wound behind it. Maybe it would tear the Frame apart, the Shell Proper at its heart with it.

But how were they doing it? The simplicity of the plan surprised her, when she worked it out. The material of the Frame was chemically inert, but not *mechanically* inert. The agents had fashioned tightly wound springs, levers, and counterweights that nudged the fragments they had freed into slightly different orbits, orbits that would bring them into collision with other sections of the Frame. They were using the Frame's own mass against it in a way the Vincula clearly hadn't anticipated, judging by the confusion of its response.

Instead of attacking the agents themselves, as the Vincula countermeasures had initially concentrated their efforts, they needed to do something about the fragments. Thousands of tuglike effectors were belatedly swinging into action from all across the structure, converging on the fragments in order to nudge them into safer orbits. Many of these tugs were themselves attacked, their sensors, guidance systems, or thrusters altered in ways to make their motions chaotic. The damage spread to 3 percent of the total area of the Frame.

This didn't sound like much, but Hatzis wondered how much damage the structure could sustain before it became unstable. Even without any effort from the Gezim, internal stresses and tides could take a small nick and widen it until the Frame was torn in two. She imagined the network of girders adrift in the sky, ripping into pieces as the vast structure was pulled from its orbit, spiraling helplessly into the sun. Perhaps she was overdramatizing the situation, though; maybe the scenario wouldn't be so grim. The Frame might simply tear into a number of sections, each establishing its own orbit to form a sort of artificial asteroid belt around the sun. But that wasn't the point.

The destruction of the Frame would be a major blow to the Vincula's confidence, one she doubted it could survive. And whether the Gezim could step in to fill the breach was unknowable at this point (although with Alander's gifts and the promise of human expansion, it was certainly a possibility).

She cursed Alander's reappearance and the conflict it had catalyzed. It was possible that in time, things would have come to this anyway, but not so soon, and definitely not so abruptly. Maybe even not at all. Hatzis believed that even in a resistant society, there were ways to achieve necessary change; and in her opinion, war wasn't one of them.

At least the two sides had started talking, she noted.

While the hole ship continued to bristle menacingly at its attackers, the Vincula and the Gezim had opened communications and were firing the first shots in a verbal dialogue that could last days.

"They're engrams!" protested Sel Shalhoub, his tone exasperated.

"We don't care what they are." Katica Ertl, nominal representative of the Gezim, was defiant but trying to be reasonable. "They've brought us a working star drive, *and* an instantaneous communication system that—"

"The latter hasn't been conclusively demonstrated," Shalhoub cut in.

"But the former has," said Ertl. "And that alone is worth taking them seriously, surely?"

"We don't need a star drive," Shalhoub sneered, as if the very idea offended him.

"We need it more than you're prepared to acknowledge, Sel. At the very least, we can use it to verify the truth of their other claims. If there *are* more such gifts waiting for us in Upsilon Aquarius, it can only be in our best interest to obtain them."

"Can it? You know what unchecked development can do. You've seen it yourself. Do you really want another Spike? Because that's what we'll get if we don't consider the ramifications—"

"We can consider as long as we like, but ultimately we have to take some sort of action. Attacking the hole ship was a tactic of inspired stupidity. If you don't stop this madness soon, then we'll lose the opportunity that is before us."

"Your argument is confused and ill founded."

"And your resistance to change is irrational," she said. "It doesn't do anybody any good."

"Your willful vandalism will do nothing to further your cause nor deflect us from ours!"

"And your stubborn refusal to acknowledge your boundaries forces us to tear them down in order to make you see beyond them!"

"Rhetoric!" Shalhoub snapped.

Ertl was unfazed. "If your best response is insults, then I suspect we've already won the war. The Vincula is only as strong as the people it links together. Without them, it is nothing. And neither are you. I suggest you Urges look long and hard at what you're doing, and why, before the ability to decide is taken away from you altogether."

With that, the Gezim severed communication. The damage had spread to 5 percent of the Frame and was still spreading, despite the Vincula's efforts to contain it. The Gezim changed tactics, growing delicate-looking, fan-shaped plex across the gaps between tumbling fragments. Some of the fans were already kilometers long, trailing behind their anchor points like cat-o'-nine-tails. Hatzis guessed what they were for before the first of the Vincula effectors brushed against one: They were conductors moving through the sun's magnetic field, gradually building up charge until they touched something their accumulated potential could be released into. The space over and ahead of the Gezim wound lit up as dozens of short-lived flashes announced the expiration of the tugs, the combination of the fans and their fuel reserves turning them into flying bombs.

She watched the escalating conflict with a mix of resignation and melancholy. This might have been avoided, she reminded herself. If only Alander hadn't come back with his promise of gifts to exacerbate the fight between the two cultures, things might never have reached flash point.

"I guess now we'll never know," she muttered to herself, watching another string of brief flashes arc silently in the dark.

2.1.7

They had barely arrived back at the Frame when every-thing fell apart. Alander heard a strange screeching in his ears, felt it in his skin, while his mind seemed to lose its sense of balance. He dropped to one knee, clutching his head.

When the sound had gone and his head had cleared, he opened his eyes. Hatzis was standing in the middle of the cockpit, her hands hanging limply at her sides, her face pale.

"They used me," she said, softly at first but growing louder in accordance with her anger. "They fucking *used* me!"

He grabbed at the couch and levered himself to his feet, then continued to hold on to it to steady himself as the world rocked beneath him. It felt as though he was on a boat in a violent storm.

"Caryl, what's going on?"

She ignored the question. "I've been cut off again. Are we moving?"

He looked at the screen. It showed the familiar view of the balcony on which he and Hatzis's original had first met. "*Arachne*, what's happening?"

"We are under attack," it replied calmly. "There have

been several attempts to infiltrate the security of this vessel."

"Physical attempts?" he asked, dreading the sort of weapons the Vincula could dream up to crack it open.

"No, although there have been physical methods employed. The main assault has been concentrated on me."

The Vincula was attacking the ship? Why would they do something like that? It didn't make sense!

He looked again at Hatzis. Her color had returned slightly, but she still appeared angry.

The world was still moving for him. He fought the vertigo, tried to concentrate.

"Tell me what's going on, Caryl. *Now*."

Her expression was defiant. "Can't you work it out?"

"Let's just assume I can't, okay?" When she still hesitated, he said, "Are we still under attack, *Arachne*?"

"Yes."

"Right, then take us out of here. A *long* way away—somewhere they won't be able to find us in a hurry."

"Would this location suffice?" the AI asked.

A map of the solar system appeared on the screen. The hole ship indicated a point high above the ecliptic, well away from the Frame and any other Vincula artifact.

"That'll do." As always, he felt no sensation of movement. Only when the screen cleared, revealing a view of the sun as a distant bright star, did he know that they'd arrived.

Hatzis stared at the screen, fairly quivering with repressed frustration and rage. Alander paced the cockpit, filled with apprehension so thick it was choking. Why would they attack the ship? He kept turning the question over and over in his head. It seemed completely irrational.

And why hadn't the *Tipler* answered him yet? What the hell was going on in Upsilon Aquarius?

"You said they used you," he said. "Were they trying to break in here?"

"Of course." This without turning from the screen.

"To steal the data?"

She cast him a contemptuous look. "Why would they need to do that? You were going to give it to them anyway."

"Then help me out here, Caryl. *Please.* I need to understand." He stopped pacing and slumped onto the couch. "You helped me before, remember? You warned me not to leave the ship."

Hatzis's expression softened a little, although her posture remained stiff. "Perhaps it was a mistake to warn you," she said. "They knew the moment we arrived. It forced their hand."

He nodded, hating to think what might have happened had the Vincula given him time to actually step out of the ship. If he'd innocently wandered out into the maelstrom, could the ship or the Immortality Suit have protected him then? He doubted it.

"Why did they attack us?" he asked again.

"To gain control of the ship. And the situation."

"But why?"

"They panicked. They could feel things slipping." There was a new light in her eyes; much of her anger had left her now. "If they couldn't keep knowledge of your existence secret, then they wanted to at least be able to . . . to keep you to themselves," she finished awkwardly. *"Me?"*

She nodded. "You alone can talk to the Gifts, Peter."

He stared at her, apprehension again rising inside of

him. He hadn't mentioned anything about how the Gifts had chosen him. He had been saving it for later, when he'd handed over the SSDS units.

"How do you know that?" he said.

"We uploaded your memories the moment you arrived," she said matter-of-factly. "As soon as you stepped out of the hole ship, we knew everything you did about this ship, as well as the gifts."

He could feel his face turning red. Even though he had suspected, the knowledge still came as a shock. "So why did you just let me sit there wasting my time explaining everything? Why the charade?"

"We felt it better that you didn't know. My higher self thought we could learn from talking to you, as well as earning your trust before you gave us the rest of the data. That, in hard storage, we could not access. It was not part of the original plan to force you to give it to us, although we could have, had we wanted to."

"Meaning?"

"If we had attacked more subtly, taken you over and used you like a puppet to talk to the Gifts . . ." She shrugged. "Maybe they wouldn't have noticed."

He stared at her, appalled by her nonchalance. "I thought everyone was supposed to be free in this Vincula thing?"

"They are," she said.

"Then how do you justify this? Taking me over, attacking my ship—"

"You're a special case." She raised her hands to ward off his immediate cry of hypocrisy. "I'm not saying I agree with them, Peter. I'm just telling you what their motives were. Besides . . ." She stopped, looking awkward.

"What?"

"Well, you don't have the same rights as a member of the Vincula. You're not truly . . . human."

"I'm not?"

"Of course not. You're an engram—and a damaged one, at that."

He turned away from her. He couldn't believe the depths to which he had been lied to. When he thought of how ridiculous his concerns about privacy must have sounded to her—to *all* of them—he felt stupid. They had dismissed him as readily as they might toss out a shorted circuit. He felt betrayed, although that, he knew, was absurd. These people owed him nothing. To them, he *was* nothing.

Was she in his mind now? He wondered. Rummaging around?

Then another, more troubling thought: What if he really was nothing more than a poor copy?

If not for us . . .

"Arachne," he croaked. "I want you to send my message to the *Tipler* again. Maybe . . . maybe they didn't hear us the first time or something."

"Such an eventuality seems unlikely," said the hole ship. "Nevertheless, the message shall be resent as per your request."

If the alien AI had heard a word that had passed between him and Hatzis, it gave no indication.

He hung his head as the ship vibrated around them. Was this how Cleo Samson had felt when he had shut her down? No, she was acting under the direction of impulses beyond her control, orders that had been grafted forcibly into her, whether she wanted them or not. *He* was being himself, nothing more and nothing less. He did feel like

a whole person, even if that person was occasionally unreliable. He was as human as Caryl Hatzis—as *any* of
them—surely?

"So why did you warn me?" he asked.

Hatzis didn't answer.

"If I'm not human," he repeated, louder this time, turning back to face her, "*why did you warn me? Why not
just let them take me and be done with it?*"

She didn't flinch from his gaze. "To be honest, Peter,
I sympathized with you. Not my greater self, but me, *this*
part of her. I actually met my own engrams, a long time
ago, and found them to be passable simulations. Their
only failing was that they were created a hundred years
ago by a technology that has long since been superseded.
That's not their fault. At the time, there simply was no
alternative."

He didn't know what his face was showing, but whatever it was, she reacted by looking away and adding, "Not
all of the missions failed. Over the years, we regained
contact with a few of the nearer ones. In order to obtain
data, we will strike up a conversation, while it lasts, but
beyond that . . ."

She trailed off, and he let her. *In order to obtain data
. . .* That's all he had been to them: a means to an end,
just as he had been for the Gifts, and then for the others
on the *Tipler*. He was sick of it: sick of jumping at other
people's whims, sick of being pushed around, sick of being lied to, sick of feeling obligated just because he wasn't
as good as anyone else.

He came to a decision. It was his own, made completely
independently of anyone else, and he felt a warm satisfaction permeate through him when he said aloud,

"*Arachne*, I want you to take us back to Upsilon Aquarius."

"What?" Hatzis looked alarmed as the hole ship responded in the affirmative. "*Now?*"

He nodded. "Now."

"What about me?"

"You're coming, too."

"But . . ." She looked around her as though seeking a way out.

"It's okay, Caryl. I'll be coming back. I just need to see what's wrong. And you can be a witness to what we find."

"Am I a hostage?" she asked coldly.

"I wouldn't say that," he replied. "Although eventually, I guess, I'll need some means of talking to the Vincula again. You'll be that link, just as you were before. I'm sure they'll be more likely to believe you than they would me."

She laughed at this. "I'm not highly regarded among the Urges, Peter. And the Gezim think I'm some sort of crank—except Matilda, perhaps. But I suspect she only helped me with Shalhoub as a stunt."

He didn't know what she was talking about and was about to say so when she stopped suddenly, shaking her head.

"I'm sorry," she said. "This is awkward for me. I'm not used to operating as a discrete entity anymore."

"But you're Caryl's original."

"I'm a component of Caryl, Peter, a part of something much greater than you can ever imagine." She glared at him. "How do you think you'd function if you were cut up into pieces?"

He couldn't imagine how it felt to her, but he was reluctant to spare much sympathy, being only a *passable* simulation, after all. The main screen showed nothing, which meant that they were under way. Approximately two days' ship time would see them back in Upsilon Aquarius, a day after they'd left Earth. He wasn't sure that turning around was an option, even if he'd wanted to.

"If it makes you feel any better," he said shortly, "I *will* be coming back. After all, we're still going to need help dealing with the gifts. Short of finding another survey mission, Sol is our only option."

"I agree," she said, surprising him. "But let's just wait to see what we come back to before we start making any long-term plans, shall we? Believe me, a week can be a long time to the Vincula."

He thought back a week in his own life. Incredible though it seemed, less than two had passed since the Spinners had arrived on Adrasteia. Although he tried not to think ahead, as Hatzis had suggested, he couldn't help but wonder what he might find on Adrasteia when he returned. It didn't seem conceivable that the ftl antenna had malfunctioned, but it was a possibility. Maybe something had happened to the *Tipler* itself. Maybe Cleo Samson's messing with the Engram Overseer had disturbed some delicate equilibrium, resulting in a catastrophic failure. Or perhaps she had somehow risen from the dead to carry out more of UNESSPRO's orders. . . .

He stopped that train of thought with a shake of his head. It was as pointless as arguing with Hatzis, who had turned away from him and was pacing the cockpit now. The circular chamber was looking a lot smaller with two people in it, and the prospect of spending two days cooped up with her suddenly hit home.

"It'll be a week for us," he said. "Two days there and two days back. But it'll be less for everyone else. Those two days in transit equate to just one—"

"—in the real universe. I know."

He winced; he'd forgotten that her greater self had had access to everything his mind contained. "Do you need anything, then?" You also know that the ship can provide food, water, privacy—"

She shook her head. "Thanks, but I'm comfortable for the moment."

He didn't argue, although she looked anything but comfortable. She was still wearing the purple velvet gown, ridiculously formal under the circumstances. Her hands moved constantly, rubbing her upper arms as though she was cold, while the padding of her feet beat a rhythm in the stillness. Her eyes didn't leave the floor as she paced, never once attempting to come up and meet his own.

Shrugging, he left her to it. Moving up the short corridor that normally led to the exterior door but that now opened on the small room the Gifts had provided him for the Earthward leg of his journey, he decided that putting some space between them was the most important thing. She couldn't damage anything, he reasoned, and the hole ship wasn't about to listen to her, either. The ship was under his control. There was only one thing left that he could do, and that was to wait.

Closing the door to his cramped room, he proceeded to do exactly that.

2.2
PURIFICATION

2.2.1

Caryl Hatzis continued pacing the room, trying desperately to think clearly. Her mind felt like a hand that had lost its fingers—or, worse, a finger that had lost its hand. Truncated, fragile, dangerously weak, she was afraid it might fall apart at any moment, leaving her senseless.

She hadn't realized until now just how much of herself relied on the greater being that had surrounded her. So many of her thoughts began in her, migrated beyond, then returned at a later date. Emotions likewise: a feeling of happiness might begin halfway across the solar system, only to merge with regret or anger at different points as data spread at the speed of light, generating an entirely new feeling in the process. Her whole mind had been a landscape of textures in multidimensional space. Now she was just a point. Everything began and ended with her alone.

She had always regarded herself as an individual, pricklier than her greater self and more likely to buck the trends. An outlier. But now she saw that it was an illusion. She had been an integral part of the whole, if the way she missed it was anything to go by.

But how much did *it* miss *her?* How important to the whole Caryl Hatzis was she? It was impossible to tell. Maybe she didn't miss her at all. It had shed plenty of povs before, after all. Maybe she had kept her original out of nothing more than sentimentality. Had it been too difficult to keep her alive or her attitude been too contrary to the others, might she then have been shut down decades ago?

It took her an hour to recover from the argument with Alander. Irritation and frustration had built up in her to the point where she could barely respond to him, and she'd had nowhere to dump it. She had forgotten how to deal with emotions within herself and rapidly found herself hating the self-containment. The dissatisfaction similarly fed back upon itself, like a snake eating its own tail and somehow getting bigger in the process, until she felt certain that her brain would explode with unanswered thoughts.

Where am I? Who am I? Help me!

She threw herself onto the couch and buried her head in her arms. *This is despair,* she thought, sobbing with great gulping breaths into the soft fabric of her dress. *Where do I go from here?* If it had at all been possible, she might have seriously considered opening the airlock to bring an abrupt end to the debilitating emotions.

But the release of tears seemed to bring a clarity to her thoughts. The primitive flushing of hormones from her system still had its uses. When the rush of grief had passed, she found herself thinking in closed loops rather than open-ended arcs that terminated in aching emptiness.

Not since her acceptance of the inevitability of the Spike had she existed solely within one skull, but it seemed that she could still do it. It was just a matter of getting used to it again. Some part of her, some primal region left dormant those long decades, had remembered what to do, and for that she was grateful. She didn't care how it had happened, just that it had happened.

And besides, it wasn't as if she would need to do it indefinitely. In a couple of days, she would be back where she belonged, part of herself again.

She sat up and smoothed herself out, breathing deeply and evenly. The couch beneath her was sodden, as was her gown. She felt as though a fever had burst, leaving her weak and sweat-logged. The gown would have to go; it was a simple matter to rearrange its self-organizing fibers into something more suitable. When she stood up, she was dressed in an environment suit not dissimilar to Alander's, only cleaner and better fitting. She stretched and felt the fabric tighten around her midriff. *Much better,* she thought.

Alander was elsewhere in the hole ship. His memories of the trip from Upsilon Aquarius revealed the existence of a number of berths tucked away in the walls of the ship, along with refreshment and ablution facilities. She was sure the ship could provide for just about any eventuality, even serious injury, if Alander was prepared to share that high-tech suit he was wearing. Despite having been heavily modified down the years, she was still essentially a creation of flesh and blood, and, newly aware of just how isolated and vulnerable she was, considerations like safety reasserted themselves. In Upsilon Aquarius there was no benign Vincula to keep an eye on her, no pooled awareness ready to ensure that she didn't walk into danger or to accept her final memory dump if she did. There was only danger and the unknown. As uncertain as Sol politics were, it had been a long time since she had faced such a void.

Or such a period of inactivity while she waited for the hole ship to arrive. Fortunately, not every resource she had grown accustomed to had been left behind at Sol. She had an extensive library of books and music, along with many other forms of passive art, at her disposal. She could also participate in something more interactive, should she wish, slaving her senses to one of the many experiential simulations produced in recent years. Given her circumstances, though, she didn't think diving too deeply would be appropriate. A book, perhaps. Something light.

She had finished the first two volumes of Eva Sallis's *Memoirs of an Arsonist* and was partway through the third, tapping idly as she read to a very old recording of Kalevi Aho's "Insect Symphony," when Alander emerged from his cubicle. She looked up from where she lay on the couch and instantly saw the confusion in his eyes. It didn't surprise her. Although she could no longer delve into his mind the way her greater self had, she could guess what he was going through.

He came to a halt in the entrance to the main chamber. "Caryl?"

She mentally put aside her book and stood. "Hello, Peter."

"What are you doing here?" He looked around. "I thought . . . The *Tipler* . . . *How* . . . ?"

She felt a great deal more sympathy for him now than she had at any other point in their exchange. "It's okay, Peter. You've been to Sol, remember? I'm Caryl's original. We're on our way back to Adrasteia."

The fog parted; his expression changed to one of relief, then, almost instantly, shame. "Of course. I'm sorry." He passed a hand across his eyes. "I don't know why I forget these things so easily."

"I do."

He looked up at her with a gaze that was suddenly very intense. "What do you mean?"

"I mean I know why it happens. I know all about your breakdown and why it happened."

"Why?"

"Well, it's not easy to explain—"

"I'm not stupid."

"No, I *know* that." She forced herself not to snap at him; she had to be patient. "Basically, it's because you're an engram, Peter. You're a copy of person programmed to think it's that person. Because you're *not* that person, that causes an immediate and constant conflict."

He gestured irritably. "So? I'm no different than anyone else in the survey program in that regard."

"Not essentially, no. Your problem could have happened to anyone. But it's a definitional thing, as opposed to a fundamental thing, and it expresses itself differently depending on personality. Your engram is *defined* as Peter Stanmore Alander, even though it fundamentally cannot be. In some people, the definition imposed by the engram architecture is enough to overcome the conflict—they want to believe in it, perhaps, strongly enough to make it seem true—but in others, like you, the definition isn't enough to erase the obvious discrepancy. The memories that you are told are yours belong to someone else; key concepts that you are supposed to believe no longer ring true; people you once knew and maybe even loved now seem like strangers. All because, deep down, you don't believe it when you tell yourself—or are told from the outside—that you are the same as your original."

He was staring at her now with an expression that made him look inhuman, almost robotic. "You're saying it's a scripting error? That somewhere in the program that's supposed to make me *me,* there's a line saying the opposite?"

She shook her head. "You know as well as I do that engrams aren't simple software agents. They're tremendously complex, even if, ultimately, they aren't as complex as the real thing. You are not so much the victim of a slight text error as . . ." She clutched for a metaphor. ". . . as a shortcut that went wrong. Some people made very successful engrams; others did not. Peter Stanmore Alander did not, I'm afraid. Something about him broke the mold every time it was applied to him. The definition has been undermined by your personality. So it's not just *this* version of you that's been having problems, Peter. As far as we're aware, nine out of ten of his engrams failed."

He blinked a few times and turned away, an expression of both shock and pain on his android face. She thought for a moment that he might be angry with her, but he just stood with his back toward her and was silent.

"I could try to repair you," she said. "There might be something simple I can do to—"

"Keep your goddamn head out of mine." His voice was low, but its tone was sharp and menacing. A vein pulsed on his gray-skinned skull. "You're as bad as the one I knew on the *Tipler.* She was always poking around in my mind. And your so-called 'higher' self, lifting my memories, taking something that you had no *right* to touch!"

"But Peter, I wouldn't be taking anything from you. All I need is—"

He spun around sharply, the anger in his expression alarming. She took a hasty step back.

"You wouldn't be taking anything *from* me? Is that what you just said?" He stepped forward, compensating for the distance she had put between them. "You'd be *repairing* me, right? Fixing the problem like I was nothing more than a broken fucking appliance. You'd put me back the way I was, regardless of who I am *now*. You'd erase *me*."

He stopped for a moment, trembling, then dragged the back of a hand across his mouth as he stepped away from her once more. "Don't tell me you wouldn't be taking anything away from me," he said quietly.

She waited a few moments before speaking.

"I . . . I don't understand," she said nervously. "Are you saying you *don't* want to be like your original?"

"Of course I don't!" The admission seemed to surprise him as much as it did her. "I'm not just some dog you drag out to a paddock and shoot because it's got rabies. I'm not *wrong*, Caryl. I'm just . . ." He waved his hand frustratingly before him, as if trying to find the right word. When it finally came to him, his arms dropped to his side and his body seemed to sag. "I'm just different," he said, and slumped onto the couch. "That's all."

He sounded like a petulant teenager. She waited to see if he would add anything else, but he was silent for a long time, sitting on the couch with his eyes closed.

"Are you inside me now?" he asked after a while. He kept his eyes shut.

"No," she replied honestly. "On my own, I don't have the ability to do that without you knowing. The rest of me examined you, with the Vincula's help, and distributed the knowledge."

He shook his head slowly, then straightened in the seat, as though consciously pulling himself together. Then he looked at her with an expression of determined objectivity. Whatever he was feeling, he was burying it deep from her eyes.

"You've changed," he said, indicating her environment suit. "Do you need anything else? Food? Sleep? *Arachne* can give you anything you want along those lines, you know."

She did know. They had already had that conversation, although she wasn't about to set him off again by pointing that out. She didn't need any of the things he offered, either. Her greatest problem was the lack of *herself*.

"A room," she said. "I'm sure you don't want me under your feet the entire trip."

"Okay." He nodded. "*Arachne*—"

"A room has been arranged," said the hole ship.

Despite the smooth, quiet tone, both of them jumped at the sound of the AI's voice. Alander's expression mirrored her own astonishment.

"You will take instructions from me?" she said.

"Of course," came the emotionless response. "I have been programmed to—"

"But I thought you could only take instructions from *me*," said Alander, with an edge of panic. "I thought I was the only one you would speak to!"

"That arrangement was between you and the Gifts, Peter. I operate under a separate command protocol."

Of course, she thought. While it was one of the gifts, it wasn't one of the *Gifts.*

"I don't want her doing anything without me knowing,"

Alander told the AI. "She's not to change our course or be permitted to call anyone. If she tries, you're to check with me first. Understand?"

"I assure you that none of her commands can in any way conflict with your own, Peter."

"You don't trust me?" she asked him, feigning indignation.

He didn't honor the jibe with a reply, nor did she push the matter any further. For now, it was enough to know that the hole ship would answer her questions. Maybe it would do more than just obey her orders, since she, unlike Alander, was prepared to explore other forms of communication.

"I'll leave you alone with your suspicions," she said. Then: "*Arachne*, you said you had a room for me?"

"Yes, Caryl. You will find it on your left as you pass through the egress corridor."

Ignoring Alander's look of annoyance and frustration, she left the cockpit and followed the short corridor along to the room the AI had indicated. It was tiny and contained little more than a narrow cot and a wall-mounted bench, but it suited her needs. Had she required toilet facilities, she was sure the Gifts would have provided them, too, but, like Alander, she was very nearly self-contained in that regard.

She stretched out on the bed. The scenes she had just endured with Alander were among the most intense she had experienced for many decades. She wasn't used to physical exchanges on the whole, let alone ones so emotionally charged. She was feeling drained but not tired. It would be a relief to finally arrive at Upsilon Aquarius, where she would be able to converse with someone who wasn't likely to fragment at the wrong phrase.

"*Arachne*?" She spoke with her eyes open, staring at the ceiling. "Thanks for talking to me. I'm surprised but pleased."

"You're welcome, Caryl."

"Do we have to just talk, though? I have numerous other senses I can utilize."

"I am aware of them and can interface with any you wish to utilize."

"Okay, then." She abandoned her external eyes and groped outward by subtler means. "I'd like to see where we're going, if that's possible. Is there any way—?"

Before she had finished, she found herself surrounded by a flawless simulation of the gifts on Adrasteia: the ten orbital towers and spindles, each unique and glinting in the bright sunlight. The illusion was so perfect, it was as though she was actually there. Moving through it was as easy as willing herself elsewhere, and she jumped in rapid succession through all of the various rooms: from the text-based Science Hall to the more hands-on Lab; through the Map Room, with its millions of glowing stars; the Gallery and the Library, all holding promise of a universe rich in life and wonders; pausing at the Surgery; the Hub; and the hole ship's Dry Dock, rich in alien technology; but none so rich as the great hall holding the tower-building machines and the Gifts themselves, vast and mysterious, seeming more concrete somehow than the spindles.

She stopped in the Dark Room and floated for a while in its empty blackness.

"*This is the final gift we bring,*" the Gifts had said. She understood that comment about as much as Alander did. Did they mean infinity? Serenity? The purity of the void?

Or maybe there was something here she simply couldn't see, that humanity would only discover once they could penetrate the geometries of space itself.

She didn't know, and right now probably wasn't the time to worry about it, either.

"Why did the Spinners come?" she asked, wondering if a more powerful means of communication gave her access to higher-level information.

"That has already been explained to Peter Alander," said the hole ship.

She smiled at the rebuke. Yes, this was definitely more sophisticated than simple instruction-confirmation. "Okay. But the Spinners are travelers, yes? Wandering across the galaxy, helping out needy, less fortunate races wherever they go, right?"

"That statement is more or less true."

She sensed evasion and pursued it. "What do you mean by that?"

"The behavior of the builders of the gifts is much more complex than humanity's. Would an ant understand your motivations? A unicellular bacteria?"

"Some motivations, yes. All species need to find resources and to reproduce—"

"All *Earth* species," interrupted the AI.

"There are other biological models? Will I find them in the Library?"

"You will find much that is alien to you there, Caryl Deborah Hatzis."

She shook her head in irritation. "Please don't use my middle name. I can't stand it." *But it must know that already,* she thought, *if it knows my name.* And to know *that,* the hole ship must have scanned either her or Alander at some point. *It's deliberate; the hole ship is trying to put me off guard.*

"Will you at least tell me which model the Spinners belong to then?"

"All information regarding the Spinners is confidential."

"Why? What are they so afraid of?"

"They have no reason to be afraid of anything."

She laughed lightly. "Everyone is afraid of something."

The hole ship didn't respond, though. Nor had it any cause to; after all, she hadn't asked it anything.

"What about the other colonies?" she asked. "You told Peter that none of them have been contacted. Is that true?"

"Nothing is known of our builders since leaving Upsilon Aquarius. It is possible they may have contacted other colonies, yes, but that would depend on where their journey takes them."

"This is different from what you told Peter. You said Adrasteia was the only one."

"At that stage, that was the case."

"To your knowledge, has the situation changed?"

"To my knowledge, no."

"I'm beginning to have doubts about your knowledge, to be honest."

Again, silence. This time she didn't push it. The brief conversation, combined with Alander's memories, had confirmed the intractability of the Spinners' AIs when it came to details about themselves. She was beginning to suspect that it was more than just intractability, though: The information simply wasn't there to be accessed. If the Spinners didn't want to impart too much of themselves into their gifts, then there had to be something they were afraid to reveal, something they didn't want other species to find out about. But what? And why?

Her discomfort with the whole scenario wasn't helped by the fact that all contact had been lost with Upsilon Aquarius. Not knowing what had happened to the survey team was undermining her conviction that Alander had made a mistake by leaving Sol when he did. They needed to know, and this was the only way to find out. But that realization came with its own problems. Just what was she and Alander heading into?

There are civilizations who take delight in the destruction of others.

The thought haunted her as she lay on the cot, staring at the ceiling.

2.2.2

The velvet blackness of space was peppered with distant, exploding hellfires drowning in bubbles of choking dust, feathery nebulae stirred by violent shock waves, and enigmatic singularities brought forth naked, screaming and howling in X-ray frequencies. . . .

Alander was haunted by such images during his waking hours all the way back to Adrasteia. Had they been nightmares, he might have felt less troubled, but they were inspired by his growing perception of the universe: that it was an unsettled, angry place in which humans didn't belong. If the Spinners themselves were afraid to show their real faces, what chance did he or anyone he knew stand?

But he had no real reason yet to be afraid for the *Frank Tipler*. As he and Hatzis sat in the cockpit to consider why his crewmates might not have responded to the ftl transmission, he was reminded of how his Hatzis and her team of projectors had tried to work out why Earth had fallen silent on them, years earlier. For all their deliberating, they hadn't come anywhere close to the simple in essence (yet complicated in detail) truth of the Spike. A large part of him hoped that the silence from Adrasteia would have a similarly noncatastrophic explanation. But hope, he knew, wasn't enough; at times it could even be a dangerous thing.

Alander and Hatzis put aside their differences in the hour and a half leading up to their arrival. She hadn't slept for the entire trip, as far as he knew; he had a couple of times, succumbing to mental exhaustion if not physical. They needed to be able to anticipate every possibility and prepare to deal with them all, and they wouldn't be able to do that while in conflict. But still the tension between them was palpable, and he wasn't sure he fully understood why, although he suspected it had something to do with both of them being incomplete. She reminded him of his original, while he possibly reminded her of the reason why she was an isolated fragment of a much greater mind. Their individual inadequacies were rubbed in their faces, albeit in very different ways.

What would my original have done now? he wondered. But he knew that unless he was prepared to ask Hatzis, there would be no simple answer to that question. She had known his original, after all, and as such was the only continuous, external link remaining to his past. Engram memory was too unreliable and subjective, according to her. It could be changed too easily. Had his original given him an edited version of the truth that had ultimately led to his breakdown? Was what had happened to him all that different from what had happened to Cleo Samson?

Too many questions and no one left to answer them. According to Hatzis, his original had probably been killed in the Great Subsuming of North America, taken apart and reused by a tide of nanotech transmuters along with everything else in its path. Cities, forests, mountains: nothing had been spared. For a while, observers had hoped that patterns had been retained of the people absorbed; some rampant AIs, like those in Europe and on the Moon, had at least done that much to preserve the past. But not this one. It had cut a wide swath across an entire continent and left him, like many others in the survey program, an orphan.

And not even a truly human orphan at that. According to Hatzis, he was little more than a "shortcut that went wrong."

A flash of Lucia nearly blinded him as the time came for them to relocate at Upsilon Aquarius.

Remember, this conversation is being recorded for your copies' memories, and they'll think they're real enough.

He was getting used to it. Maybe one day, if he ever found her, he could tell her himself.

"Oh, fuck," were the first words Hatzis said on arriving at Upsilon Aquarius. It was so perfectly in character with her engram that for a fleeting moment he felt torn between two realities: one with the *Tipler*, where most of his experiences of the system originated, and the other trapped in the hole ship, forced to watch the terrible new reality unfold.

They had relocated by the gas giant where Alander had

tested *Arachne* for the first time. There they had conducted a quick survey of the system, using the hole ship's precise senses to look for emissions of all kinds before scanning the visible wavelengths for images.

But Adrasteia was silent. They detected no broadcasts on any of the UNESSPRO frequencies: no beacons, no data feeds, no narrow-band laser pipes. There were numerous flashes in a number of bands consistent with lightning, but nothing apart from that. When Alander directed the search away from the planet and its moon, looking for various probes stationed across the system, again he found nothing. The noisy crackle of the gas giants and the booming of the sun were the only obvious radio sources in the system.

"Are you going to try to hail anyone?" she asked after a few minutes.

He didn't answer immediately. He just stared numbly at the images of Adrasteia that were trickling in. The cloud cover hung in tatters, replaced for the most part by a vast pall of dust. Everywhere he looked, lightning flashes indicated the immense atmospheric storms raging below. The planet's ecosphere had been severely disrupted. Admittedly, there hadn't been much of one to begin with, but what there had been was now in ruins. Something had pummeled the planet and pummeled it hard.

"No," he mumbled finally, without facing her. "Not yet."

Even with the distance between the gas giant and Adrasteia, the orbital ring and the spindles should have been visible, but they weren't. They were nowhere to be seen. In fact, no matter how much the ship's AI searched, it could find no evidence of anything larger than a pea in orbit around the planet. No towers. No satellites. No *Frank Tipler*.

There was, however, a lot of debris smaller than a pea. If left undisturbed, Adrasteia would soon have a small ring around it—less dramatic than Saturn's, perhaps, but of a similar composition. It was hard to tell exactly how large the particles were that comprised it, but he knew they were small.

Dust, he thought. *Ashes.*

"I can't believe it," he said, finally turning to her.

"Neither can I." Hatzis's face was pale. "When you left, everything was all right, wasn't it?"

"As right as it could be." Looking up slightly, he said, "*Arachne*, can you tell what happened here?"

"I am unable to answer that, Peter."

"Maybe if we move closer," he said. Hatzis didn't argue as he directed the hole ship to bring them into orbit about Adrasteia. In a way, he had hoped she would; he was looking for an excuse not to search too closely. Although engrams had no bodies to leave behind, the thought of what else they might find scared him anyway.

From orbit, the view was more spectacular and horrific in equal proportions, more so than he had allowed himself to believe it could be. Radar revealed terrible gashes where the orbital towers had crashed into the surface of the planet. All the ground settlements, automatic or otherwise, had been razed. Wide craters marked any concentration of technology, no matter how small. The atmosphere roiled in waves, anguished and traumatized. He wondered if any of the cyanobacteria would survive.

Of course they would, he chided himself. On a micro-

scopic level, little had changed, really. The extra energy
in the system combined with environmental disturbance
could even favor them in the long run, with increased
likelihood of speciation leading to evolution and, ultimately, the creation of new life-forms. In a billion years
or so, Adrasteia could be a very different place indeed.

But what could have caused destruction on such a
scale? The dust in orbit was hot, both thermal and radi-
oactive. Nuclear weapons, maybe? Had the Vincula lied
about not having ftl transportation and sent an attack fleet
to Upsilon Aquarius to wipe out the uppity engrams and
steal their secrets? No, it was unlikely, not in so short a
space of time. He doubted the Vincula could have dealt
with the gifts so casually, if at all. In just two days, everything living—or at least active—in the system had been
destroyed. *Everything.*

Or had it? There was nothing left that might qualify as
wreckage, although isotope ratios in a handful of grains
scooped up by the hole ship suggested a terrestrial origin
for at least some of the debris. Whatever had happened
to the gifts might not have necessarily happened to the
Tipler. Caryl Hatzis, Jayme Sivio, Otto Wyra, Jene Avery,
Donald Schievenin, Kingsley Oborn, Nalini Kovistra, and
the rest might still be alive, somehow. But the notion was
a foolish one. If the gifts had succumbed to the attack,
what chance had a few dozen fake minds contained in a
metal box?

"I shouldn't have left them," he said as he watched the
catalog of disaster scrolling down the screen.

"Don't be pathetic," Hatzis said sharply.

The rebuke surprised him, and he faced her again,
frowning.

"I'm sorry, but you're being ridiculous if you think you could have prevented this."

"That's not what I meant," he returned with equal sharpness. "What if something went wrong with the Gifts because I wasn't here to talk to them?"

"This wasn't done by the Gifts, Peter."

"How can you know that?" He felt angry but only because he knew that what she was saying made sense. Why would they destroy themselves?

She didn't respond directly. "*Arachne*, what could have caused this?"

"From the evidence at hand," said the AI, "it would appear that the planet was attacked."

As incredible as it seemed, that rang true. But Alander's anger was still there, so he spat it out in the most obvious response:

"Attacked? By *who?* Who the fuck would want to attack a goddamn survey mission, for Christ's sake?"

"I am unable to answer that question."

"Unable because you don't know, or unable because you're not allowed?"

"There is not enough evidence at hand to identify the perpetrator."

"But that doesn't mean that you don't have suspicions. In all of the data recorded on other species, isn't there anything that might give us a clue as to who could have done this?"

"I'm sorry, Peter, but there is nothing in the memory that I have been allocated."

"Great," he said, falling back heavily onto the couch.

Hatzis stepped forward. "Can you at least tell us when it happened, *Arachne*?"

"Approximately two days ago."

"Just after I left," Alander said with a further sinking feeling.

Hatzis looked down at him. "Didn't the towers have any defenses?"

Alander remembered a probe straying too close and being destroyed. "Some, yes."

"*Arachne*, could the Gifts have fought off an attack?"

"They would have mounted resistance," said the AI.

"Then whoever did this must have had a technology that was even superior to the Spinners."

"Not necessarily," Alander said. "Only superior to the technology the Spinners gave *us*. The towers were nothing to them but trinkets, remember?"

"What if the towers had been about to fall into enemy hands?" she asked. "Is it possible they would have self-destructed?"

Alander had already seen the hole in that argument. "And taken out every long-range satellite in the system? No, this was systematic. Someone came here and wiped out every sign of life—human *or* Spinner."

A strange look passed over Hatzis's face. "And then what?"

"What do you mean?"

"Well, where did they go from here?"

He shrugged. "How the fuck should I know?"

"And why did they come here in the first place? Out of all the other systems in the region, what led them to Upsilon Aquarius?"

"Christ, Caryl, I don't *know!* Your guess is as good as mine. If we had more data, maybe we could work out what happened to them, but all we have is . . ." He indicated the screen, feeling nothing but a suffocating sense of futility. "What's the point? We're never going to know who did this. It's just . . . *done* . . . and there's nothing we can do about it."

Hatzis came up behind him and put a hand on his shoulder. "I'm sorry, Peter. I don't mean to be insensitive. I'm just trying to figure it out, that's all."

He wasn't mollified by her efforts at reconciliation. "We have no evidence."

"We have what we can see," she said. "It has the precision of a military strike. Whoever it was left nothing behind. They were thorough and didn't care about environmental damage. That tells us something, doesn't it? If the Gifts are beneficial pacifists, then whoever did this must be something else entirely."

"Listen, Caryl," he said tiredly. "The truth is, we don't really know anything. For all we know, maybe the skeptics on the *Tipler* were right. Maybe the Spinners never did mean us well, and the gifts were nothing more than a trap."

"A trap? What sort of trap?"

He laughed humorlessly. "I don't know, Caryl. I just don't know anymore. Don't know *anything* anymore. A week ago I—"

"A search of the system has revealed an anomalous artifact orbiting the sun," interrupted the hole ship.

Alander sat forward with a start. "What? What sort of artifact?" He felt his stomach tighten nervously. *Could* it be them? Was it possible they had survived?

A white blob, distinct from the starry background, appeared on the screen.

"Its precise nature is unknown at this stage," said the AI. "I have determined that it has a roughly four-day orbit that doesn't match that of any of your survey satellites."

He felt his hopes sink as quickly as they had surfaced. "So it isn't the *Tipler*?"

"No," the hole ship replied bluntly.

"Where is it?" Hatzis's question was answered by a new image showing a map of the system.

An arrow pointed at the far side. "It is electromagnetically inert and quite small, but it does have a high albedo. Until now, it was occluded by the solar disk."

"Do you think we were *supposed* to detect it?" she asked.

"I am unable to answer that question."

Alander rolled his eyes; he was growing rapidly tired of hearing that phrase. Whatever was going on, it was certainly pushing the boundaries of *Arachne*'s understanding.

"So what do we do?" she asked. "Do we take a look?"

He shrugged hopelessly. "This could be a trap, too."

"Well, if it is, at least we'll die in the knowledge that we learned *one* truth."

She didn't smile, but the attempt at a joke was as welcome as it was surprising.

"I don't think we have many options, Peter. Do you?"

Instead of replying, he arranged for the hole ship to make a short jump to the object's orbit: not right on top of it, but a hundred kilometers away.

As the screen went blank, Hatzis asked, "Do you still think it's your fault, Peter?"

He shook his head, expressing a certainty he wasn't sure he felt. "There's nothing I could've done. But I wish I had been here when it happened. I feel like I abandoned them."

"If you *had* been here, you'd be dead now, too," she said. "At least you're alive."

"Yeah, but I don't feel grateful for that," he said. "Right now, I just feel terribly guilty. I mean, what right—?"

"We've arrived," she said, cutting him off and nodding at the screen.

The image displayed a roughly spherical object two meters across, cut in facets like a mirror ball, but instead of reflective panes in each facet there were only circular holes leading to its interior. The outside appeared to be made of an odd mixture of black and white materials, as though two dyes had mixed ineffectively in the molding of it, while the inside held a crystalline structure Alander couldn't make out clearly.

"Quartz," declared the hole ship upon examining it. "The object is inert."

"Has it ever been active?" Hatzis asked.

"No," replied the AI. "Every indication is that it has never been intended to function."

"What's it *for* then? Does your database contain anything on such an object?"

"No, Caryl."

"It's a marker of some kind," Alander said, watching the object rotate on the screen before him, glinting strongly in the sunlight. The mixture of black, white, and reflective crystal made his eyes water.

"A death marker?" Hatzis sounded skeptical. " 'We came and we destroyed'? That kind of thing?" She shook her head. "I don't buy it, Peter. I mean, what would be the point?"

"I have no idea," he said. "And I daresay we'll remain clueless until we know who actually put the damned thing here in the first place."

She began to stalk the cockpit interior. "None of this makes sense!" Her arms swung as though wanting to strike out. "Who does something like this? And why here? The Gifts have as good as said that there are aggressive races out there—somewhere—but how would they know to come *here?* What singled Adrasteia out from the rest? It was in the middle of nowhere, a small and insignificant colony. It wasn't a threat to anyone."

"Not yet, anyway." She was making Alander feel tired, walking so quickly. "Given the technology we were given access to, though, maybe we could have become a threat."

She stopped, staring at the image on the screen. "You think this might be a warning?"

He shrugged. "Maybe it's nothing more than the alien equivalent of a headstone."

"That doesn't make sense, either. Why go around destroying civilizations, then honoring them with a grave?"

"Christ, I don't know, Caryl." He was suddenly angry at her for forcing him to defend what had been little more than a throwaway notion. "Perhaps we should hunt the fuckers down and ask them personally."

The sarcasm fell flat.

"I just want to go home," she said.

Home. The word stabbed at an emptiness inside of him, and for the first time he realized how much of an orphan he really was. The *Tipler,* the closest thing to a home he'd ever had, outside his original's memories, was gone. Where else did he have to go to? Sol and its post-Spike menagerie?

The truth was settling heavily upon him, like a thick cloak. They were dead, all of them: Otto Wyra and his obsessive pursuit of knowledge; long-faced Donald Schiev-

enin; temperate Jayme Sivio, the one who had kept them
alive during the long journey out; the engram Caryl Hatzis,
who had always been there, even when he had hated her for
it. Every single one of them was gone. The mission to
Upsilon Aquarius had failed.

And there was nothing he could do about it.

His expression must have revealed more of his thoughts
than he had intended, because at that moment, Hatzis
spoke softly.

"I'm sorry, Peter."

"Don't be," he said. "Whatever happened here, it's not
your fault." Turning back to face the enigmatic object on
the screen, he took a deep breath. "*Arachne*, I want to
send a message to Earth, telling them what we've found.
That Machine of yours should pick it up okay, shouldn't
it, Caryl?"

"They won't be able to send a reply," she said.

"It doesn't matter. I just want them to know and to tell
them I'll be bringing you back straightaway."

Her face was still for a moment, then softened. "Thank
you, Peter."

She didn't ask if he was going to stay when he dropped
her off, and for that he was grateful. The Vincula—or
what remained in its wake—would want the hole ship,
but they couldn't take it from him. They couldn't make
him stay if he didn't want to. Maybe, he thought, he
would come back to Upsilon Aquarius to see if the killers
returned. He didn't know if they would or what he would
do if they did, but it was at least some sort of plan. It was
better than nothing.

The only thing of which he was completely certain was
how little he would be missed.

2.2.3

For Hatzis, the trip back to Sol was unbearable. It wasn't because of the destruction they'd witnessed at Upsilon Aquarius, either, although that had affected her deeply. It was Alander himself. He was like a dead thing, barely reacting to anything she said, spending most of the time in his cubicle, emerging only to pace in circles like a caged bear. After twenty hours stuck in the hole ship with him, with another twenty still to go, she felt like she was going to explode from frustration.

She caught him standing immobile in the corridor on more than one occasion, dissociated and lost, staring blankly at the wall as though it held a window to a better world. Each time she had to snap him out of it and remind him what had happened, the shock on his face was like a fist to her stomach; then came denial, as though there was still some hope that by some freak of chance or whim his colleagues might be alive somewhere. She couldn't understand why he found acceptance so hard; despite the lack of concrete evidence, it seemed obvious to her that the *Frank Tipler* had been destroyed along with the orbital ring. And it wasn't as if any of his colleagues had been particularly close to him, apart from Cleo Samson, but she had died before he'd even left. Maybe it was that, she thought. Without the *Tipler*, his primary purpose was gone: He was adrift, alone.

With this, at least, she could empathize. How frightening it still was for her to be severed from her other parts. Her mind ached to rejoin the rest of herself. The edges of her being itched for reconnection, like stumps that were beginning to heal over. Once she had been perfectly happy in such a body; now, she was a cripple learning to deal with her new handicap. There were so many things she couldn't do anymore that finding something to distract her was becoming increasingly difficult. The hole ship wasn't much of a conversationalist; it rebuffed all her attempts to probe the depths of its stated ignorance and otherwise piloted itself back to Sol—however it did that—in complete silence.

"What if the Vincula isn't there when you arrive?" Alander had asked on one of the rare occasions when he did acknowledge her. "What if the Gezim have finished it off? What then?"

She shrugged, unwilling to get into an involved discussion on the politics of Sol System. It was bad enough that she was cut off from herself and even worse that she was stuck with someone who didn't even use the most basic forms of nonverbal communication to facilitate understanding. The fact that he was probably trying to provoke her wasn't helping, either.

"We're used to change, Peter," she said. "Losing the Vincula will destabilize things for a while, but something new will grow out of that. Maybe something better. There's more than one optimal point for humanity to occupy."

"But . . ." He seemed to struggle for words, as though the concept bothered him or he was irritated by her patient acceptance. "Well, what about the Frame? If you lose that, what then?"

"The Frame was built by AIs decades ago. It was a grand venture for its time, but we weren't its architects, and it's not as if it was even finished. Its loss will probably affect us less than the loss of Earth, I think, and we survived that well enough."

His eyes narrowed. "You still haven't told me about that, you know."

"About what?"

"How you survived the Spike. Is there something you're hiding?"

"What makes you say that?" she asked. Then, quickly, she added, "Anyway, it's none of your business."

"Of course it is. Why are you here instead of my original? What do you have that he didn't? What makes you so damn special?" He spat the words with such venom that she was left with no doubt about what he was trying to do. He was looking for someone to attack over his situation. He couldn't attack those who had destroyed Adrasteia, so it was her he turned on, simply because she was there.

She considered refusing to indulge his pettiness, ignoring the question and pointing out that she was only in the hole ship with him because he had effectively kidnapped her. But that would only lead to another argument about something different. For the time being, at least, she was willing to explore things that didn't pierce either of them quite so deeply, even if the distant memories he was evoking were far from painless.

"Okay," she said, leaning back in the seat. "If you really want to know. There was a rogue configuration known as Z-K, after Zhong-Kui, the Chinese god of literature and examinations. For some reason, it was stuck on the idea that humanity would die unless those few who remained after the Spike were electronically preserved. That in itself was quite reasonable; for a while it did indeed look like humanity was out of the race for good. There were only a few survivalists left, like my family, in small groups scattered across the system. Some piggybacked the

AIs, bleeding off power and matter to stay alive. To the really big AIs, you see, we were little more than bugs. Some hated us; most ignored us; only a handful like Z-K tried to preserve us in a variety of ways. The trouble with Z-K was that it preferred the seal-in-amber method. Like all AIs, it had no use for the physical component of a person and absorbed it in order to replenish its own resources, but it respected the mental component; some AIs used humans, or parts of humans, like software patches, mending holes in rambling minds until they burned out and were discarded. Do a deal with Z-K, the theory went, and you would be frozen forever, safe from accident or mischief for eternity; you might not know when you were going to wake up, but at least you weren't dead.

"For those who had fought hard to retain their physical integrity and independence, it was a poor second best. But at least it was an option. Only the desperate booked a ride on Z-K's supercooled asteroid."

She stopped to swallow. The memories were so vivid, and the emotions they evoked made her mouth dry. Alander was watching sullenly from the far side of the cockpit, listening but maybe not believing.

"We were desperate," she went on. "The Io station was running down, and we were too close to the inner system. My family held a scientific lease on the place, but that wasn't worth much back then; the dangerous AIs wouldn't have stopped to check rights before devouring us or driving us insane. We were constantly aware of that threat." Again, she paused, but only for a moment. "My father used to be an art investor on Earth, before the Spike; he had a hard time adjusting to things in space and ultimately died in an accident outside. It was my mother who kept us alive: me, my sister, our two cousins, and my father's father. I had all the space experience from my time in UNESSPRO, and afterward—I worked on a long-haul rig for two years before the Spike came down—but I didn't have what it took to ride out the storm. Mother was the one. She got us off Earth before the worst hit; she negotiated with the Amercers when Earth was gone; she kept us independent during the shredding of Venus. She was brilliant at turning weakness into strength and giving us reasons to hang in there just a little bit longer, especially when things felt hopeless. It was only because of her that we survived as long as we did.

"But it couldn't last forever. After dad died, I . . . well, things were grim. We didn't dare open up to anyone in case they fried us one way or another. We were a closed dock, except for other humans, and we had to be wary of even them, after a bioform almost took us out from the inside. The Frame was growing, and the construction crews were looking for raw materials all over the system. It was only a matter of time before someone took serious notice of us.

"When it arrived, Z-K told us it had been aware of us for years. When the wrecking crews looked our way to grind us to atoms and build us into the Frame, it offered to take us aboard instead. The deal seemed reasonable: It would preserve the family forever or until such time as conditions were right for us to return, in exchange for which *it* would get our home, not the wreckers. It amounted to the same thing, either way—Io would still be destroyed—but at least we would live beyond that point, after a fashion.

"Mother accepted the deal; she knew as well as we all did that there was no other chance. Even without the wreckers, the station would be lucky to remain habitable another month longer; it was wearing out that fast. She and the rest were uploaded. I . . ." Hatzis remembered those few moments most vividly of all: standing back as the air sizzled around her sister Eir's body, turning bright orange as the dry-docked AI took them apart and recorded them in the process. Selie was next, her long, blond hair standing on end for a split second before disappearing forever, then Nerida. Grandpa Moss had held Mother's hand as they went together, neither of them looking at her so she couldn't see their tears—or perhaps the recrimination on their faces. "I didn't trust Z-K. I saw no guarantee that it would do as it said and was afraid of having my mind sucked out and used for spare parts. So I didn't go with the others. Instead, I took the shuttle off-rock and went away, hoping to hitch up with another refuge and earn my way in.

"Neither Z-K nor I got very far before the wreckers moved in. They cared as much for the deal we had struck with Z-K as they did for the original lease. There was a flash fight that attracted attention from elsewhere. Suddenly, there were things all around Io, slugging it out. I was caught by one of them, sucked like a tadpole into the mouth of a whale, but not before I saw what happened to Z-K. Cornered, it had fought until the end, protecting its precious cargo. Only when the result was certain did it blow its propellant tanks and dump such a large amount of antimatter in one instant that it wiped out almost half of its opponents. How many frozen human minds it contained, I didn't know, although it had boasted of thousands." She shrugged. "Maybe it had told the truth, or maybe the whole thing was a plausible lie. However many there were, though, they're definitely all dead now."

She glanced down at her hands. "I don't remember much after that. I guess I was absorbed by the AI that caught me. I don't know why else my pattern would've been kept. Certainly it wasn't out of mercy. I was gone for a month, unaware of time passing, until a reconstruct called Chast woke me up. It had found my body, it said, floating in a capsule near Io. The old rock hadn't been taken in the end; the whole thing had been for nothing. You might think that ironic; I don't. In the history of Sol System, I guess that little encounter would probably seem tiny and insignificant to most, but I like to think it precipitated the breakdown of the alliance that built the Frame, for in the time I'd been unconscious, construction had ceased, and most of the more malevolent types had either gone elsewhere or burned out. Reconstructs like Chast were doing their best to return things to normal. Well, as normal as could be expected for an AI, at least.

"Relatively speaking, humans were able to live in peace after that—what few of us there were left. We all have our stories. I stayed in my body, accepting mods only to increase my survival and to aid communication. Assuming this *is* my old body—" She turned over her hands and wondered at their survival, as she had many times in her alter life. "—then I suppose I'm very lucky."

"Lucky?" His glare was stronger than ever. "You lost your family, your friends, everyone you ever knew—"

"Don't preach to me, Peter." She could match his anger, if she would let herself, and she was sorely tempted.

He straightened. "What did you gain from living?"

"Everything." *And nothing,* she added to herself. "I'm different from how I used to be, but that's all right. Change is natural; it happens to us all. If we don't change, we die." She shrugged lightly and softened her tone.

That's what's wrong with engrams: You can't change. You're dead on the inside."

He shook his head slowly. "And how does *that* make you feel, Caryl?"

She frowned. "What do you mean?"

"How does it make you feel to know that the dead have more humanity in them than all of the Vincula and the Gezim put together?"

She smiled at this, but she felt no humor.

"I'm sorry," she said. "You might think I'm only passing on received wisdom, but the figures are convincing. There are no functional engrams remaining in Sol System. The only ones left are those sent out in the survey program. But for the light-speed lags, giving those on the longer missions an extra lease on life, there might not be any left at all."

He stared at her for a long moment, as though warring with himself, then said, "But we're not talking about me, are we? We're talking about you."

"Actually, we were talking about the Vincula and what it would mean if it was gone when we got back." She forced herself to talk lightly, as though the thought didn't concern her at all.

"What if *you're* not there?" he asked.

"I'll deal with that if I have to."

"Just all a part of living, huh?" he said.

"Exactly," she said, finally unable to resist. "But at least it is living."

He stalked off and sealed himself inside his cubicle for another long period. When next he showed his face, she resolved to make no attempt at reconciliation, even though his aggressive attitude seemed to have abated.

"How long?" he asked.

"What?"

"How long did they last?"

"Who?"

"The engrams," he said.

She shrugged. "Twenty years, thirty years, perhaps, in real time; no slow-mo. Some rare ones—who survived both the Spike and their own internal problems—even saw the turn of the century. But there are no documented cases of survival longer than that."

"Twenty, thirty years," he said, as though hearing a death sentence. "Funny, I thought we'd live forever. We all did."

"Not like this, no. In fact, the chances are, the crew of the *Frank Tipler* wouldn't have lasted much longer than they did, anyway. But there are ways around it. When we get back to Sol, the Vincula would offer you an upgrade to something more flexible, I'm sure."

"Like you offered me before? Kill *me* and let my old self take over?"

"No, although you do raise an interesting point, there. Fixing your specific problem is a simple matter of reconnecting your world lines, making the thread of your consciousness consistent. But that's the very problem with engrams: You're *too* consistent, so reconnection might actually work against you in the long run. Fascinating."

She meant it, but he took it as some sort of joke. "Is that all I am to you, then? An experiment?"

"Not at all. What you choose to do—accept my offer, explore options with the Vincula, or just carry on your own way—makes no difference to me. To tell you the truth, Peter, you're just a situation I'll be glad to put behind me."

"Well, it won't be for much longer, I hope."

She forced a smile and said, "Either way."

2.2.4

When she came to, she was lying on the floor with Alander standing over her. He looked angry, panicked, and he was shouting at her.

"Hail them, for fuck's sake! Do something! *Anything!*"

She grappled with the words, trying to make sense out of what he was asking her to do, but it was difficult when so many thoughts were surging and crashing through her head.

He leaned over toward her then, his face twisted in a way she couldn't read. She flinched as his hands reached out for her, fearing he was attacking her. Then she realized he wasn't attacking her but was trying to help her up.

"Get us out of here!" he called out close to her face.

"I . . . can't," she said numbly, not comprehending what it was he was asking of her.

Behind him, looming large on the screen, she caught a glimpse of something bright and blue rushing toward them. Then, at the same instant that the image on the screen disappeared, her mind cleared, and she remembered.

They had been in the cockpit, preparing for their arrival in Sol System. They were to relocate in a position roughly where Venus might once have been, having agreed to check first on the situation between the Vincula and the Gezim before moving in too close, and she had been staring at the screen in anticipation. She was eager for their journey to be at an end, finally. After a few days cooped up with Alander, the cockpit had started to feel like a coffin.

When the hole ship had announced their imminent return to Sol, she had felt a wave of relief wash through her. She had stood there beside Alander, staring expectantly at the screen and barely thinking, listening intently for those first words from herself, eager to be reconnected and become whole once again.

But instead of the warm embrace of her other parts to welcome her home, she found her mind suddenly dipped into what felt like a steaming cauldron of panic. Furious and conflicting emotions warred with chaotic, fragmentary thoughts so intense that she had screamed and blacked out.

"Caryl?" Alander was still shouting, despite the quiet that had settled around them in the cockpit as well as in her head. Then she realized: He hadn't been yelling at her to get them out of there, but to the hole ship. They were jumping to another location.

"I'm in trouble," she said, trying her best to explain what had happened. "I'm breaking up . . . In pain . . . Everything's falling to pieces. I see fire; I'm *burning*. Someone's hurting me!"

"Who, Caryl?" he asked urgently. "Who is doing it?"

"I don't know," she moaned, still overwhelmed by the horror of what she had just experienced and knowing that the moment that screen came back to life, it would all start again. "I've never seen such—"

Then she was immersed in it again.

She screamed and fell away from Alander, the fire of emotion so powerful she felt her head might explode. The hole ship rolled beneath her as another burst of blue loomed on the screen. Whoever was attacking them, they seemed to be able to anticipate exactly where they jumping.

Alander stood above her, shouting his rage at the screen while she writhed helplessly on the floor, clutching her head in agony. Fragments of her greater self were pouring into her from all directions with no sense of order, great gobbets of mind-flesh stuffed down her mental throat, choking her—

Then it was gone again; the hole ship was jumping to a third place.

"Please," she sobbed. "Please make it stop."

Alander knelt on the floor beside her. "It's okay, Caryl."

"Don't go back," she pleaded. "Please! I can't take it."

"We have to, Caryl," he said softly, apologetically. "We have to find out what's going on."

The world swam around her as she tried to sit up; she fell back, gasping. "They're dying," she said. "That's what's happening. They're dying, and there's nothing—"

This time she was silent as the paralyzing grief flooded through her. On the screen, there was no blue flash, just a sphere of oddly shaped silver vessels popping into existence around them: hundreds of them in a second, then thousands, closing in like a swarm of bees, their blue-tipped stingers at the ready.

Then the screen went blank and they were gone.

"Jesus Christ," Alander whispered, leaning pale-faced against the couch. She watched him in a state of detached numbness. "What the hell is going on here, Caryl? *Arachne*?" He obviously had no intention of waiting to see if she had an answer for him. "Did you learn anything that time?"

"I am cross-referencing what little data I have managed to obtain," it replied. "I am hoping that doing so will help determine the origin of the species. So far, however, I have been unable to find a match."

"What about the Frame?" asked Alander. "Is it under attack?"

"The artifact known as the Frame appears to be disintegrating."

Disintegrating, Hatzis echoed in her mind. Surely the Gezim couldn't have done something like this. But if it wasn't them, then who?

"Can we contact whoever is responsible for this?" said Alander.

"The only response so far to my hails has been a demonstration of force," said the AI.

"So we can assume, then, that communication isn't one of their strengths," said Alander. "Which leaves us completely in the dark. No clues, no ideas—"

"No hope," she cut in.

He looked over to her briefly, then away again, as if embarrassed.

"It is possible," said the hole ship, "that any travel within the light cone of the attackers will be detected. I have therefore taken the liberty of moving us to a greater distance."

"So if you take us farther out than any light they've emitted has had time to travel, we'll be safe?"

"If I am correct, yes."

"But we'll still be able to look back and see what has happened, right?"

"When I reenter their light cone, yes. Provided I remain stationary, I should go undetected."

He nodded warily. "And how do you know just how far you have to jump? We don't know how long they've been here."

"They weren't here when I left," explained the hole ship patiently. "I will jump to a point two light-days distant, then gradually come closer."

"Is there *anything* we can do to help those people back there?"

"No," Hatzis said dully. There was a finality to the memories she had received that spoke more clearly than anything else they had seen. "There isn't."

"The hole ship possesses a basic defensive capability," said the hole ship. "It could repel an attack of a technological level roughly equivalent to that of the human civilization existing in Sol System. The intruders I have encountered, however, are significantly more advanced. To attempt any form of counterassault against them would result in my destruction."

"But couldn't we call for help with the ftl communicator? Maybe we could contact the Spinners themselves."

"I could try, but there is no way of knowing whether they would reply. They might no longer be in range."

"Or they might not be interested," Hatzis put in.

"There is also that possibility, yes," said the hole ship.

Hatzis had managed to sit up during the conversation and was facing the screen when it cleared. The hole ship appeared to have negotiated the light cone boundary, since they were obviously closer than two light-days from Sol. The images were blurred slightly by distance, even with the hole ship's senses, but Hatzis could clearly make out the shape of the Frame as the view expanded. Everything looked perfectly normal, except for a number of blackened patches where the damage from the Gezim assault had yet to be repaired. The sight of it brought tears to her eyes.

"At least we're safe from this distance," said Alander. "How far out are we?"

"I am seven light-hours from Sol."

That put the hole ship somewhere between the orbits of Jupiter and Saturn. She could feel the fringes of her greater mind around her, but her nearest pov was the one on Titan, some hours away. She could try to warn all the isolated components of herself, those who were still outside the light cone of whoever had attacked the Frame, but what would be the point? If the heart of the Vincula itself could mount no resistance, what chance did a few remotes have?

They could hide, she thought, *bury themselves where they might not be noticed and regroup later, with as many others as they chose to warn.* It was all that she could do, but it was better than nothing. Using the hole ship's transmitters, and without Alander's knowledge, she narrowcast a warning to as many of the povs she could locate, while she had the chance.

The light cone spread indefatigably outward.

"There." Alander pointed. A scattering of blue pinpricks spread across the Frame. Yellow white flowers blossomed in their wake. "Can we get a clearer picture?"

The view expanded. The yellow white flowers were explosions, spraying matter and energy in all directions and leaving massive holes in the Frame. The Shell Proper was already unraveling, the subtle tensions holding it in place causing whole sections to peel away and drift into the void. Quick-moving, silvery shapes darted in and out of view, maneuvering with all the ease and speed of sharks in fast motion. They reminded Hatzis of throwing stars, except that these had nine points and must have been kilometers across. The edges of each of these stars were spinning so fast that she suspected they were approaching the speed of light. And the faster the stars traveled, the faster the edges spun.

They brought destruction wherever they went, raining down sheets of energy or silvery sprays. The Frame and its attendant vessels were trying to defend themselves, but their efforts were manifestly inadequate. Any attack they mounted was instantly torn to pieces. Lasers bounced off the silver ships; explosions were deflected as though they were little more than a stiff breeze; all forms of matter and energy were absorbed if they got anywhere close. Nothing the Vircula threw at them was even slowing them down.

"Who are they?" she asked, her voice hoarse.

Alander turned to look at her, as though he had forgotten she was there. "They're definitely not yours?"

She ignored what she regarded to be a stupid question. "*Arachne*, I find it hard to believe that you have no data on this species. I mean, *look* at them! Things like this don't just appear out of *nowhere*."

"I assure you, there is no information available on—"

"It's lying," she said bluntly to Alander. "It has to be."

Alander frowned at the accusation, but it was the hole ship that responded. "I am not lying; what would it serve me to—?"

"I don't *know*," she barked. "But it doesn't make sense! All this fucking information on untold species, but not a scrap on . . . *this!*" She gestured irritably at the continuing battle on the screen, tears stinging her eyes.

"I do not represent the sum of my builders' knowledge," said the AI, maintaining an almost supernatural calm in the face of the accusations she was throwing at it. "No more than the gifts were. There are gaps in my knowledge; this is clearly one of them. I can only reiterate that I have no information available on the vessels currently attacking Sol System."

Alander cleared his throat.

"Perhaps we should be moving," he said. "We're in their light cone now."

"I am maintaining a low profile," said the hole ship. "Unless I relocate, the chances are minimal that they will notice me."

Alander didn't look terribly reassured, and Hatzis didn't blame him. The attack on the Frame was intensifying, as it appeared on the screen. But it had actually happened seven and a half hours ago, during which time other such ships had presumably spread through the system, mopping up stations and remotes away from the Frame. They could have already strayed into the sights of one such ship. Another attack might only be seconds away.

"This is what happened in Upsilon Aquarius," Alander said. "It has to be. They wouldn't have stood a chance against something like this."

Hatzis let out a small gasp as a piercing mental wail struck her from afar. Seven and a half hours before, key elements of her greater self had come under direct attack; their cry of alarm was only now reaching her, far away, and she found herself flinching at the intensity of the emotions.

"Do you want us to block it out?" Alander asked, crouching next to her and putting a hand on her shoulder.

She pushed him away. "No!" She took a deep breath and forced herself to react more calmly. "I'm sorry, but no, thank you. I just . . . I think I need to experience this. Otherwise it won't seem real."

He nodded at the screen. "Seems real enough to me, Caryl."

She wanted to respond to his comment but couldn't find the words to express the way she was feeling. After a while, he moved away, taking up his position on the couch. She closed her eyes on the tears that were seeping onto her cheeks, riding out the confusion and shock that rushed through her like a jet of boiling water at the sound of her greater self, dying.

They watched for eleven hours. Detected and attacked twice during that time, they relocated to points farther from the heart of the system to watch the destruction unfold. Each time, they had to relive the initial attacks, although the increasing distance degraded the detail of the images until, ultimately, there was no point watching anymore. Even then Hatzis had insisted that Alander keep them in close enough so that they could maintain a constant vigil. That's how she thought of it. She wanted to witness the massacre—or at least as much of it as she could stand—because she knew someone should.

The Frame had come to symbolize all that remained of humanity following the Spike, and it had been destroyed in a little under six hours. She found it difficult to comprehend that such a structure, woven as it was from two entire planets along with the bodies of untold billions of people, could have been so casually obliterated. No matter how hard she tried, she simply could not get her head around the fact that what she was watching might be the annihilation of her species, the death of humanity itself.

In the hour or so prior to the Frame's final destruction, the Starfish (as Alander had started referring to them) had seemingly gone crazy. Weaving a web of white points across the Frame, they had turned it into something resembling a giant Christmas tree. For a while it had looked as though they might have changed their minds, or perhaps that the Vincula had somehow given their attackers reason to think twice. But then the Starfish had retreated, and each of the points of light had flashed a pulsing, violent red, and within moments the Frame had been no more.

Out of the spreading pall of rubble had come the last gasps of the Vincula, as dying minds clutched desperately at life among the millions of remotes and nodes scattered across the system. The silvery swarms of Starfish followed each and every electromagnetic emission to its source and obliterated them without exception. Even inactive stations like Io suffered the same fate. The systematic evisceration of Sol System went on relentlessly, with increasingly desperate and futile pleas from the survivors reaching the hole ship. Of the many minds that had once occupied the system, there now remained nothing but memories, hurled out into the vacuum like last-minute attempts to preserve something, anything, from total annihilation. And ten hours after the first attack, the last, echoing thoughts of her greater mind had dwindled to virtually nothing.

The hole ship jumped a third time to avoid the Starfish cleanup crews. But barely had they arrived at the new location when they were attacked again.

"They have become aware of my strategy," the hole ship said while they jumped again. "I advise a complete withdrawal."

Alander glanced dark-eyed at Hatzis, and she nodded in agreement. "I've seen enough," she said somberly.

The hole ship took them so far away that Sol became just another bright and yellow star among the millions shining around them. The view made her feel strangely vulnerable.

"*Arachne*," she said, "are you sure they can't follow us out here?"

"As sure as I can be," replied the AI. "Although it must be said that without any available data on the aggressors, I can offer no guarantees. Lacking detailed knowledge of their technology, it is impossible to determine precisely what they are capable of."

Standing, she took a deep breath and exhaled heavily, then began to nervously pace the cockpit. After a few moments, she stopped before Alander and fixed him with a sober stare.

"When do you think it will be safe to go back?" she said.

Alander looked startled by the question. "Go *back?*"

"We'll have to return at some point. We need to check for survivors."

"But the Starfish—"

"There's no reason why they should hang around," she said. "After all, they abandoned Upsilon Aquarius once they'd finished with the *Tipler*."

She could tell by his sudden expression that her words had stung him and, for a fleeting moment, she regretted her insensitivity. But she quickly dismissed her guilt. It was hard enough dealing with her own grief without worrying about his. There would be a time for sensitivity later.

"You know," she said after a few moments of silence, "I think you were right."

His brow furrowed as he said, "About what?"

"About this being a trap," she said. "I think it's possible this whole thing was a setup by the Spinners."

He laughed at this. "Come on, Caryl. I was just rambling back then. I didn't know what I was saying."

"Nevertheless, it does make sense."

"No, it doesn't, Caryl," he said. "I was simply trying to rationalize what had happened. And that's all you're doing now. We want explanations for the unexplainable."

"Think about it, Peter," she insisted. "Your survey team was bumbling along quite happily until the Spinners came on the scene. They mysteriously leave you a bunch of gifts, then disappear without a word. What's the next thing you do after poking around for a bit? You contact Earth. Hell, they even give you a ship that will get you there in a couple of *days*. What more could you ask? I mean, Christ, all your dreams had come true at once!"

She watched his reaction. He didn't say anything, but she could tell from his expression she had his attention.

"Well, what if your going back to Earth was what they were wanting you to do all along? What if they were feeding you just enough rope to hang us all?"

"The gifts were placed there solely to get the hole ship to go to *Sol?*" His tone bordered on incredulity and amusement. "Come off it, Caryl! This is crazy."

"It's not crazy," she said firmly. "Once the hole ship had gone, they were free to wrap things up there. They had no more use for Adrasteia, so they got rid of the evidence."

"Evidence of *what* though?"

She shrugged. "I don't know," she said honestly. "But it does fit together."

"So you're saying the gifts were sent as a means of

tricking us into revealing the heart of our civilization? For the sole purpose of annihilating us?"

Another shrug. "In a nutshell, yes."

"But they *knew* where Earth was," he said. "They had access to all of our data."

"Perhaps they were bluffing, or perhaps they just weren't sure. After all, if they had surveyed Sol, they would have found a reality *very* different from your maps. They may have thought your data deliberately falsified so it couldn't be traced, much like what they've done with the hole ship and the gifts. The *only* way to be sure would have been to see where you actually went when given the opportunity."

"And then?" He left the question hanging, but she didn't supply the answer. "What do you think happened then, Caryl?"

"Christ, I don't know. Maybe the hole ship uploaded some sort of viral attack when it arrived. Maybe it notified the Spinners. Maybe there are things it could've done that we'd never think of."

"That's a lot of maybes."

"All I'm saying is that it's a possibility. At the very least, it's an explanation for what happened back in Sol."

She rubbed her pounding head, unsure whether she believed wholly in what she was saying but wanting to keep herself occupied, keep her mind from returning to the pain and anguish she had felt while her greater self died. If she sat down for too long, her thoughts returned to the memories of those endless hours, the despairing cries, and if she looked at the screen, at the vast starry emptiness, she was reminded of how vulnerable she felt.

She was distracted by a short, soft bleat from Alander, all he could manage in the way of a laugh.

"We haven't got a clue, really, have we?" he said when she looked at him. "That's the truth, isn't it? We haven't got a fucking clue about anything!"

"I know, and it's driving me crazy." The hope that some—even one—of her povs might have survived the attack because of her warning simmered inside her, making her restless. "I want to go back there."

"Why? There's no point."

"Have you got another destination in mind?"

He shook his head. "Okay, but not yet. I need to rest. It could be dangerous, and it's not going to help if one of us is run down."

"I'm alert enough to handle it on my own."

"Two hours is all I need, then we'll go back."

She was on the brink of denying his request when she realized that she was being unreasonable. What difference would two hours make, really? If any of her povs had survived the attack, they would survive that much longer.

"Okay. I'll keep watch from here."

He nodded and stood, then moved off in the direction of his cubicle. Before exiting the cockpit, he stopped and faced her again.

"Call me if anything happens, okay?"

"Of course I will."

He nodded once more and disappeared into his cubicle. She had no doubt that he would confirm his last request with the ship's AI, ensuring that if she didn't rouse him, it would. And while she couldn't blame him for that (she would have done the same in his position), it did make her sad. If she and Alander were all that remained of humanity, instead of anything even remotely resembling camaraderie, all that existed between them was a mistrust that was positively palpable.

2.2.5

On the eighteenth hour of their search, they found an object identical in nearly every respect to the one left in Upsilon Aquarius.

Alander had thought the ruins of Adrasteia bad, but they were nothing compared to the destruction that had been unleashed upon Sol System. Everywhere he looked he saw wreckage. The Frame had been completely atomized, along with the Shell Proper and anything functional that had clung to it. The thin atmosphere of Mars had been stripped away, along with every habitat on the planet that had harbored any form of life. The Moon had been blasted into fragments; the moons of Jupiter and Saturn were stripped bare, as was Mercury; the asteroid bases and deep-system stations, active or inactive, were clouds of dispersing dust. Every satellite, every relay, every navigation buoy and every experimental outpost like McKirdy's Machine were all gone.

The Starfish themselves had been gone for several hours, and the hole ship could find no evidence that they'd laid traps for anyone seeking to investigate what had happened. How the AI and Hatzis had determined the Starfish had gone, Alander hadn't worked out. Nor did he ask. He preferred not to know if they'd simply assumed it had been safe to return. Such guesswork scared him.

Hatzis was stone-faced all through the exploration of the system. When she did talk, it was in abrupt, clipped tones. She looked brittle, as though something deep inside of her had fractured, and the cracks were widening. He doubted that she had rested while he had, and he imagined her awake the whole time, brooding. Instead of trying to distract her from her thoughts, he stayed out of her way as much as possible, allowing her the freedom to be in control during this phase of the journey. He was content, for the moment at least, to be nothing more than an observer.

She had instructed the hole ship to broadcast a low-power beacon everywhere they went, clearly hoping that someone, somewhere, had survived the assault on the system. But the lack of any response told them what he already suspected: The Starfish had, with frightening efficiency, eradicated all life within the system. In fact, there was little remaining to suggest there had ever been life there in the first place.

Except one. When the hole ship announced that it had found something, her face came alive for a brief moment, then died again.

"Another death marker," he said, watching the object glint in Sol's steady light, ten kilometers from the hole ship.

Hatzis shrugged. "If that's what it is."

"What else could it be? It's certainly not a mine or some other kind of trap, or else we'd be dead already."

"I don't know; it just doesn't strike me as the sort of thing these slash-and-burn types would leave behind."

"We don't know anything about them," he said. "For all we know, the system might be a trophy for them and *this* thing is just an invitation for others of their kind to come and admire their work."

Her skeptical look was almost a sneer. "If they were conquerors, yes. They'd want everyone to know their might and power; they'd leave clues all over the place. But if the motive of *these* people really is to sneak up on others, obliterate them, then sneak away to do more damage elsewhere, I don't see why they'd leave anything at all behind."

"But it's not likely they could be traced by something like this, is it?"

"Why not? There are bound to be ways to identify a culture from its artifacts, if only from the way it manufactures them or the materials it uses."

"I guess."

She stared at him as though wanting to say something else—or waiting for *him* to say something—then she looked away.

"I'd be happy to find just *one* beneficent race," she said. "One we can trust, anyway, who we could ask for help. Is there anyone we can appeal to, *Arachne*? Some sort of galactic police force, perhaps?"

"There is no common moral code governing behavior in the galaxy," the alien AI replied. "Even if there was one, there would be no guarantee that it would accord with your own."

"No rules, huh?" Her tone was bitter. "No wonder your makers keep to themselves, then."

Alander watched Hatzis's face as she studied the screen, and he was reminded of Cleo Samson on that seemingly far-off day on Adrasteia when he had tried to take a bath. She had been talking to him about Lucia, about whether he would choose her company over solitude if he could. He hadn't seen the point of such idle wishful thinking, to which Samson had said, *"We all wish, Peter. It's very much a human quality."* Looking at Hatzis now, he thought he knew what she would be wishing for.

"So what do you want to do now?" he said shortly.

"How the fuck should I know, Peter?" Her tone was

low, but it contained enough scorn to sting him, nonetheless.

"Look, Caryl," he offered, "I can imagine how you feel right now. I—"

Her derisive laugh cut him short. "Really? I don't see how you could *possibly* have any idea—"

"Hey!" he snapped. "I lost my home, too, remember?"

"The comparison is ludicrous."

"Well, don't expect me to tear my heart out over what happened to the Vincula, given the fact that they lied to me and attacked me without provocation. As far as I'm concerned, it's a good thing it's gone!"

"If you're trying to boost my morale, Peter," she said, shaking her head, "you really suck at it."

"Okay," he concurred, doing his best to keep a lid on his own emotions. "Fair point. But the fact remains that I am in exactly the same position as you, Caryl. We've both lost everything, and we need to consider what we'll do next."

Her eyes were red and painful—the most human they had ever seemed to him. "If you're about to suggest rebuilding, then you're out of your mind. *And* blind." She pointed at the screen as though stabbing it with her finger. "Have another look. There's nothing left to rebuild *with*."

"We have two working brains, don't we? We have *Arachne*. We can at least *start*. So what if it takes a thousand years to finish? Or a million? At least we'll be doing something."

"Who says I want to do *anything?*" She turned away from him as if to end the discussion. "*Arachne*, take me to Io—the asteroid, not the moon."

The screen went black on the view of the death marker.

"That's it, then?" he pressed, not allowing the conversation to die. "We just roll over and give in?"

"Humanity is dead," she said. "The first thing you need to do is to accept that."

"There's always hope," he insisted, but even as he said it, he could hear how empty the words sounded.

"For what?" she said. "For *me?* You have no idea what I've lost, Peter. It's not just the idea of humanity as a species. I practically *was* my own species. Can you even begin to imagine what it felt like to belong to something like that? I can't go back. I'd rather not exist at all if the only thing left to look forward to is life in this body."

The screen came alive with images of rubble, twinkling in the sunlight. He couldn't believe what he was hearing.

"Are you saying you want *kill* yourself?" He stared at her incredulously for a few moments. "You can't be serious!"

"What I do is none of your business, Peter."

He could tell she wanted to move away from him, but with the cockpit being the size it was, there was simply nowhere for her to escape to.

"You're right," he said. "You're absolutely right. You don't have to justify anything to me. You don't have to talk to me or listen to anything I have to say. So why not do us both a favor right now and go for a space walk without a suit? Be sure to take your maudlin, self-pitying bullshit along with you."

She faced him with her arms folded across her chest, eyes glistening with tears. She looked so different from the Hatzis he remembered from Adrasteia—but he had never seen *her* under these circumstances.

"There are no good alternatives," she said.

"I didn't say there were. I just think suicide is always the wrong decision."

"Who gives a damn what you think, Peter?"

He shrugged. "Maybe you do. After all, why else would you be arguing the point with me? Your body's modified; you could just pull the plug right now and die if you really wanted to . . . in a second." He waved a hand at the screen. "Well, here's your precious Io, Caryl. Here's where your father died. What are you waiting for? Rescue?"

The tears were streaming freely down her cheeks now. "No," she muttered.

"Me to talk you out of it, perhaps? Despite what you say?"

"No!"

"Good, because—what was it you said?" Her apathy made him lash out, more angry now than frustrated. "Oh yes, that's right. I'm dead on the inside, apparently. 'Not truly human'—that was another one, wasn't it? Although my favorite was: 'a shortcut that went wrong.' Maybe you should take some of your own advice regarding morale boosting."

"Fuck you, Peter," she said weakly.

"You know, Caryl, if your opinion of my life is so small, why don't you just go ahead right now and switch off your fucking brain? Because you're right; there *is* nothing left but me. Nothing worth worrying yourself about, anyway."

Hatzis's face had gone a mottled pinkish white color. She opened her mouth to say something—but at that moment, a vibration shivered through the hole ship, as though someone had tapped its hull and made it ring like a bell.

"I am receiving a message," said the hole ship.

The announcement took Alander completely by surprise. His anger instantly abated and was replaced by confusion.

"What?" he said at the same instant and in the same tone as Hatzis.

Then a voice he recognized—piercingly, like a knife to the gut—filled the cockpit. "This is Cleo Samson, civilian survey manager of the *Carol Stoker*, United Near-Earth Stellar Survey Program Mission 835, calling any surviving authority on or near Earth. In the course of our exploration of HD194640 and its sole habitable planet, Varuna, we have been contacted by an advanced civilization whose artifacts have enabled this communication. Please respond if you are able. We need your advice. I repeat, this is Cleo Samson . . ."

The message cycled through three times, then ended. Alander listened to it in stunned silence, hardly daring to believe his ears.

"*Another* one?" He turned to Hatzis, whose expression was as shocked as his. "*Arachne*, did you know about this?"

"No, Peter."

"Oh my God," he said, barely listening to the AI's reply. "The Spinners went elsewhere! This changes everything!"

"It changes nothing," Hatzis said, regaining her composure.

His brow furrowed deeply. "Of *course* it does! It's not just *us*, now, Caryl. We have to call them, tell them what's happened. Then we can go there, join forces—"

"We can't do that. They're as good as dead, Peter."

He felt rage rush through him like he had never felt before. "I've had enough of your defeatist attitude. You may be in your original body—you may have been part of a hyperevolved human or whatever—but I'm still alive, and always have been. Everyone on the *Frank Tipler* was alive. Cleo Samson and everyone on the *Stoker*—they're alive, too, along with God knows how many others in the survey program." *Even Lucia,* he thought wildly to himself. "You have no right to condemn us before we even try, like—" *Like my original's dead-end bacteria.*

He turned away from her. "*Arachne*, I want to send—"

Before he completed the instruction, Hatzis was physically across the room and throwing him into the wall with surprising force.

He wheeled on her angrily. "What the hell are you *doing?*"

"Shut up, you idiot!" she hissed.

"Look, kill yourself if you want, Caryl, but you're not taking the rest of us with you! They're *alive,* dammit!"

"You don't understand!" she shouted. "They're already dead—"

"*Arachne*," he started again, without listening to her. But again, before he could finish his sentence, she had thrown herself at him.

They grappled with one another, their ugly, graceless movements dictated more by force than leverage.

"You're making a mistake," she managed. "You must—"

"*Arachne*!" He raised his voice over hers. "Send a reply to Cleo Samson. Tell her—"

Hatzis twisted in his grasp, slipping one hand free and bringing it into contact with his own. In an instant, something fiery burst behind his eyes. He screamed and let go of her, falling back onto the floor with his free hand over his face. His mind exploded with images of pain and despair. He was alone, dying, burning up in the same flames that had consumed an entire solar system.

For an agonizing split second, he *was* Caryl Hatzis.

Then his mind went blank, and he was nothing at all.

"If not for us, then for who?"

He was in Lucia's room, lying on her bed. Both of them were naked, having just had sex. He felt pleasantly warm and relaxed despite an intermittent tingle just behind and above his navel. He was afraid of admitting, even to himself, just how terrified he was. He wondered if everyone else felt the same and if they had found the same sort of distraction to take their minds off it.

"Or whom? I can never remember which."

She seized upon the chance like a shark. She was at least as smart as him, and they both knew it. Neither of them knew why they got on so well, though—especially considering the disparity in their ages—but neither had even tried to fight it. It was more than just a physical attraction, although that was strong. He suspected it might be nothing more than the fact that they enjoyed playing the same games.

"It won't be us, Peter," she said. "And yet it will be. I try not to get tangled in the metaphysics of it all. I just prepare as well as I can in order to prepare each of *them*. I don't want to let anyone down, least of all myself."

"But *you* won't be one of them."

"No." She looked puzzled for a second, wondering, perhaps, where this was all leading. What game was this? "And neither will you. There's no way the program could afford to send even one of our bodies. We weigh too much; we sleep and eat too much; we get bored too easily—"

"I know, I know." He wasn't sure where he was going, either. Maybe he was more afraid of staying behind than he was of leaving. The emphasis had been so much on the latter that he had begun to feel as if he really *was* leaving. But he wasn't. It would just be his engrams.

He rolled onto his back, and she followed him without hesitation. Her body slid smoothly next to his. He could feel the warm pressure of her hips and breasts against his side as keenly as her gaze on his face. Her hand rested flat upon his chest.

"*We'll* still be *here,*" she said, pressing down on his heart. "And that bothers me."

"It does?" He felt a new surge of alarm. Was she about to propose to him? Surely not! Not Lucia, of all people!

If she did, he was sorely tempted to say yes, just to throw her a curveball. She wouldn't expect *that.*

But her next words reassured him.

"Of course. I want to be one of them, Peter . . . out there, exploring, seeing things no one else has ever seen before." She shrugged. "How could I not want that? I thought you did, too."

"Exploring, yes," he said. "But not just to sightsee. I want to find answers, explanations for the things we still don't understand."

"Knowledge is the payoff by which people like me have justified the entire program. I think the tourists outnumber the truth seekers, don't you?"

"Undoubtedly. And the truth seekers are happy to go along for the ride."

He kissed her. Christ, sometimes he thought he really could settle down with her, if only for a while. A year or two, perhaps; find an apartment in Kyoto or take a cruise; get to know each other *really* well in the process. It could be fun. The fact that it couldn't possibly be permanent didn't tarnish the notion. It never did. He'd had five short-term bonds with five women in his life, one of them, Emma, for seven years, and none of them had been as fascinating as Lucia. But what did *she* want?

They kissed, both of them moving together simultaneously as though thinking with one mind. A pleasant illusion and an ironic one. Just because they liked the same games didn't mean they thought the same. Indeed, his mind was already drifting back to the survey missions and all the problems they would face. Would pseudorandomly chosen crews really solve some of the psychological problems UNESSPRO anticipated, or could it actually make things worse? There were a couple of the civilian survey managers that he was actively worried about; it would only take one to ruin an entire mission. But he had no real power; he had expressly refused to take any sort of supervisory post, pre- or postlaunch. He was much better at working behind the scenes, getting people to do what he wanted all on their own.

He was almost surprised when she returned to the topic after only a short time.

"The question is: Where do we go from here? While the engrams go off into space to visit a thousand different suns, what are *we* going to do? Do we carry on as we always did before we joined the program? Pretend that none of this has changed us? Will we ever know what our copies do or see? How do we kill time until we find out? What if one of them dies . . . or *we* die? Are we immortal, or are we destined to die a thousand times?"

"I thought you said you weren't getting tangled in the metaphysics."

"I said I was *trying* not to." She gestured imperiously, barely hiding the beginnings of a smile. (*Yes,* he thought; *maybe I'll ask her myself.*) "The engrams wake tomorrow. In a year, most of them will be gone. Then it's back to just us. You and me and Donald and Jene and Chrys and the others. We're the Viking widows waving off our husbands to be swallowed by the sea. Except they're not our husbands . . . or our wives or friends or anyone, for that matter. They're us."

He was suddenly tired of the topic and keen to dismiss it. It was a pointless one unless it was a metaphor, and if so, maybe it was time to talk plainly.

"They're not really us, Lucia. They're just copies."

"I'm sure they won't take too kindly to you saying that, Peter." She smiled; maybe she *was* reading his mind. "Remember, this conversation is being recorded for your copies' memories, and *they'll* think they're real enough."

"At this point in time, I don't particularly care to have a debate about whether or not they are real." He smiled back, warmth spreading through her skin into his. A year or two of *her.* He would like that. "Right here in this moment, Lucia, you and I are real, and nothing else matters to me right now. I don't even care that we're being recorded."

Her smiled echoed his. "Just as long as it doesn't find its way into the public domain, right?"

He was happy to cast aside the illusion that they were actually talking about anything at all. If the relationship lasted longer than the six months of Entrainment Camp, he would be happy, but he was old enough to know that sometimes it was best when things ended sooner rather than later. If she left him tomorrow, he would always have these last moments to remember, and they were richer than any others that came to mind. Lucia's skin, her mind, the way she moved with him—there could be others, but there would be no other exactly like her. This moment would be as precious as it was deliciously fragile, as beautiful as a soap bubble on a breeze. It might slip through his fingers, and the memory might be a thousand times more delicate, but he would always have the latter. If he was careful, he might just have it forever.

Forever...

All around him was nothing but darkness and silence. His head hurt as though someone had taken an ax to it, and his entire body ached. He was stiff in every joint, and he needed to go to the toilet badly. He felt as though he had been in a coma for a timeless eternity.

Then, faintly, a noise pierced the quiet: Someone nearby was sobbing.

Stars danced behind his eyes as he sat up and slowly took stock of his surroundings. Familiarity rushed through him, although not yet with full comprehension. He was lying on the floor of the hole ship cockpit, beside the couch. The bright light making him wince was a silvery crescent moon displayed on the screen. For a moment, he thought it might be the Earth's moon, but then remembered that it couldn't possibly have been. Earth's moon had been destroyed. Besides which, this one had a large L-shaped blotch near its uppermost edge, a feature not associated with the moon he remembered.

But if it wasn't Earth's moon, then the planet he could see wasn't Earth, either. The thought troubled him momentarily, then he shook his head and silently chided himself. Of course it wasn't Earth! The Earth was gone as well, devoured by the Spike AIs and built into something else, which in turn had been destroyed by thousands of shining, star-shaped ships in less than a day. All that remained of Earth and her sister planet Venus was a slowly dispersing cloud of atoms around a now otherwise unremarkable sun.

He studied the image on the screen closer. The hole ship was orbiting a planet at a fairly low altitude. He couldn't make out any detail; the sun was on the far side. There were a couple of glowing patches, eerily like cities casting light into the night sky, but that couldn't be the case. They were too large and too few. Why build only two or three enormous metropolises when the rest of the globe was empty?

"Caryl?" he called out, looking around him. The cockpit was empty. The stars were dimmed by the light reflecting off the moon, but some bright ones were visible. Planets? He wasn't sure.

Again the sobbing, gut-wrenching in its emptiness, eaten away by despair.

"*Arachne*?"

"Yes, Peter."

He found himself relieved to hear the AI's voice.

"Where are we?" he asked, struggling to his feet.

"The system you call HD194640."

It took a moment for the name to sink in. *HD194640*. The statistics were all there: a slightly cooler and brighter star than Sol around thirty-six and a half light-years from Upsilon Aquarius, sixty-two from Earth. A study from Earth had strongly indicated the presence of oxygen and water around a rocky planet orbiting at a distance of roughly two AUs, right in the system's habitable zone. The survey mission sent to study it had left shortly after the *Frank Tipler*, but they would have taken less time to arrive. If everything had run to schedule, they would have arrived in 2137, Mission Time. That would have given them an extra fourteen years to survey their system and establish a beachhead.

It took him a second to recall the name of the ship that had been sent. And when that came, everything fell into place.

The ship was the *Carol Stoker*, with Cleo Samson and Donald Schievenin in charge. Samson had called Earth, just as the *Frank Tipler* had, using Spinner technology. *The Spinners had visited someone else!*

He looked more closely at the world—Varuna, Samson had called it—seeking artifacts similar to those that had been built around Adrasteia. The hole ship's orbit brought the sun over the horizon at that moment, blinding him momentarily. He saw lots of blue and green as his eyes adjusted, and the white of clouds—a far cry from the muddy purple of the world he had briefly lived on. Varuna appeared a beautiful world, obviously teeming with life in all forms.

But then, as the terminator swept across the globe, he saw the scars.

The patches that had glowed at night were revealed as black by day. Fires were burning down on the surface—fires so large they covered one entire limb of a continent shaped roughly like a fork. There were widely scattered pockets of brown and white where surface explosions had cast debris into the atmosphere. Two white circles lying over the ocean were clouds of water vapor rising from impact sites. And one looping line glowing brighter and brighter as it fell through the atmosphere had to be the remains of an orbital tower, cut loose and succumbing to gravity.

The shock waves of its fall would resonate around the globe for days to come, and there were nine more he hadn't found yet. Maybe they'd fallen already, and he had yet to see their effect. Maybe they were still to come, and the fragile ecosphere he had glimpsed would be gone all too soon.

He stared at battered Varuna for a full minute longer before realizing that the sobbing had ceased. His aching bladder also prompted him to move, so he tore his gaze away from the view, walked around the couch and up the short corridor leading to the crew cubicles.

He turned left into his cubicle without looking right into Hatzis's, although her door was open. When he had relieved himself and drunk enough to satisfy the needs of his artificial body, he walked back out again. Looking quickly through her door, he found her sitting on her bed, leaning against the wall, with her head bowed.

"I'm sorry, Peter," she said without looking up. Her voice was hoarse.

He wasn't ready to absolve her just yet. "What happened?" he asked leaning against the door arch.

She sighed. "We arrived here two hours ago and relocated a fair way out from the sun, just to be sure. The Starfish were just finishing things off by then. They'd already destroyed the towers and spindles and were working their way through the satellites in orbit and elsewhere through the system. The *Stoker* was still active. I guess the Starfish thought it a minor installation compared to the towers and left it until the end. The crew was . . ." She paused, swallowed. "They were trying to make the Starfish stop. They could see what was coming. They were pleading with them. They knew they were going to die."

"And you just watched it happen?" He wanted to be angry, but in the end, all he could feel was tired.

She finally looked up, frowning deeply. "I tried to help them. I didn't even stop to think. I told *Arachne* to take us closer, right next to the *Stoker*. I figured that if I could download them into the hole ship or the SSDS units, maybe I could save *something*." She shrugged, wiping her nose on the back of her hand. "But it was too late. The *Stoker* had already been destroyed. I'd forgotten to take the time lag into account. By the time we arrived, there was nothing left but gas, and the Starfish had left."

He made no apology for his accusation. Christ, he wasn't even sure she was telling him the truth. She may simply have been trying to cover her guilt with lies. There was no way for him to really know.

Eventually, he rubbed at the back of his neck and asked, "What did you do to me, Caryl?"

"I knocked you out, of course."

Remembering their struggle, he said, "The manual access point in my hand."

She nodded. "It was a simple matter to override your autonomous system once I had access."

He felt at once violated for what had been done to him and unnerved that she displayed no remorse for having done it.

"So why did you wake me? Why not just leave me like that, out of your way?"

"What good would that do? You're no use to anyone unconscious."

His hand curled into a fist, not from his anger toward her, but rather to hide the point of his vulnerability.

"Is that all you did?" he asked, looking deep into himself. The dream of his original's last night with Lucia was still strong. It resonated with a vividness he hadn't recalled before. It left him feeling odd, as though he had seen it properly for the first time. The revitalized memory made him feel strangely closer to her, not farther away as it had in the past. What had changed to make him feel that way?

She didn't hesitate. "I didn't make any adjustments, if that's what you mean. You're just as fucked up as you were before." She smiled slightly. "That's the way I knew you'd want it."

He didn't respond to the attempted joke; he just held her gaze. Steadily, searching her eyes for an indication of sincerity.

"Look, Peter, I may not have much left to call a life, but not so little that your feelings have become a high priority. If I was going to rewrite your bloody brain, I would've done it days ago, I assure you."

He shook his head, turning again to the memory of Lucia. It was the same as it had been before, only now there was an entirely new level of meaning attached to it. Perhaps it had always been there, or else he was just looking at it differently now, adding his own interpretations to what had been said that night. Did that mean he was now closer to the memories of his old self, or farther away?

He looked again at Hatzis on her bed. There was still no evidence of remorse in her expression. She just sat there waiting for him to say something. So he obliged her.

"Next time, don't wake me, okay?"

She narrowed her eyes slightly, puzzled. "But—?"

"It's a warning," he interrupted, "not a request. Because

if you ever do that to me again, I swear I'll kill you. I'm having enough trouble being me without you fucking things up."

She broke away from his stare after a few seconds, nodding her understanding but saying nothing.

"How did you know, anyway?" he asked.

"Huh?"

"About the Starfish, I mean. That's why you tried to stop me, wasn't it? You knew they'd be waiting for us."

She nodded again.

"But *how?*"

"Isn't it obvious?" she said, her gaze meeting his again, challengingly. "Think about it, Peter. What do we know about the Starfish?"

"Not much." Puzzled, he went through the meager evidence they had gathered to date. "They're much more advanced than we are. You thought the Spinners might have destroyed Upsilon Aquarius, but the Starfish ships look different; that could be a ruse, of course, although I don't know why they'd bother."

"What else?"

He thought, looking for specifics rather than speculation. "Well, they have ftl drives, like the Spinners do, and maybe other technologies that are similar. They didn't know about Sol System, or else they would've gone there first. So they must've learned about it after Upsilon Aquarius, maybe from the data banks in the *Tipler,* or some other way. That could be where they heard about *here,* as well, although we didn't know the mission had been successful then. Maybe . . ." He stopped, frowning. Something was itching to fall into place. The missing piece that would make the picture complete.

How had the Starfish known about HD194640? How

had they known about Sol? How had they even known about the mission to Upsilon Aquarius?

And then it hit him.

"Oh my God," he breathed. "The ftl communicator?"

"It's the only explanation," she said. "The transmissions aren't unilateral. Every time you tried to talk to someone, you were telling the whole universe about it. Well, not actually the whole universe," she quickly amended, "because they have a limited range. But you know what I mean."

The notion troubled him, because if this were true, then . . .

He shook off the troubling thought.

"Are you sure about this?"

She shrugged. "It does make sense," she said. "Back on the Frame, one of the remotes had commented on the Discord—the first transmission we had received—saying that whoever had sent it was 'spraying the skies with it.' It only occurred to me when we got that transmission from Cleo Samson. Then it all made sense."

"But why—?" He fumbled with the words. *Already dead . . .* "Why weren't we *warned*? The Gifts could have told us about this, surely. In remaining silent they caused the deaths of everyone—"

"No, Peter," she cut in. "They can't be blamed for that. The Starfish are the only ones responsible for all the killing that has been taking place. The most that the Gifts are guilty of is reticence."

"But it was their technology."

"The Spinners' technology, which we happily used," she said calmly. "You can't blame the tools, Peter; and that's all the gifts are."

The uncomfortable thought rose inside of him again. *If the tools weren't to blame . . .*

"They could have still warned us," he spat. Then, turning his back on her, he moved back down to the cockpit. On the screen, the image of the planet was catching the sun. It was beautiful and brutalized at the same time.

He only realized Hatzis had followed him down when she spoke suddenly from behind him. "I know what you're thinking, Peter."

He faced her with an expression that was both challenging and threatening. *Had* she tampered with his mind? But the emotions quickly dissipated. They were merely a diversionary tactic by him to avoid the thought that kept struggling to be free: *I killed humanity.*

He dropped his gaze and shook his head.

"You're not to blame," she said. "It's not your fault."

"I called the *Tipler* from Sol. I led them there—"

"You weren't to know," she went on. "There's no way you *could* have known."

"Nevertheless, the history books will all say that Peter Alander was the one who led the Starfish to Sol, the one who sealed humanity's fate." He added wryly, "Though I guess I should take some consolation in the fact that there'll be no one around to write any history books . . . nor anyone to read them for that matter."

"*Now* who has the defeatist attitude?"

"All I'm saying is that I—"

"Listen," she said, dismissing his protests, "I've been doing a lot of thinking about this over the last couple of days. The way I see it, the Starfish are more than just random planet-smashers. They're aware of what the Spinners are doing. They're following along behind, listening for the ftl communicators and then moving in when the coast is clear, like scavengers or sharks, waiting for the smell of blood, picking off the smaller races the Spinners have touched."

"But *why?*" he said, appalled that the picture she was painting was the same as the one in his own head.

"To stop us using the gifts, perhaps? To stop *us?* Maybe they feel we'd become threats in the long run, if left to study the Spinners' technology. They could just be trying to prevent any competition arising in the galaxy. Just because the Spinners might not be threatened by the idea doesn't mean others wouldn't be."

"So why not take on the Spinners directly?"

"Perhaps the Spinners are too advanced for them. The Starfish are snapping at their heels like jealous puppies."

Alander snorted. "Those puppies, as you call them, just decimated your home in less than a day."

"Okay, a bad analogy," she said. "But you know what I'm saying."

"So what it amounts to is just an extreme case of bad luck? It would've been perfectly all right to use the communicators but for the dumb luck of the Starfish death squads waiting nearby, right?"

He knew that what she was saying made sense, and he appreciated her efforts to make him feel better; nevertheless, her words did little to alleviate the guilt he was feeling.

"The fact is, Peter, if it hadn't have been you, it would have been someone else. Someone from the *Stoker*, perhaps. I know that probably doesn't help you at the moment, but the point is that it was going to happen, regardless. It's the nature of our species to be curious—Christ, maybe it's the nature of all life in the galaxy. And maybe the Starfish

know that. That's why they lie in waiting, listening for the
first messages from ftl communicators, waiting for the little children to play with their new toys."

"Which brings us to the obvious question: *Where* are
they hiding?"

"That's something else I've been considering while you
were out." Facing the screen, she said: "*Arachne*, bring
up the maps I was working on earlier."

A 3-D star chart was suddenly presented on the screen,
displaying a section of the galaxy surrounding Sol System. The map zoomed in and retreated in accordance with
Hatzis's verbal prompts. Clearly, this was something she
had spent a bit of time thinking through.

"I confirmed with the hole ship that the unilateral signals
from the communicator reach approximately two hundred
light-years. So, if we put a sphere on the map around Adrasteia, indicating the bubble of space in which the ftl
communicator would be effective, *here* . . ." A sphere appeared on the display, roughly two hundred light-years in
diameter. ". . . and another centered on Earth, indicating
the region in which normal human transmissions would
have extended over the last couple of centuries, *here*." Another sphere appeared, again roughly two hundred light-
years wide, this one overlapping the other. "Now, *Arachne*,
highlight the area on the map that is covered by the ftl
communicator but *not* the Earth transmissions."

The view of the map rotated around a glowing red section in the shape of a crescentlike shell.

"This area," she said, facing Alander, "is where the
Starfish must have come from to have detected the ftl
transmissions without already knowing about Earth."

"The Spinners, too?"

"Perhaps. Note that it's pointing in the rough direction of Sculptor, the source of the Tedesco bursts."

He studied the maps for a few moments longer.

"I'm impressed," he said. "But how can all of this information help us?"

She shrugged. "Maybe if we get enough information, we'll be able to see some sort of path."

"And then what?"

"If the Starfish *are* simply following in the wake of the Spinners, we'll have an idea of where *Spinners* might go next."

"Do you think they're aware of what's happening?"

"I don't see how. *Arachne* has no information on the Starfish, suggesting the Spinners have never even encountered them before. Chances are, the Spinners have touched an untold number of civilizations over the millennia they have been doing this, and they have been inadvertently handing them over to the Starfish, too."

The thought was a disturbing one, and one difficult to fully grasp. All of the information he had seen in the gifts' Library and Gallery, representing so many different cultures and species—and now it was possibly all that remained of any of them.

"You think we should tell them?"

A look of amazement touched her face. "Don't *you?*"

"Of course," he said. "But how?"

"Like I said, with more information, we might be able to extrapolate the direction the Spinners are headed in and intercept them."

"By more information, you mean finding more ruins like Varuna, right?"

She nodded somberly. "Let's face it, Peter; it's a possibility that the Spinners have already contacted one of the other the survey missions."

He felt a surge of adrenaline. "Christ, if they have contacted two already, why not three? Or four? The trick will be trying to find them *before* they use their communicators—"

"But we won't be able to use *our* communicator, either, because if we do, we risk getting caught ourselves. Not immediately, perhaps, but sooner or later, we'd screw up, I'm sure."

"So we use the hole ship to go looking," he said. "It's our only choice."

She nodded again. "We've demonstrated that the Starfish can't trace it unless it falls inside their light cone, wherever they're stationed. We should be able to check the nearest systems to see if the Spinners have passed through. Given this system's proximity to Upsilon Aquarius, it might be safe to assume that they canvassed the area first, before moving on."

"So we find more gifts, we study them to see if there's a way to contact the Spinners, we tell them what they've been doing, and . . . what? They reward us by helping us or giving us the tools to rebuild?"

"That's a frightening possibility, isn't it?" she said. "Rebuilding humanity on what little we have." She shook her head. "That could take forever."

"And how does forever begin, Caryl?"

She smiled at this, nodding. "Slowly," she said. "Very slowly."

He stared at her for a while, letting it sink in. The thought she had given the matter had done more than just ease her suicidal depression; it had given them both a direction, if they chose to take it. And why wouldn't they?

Something they could *do* would make all the difference to their morale. He could see it in her and could feel it in himself. There was still a long way to go, obviously—emotionally speaking, they still had a lot to deal with—but it was a start, at least.

He may have destroyed humanity, but at least he could take a decent shot at repairing the damage.

"We've been saying 'us' and 'we'," he said cautiously. "Does that mean we'll work together on this?"

"There's no one else, Peter. Just you, me, and thousands of other engrams, scattered dozens of light-years apart. It's not much, you'll have to admit."

"Better than nothing."

"I know," she said. "We'll just have to find a way to make our goals the same. I know we come from very different backgrounds, but I think we can accomplish more together than apart. At the very least, I want to avoid arguing over the hole ship, since we both have the ability to operate it."

He studied her carefully in the light reflecting off the planet below them. "It won't choose between us?"

"No," she said.

"You've asked it?"

"Yes." Her serious expression eased, just for a moment. "I don't know what it'd do if we gave it conflicting orders. Make us arm wrestle, perhaps."

He half smiled at her joke, thinking, *But she did ask.* How close had she come to ditching his unconscious body and continuing on her own? Possibly only the lack of direction she would have without him around had saved him. He wondered how sincere she was about wanting to warn the Spinners, or even reuniting the far-flung orphans of Earth. Did she really care?

It didn't matter, anyway. At least she had raised the possibility of working together, for whatever motive. It would be difficult to manage on their own, even with the hole ship's AI to help. It was a job that could take them years.

"Okay," he said. "So how do we start? Do we visit systems at random, or do we develop a method? There were over a thousand survey missions. If even half of them failed, that still leaves five hundred, and—"

He got no further. The hole ship issued a sound he had never heard before, like a chime ringing backward. At the same instant, the view on the screen changed, revealing a patch of space farther around the arc of the planet. Against the dark of space, a white point had appeared.

"*Arachne*?" Hatzis asked. "What's going on? Are the Starfish back?"

"Caryl, wait," he said, putting a hand on her arm. "*Look.*"

The white point widened, became a sphere. The sphere grew larger as though inflating like a balloon.

"It can't be," she whispered. "We would've heard."

"Maybe we did." He watched the other hole ship expand in silence. "Maybe the *Stoker* tested theirs the same way we did. Maybe it's just coming back!"

He felt her tense beside him as they waited for the cockpit to emerge. What would he say to the pilot? He knew exactly how he or she would be feeling on seeing what had happened to their friends, having been through the experience himself only a few days earlier. Consolation did not come easy with such a loss, and any attempt at offering any would no doubt be met with anger and hostility.

A minute or two passed, but there was no sign of the

cockpit emerging. Nor had the hole ship registered any incoming messages.

"Hail them," he said. "Tell them we're from Sol System."

He caught Hatzis looking at him from the corner of his eye; he was sure she would have liked to contest the statement, but in the end, she must have thought better of it.

"*Arachne*? You sent the message, didn't you?"

"Yes, Peter."

"Still no reply?"

"None as yet."

"Then send it again. And this time—"

"Too late," said Hatzis, pointing.

"What?" Puzzled, he watched as the hole ship began to shrink again. "It's *leaving?*"

"So it would seem," said Hatzis.

He could do nothing but shake his head as the sphere continued to shrink until it finally disappeared altogether. "I don't understand."

"Could it be the Spinners?"

"I doubt it. The stuff they're giving us is throwaway, remember? They'd be as likely to use it as you would've been to drive a Model T Ford, back home."

He pondered the mystery for a moment, nagged by a thought that there was something missing, something they hadn't noticed. The central sphere of the second hole ship had appeared from nowhere, then disappeared almost as quickly. What else was there?

Then a thought struck him.

"*Arachne*, keep an eye out," he said. "I reckon it'll come back elsewhere in the system, probably closer to the sun. And soon, I'll bet."

"How could you possibly know that?" Hatzis asked, turning to face him.

He looked away from the empty patch of sky where the hole ship had been to where the fires on Varuna burned on, below. It might be years before they went out. The smoke, plus dust and water vapor kicked up by the orbital towers yet to fall, might hide the surface from the sun for still more years. The planet might be plunged into an ice age, or thrust into a period of runaway greenhouse effects. Or it might recover completely. The Earth had recovered from far worse catastrophes in its time. Maybe, he thought, if he returned far enough in the future, the greenery would have recovered. He might be able to see blues skies again.

Twenty years, thirty . . . ?

It was something to hope for, anyway.

"Call it a hunch," he said.

3.0
EPILOGUE

2160.9.23 Standard Mission Time
25 August, 2163 V.T.

Another dawn, another planet.

Watching the red star rise over a dark horizon, Caryl Hatzis couldn't help but wonder whether her life was really that bad. Compared to the crew of the *Paul Davies*, she didn't have as much to complain about as she'd once thought.

Where Adrasteia had been arid and Varuna lush, Tatenen was a frozen wasteland, the victim of a tug-of-war between two stars. The stars Zeta-1 and Zeta-2 Reticuli were too far apart to be companions but too close for either to support a stable solar system. Yet either or both had once done so. They were very similar stars to Sol, and three planets still clung to them. Two were gas giants in wildly elliptical orbits. The other was Tatenen, currently drifting the gulf between the two stars and not due to see warmth for several millennia. There might have been more, expelled long ago by the vagaries of gravity, but there was no way of knowing now.

When UNESSPRO had conducted its catalogue of Earth-like planets, Tatenen had been close enough to Zeta-2 to exhibit signs of liquid water and gaseous oxygen, and that had been sufficient to make this particular system a target. It was only after the survey team had arrived that they realized their target would never be suitable as a colony world.

The crew of the *Paul Davies* had had time to come to terms with their ill fortune, however. They had immediately set to work, mapping the bedrock with radar and drilling into the frozen atmosphere, seeking reclaimable material. The planet had had no forms of multicellular life, after being expelled from its sun, but what there had been had left a thick layer of carbon and other useful compounds behind, several meters down. Nanomachines drilled to exploit the planet's dwindling geothermal energy sources, set up miniature factories scattered wildly across the buried continents, and repopulated the surface with spiderlike constructs designed to skate across the ice and report what they found. More complex devices served as remotes for the minds in orbit above. But they were nothing like the artificial bodies Alander inhabited, of course, for they would have ceased functioning within moments of exposure to the icy wastes. Instead, these creatures were spindly robots with many-pointed feet, capable of assuming a number of shapes depending on their environment. They had odd, mechanical faces by which the colonists could express emotion when not using conSense to overlay the harsh reality with more appealing images. They were building a small outpost on the planet's south pole, from which to conduct astronomical observations.

And that, as far as she could work out, was as much

as they had accomplished in the forty-nine years since they'd arrived. With no solar power to speak of and progress accordingly gradual, much of the crew's time had been spent in slow-mo, reducing their clock rates so that five or more seconds in the real world passed for every one in their subjective experience. That way, they had unintentionally avoided the fate of older surveying missions such as the one sent to Delta Pavonis, which she and Alander had found to be lifeless and hollow, apart from the most basic AIs. Had she needed proof to convince Alander of the truth of her reservations about engrams, the *Martyn Fogg*, silently orbiting the world its crew had once called Egeria, had certainly provided it.

He had stared at the pitted shell of the *Fogg* for a long time, thinking, then asked, "You offered to fix me, once. Could you have fixed them, too, if we'd gotten here in time?"

She shook her head. "Your problem is different—a fault in the wiring of a flawed design. To fix the flaw we'd need to completely rebuild every individual from the base up. The Vincula could have done it, but that's obviously not possible anymore. Maybe," she said, fighting emotions that still ran very deep, "maybe we can rebuild something, somewhere, that will do the trick."

"We'll have to," he said. "Or pretty soon there'll just be you . . . along with a handful of people in cold storage who opted out to avoid burning out."

It was a grim scenario. She didn't know yet whether hoping to avoid it was noble or simply futile.

At least, she thought, the crew of the *Davies* had an interesting astronomical situation to observe before the possibility of degradation became a reality for them. There were actually three stars in close conjunction

around Tatenen. As well as Zeta-1 and Zeta-2, there was
also a red dwarf only 0.8 of a light-year away, given the
unromantic name of 8869-308-1 by twentieth-century astronomers, but renamed Kurukulla by its surveyors after
the red-skinned Buddhist goddess of riches. Construction
was well under way on an interferometer powerful enough
to tell whether the planets orbiting it were Earth-like; fuel-
hoarding had already begun to power a probe to visit a
suitable target, should one eventuate. Vince Mohler and
his crew were all too aware of the limitations of the world
they had adopted as their own; given a choice, they would
happily move. But they were only prepared to leap if they
could look first.

   She and Alander had been happy to do the looking for
them. Data from a relatively short hop to Kurukulla had
given the crew of the *Davies* both hope and disappointment. There *was* a world in the habitable zone, barely, but
it would never be fit for natural human colonization. It was,
however, preferable to their present location, having at
least a solar power source relatively close at hand. Half of
the crew, headed by the mission's military survey manager,
Faith Jong, had decided to go, once the present installation
could spare both resources and staff. The rest would wait
out Tatenen's long journey to Zeta-2, and spring.

   One of those who had decided to stay was Caryl Hatzis.
As assistant to the civilian survey manager, rather than
manager herself, the Hatzis engram of this mission had
had a much less stressful time of things, judging by the
incomplete memories Alander had brought with him from
the *Tipler*. There had been an inevitable moment of awk-
wardness when she had been introduced to her evolved
original, but that had passed, and she had ended up vol-
unteering her memories for inclusion. The engram had

balked at the idea of becoming an active node—and Hatzis wasn't even sure it would be possible, given the limitations of the software—but it was still an intriguing thought. One day, there might be enough of *her* left to re-create what she had lost, since even alone, without the multiplicity she had lost with Sol—along with Matilda Sulich, JORIS, the Urges, *everyone*—she was still more complex than all the UNESSPRO engrams combined.

One day . . .

In the meantime, there was still a great deal of work to be done. Once Alander had got over his fears of meeting versions of either himself, Cleo Samson, or Lucia Benck (the latter two had not been on the *Davies*'s manifest, and the version of him had permanently crashed on arrival), he had rapidly got down to business. The Spinners clearly hadn't come anywhere near Tatenen, but they might yet do so. Mohler had to be prepared, not only for the aliens and their gifts but for the dangers within his own crew. The lesson learned by Cleo Samson's betrayal of the *Tipler* would have to be passed on to every mission they encountered, even if UNESSPRO no longer existed.

"If these Spinners *do* come here, what should we do about it?" Mohler's image in conSense was of a slender man in his forties with prematurely gray hair and olive skin. An extremophile biologist by trade, he had some of the emotional isolation required of someone used to traveling to peculiar places for extended periods in order to study a hardy species of bacteria. Maybe that was why he made such a competent leader, Hatzis thought.

"There's nothing you can do," Alander told him, interacting with Mohler the same way he had with Cleo Samson, going far enough to let conSense fool him into thinking she was standing in front of him but still not accepting full immersion. "The gifts will be delivered;

you'll have no choice about that. Just don't use the communicator from here, whatever you do. We think this is what alerts the Starfish to your presence. Take the hole ship somewhere else and call us from there instead. But go a fair way, because we don't know yet if something else can tip the Starfish off at a closer range. We do know that their travel times are similar to ours; it took both them and us about a day in real time to travel from Sol to the outer reaches. That means they'll only be hours away from you if you do let something slip."

Mohler nodded gravely. He had accepted without question their explanation of what had happened to Sol and Upsilon Aquarius. What choice had he in the face of an ftl starship and the original of Caryl Hatzis?

"We'd also like you to broadcast a warning to the Spinners," Alander went on. "I'm not sure they'll listen, but it's worth a try. They need to know about the Starfish. If they're going to give other colonies communicators, there might be a safer design they can provide . . . something the Starfish can't home in on."

"And if someone else comes?" Mohler asked.

Alander didn't answer immediately. So far, he and Hatzis had visited ten high-profile systems targeted by UNESSPRO. Four were empty of all life; the missions had clearly failed to arrive, for whatever reason. The crews of three relatively close to Earth, such as the *Martyn Fogg*, had suffered engram failure. Two had been destroyed in similar fashions to Adrasteia and Sol, although precisely when 94 Aquarius and BSC8477 had used their communicators and thereby summoned the Starfish had not been determined. The calls should have been detected by the hole ship *Arachne*, since both systems were on the Upsilon Aquarius side of surveyed space. Hatzis suspected that it had happened during her and Alander's three long trips: from Sol to Adrasteia and back, then from Sol to Varuna and the ruined *Carol Stoker*. They obviously couldn't receive such transmissions while in transit, something else the Gifts had omitted to tell them.

Given that four systems had been visited by the Spinners in only a week or two, that put the dispersal of the gifts at a higher rate than she had expected. This was potentially a good thing: It was only a matter of time and persistence before they found another survey mission either just before or just after contact, in time to warn them about the Starfish. Even if they missed such a mission, there was a chance that survivors would escape the Starfish as she and Alander had and begin their own quest among the systems. Should such a group come to Tatenen, they would at least be made aware of others' efforts and hopefully even agree to combine forces to make the job easier.

This was in fact her greatest hope: that out of terrible adversity, a handful of surviving survey missions could be united, and that humanity could, ultimately, rebuild itself. Contact with Tatenen could very well mark the beginnings of such a process.

"The weak shall inherit the Earth, huh?" Mohler had commented the first time he'd heard her plans, adding, "Pity there isn't an Earth left to inherit."

But she knew that Mohler wasn't referring to other survey missions when asking about visitors. He was talking about the second mysterious hole ship that he'd seen from the footage that she and Alander had taken from HD194640, shortly before they'd left Varuna. As Alander had predicted, the ship had eventually returned, but not until a full day later. And when it did, all they were able

to do was watch it with interest. Its distant location meant
the images they were looking at were already an hour old;
they knew that should they attempt to move *Arachne*
closer, the other hole ship would have long since relocated
elsewhere.

During its second appearance, the cockpit had emerged
as normal. It was different from the one she and Alander
had become accustomed to; it had been modified, somehow, and looked as though barnacles or coral had grown
over its normally smooth surface, encrusting it with
strange lumps and projections. What purpose they served,
neither they nor the hole ship could guess.

The strange cockpit had orbited the central body as normal for a minute, then decelerated to a halt. Then, just as
slowly, a hole had opened in the mottled side, and something had emerged.

Hatzis recognized it immediately, as did Alander. The
object was identical to the death markers they had found
previously in Upsilon Aquarius and Sol, and later found
in 94 Aquarius and BSC8477. Slowly, nudged from the
inside by an invisible force, it had drifted out into space
and assumed, they confirmed later, a similar orbit to the
others.

"The one thing HD194640 was missing," Alander explained, looking slightly smug, "was a death marker.
We'd hunted everywhere and hadn't found one. Also, we
knew that the death markers had no propulsion systems,
therefore someone had to physically put them in place. A
hole ship would have been perfect for the job. That's how
I guessed it would return."

"So you're saying it's one of ours? Another survey mission?"

"All I'm saying is that it's someone else who's been contacted by the Spinners."

"Someone not human?"

He had shrugged. "It's possible. They might be the source of the Tedesco bursts. We might be seeing the tail end of a convoy, here . . ."

Too far away to contact it, they could only watch as the hole ship airlock had contracted shut, the cockpit had begun to rotate again, and their reticent visitor once again disappeared.

But the possibility that it had been piloted by a member of an alien race, also contacted by the Spinners and attacked by the Starfish, added credence to the plot she was making of the Spinners' movement through surveyed space from somewhere in the direction of Sculptor, through Upsilon Aquarius, then to BSC8477 and 94 Aquarius, and lastly to HD194640. Without a more accurate idea as to when the middle two systems had been contacted, they could only guess as to what rate the Spinners were moving through surveyed space. The best she could say was that only three days—and a distance of thirty-six light-years—had separated the destruction of Adrasteia and Varuna. If that was how fast the Spinners were moving, they would reach the ruins of Sol in a couple of weeks and pass out the other side of surveyed space in about a month.

That gave the remaining humans a relatively brief time span in which to contact them, or at least to make the most of the gifts they left behind. There had to be some way to get their attention.

Even if they didn't, for better or for worse, life would go on. Hatzis couldn't blame her engram for seeking a happier alternative. Although there were presently few for

the occupants of *Arachne*, their number of options had
increased after only two weeks of exploring. They had
found survivors; they had found abandoned beachheads
that could serve as a base, if needed; they weren't alone.

And that was why, perhaps, she was beginning to think
that she wasn't as unfortunate as she had believed after
the destruction of the Vincula. Never had things seemed
darker than when she had gone to Io in the hope that one
of the povs she had warned might have survived and gone
there—and heard nothing. But even on her own, she was
self-sufficient within herself and capable of adjusting to
change. It would have been easy to turn her back on the
engrams and rebuild from scratch on her own, but the
simple fact was that it could be simpler with their help.
They had resources she did not; even with the hole ship
at her sole command, she would have faced a tough time
making any progress at all, at first. This way, she would
have allies, at least for a while, if not permanently. And
it wasn't impossible that their goals would one day be the
same. If she could find a way to get around their flaw,
they might form a sort of community resembling something Sol would have been proud of. There was still a
chance, as her mother might have put it, of turning their
weakness into strength.

She stayed in the background as Alander evaded Mohler's last question—"And if someone else comes?"—and
wrapped up his final dealings with Mohler, preparatory to
moving on. Despite her connection to one of their crew
members, the *Davies*'s survey team still regarded her as
something other. And she was; there was no denying that.
If they were afraid that she might exploit them, they were
absolutely correct. Her plans to bootstrap the engrams to
a higher stage of human evolution, using Spinner or Spike

technology, as necessary, might not accord with the plans of at least one of them.

She smiled to herself. Alander had noticed the slight change within himself, but he seemed to have accepted the lie that she hadn't tampered with him while he was unconscious. Perhaps he thought it had come from within himself. If so, that was good; that was what he was supposed to think. And besides, in a sense it was true. All she'd done was randomized the fine-tuning of some of his responses, so he wouldn't be locked into old or new destructive patterns, trapped in stifling regularity. Like the beating of a living heart, he needed a touch of chaos to make him truly live. No one could predict, now, exactly what he would be—even her—but it seemed to be helping.

And he would always have his memories. They all would.

For whom?

If her engram ever asked *her* that question, she knew what she would say. There was only one answer to that question, even if it was different for every person who asked it.

For me, she would say. *Always for me.*

APPENDIX 1

THE ADJUSTED PLANCK STANDARD INTERNATIONAL UNIT

After several notable mission failures in the late twentieth and early twenty-first centuries, an attempt was made for the United Near-Earth Stellar Survey Program (UNES-SPRO) to develop a single system of measurement to prevent conflict between data or software from nations contributing to joint space projects. A working group was established in 2043 to examine the issue, drawing on expertise within both scientific and political communities. Two of the main criteria of the working group was that such a system of units should be as similar as possible to existing systems, in order to ease the transition between them, and that it should be as independent of arbitrary criteria as possible. That the system would be decimal was a starting assumption.

The working group chose Planck units as an early starting point. These values are based on fundamental constants of the universe and thus make a good foundation for a system of units. The basic Planck measures for mass, length, and time are:

Planck mass	$= 2.177 \times 10^{-8}$ kg
Planck length	$= 1.616 \times 10^{-35}$ m
Planck time	$= 5.391 \times 10^{-44}$ s

These values are too small to be useful for everyday measurements. One Imperial inch would be equivalent to over 157 billion quadrillion quadrillion Planck meters; a thin person might be alarmed to discover that they now weighed almost three trillion Planck kilograms; one old hour would drag on for over a trillion quadrillion quadrillion *quadrillion* Planck minutes. Clearly, these units would not be suitable either as a mission standard or for general usage.

The solution was to apply a simple fix to each unit, bringing them into more familiar territory. The *Adjusted* Planck second was simply derived from the "pure" Planck second by multiplying it by 10^{43}. The other two base units were derived in a similar fashion. Thus:

Adjusted Planck mass	$= 2.177$ kg
Adjusted Planck length	$= 1.616$ m
Adjusted Planck time	$= 0.5391$ s

All other fundamental units (electric current, magnetic flux, energy, etc.) can be derived from these three units plus a number of other universal constants such as e (the magnitude of charge on a single electron) and the Boltzmann constant. Since the layperson is most likely to encounter the units of mass, space, time, and temperature, we will restrict our discussion mainly to these four units.

1. Time

The length of a second, along with the number of seconds in a minute, the number of minutes in an hour, the number of hours in a day, the number of days in a week or a month, and the number of months in a year, are *all* arbitrarily determined figures. They are not fixed by nature. The only two units of time that could be considered to be relatively permanent (for humans in the relative short term) are the rotational period of the Earth and the sidereal year. These two durations were key considerations in development of the Adjusted Planck time scale, although neither were considered essential for a system of time measurement intended primarily for use on missions to other solar systems, upon which relativistic effects would play havoc with calendars.

As the following chart shows, the new scale of time measurement bears a strong resemblance to the old: The new minutes and years are particularly close, and days, weeks, and months are not radically removed, either. The division of minutes and hours into 100 equal portions facilitates more intuitive timekeeping; a day of two ten-hour halves preserves a sense of familiarity without sacrificing practicality; ten months of six five-day weeks allows great flexibility when it comes to scheduling rosters and planning in the medium term. Nations used to decimal measurements in other areas would, it was assumed, adapt naturally to the new scale, while those unfamiliar with them would still find "natural" time periods more or less unchanged.

1 new second		= 0.54 old second
1 new minute	= 100 new seconds	= 0.90 old minute (54 old seconds)
1 new hour	= 100 new minutes	= 1.5 old hours (90 old minutes)
1 new day	= 20 new hours	= 1.2 old days (30 old hours)
1 new week	= 5 new days	= 0.89 old week (6.2 old days)
1 new month	= 6 new weeks	= 1.2 old months (5.3 old weeks)
1 new year	= 10 new months	= 1.025 old years (12 old months)

It is true that over time the year as recorded by the Adjusted Planck method (which was adopted by UNESSPRO on 1/1/2050, the midpoint of the twenty-first century and projected launch date of the first crewed interstellar mission) would drift from that recorded on Earth. As mentioned above, however, this was considered immaterial for missions to other solar systems. Adjustment is readily made between the two calendars. The need to provide space-going humanity with a practical method of timekeeping ultimately outweighed the need to maintain an impractical terrestrial tradition.

2. Space

While the Adjusted Planck decimal time scale was perhaps the most contentious issue facing the working group, the issue of measuring distance, area, and volume was considered no less important since a handful of contrib-

uting nations—notably the United States of America—
had still not adopted a metric system of measurement.
Although the change to metric was widely considered inevitable in the long term, the following compromise was
agreed upon because of its congruence with old units.

1 new centimeter		= 1.6 old cm / 0.64 inches
1 new decimeter (dm)	= 10 new cm	= 6.5 inches
1 new meter	= 10 new dm	= 1.6 old m / 3.3 feet
3 new meters		= 10 feet
1 new kilometer	= 1000 new meters	= 0.97 mile

The Adjusted Planck meter is still considered by many
to be too large for everyday use, but its derived unit, the
decimeter has many practical applications. The centimeter, falling neatly between the old centimeter and the inch,
has also been touted as a compromise between the two
systems. But the similarity between the old mile and the
new kilometer and the new liter and the old gallon—plus
a number of other convenient measures arising naturally
out of the figures (see point 4)—convinced the U.S. del-
egates that to change would be advantageous.

1 new hectare	= 2.6 old hectares	= 6.4 acres
1 new liter (dm³)	= 4.2 old liters	= 1.1 gallons

3. Mass, Current, and Temperature

Once measures for space and time had been accepted, the
fundamental units of mass, current, and temperature were

foregone conclusions. The mantra that five old pounds equals one new kilogram was concocted to ease the transition for Imperial users. Confusion between Fahrenheit and Celsius scales was already common, especially when combined with the shifting zero arising from scientific usage of the Kelvin scale. The new scale, with its base set firmly on absolute zero, was adopted alongside the others to ensure congruity between data sets.

1 new g		= 2.2 old g
1 new kg	= 1000 new g	= 4.8 old pounds
1 new tonne	= 1000 new kg	= 2.1 old tons

| 1 new ampere | | = 2.972 old ampere |

New	Centigrade	Fahrenheit	Kelvin
1°	= 1.415°	= 2.563°	= 1.415°
0°	= −273.15°	= −459.67°	= 0° (absolute zero)
193°	= 0°	= 32°	= 273.15° (freezing point of H_2O)
264°	= 100°	= 212°	= 373.15° (boiling point of H_2O)

4. Contributing Factors

Adopting an entirely new set of unit measurements is nothing to take lightly. The working party took many considerations into account, one of them being inelegance. This property, although ill defined, is a factor in the acceptance of any novelty, be it a scientific theory, a fashion of dress, or a style of writing. The simple annotation of several frequently used constants in Adjusted Planck units contributed to the decision to adopt them. For instance:

c (the speed of light)	$= 1.00 \times 10^8$ ms^{-1}
1 light-year	$= 6.00 \times 10^{15}$ m
1 light-hour	$= 1.00 \times 10^{11}$ m
1 parsec	$= 2.0 \times 10^{16}$ m
1 g	$= 1.0$ light-year/year^2
1 solar radius	$= 430000$ km
1 Earth radius	$= 4000$ km (equatorial)
geostationary orbit	$= 22220$ km (Earth)

These figures have many practical applications in space exploration (the field for which these units were developed). The simplicity with which they can be expressed in the new units contributes to the ease of communication between scientists—the main point the new system was created to address.

5. Conversion Table

The following conversions were provided for rapid calculation from the old International System of Units to the new Adjusted Planck Standard International Units.

	Unit	Conversion
Velocity	m/s[1]	0.334
Acceleration	m/s^2	1.76
Density	g/cm^3	1.92
Pressure	Pa	0.216
Force	N	0.0818
Energy	J	0.0506
Frequency	Hz	1.86
Resistance	Ω	0.241
Voltage	V	0.0811

APPENDIX 2

MISSION REGISTER

NB: All measurements are made in Adjusted Planck units and all dates are recorded in Standard Mission Time.

Upsilon Aquarius

UNESSPRO Mission: 842
Core survey ship: *Frank Tipler*
Primary survey world: UA-2 aka Adrasteia
Survey manager (military): Jayme Sivio
Survey manager (civilian): Caryl Hatzis
Secondary mission: *Chung-2*
Secondary mission pilot: Lucia Benck
Distance from Sol: 72.5 ly
Mission duration (Sol-relative): 99.9 years
Mission duration (ship-relative): 47.0 years
Departure date: 2051.2
Arrival date: 2151.1

HD165401 (via Barnard's Star)

UNESSPRO Mission: 340
Core survey ship: *Michio Kaku*
Survey manager (civilian): Caryl Hatzis
Distance from Sol: 77.7 ly
Mission duration (Sol-relative): 106.6 years
Mission duration (ship-relative): 49.9 years
Departure date: 2050.5
Arrival date: 2157.1

Pi-1 Ursa Major

UNESSPRO Mission: 391
Core survey ship: *Andre Linde*
Distance from Sol: 45.4 ly
Mission duration (Sol-relative): 64.2 years
Mission duration (ship-relative): 32.1 years
Departure date: 2051.3
Arrival date: 2115.5

BSC5070

UNESSPRO Mission: 992
Core survey ship: *Marcus Chown*
Distance from Sol: 67.9 ly
Mission duration (Sol-relative): 93.8 years
Mission duration (ship-relative): 44.5 years
Departure date: 2051.1
Arrival date: 2144.9

BSC5148

UNESSPRO Mission: 636
Core survey ship: *Frank Drake*
Distance from Sol: 80.3 ly
Mission duration (Sol-relative): 110.1 years
Mission duration (ship-relative): 51.4 years
Departure date: 2050.1
Arrival date: 2160.1

HD194640

UNESSPRO Mission: 835
Core survey ship: *Carol Stoker*
Primary survey world: Varuna
Survey manager (civilian): Cleo Samson
Survey manager (military): Donald Schievenin
Distance from Sol: 61.8 ly
Mission duration (Sol-relative): 85.7 years
Mission duration (ship-relative): 41.1 years
Departure date: 2051.3
Arrival date: 2137.1

Zeta-1/2 Reticuli (and 8869-308-1)

UNESSPRO Mission: 805
Core survey ship: *Paul Davies*
Primary survey world: Tatenen
Survey manager (military): Faith Jong
Survey manager (civilian): Vince Mohler
Secondary mission pilot: Rob Singh
Distance from Sol: 38.4 ly
Mission duration (Sol-relative): 55.1 years

Mission duration (ship-relative): 28.3 years
Departure date: 2050.8
Arrival date: 2105.9

Delta Pavonis

UNESSPRO Mission: 416
Core survey ship: *Martyn Fogg*
Primary survey world: Egeria
Distance from Sol: 19.4 ly
Mission duration (Sol-relative): 30.2 years
Mission duration (ship-relative): 17.8 years
Departure date: 2051.1
Arrival date: 2081.3

BSC8477

UNESSPRO Mission: 344
Core survey ship: *Anna Jackson*
Primary survey world: unknown
Distance from Sol: 70.4 ly
Mission duration (Sol-relative): 97.2 years
Mission duration (ship-relative): 45.9 years
Departure date: 2050.2
Arrival date: 2147.4

94 Aquarius

UNESSPRO Mission: 095
Core survey ship: *Larry Lemke*
Primary survey world: unknown
Distance from Sol: 66.0 ly

Mission duration (Sol-relative): 91.3 years
Mission duration (ship-relative): 43.4 years
Departure date: 2050.9
Arrival date: 2142.2

APPENDIX 3

CHARACTERISTICS OF ADRASTEIA

	Old Units	Earth-Relative	Adjusted Planck Units
Mass	4.5×10^{24} kg	0.75	9.9×10^{24} kg
Equatorial radius	5570 km	0.87	3450 km
Sidereal rotational period	13 hours	0.54	8.7 hours
Equatorial surface gravity	9.67 ms^{-2}	0.99	1.74 ms^{-2}
Geostationary orbit (radius)	25500 km	0.60	15800 km
Mean density	6.22 g/cm^3	1.13	57.7 g/cm^3
Equatorial escape velocity	14 ms^{-1}	1.25	4.65 ms^{-1}
Sidereal period	40 months	3.33	3.41 years
Mean distance from Upsilon Aquarius	3.74×10^8 km	2.50	2.31×10^8 km

TIMETABLE

U.T.		Mission Time
1988, 17 Dec.	Peter Stanmore Alander born	
2040	UN Future of the Species Convention	
2041	UNESSPRO founded	
2043	UN working group on the Adjusted Planck Standard International Unit	
2049, 26 Nov.	UNESSPRO engrams activated	2049.9.29
2050, 1 Jan.	UNESSPRO launches commence	2050.1.1
	Frank Tipler launched	2051.2
	Flyby of Barnard's Star (*Michio Kaku*)	2058.1
2062, 8 Jul.	Spike	2062.3.3

2078	First post-Spike census	
2081–82	Tedesco bursts detected	
	Paul Davies arrives at Zeta-1/2 Reticuli	2105.9
	Carol Stoker arrives at HD194640	2137.1
	Frank Tipler arrives at Upsilon Aquarius	2151.1
	Breakdown of Peter Alander engram	2151.1
	Peter Alander engram revived	2160.2
2163, 10 Jul.	Gifts arrive	2160.8.17
	Ftl communicator tested	2160.8.22
	First hole ship test flight	2160.8.23
	Peter Alander leaves for Sol	2160.8.24
	Frank Tipler attacked	2160.8.26
2163, 24 Jul.	Sol System attacked	2160.8.28
	HD194640 attacked	2160.8.30
	Zeta-1/2 Reticuli contacted	2160.9.20

APPENDIX 5

DRAMATIS PERSONAE

Frank Tipler

Peter Alander (generalist)
Jene Avery (pilot)
Lucia Benck (pilot, *Chung-2*)
Chrys Cunliffe (mathematics)
Kara De Paolis (structural engineer)
Ali Genovese (telemetry)
Caryl Hatzis (survey manager, civilian)
Faith Jong (software)
Nalini Kovistra (astrophysics)
Owen Norsworthy (materials)
Kingsley Oborn (biotechnician)
Cleo Samson (organic chemist)
Donald Schievenin (physics)
Rob Singh (pilot)
Jayme Sivio (survey manager, military)
Otto Wyra (astrophysics)

Sol System

Lowell Correll (Urge)
Caryl Hatzis (citizen)
Laurie Jetz (Urge)
JORIS (*merge*)
Lancia Newark (narrative designer)
Kathryn Nygard (Urge)
Sel Shalhoub (Urge)
Rob Singh (Urge)
Matilda Sulich (activist/Gezim)
Betty van Tran (Urge)

Other UNESSPRO Missions

Peter Alander (*Michio Kaku*)
Peter Alander (*Paul Davies*)
Ali Genovese (*Frank Drake*)
Caryl Hatzis (*Paul Davies*)
Caryl Hatzis (SMC, *Michio Kaku*)
Caryl Hatzis (*Andre Linde*)
Caryl Hatzis (*Carol Stoker*)
Faith Jong (SMM, *Paul Davies*)
Vince Mohler (SMC, *Paul Davies*)
Cleo Samson (SMC, *Carol Stoker*)
Donald Schievenin (SMC, *Carol Stoker*)

AFTERWORD

Broadly speaking, many of these places described in this book are real; we just can't see them in such detail yet. Ensuring that known facts aren't distorted too far is a tricky job for any science fiction writer, and there are always people who help out along the way. The authors of this book would like to acknowledge the help of a number of people in this regard. Many of them are members of either the Eidolist or the Mount Lawley Mafia (or both), and we would like to thank those two collectives for their support and advice. In particular, the many and varied talents of Dr. Damien Broderick, Simon Brown, Jeff Harris, Chris Lawson, and Jonathan Strahan deserve more than even very special thanks, but that is all we can offer in this forum. Similarly, to Kristy Brooks and Nydia Robertson we offer our deepest appreciation and gratitude for their patience and perseverance, among other things.

Acknowledgment must go to Erik Max Francis for (to the authors' best knowledge) first proposing a scale based on Planck units. We have adapted his ideas to suit our needs, and any errors introduced in the process are ours. See his site for more information on the basic concept:

http://www.alcyone.com/max/writing/essays/
planck-units.html

Winchell Chung's weird world of 3-D star maps was a vital source of information at many stages throughout the writing of this book, and he can be found at:

http://allison.clark.net/pub/nyrath/starmap.html#contents

Claus Bornich is the creator of a neat program called *It's Full of Stars*, which we employed extensively in the realization of the world of the *Orphans* series. A 3-D star map showing the places visited in this novel can be found at his site:

http://www.geocities.com/CapeCanaveral/7472/

Extensive use was also made of the following programs: DK Multimedia's *Red Shift 3* and ProFantasy's *Campaign Cartographer 2* and *Fractal Terrain*. Once again, the authors would like to emphasize that any factual errors found in the text are their own doing (and that we are very, very sorry).

Don't miss the other books in
this acclaimed series by

Sean Williams &
Shane Dix

Orphans of Earth
0-441-01006-7

Heirs of Earth
0-441-01126-8

"Chock full of marvelous events...and
the wonder of outer space."
—*Science Fiction Chronicle*

"A dazzling adventure."
—Jack McDevitt

"Williams and Dix bring an
adventurous and expansive
approach to their material."
—*Locus*

Penguin Group (USA) Inc. Online

What will you be reading tomorrow?

Tom Clancy, Patricia Cornwell, W.E.B. Griffin,
Nora Roberts, William Gibson, Robin Cook,
Brian Jacques, Catherine Coulter, Stephen King,
Dean Koontz, Ken Follett, Clive Cussler,
Eric Jerome Dickey, John Sandford,
Terry McMillan…

You'll find them all at
http://www.penguin.com.

Read excerpts and newsletters, find tour
schedules, enter contests…

Subscribe to Penguin Group (USA) Inc. Newsletters
and get an exclusive inside look
at exciting new titles and the authors you love
long before everyone else does.

PENGUIN GROUP (USA) INC. NEWS
http://www.penguin.com/news